TWENTY-ONE

THE BEST OF GRANTA MAGAZINE

Granta Books
London · New York

Granta Publications, 2/3 Hanover Yard, London N1 8BE

Published in Great Britain by Granta Books 2001
Copyright © 2001 by Granta Books

Contents

Introduction

In 1979, a few postgraduate students at Cambridge decided to revive a recently defunct student periodical and under its name—the old name for the River Cam—to publish a literary magazine with high ambitions, which would attract writers and readers well beyond the boundaries of the university, its lawns, punts and ancient colleges. This was a brave idea. All literary magazines are brave ideas; often—perhaps usually—they become broken, brave ideas, or brave ideas that remain only that and never reach a printer, far less an audience. The founders of the new *Granta*, however, had a mission. Again, missions are common enough—if only the mission to publish work by one's friends. The difference here was that the new *Granta*'s founders were, in the first sense of the word, missionaries. Three out of the five people listed on the original masthead were American (one of them, Bill Buford, edited the magazine for the next sixteen years). They had looked at contemporary English fiction and found most of it wanting. It was 'insulated' and 'enclosed'. The magazine's first editorial began:

> It is increasingly a discomforting commonplace that today's British novel is neither remarkable nor remarkably interesting. Current fiction does not startle, does not surprise, is not the source of controversy or contention: what is written today, what has been written since the time of the Second World War, can hardly rival what was written in the time immediately before it. And so the complaint: British fiction of the Fifties, Sixties, and even most of the Seventies variously appears as a montonously protracted, realistically rendered monologue. It lacks excitement, wants drive, provides comforts not challenges.

There were some exceptions: the editorial mentioned Malcolm Bradbury, Roald Dahl and Ian McEwan among others. But where was a more general salvation to come from? Granta had no doubts: the United States, the home of 'some of the most challenging, diversified and adventurous writing today'. The new *Granta*'s first issue was called *New American Writing* and introduced writers such as Joyce Carol Oates and Donald Barthelme who were at that time barely known in Britain, in the hope that British writing would be invigorated by their example. *Granta* would be 'dedicated to an exchange of fiction and discussions about it...devoted to the idea of the dialogue in prose about prose'.

It is interesting to look back at that first issue, at the beginnings of a magazine which has become—and I think this can be fairly said—probably the most successful of its kind in the English language, to the extent that today certain styles of writing are sometimes described (sometimes mystifyingly to those of us who work on the magazine) as '*Granta*esque' or 'typically *Granta*'. Despite its manifesto, *Granta* never became a forum for literary discussions—outside the pages of its first few issues it has mainly eschewed 'writing about writing'—and almost certainly would not have survived had it done so. Nor did it do much to promote 'postmodern' American writers such as Thomas Pynchon and John Barth who were then thought to be at the cutting edge of experimentation with the non-linear, anti-narrative novel. Instead, issue by issue, it began to feel its way towards publishing what it liked (rather than abusing what it didn't); a liking for and belief in what could be crudely summarized as new and interesting, but rarely complicated or confusing, ways of telling stories. Urgency and clarity became important qualities, as did the subject, what the stories were *about*. In 1979 (and even to the editors of *Granta*), artistically ambitious 'new writing' still meant 'fiction'. Only a few years later, *Granta* was publishing just as much non-fiction as fiction and according it the same prominence and esteem. The devices that made good fiction compelling could be harnessed to other forms which still stood outside the gates of the kingdom known as 'literature': reporting, travel, memoir, narrative history. Of course, *Granta* did not invent this cross-fertilization, but throughout the 1980s and 90s it played a large part in shaping new forms of documentary story writing and creating a public appetite for them.

In 1983, *Granta* published two issues in which you can see the magazine discovering both its self-belief and purpose. The first was *Dirty Realism*, in which Americans such as Raymond Carver, Richard Ford and Jayne Anne Phillips were brought together, quite convincingly, under a label that has stuck. The second, *Travel Writing*, contained writers as diverse as Gabriel García Márquez, Martha Gellhorn and Bruce Chatwin. The first was fiction, the second documentary, but taken together they reveal the power and urgency of the realistic narrative—for lack of a better phrase—at its best; how it can illuminate hidden lives and hidden places, and how it can grip. After its first issue, *Granta* published no more mission statements, but the pieces in those issues (and in this anthology) are exemplars of what it is about.

Twenty-one years separate the first and last pieces in the pages that follow. The world has changed, and so has the business of writing and publishing. In 1979, modern marketing had hardly touched the book trade. There were few bookselling chain stores. Authors, other than their appearances on book jackets, were almost invisible. In the Eighties, both books and authors became fashionable objects. You can be sceptical about the virtues of this, but it would be hard to argue today that writing in Britain is immune to American (or for that matter European, Indian or African) influence, or vice versa, or that it is dull and reclusive. Who can say what part *Granta* played in this, but some part certainly.

Selecting the pieces for this anthology, one piece for each year of the magazine's history, was a maddening task. Many other writers should also be here (some of them appear in other *Granta* anthologies—the *Granta* Books of *Travel*, *Reportage*, and *The Family*). But the variety and strength of these pieces are true to the magazine's history. Each has a primary purpose: to be enjoyed.

Ian Jack

1979
The Men's Club
Leonard Michaels

Women wanted to talk about anger, identity, politics, etc. I saw posters in Berkeley urging them to join groups. I saw their leaders on TV. Strong, articulate faces. So when Cavanaugh phoned and invited me to join a men's club, I laughed. Slowly, not laughing, he repeated himself. He was six foot nine. The size and weight entered his voice. He and some friends wanted a club. 'A regular social possibility outside our jobs and marriages. Nothing to do with women's groups.' One man was a tax accountant, another was a lawyer. There was also a college teacher like me and two psychotherapists. Solid types. I supposed there could be virtues in a men's club, a regular social possibility. I should have said yes immediately, but something in me resisted. The prospect of leaving my house after dinner. Blood is heavy then. Brain is slow. Besides, wasn't this club idea corny? Like trying to recapture high school days. Locker room fun. Wet naked boys snapping towels at each other's genitals. It didn't feel exactly right. To be wretchedly truthful, any social possibility unrelated to wife, kids, house and work felt like a form of adultery. Not criminal. Not legitimate.

'Cavanaugh, I don't even go to the movies any more.'

'I'm talking about a men's club. Good company. You talk about women's groups. Movies. Can't you hear me?'

'When the phone rings it's like an attack on my life. I get confused. Say it again.'

'Look, you're one of my best friends. You live less than a mile away. Do we see each other three times a year?'

'I lose over a month every year just working to pay property taxes. Friendship is a luxury. Unless you're so poor it makes no difference how you spend your time.'

'A men's club. Good company.'

'I hear you.'

But I was thinking about good company. Some of my married colleagues have love affairs, usually with students. You could call it a regular social possibility. It included emotion chaos. Gonorrhoea. Even guilt. They would have been better off in a men's club.

'What do you say? Can we expect you?'

'I'll go to the first meeting. I can't promise more. I'm very busy.'

'Yeah, yeah,' said Cavanaugh and gave me an address in the Berkeley flats.

The night of the meeting I told my wife I'd be home before midnight. She said, 'Take out the garbage.' Big sticky bag felt unpropitious and my hands soon smelled of tuna fish. After driving five minutes I found the place. The front of the house, vine covered, seemed to brood in lunatic privacy. Nobody answered when I knocked, but I heard voices, took hold of a wrought iron handle and pushed, discovering a large Berkeley living room and six men. I saw dark wood panelling and potted ferns dangling from exposed beams. Other plants along the window ledges. A potted tree in a far corner, skinny, spinsterish looking. Nervous yellow leaves filled its head. Various ceramics, bowls on table tops and plates on the walls beside huge acrylic paintings, abstractions like glistening viscera splashed off a butcher block. There was an amazing rug, but I couldn't take it in. A man was rising from a pillow on the floor, coming toward me, smiling.

'I knocked,' I said.

'Come in, man. I'm Harry Kramer.'

'I'm Cavanaugh's friend.'

'Who isn't?'

'Really,' I said, giving it the LA inflection to suggest sympathetic understanding, not wonder. Kramer registered the nuance and glanced at me as at a potential brother. His heavy black hair was controlled by a style, parted in the middle, shaped to cup his ears with a feeling that once belonged to little girls and now was common among TV actors and rock musicians. It was contradicted by black force in his eyes, handshake like a bite, and tattooed forearms. Blue winged snake. Blue dagger amid roses. They spoke for an earlier life, I supposed, but Kramer wore his sleeves rolled to the elbow. It was impossible to connect him with his rug, which I began to appreciate as spongy and sensuous. Orange. I felt myself wading through it as Kramer led me toward the men.

Shaking hands, nodding hello, saying my name, each man was a complex flash—eyes, hand, names—but one had definition. Solly Berliner. Tall. Wearing a suit. Dead white hair and big greenish light in his eyes. The face of an infant surprised by senility. His suit was grey polyester, conservative and sleazy. Kramer left me with Berliner beside the potted tree, a beer in my hand. A man about five foot six with an eager face came right up to us. 'Care for a taste?' In his palm lay two brown marijuanas, slick with spittle. I declined. Berliner said, 'Thanks, thanks,' with frightening gratitude and took both cigarettes. We laughed as he dropped one back into the man's palm. The little face turned toward the other men. 'Anybody care for a taste?'

The sound of Berliner's voice lingered after the joke. Maybe he felt uneasy. Out of his natural environment. I couldn't guess where that might be. He was a confusion of clues. The suit wasn't Berkeley. The eyes were worlds of feeling. His speedy voice flew from nerves. Maybe the living room affected him. A men's club would have been more authentic, more properly convened, elsewhere. What did I have in mind? A cold ditch? I supposed Kramer's wife, exiled for the evening, had cultivated the plants and picked the orange rug and the luscious fabrics on the couches and chairs. Ideas of happiness. Berliner and I remained standing as if the fabrics—heavy velvets, beige tones— were nothing to violate with our behinds. It was a woman's room, but the point of the club was to be with men, not to escape from women, so I turned to Berliner and asked what he did for a living.

'Real estate,' he said, grinning ferociously, as if extreme types were into that. Wild fellows. 'I drove in from San Jose.' He spoke with rapid little shrugs, as if readjusting his vertebrae. His eyes were full of green distance after two drags on the cigarette. He was already driving back to San Jose, I figured, but then he said, 'Forgive me for saying this, but, a minute ago when Kramer introduced us, I had a weird thought.' His eyes returned.

'You did?'

I'd seen the look before. It signalled the California plunge into truth, a conversational style developed in encounter groups where sensitivity training occurs.

'I hope this doesn't bother you. But I thought you had a withered leg.'

4

'You did.

'I see you

'Weird that I

'I thought your

I wiggled my legs.

unusual depths, waiting

air like a fish. I said noth

'You look much younger.

hair, he also looked older.

'I stay in shape,' he answered,

his nostrils. 'Nobody,' he said,

crackling sheets of snot, 'nobody else

I'm oldest. I asked the guys.'

He gagged a little, then released the sm   it through
compressed lips. 'Kramer is thirty-eigh   wondered if
conversation had ever been more like medical e..perience, so rich
in gas and mucous. 'I'm always the oldest. Ever since I was a
kid I was the oldest.' He giggled and intensified his stare. I
giggled, too, in a social way. Then the door opened and
Cavanaugh walked in.

'Excuse me,' I said, intimating regret but moving quickly
away to greet Cavanaugh.

Cavanaugh, big and good-looking, had heroic charisma. He'd
once been a professional basketball player. Now he worked at
the university in special undergraduate programs, matters of
policy and funding. Nine to five, jacket and tie. To remember
his former work—the great naked shoulders and legs flying
through the air—was saddening. In restaurants and airports
people still asked for his autograph.

Things felt better, more natural, healthier, with the big man
in the room. Kramer reached him before I did. They slapped
each other's arms, laughing, pleased at how they felt to each
other. Solid. Real. I watched, thinking I'd often watched
Cavanaugh. Ever since college, in fact, when he'd become
famous. To see him burn his opponent and score was like a
miracle of justice. Now, in civilian clothes, he was faintly
disorienting. Especially his wristwatch, a golden, complicated
band. A symbolic manacle. Cavanaugh's submission to ordinary

…nt my kids to grow up like me, … He wanted his kids in jackets and

… slapping Kramer's arms, but Kramer continued … him. Kramer looked as though he might soon pee in … pants. People love athletics. Where else these days do they see such mythic drama? Images of unimpeachable excellence. I was infected by Kramer's enthusiasm. When Kramer left to get Cavanaugh a beer, we shook hands. He said, 'I didn't think I'd see you tonight.' There was mockery in his smile.

'It's not so easy getting out of the house. Nobody but you could have dragged me to this.'

'You open the door, you're out.'

'Tell me about it.'

'I'm glad you're here. Anything happen yet? I'm late because Sarah thinks the club idea is wrong. I'm wrong to be here. We argued a little at dinner.' He whispered then, 'Maybe it isn't easy,' and looked at his wristwatch, frowning, as if it were his mind. Kramer returned with the beer just as a phone started ringing.

'I'll be right back,' said Kramer, turning toward the ringing.

Sarah's word 'wrong' made me wonder. If something was wrong with Cavanaugh, it was wrong with the universe. Men could understand that. When Cavanaugh needed a loan to buy his house, the bank gave him no problem. You could see his credit was good; he was six foot nine and could run a hundred yards in ten seconds. The loan officer, a man, recognized Cavanaugh and felt privileged to help him with financial negotiations. He didn't ask about Cavanaugh's recent divorce, his alimony payments.

Men's clubs. Women's groups. They suggest incurable disorders. I remembered Socrates—how the boys, not his wife, adored him. And Karl Marx running around with Engels while Jenny stayed home with the kids. Maybe men played more than women. A men's club, compared to women's groups, was play. Frivolous; virtually insulting. It excluded women. But I was thinking in circles. A men's club didn't exclude women. It also didn't exclude kangaroos. It included only men. I tried to imagine explaining this to Sarah. 'You see, men love to play.' It didn't feel convincing. She had strong opinions and a bad temper. When Cavanaugh decided to quit basketball, it was his decision, but I blamed her anyway. She wanted him home. The king became the dean.

Kramer shouted from another room, 'Is anybody here named Terry? His wife is on the phone. She's crying.' Shouting again, more loudly, as if to make sure the woman on the phone would hear him, Kramer said, 'Is anybody in this house named Terry?'

Nobody admitted to being named Terry. I heard Kramer, still shouting, say, 'Terry isn't here. If Terry shows up, I'll tell him to phone you right away. No, I won't forget. I'll tell Terry to phone you right away.'

When Kramer returned he said, 'You guys sure none of you is named Terry?'

Cavanaugh muttered, 'We're all named Terry.'

We made a circle, some men sitting on the rug. Kramer settled into his pillow, legs folded and crossed. He began talking to us in a slow rational voice. The black eyes darkened his face. His words became darker, heavier, because of them.

'What is the purpose of this club?'

To make women cry, I thought. Kramer's beginning was not very brilliant, but he looked so deep that I resisted judgement.

'Some of us—Solly Berliner, Paul, Cavanaugh—had a discussion a few weeks ago. We agreed it would be a good idea...' Paul was the short, marijuana man with the eager face. Kramer nodded to him when he said his name. He went on about the good idea, but I wasn't listening.

I thought again about the women. Anger, identity, politics, rights, wrongs. I envied them. It seemed attractive to be deprived in our society. Deprivation gives you something to fight for, it makes you morally superior, it makes you serious. What was left for men these days? They already had everything. Did they need clubs? The mere sight of two men together suggests a club. Consider Damon and Pythias, Huck and Jim, Hamlet and Horatio. The list is familiar. Even the Lone Ranger wasn't lonely. He had Tonto. There is Gertrude Stein and Alice B. Toklas, but generally, two women suggest gossip and a kiss goodbye. Kramer, talking, meandered in a sea of non-existent purpose. I

7

said, 'Why are you talking about our purpose? We're all here. Let's just say what we want to do.' I'd stopped him mid-meander. He looked relieved—a little surprised, not offended. 'Can you offer a suggestion?' he asked.

I glanced at the other faces, particularly Cavanaugh's. I didn't want to embarrass him. I was his guest and I'd been too aggressive maybe. He said, 'Go on.'

'I suggest each of us tell the story of his life.'

The instant I said it I laughed, as if I'd intended a joke. What else could it be? I didn't tell the story of my life to strangers. Maybe I'd lived too long in California, or I'd given too many lectures at the University. Perhaps I'd been influenced by Berliner, becoming like him, a confessional person. Nobody else laughed. Cavanaugh looked at me with approval. Berliner grinned, his rigid ferocity. He loved the suggestion. He could hardly wait to begin. Kramer, however, said, 'I'll go first.'

'You want to? You do like the idea?'

'One of us can talk at each meeting. I have listened in this room to numerous life stories.' Kramer, apparently, was a psychotherapist.

'It will be good for me,' he said, 'to tell the story of my life, especially in a non-professional context. It will be a challenge. I'm going to put it on tape. I will tape each of us.'

Suddenly I imagined him sitting among his plants listening to life—stories, his tape recorder going, his dark face and tattoos presiding over everything.

'Oh, come on. Let's talk to one another, Kramer. No machines.'

To my dismay, Kramer yelled, 'Why the hell not? I have so much talk on my tapes—friends, clients, lovers—that I don't even know what I have. So much I don't even remember.'

Apparently, I'd struck at something he cherished. I didn't know him well enough to do that, but I heard myself yelling back at him, a man who looked angry, even dangerous, 'If you didn't put it on tape, you'd remember.'

Everyone laughed, including Kramer. He said, 'That's good, that's good.' No anger at all. I was strangely pleased by this violence. I liked Kramer for laughing.

'That's good,' he said. 'I'm going to write that down.'

'Yeah,' said Cavanaugh, 'no tape recorder. But I want an idea of what this life-story business is like.'

Berliner said, 'You know what it's like, Cavanaugh. It's like in the old movies. Lauren Bacall tells Humphrey Bogart about herself. Who she is. Where she's been. Then they screw.'

A blond man with plastic-framed glasses and a pastel-blue sweater strained forward in his chair, saying, 'I saw that movie on *The Late Show*, right?' He looked youthful, exceptionally clean. He wore cherry-red jogging shoes.

The faces became silent. He retreated. 'Maybe it was another movie.'

Berliner's face seemed to swell with astonishment, then tighten into eerie screeing, tortured noises, screeing, screeing. 'Oh man what is your name?' He pointed at the blond. Kramer, hugging himself, contained his laughter. The blond said, 'Harold.' Tears, like bits of glass, formed in his eyes as he smiled.

'Oh Harold,' shouted Berliner, 'the name is the whole story of my life. My mother used to say, "Solly Berliner, why can't you be like Harold." Harold Himmel was the smartest, nicest kid in Brooklyn.'

'My name is Harold Canterbury.'

'Right, man. Forgive me. A minute ago when you were talking I had a weird thought. I thought—forgive me, man—you had a withered hand.'

Harold raised his hands for everyone to see.

Kramer said, 'Don't listen to that jackass, Harold. Nothing wrong with your hands. I'm getting more beer.'

As he walked toward the kitchen, Cavanaugh followed, saying, 'I don't know what this life-story business is about, but it sounds good.' Kramer said, 'I'll show you what it's about. You get the beers.' Cavanaugh returned with the beers and Kramer with a metal footlocker, dragging it into the centre of our circle. A padlock banged against the front. Kramer, squatting, tried to fit a key into the lock. His hands began shaking. Cavanaugh bent beside him. 'You need a little help?' Kramer handed him the key, saying, 'Do it.'

Cavanaugh inserted the key and the lock snapped open as if shocked by love.

Kramer removed the lock, heaved back the lid of the footlocker, then withdrew to his pillow, quickly lighting a cigarette, his hands still shaking, 'This is it, my life story.' His voice, slower than before, laboured against feeling. 'You guys can see my junk, my trinkets. Photos, diaries, papers of every kind.' Had Kramer left the room it would have been easier to look, but he remained on his pillow, a dark pasha, urging us to look. Paul suddenly scrambled on hands and knees to the footlocker, looked, then plucked out a handful of bleary, cracked snapshots and fanned them across the rug. We could see inscriptions. Paul read aloud, 'Coney Island, 1953, Tina. Party at Josephine's, New Year's, 1965. Holiday Inn, New Orleans, 1975, Gwen.' He looked from the photos to Kramer, smiling. 'All these pictures in your box of women?'

Kramer, in the difficult voice, answered, 'I have many photos. I have my Navy discharge papers, my high school diploma, my first driver's licence. I have all my elementary school notebooks, even spelling exams from the third grade. I have maybe twenty-five fountain pens. All my old passports; everything is in that box.'

Paul, nodding, smiling, said, 'But these photos, Kramer. All these photos women?'

'I have had 622 women.'

'Right on,' shouted Berliner, his soul projecting toward Kramer through the big green eyes, dog-like, waiting for a signal. Paul took out more photos and dropped them among the others on the rug. Over a hundred now, women in bathing suits, in winter coats, in Fifties styles, Sixties styles, Seventies styles. Spirits of the decades. If men make history, women wear its look; even in their faces and figures. But, to me, Kramer's women looked fundamentally the same. One poor sweetie between twenty and thirty years old forever. On a beach, leaning against a railing, a tree, a brick wall, with sun in her eyes, squinting at the camera. A hundred fragments, each of them complete if you cared to scrutinize. A whole person who could say her name. Maybe love Kramer. That she squinted touched me.

Kramer, with his meticulously sculpted hair, cigarette trembling in his fingers, waited. Nobody spoke, not even Berliner. Looking at the pictures, I was reminded of flashers. See

10

this. It is my entire crotch. Have a scream.'

Berliner suddenly blurted, 'Great. Great. Let's all do it. Let's all talk about our sexual experience.' His face jerked in every direction, seeking encouragement.

As if he'd heard nothing, Kramer said, 'I was born in Trenton, New Jersey. My father was a union organizer. In those days it was dangerous work. He was a Communist, he lived for an idea. My mother believed in everything he said, but she was always depressed and she sat in the bedroom, in her robe, smoking cigarettes. She never cleaned the house. When I was six years old I was shopping and cooking, like my mother's mother. I cannot remember one minute which I can call my childhood. I was my mother's mother. I had a life with no beginning, no childhood.'

'Right,' said Berliner. 'You had your childhood later. Six hundred and twenty-two mothers. Right?'

'The women were women. Eventually I'll have another 600. I don't know where my father is, but when I hear the word "workers" or the word "struggle", I think of him. If I see a hardhat carrying a lunch pail, I think he's struggling. My mother now lives in New York. Twice a year I phone New York and get migraine headaches. Blindness and nausea. Just say the area code, 212, and I feel pain in my eyes.'

I'd been looking at Kramer all evening, but now, to my surprise, I noticed that his eyes didn't focus steadily. The right eye was slightly askew. He blinked hard and brought it into line with the other eye. After a while it drifted away. He'd let it go for a moment, then blink hard again. His voice was trance-like, compulsive, as if he'd been trying to tell us something before he would be overwhelmed by doubt and confusion.

Cavanaugh said, 'What about Nancy?'

'What about her?' Kramer sounded surprised, as if unsure who Nancy was.

'Nancy Kramer. These are her plants, aren't they?' Cavanaugh was looking at the photos on the rug, not the plants.

'You mean the women? What does Nancy think about my women?'

'That's right.'

'We have a good understanding. Nancy goes out, too. It's cool. The plants are mine.'

'Yours?' I said.

'Yes. I love them. I've even got them on my tape recorder. I could play you the fig tree in the corner.' Kramer said this to me with a sly, dopey look, as if trying to change the mood, trying to make a joke.

'Too much. Too much, Kramer,' said Berliner. 'My wife and me are exactly the same. I mean we also have an understanding.'

I said, 'Let Kramer talk.'

Kramer shook his head and bent toward Berliner, saying, 'That's all right. Do you want to say more, Solly?'

Berliner looked down at his knees. 'No. You go on, Kramer. I'm sorry I interrupted.'

Cavanaugh, imitating Kramer, bent toward Berliner. 'Solly, aren't you jealous when your wife is making it with another guy?'

Berliner raised his face toward Cavanaugh. 'Jealous?'

'Yeah, jealous.'

'No, man, I'm liberated.'

'What the hell does that mean?' I said.

Looking at me now, Berliner said, as if it were obvious, 'I don't feel anything.'

'Yeah,' said Berliner. 'I'm liberated.'

'Liberated means you don't feel anything?'

Harold, with a huge stare of pleasure, began repeating, 'You don't feel anything. You don't feel anything.'

Berliner shrugged. 'Once, I felt something.'

Writhing in his creamy slacks, Harold said, 'Tell us about that, please.'

The little tears were in his eyes again. 'Tell us about the time you felt something.'

'Does everyone want to hear?' said Berliner, looking at me. I said, 'Yes.'

He smiled. His voice was full of accommodation. 'We had a weekend in the mountains with another couple. A ski cabin near Lake Tahoe. The first night we became a little drunk after dinner

12

and somebody—maybe me—yeah, yeah, me—I said let's trade partners. It was my own idea, right? So we traded. It was OK. It wasn't the first time we did it. But then I heard my wife moaning. I couldn't help hearing her. A small cabin. And that was OK. But she was not just moaning, you know what I mean. You know? It was love.'

'Love?' said Kramer.

'Yeah, I didn't like it. She was moaning with love. Moaning is OK. But she was going too far, you know what I mean. She was doing love. I wanted to kill her.'

Cavanaugh reached over and squeezed Berliner's elbow. Berliner was still smiling, the big green eyes searching our faces for the meaning of what he'd said. 'Is that what you wanted to know, Harold?'

'Did it ruin your weekend?'

'It was horrible, man. I lost my erection.'

Berliner began screeing again and I heard myself doing it, too, just like him, making that creepy sound.

'It was horrible, horrible. I was ashamed. I ran out of the cabin and sat on a rock. My wife started calling though the door, "Solly, Solly, Solly Berliner." Then she came outside, laughing, and found me. I showed her what she had done to me. She said it wasn't her fault. She said it was my idea. I hit her and said that was my idea, too. She started crying. Soon as she started crying, my erection came back.'

Kramer said, 'What happened next?'

'But you were talking, Kramer,' I said. 'You know what happened next. Next she hit him and then they made it together. It's a cliché. You should finish telling your story. You should have a full turn.' I wanted things done according to my idea, one man at a time.

Berliner, incoherent with excitement, shouted at me, 'How the hell do you know? I'm telling what happened to me. Me. Me.'

'All right, all right. What happened next?'

'Next she hit me and we made it together.'

Cavanaugh, with two fists, began hammering the rug until everyone quieted. Then he said, 'Look at Kramer.' Kramer was slumped in his pillow, elbows on his knees, the dark face hanging, glancing vaguely back at Cavanaugh.

'Let's let him alone,' said Cavanaugh. 'Maybe he'll want to go on later tonight. I'll tell you guys a love story. OK?'

I said, 'Kramer tells us he made it with 600 women. Berliner says he traded his wife, then beat her up and had an erection. You call that love?'

Cavanaugh gave me a flat look, as if I'd become strange to him. 'Yeah, why not? Hey, man, what do you want to hear about? Toothpaste and deodorants?'

'You're right, Cavanaugh. I give up. I'll bet your story's about how you made it with 10,000 high school cheerleaders.'

Cavanaugh stared at the place in the rug he had just hammered. The big body and big face were immobilized, getting things in order, remembering his story, and then his voice was simply there.

'About three months after we got married my second wife and I started having arguments. Bad scenes. We would go to bed every night hating each other. There were months with no sex. I didn't know who was more miserable. I was making a lot of money playing ball and I was playing good. It should have been good for us altogether. The marriage should have been fine. In the middle of a game with the crowd screaming, I'd think this was no fantastic deal, because I had no love at home. Soon there was nothing in my body but anger. I got into fights with my own teammates. I couldn't take a shave without slicing my face. I was smoking cigarettes. I had something against my body and wanted to hurt it. When I told my wife I was moving out, she said, "Great." She wanted to live alone. I moved out and stayed with a friend until I found an apartment. One day in the grocery store, I was throwing every kind of thing into my shopping cart. I was making sure nothing I needed would show up later as being not there. And this woman, I notice, is pushing her cart behind me, up and down the aisles, giggling. I knew she was giggling at me. When I got to the cashier she is behind me in line, still giggling, and then she says, very sweet and tickled, "You must have a station wagon waiting for you." I said, "I have a pickup truck. Do you want a ride?" A man buying so much food, she

14

figured, has a family. Safe to ask for a ride. She didn't have a car. I gave her a ride and carried her groceries up to her apartment. A little boy was sitting on the floor watching TV. She introduced us and offered me a drink and we sat in another room talking. The boy took care of himself. Just like in Kramer's story. He cooked dinner for himself. He gave himself a bath. Then went to bed. But his mother wasn't depressed like Kramer's. She laughed and teased me and asked a lot of questions. I talked about myself for five or six hours. We ate dinner around midnight, and then, at four in the morning, I woke up in her bed, thinking about my ton of groceries rotting in the pickup. But that wasn't what woke me. What woke me was the feeling I wanted to go home. Back to my apartment, my own bed. I hadn't left one woman to sleep with another. I didn't know what I was doing in this woman's bed. I got up and dressed and left. As I was about to drive away she comes running to the window of my pickup, naked. "Where are you going?" she says. I told her she had nothing on. She says, "Where are you going at this hour?" I said I wanted to go home. She says, "Oh, OK, I'll come with you." I told her no and said I would phone her. She said OK and smiled and said goodnight. She was like that little boy. Or he was like her. Easy. OK. OK goodnight. I didn't think I would phone her. Now this is my story. I woke up the next afternoon. I liked it, waking up alone. I liked it very much, but I felt something strange. I wanted something. Then I remembered the woman and I knew what I wanted, I wanted to phone her. So I went to the phone and I realized I didn't know her number. I didn't even know her name. Well, I showered and got dressed and stopped thinking about her. I went out for something. I didn't know what. I had everything I needed in the apartment. But I started driving and right away I was driving back to the grocery store, as if the car had a mind of its own. I was just holding the wheel. I didn't get further than the grocery store, because I didn't remember where she lived. I remembered leaving the store with her, driving toward the bay and that's all. She said, "Turn right, turn left, and go straight," but I never noticed street names or anything. Now I wanted to see that woman more and more. The next day I went back to the grocery store and hung around the parking lot. I did that every day for a week, at different times. I thought I remembered how she looked talking to me through the window of my pickup, how she smiled and said OK. I wanted to see her again badly. But I wasn't sure that I could recognize her in the street, looking normal. She was wearing gold loop earrings, jeans and sandals. What if she came along in a skirt and heels? Anyhow, I never saw her again.'

Cavanaugh stopped. It was obvious he had no more to say, but Kramer said, 'Is that your story?'

'Yes.' Cavanaugh smiled, leaning back, watching us.

'That's your love story?' I asked.

'Right,' he answered, nodding. 'I fell in love with a woman I couldn't find the next day. She might live around the corner, man.'

'You still love her?' asked Paul, tremendous delicacy in his voice, the slight small body poised, full of tenderness and tension.

Cavanaugh smiled at him with melancholy eyes, the whole expression of his great face and body suggested that he'd been humbled by fate.

Paul said, 'That can't be it, that can't be the end.'

'The end.'

'Cavanaugh,' Paul said, pleading, 'I've known you for years. How come you never told me that story?'

'I never told anyone. Maybe I'm not sure it happened.'

'You did go back to the grocery?'

'So what?'

I said, 'Paul means, if you looked for her, it happened.'

'I still look. When Sarah sends me out to do the shopping, she doesn't know the risk she's taking.'

'Cavanaugh,' I said, 'do you think you ever passed her in the street and she recognized you, but you didn't recognize her?'

Immediately, Kramer said, 'Not recognize Cavanaugh? I'd recognize him even if I never saw him before.'

'How would you recognize me?'

'From your picture in the papers.'

'She didn't read the sport pages.'

'Hey,' said Berliner, 'I have an idea. We can all look for her. What do you say?'

Paul said, 'Shut up.'

'Why is everyone telling me to shut up? I drove here from San Jose and everyone tells me to shut up.' Berliner was sighing in a philosophical way. He'd just seen into the nature of life. 'Looking for Cavanaugh's woman. To me it's a good idea. Hey, man, I have a better idea. Cavanaugh, take a quick look through Kramer's snapshots.'

Cavanaugh smirked. 'She wasn't one of them. She was a queen.'

'Queen what?' shouted Kramer. 'My women have names. What did you call her? You call her Queen; Berliner, got me my telephone directory. I'll find her. How many women in Berkeley can be named Queen?'

'I'm sorry, Kramer. Take it easy. I didn't intend to crap on your 600 women. He thinks I crapped on his harem.'

I said, 'Let me talk, I want to tell a love story.'

'Great,' said Berliner. 'Everybody shut up. Go, man. Sing the blues.'

'You don't want to hear my story? I listened to yours, Berliner.'

'Yes he does,' said Kramer. 'Let him talk, Solly.'

'I didn't try to stop him.'

Cavanaugh said, 'Just begin.'

'Yeah,' said Berliner, grinning in an animal way, brilliant, stiff with teeth.

'So far,' I said, 'I've heard three stories about one thing. Cavanaugh calls it love. I call it stories about the other woman. By which I mean the one who is not the wife. To you guys only the other woman is interesting. If there wasn't first a wife, there couldn't be the other woman. Especially you, Berliner; especially in your case. Moaning, just moaning in the other room, your wife is only your wife. Moaning with love, she's the other woman. And Kramer with the snapshots. Look at them, Kramer spent most of his life trying to photograph the other woman, not knowing that every time he snapped a picture it was like getting married. Like permanently eliminating another woman from the possibility of being the other woman. As for Cavanaugh, why can't he find his woman? Because he doesn't

17

want to. If he finds her, she won't be the other woman any more. This way he can protect his marriage. Every time he goes to the grocery store and doesn't see the other woman, which is every single time, his marriage is stronger.'

Cavanaugh, frowning at me, said, 'What are you trying to tell us? What's all this business about the other woman? Why don't you just say it, man?'

Kramer then said, 'You're trying to tell us you love your wife. You think I don't love mine? You think Solly doesn't love his wife?'

Berliner cried, 'If that's all you think, you're right. I hate my wife.'

'Tell your story,' said Cavanaugh. 'Enough philosophy.'

'I don't know if I can tell it. I never told it before. It's about a woman who was my friend in high school and college. Her name is Marilyn. We practically grew up together. She lives in Chicago now. She's a violinist in a symphony orchestra. I spent more time with her than with any other woman except maybe my mother. She wasn't like a sister. She was like a friend, I couldn't have had such a friendship with a very close man. We'd go out together a lot and if I brought her home late, I'd stay over at her place, in the same bed. Nothing sexual. Between us it would have been a crime. We would fight plenty, say terrible things to each other, but we were close. She phoned me every day. We stayed on the phone for an hour. We went to parties together when neither of us had a date. I liked showing up with her because she was attractive. Showing up with her increased my chances of meeting some girl. It gave me a kind of power, walking in with Marilyn, feeling free to pick up somebody else. She had the same power. Anyhow, we never analysed our relationship, but we joked about what other people thought. My mother would sometimes answer the phone and, if she heard Marilyn's voice, she would say, "It's your future wife." She used to worry about us. She used to warn me that any woman I was serious about would object to Marilyn. Or she'd say it wasn't nice, me and Marilyn being so thick with each other, because I was ruining her chances of meeting a man. That wasn't true.

Marilyn had plenty of affairs. All of them ended badly, but I had nothing to do with it. One of her men scissored her dresses into rags. Another flung her Siamese cat out the window. She would manage to find some man who was well educated, had pleasant manners, and turned out to be a brute. She suffered, but nothing destroyed her. She had her violin. She also had me. When I was out of a job and not going to school, she loaned me money and let me stay at her place for weeks. I didn't have to ask. I just showed up one day with my suitcase. One weekend, while I was staying at her place, she came home with a friend, a girl who looked something like her. Lean, with curly brown hair, with beautiful skin faintly olive-coloured, like Marilyn's. Before dinner was over, Marilyn remembered something important she had to do. She excused herself and went to a movie. Her friend and I were alone in the apartment. It was glorious. Two weeks later, when I was talking to Marilyn about this and that, I mentioned her friend. Marilyn said she didn't want to hear about her. She said that friendship was over and it was something she couldn't discuss. Furthermore, she said I had acted badly that night at dinner, driving her out of her own apartment. I said, "I thought you left as a favour to me. I thought you did it deliberately." She said she did do it deliberately, but only because I made it extremely obvious that I was hot for her friend and I acted like a slob. Now I began to feel angry. I told her she didn't have to leave her apartment for my sake and it was rotten of her to make me feel guilty about it two weeks after I'd started having very strong feelings about her friend, so strong in fact we had been talking about marriage. I thought this would change everything. Marilyn would laugh and give me a hug. Instead she lights a cigarette and begins smoking with quick, half-drags, flicking ashes all over her couch. Then she says, "Why don't you just say that you consider me physically disgusting and you always have." This was my old friend Marilyn speaking, but it seemed like science fiction. It looked like her. It sounded like her. It was her, but it wasn't. Some weird mongoose had seized her soul. Then she starts telling me about what is inside my head, things she has always known though I tried to hide them from her. Her voice is getting bitter and nasty. She says she knows I can't stand her breasts and the birthmark on her neck sickens me. I said, "What birthmark?" She says, "Who are you trying to kid? I've seen you looking at it a thousand times when you thought I didn't notice." I sat down beside her on the couch. She says, "Get away from me, you pig." I felt confused. Ashamed and frightened at the same time. Then she jumps off the couch and strides out of the room. I hear her slamming around in the toilet, bottles toppling out of her medicine cabinet into the sink. Smashing. I said. "Marilyn, are you all right?" No answer. She finally comes out, wearing a bathrobe with nothing underneath and the robe is open. But she's standing there as if nothing has changed since she left the room, and she talks to me again in the same nasty voice. She sneers and accuses me of things I couldn't have imagined, let alone thought about her, as she says I did, every day, all the time, pretending I was her friend. Suddenly, I'm full of a new feeling. Feeling I've never had before. Not what a normal person would call sexual feeling, but what does a penis know? It isn't a connoisseur of normal feeling. Besides, I was a lot younger, still mystified by life, especially my own chemicals. I leap off the couch and grab her. No, I find myself leaping, grabbing her, and she's twisting, trying to hit me, really fighting. I feel she's seriously trying to hurt me, but there's no screaming or cursing, there's nothing but the two of us breathing and sweating and then she begins to collapse, to slide toward the floor. Next thing I'm on top of her. I'm wearing my clothes, she lying on her open robe. It's supernaturally exciting. Both of us are shivering and wild. We fell asleep like that and we slept at least an hour. I woke when I felt her moving. The lights were on. We were looking at each other. She says, "This is very discouraging." Then she went to her bedroom and shut the door. I got up and followed her and knocked at the door. She opens it and lets me kiss her. Then she shut the door again. I went home. Six months later she phoned me from Chicago to tell me about her new job and to give me her address. After a while she asked about her friend. I told her it was finished between her friend and me. I was seeing somebody else. She changed the subject. Now every few months I get a letter. I write to her also. Some day, if I happen to be in Chicago, I'll visit her.'

In the silence following my story, I began to regret having told it. Then a man who had said nothing all evening asked, 'Did you make it that night with Marilyn?'

'No. Nothing changed. I don't think it ever will. I could show up tomorrow in Chicago with my suitcase and move into her place.'

The man shook his head softly and started to say something, then stopped.

'Go on,' I said. 'Do you have a question?'

He smiled.

We waited. It was clear that he was a shy man. Then he said, 'Was it a true story?'

'Yes.'

He shrugged and smiled and said, 'I liked Marilyn.'

I said, 'I like her, too. Maybe I can fix you up with her. What's your name?'

'Terry.'

'Terry?' shrieked Berliner. 'Terry, you're supposed to phone your wife.'

Grinning at Berliner, Terry seemed less a shy man than a man surprised.

'It's not my wife,' he said, intimating complexities. Old confusions. As if to forbid himself another word, he shook his head. Long and bald. Sandy tufts of hair beside the ears, like baby feathers. His eyes were light brown. His nose was a straight, thick pull. 'I mustn't bore you fellows with my situation.' He nodded at me as if we had a special understanding. 'We're enjoying ourselves, telling melancholy stories about love.' He continued nodding. For no reason, I nodded back.

Cavanaugh said, 'Talk about anything you like, Terry. You say the woman who phoned isn't your wife?'

He grinned. 'I'm a haunted house. For me, yesterday is today. The woman who phoned is my former wife. A strange expression, but what else can I call her? Ex-wife?'

'Call her by her name,' I said.

'Her name is Nicki.'

21

'How long have you been divorced?' asked Cavanaugh.

'Usually one asks how long you've been married. Nicki and I have been divorced ten years. Nicki...'

'It's better,' said Berliner, 'if you say former wife. Nicki, Nicki—you sound like a ping-pong game.'

'All right. After ten years of divorce we're closer than during our marriage. If you don't remarry, this is natural. She phones me two or three times a week. Listen to how personal I'm becoming. Why is everything personal so funny?'

'Who is laughing?' said Berliner. 'Do you sleep together? To sleep with your former wife, I think—I mean just to me—it is immoral. I couldn't do it.'

'You couldn't do it,' I said. 'Who asked you to?'

'He's right. I'm sorry, Terry. Go on.'

'It doesn't happen often. Nicki has a boyfriend. His name is Harrison. But they don't live together. Nicki can't get along with kids. She doesn't like kids. More complicated yet, Harrison's daughter, eleven years old, is a very sad fat girl. His boy, six years old, has learning problems. Harrison phones me, too. I meet him now and then to talk about his kids.'

'He wants to talk to you?' I said.

'I'm a doctor. Even at parties people come up to me for an opinion. "Terry, I shouldn't discuss professional matters in these circumstances, but my aged aunt Sophie has a black wart on her buttock. She wants you to know. She says to tell you it is beginning to grow hair."'

'So what about Nicki? She was crying on the phone,' Kramer says.

'She always does. Your Marilyn story reminded me of a fight we had when I was in medical school in Montreal. We lived in a two-room flat above a grocery store. It was a Saturday morning. I was studying at the kitchen table. Can I tell this story?'

Berliner said, 'Only if it's miserable.'

'Anyhow, a blizzard had been building for days. I watched it through the kitchen window as it attacked the city. The sky disappeared. The streets were dead. Nothing moved but wind and snow. In this deadly blizzard, Nicki decided to go out. She had been saving money for a particular pair of boots. Fine soft leather. Tight. Knee-high. They had a red brown tone, like dried blood, but slightly glossy. Totally impractical and too elegant. The wind would tear them off her legs. Nobody in our crowd owned such boots. Our friends in Montreal were like us— students, poor, always working, always worried about money. Nicki had worked as a secretary all that year and she never bought presents for herself. Her salary paid for our rent and food. I had a tiny scholarship that covered books and incidental tuition fees. We were badly in debt, but she wanted these boots. I don't know how she saved a penny for them. I pleaded with her not to go out in the blizzard. Something in my voice, maybe, suggested more anxiety about the price of the boots than her safety. The more I pleaded the more determined she became.'

'Why didn't you go with her?' I asked.

'I wanted to. But the idea of the boots—so trivial, such a luxury—and her wanting to go get them that morning—made me furious. I could sympathize with her desire for beautiful boots. She deserved a reward. But why that minute did she have to go get them? I was trying to study. My papers and books were on the kitchen table. Also a box of slides and a microscope I carried home from the laboratory. Today, though I own a house with ten rooms, I still use the kitchen table when I read medical journals or write an article. Anyhow, I was trying to study. I needed the time. It's difficult for me to memorize things, but I can do it if there is peace and quiet and no bad feelings in the air. You don't have to be a genius to be a doctor. But now I was furious. I yelled, "Go on, do what you like. Buy the stupid boots. Just leave me alone." She slammed the door.

'For a while I sat with my papers and books. Outside the blizzard was hysterical. Inside it was warm and quiet. I worried about her, but my fury cancelled the worry. Soon I began really to study and I forgot about Nicki. Maybe three hours passed and, suddenly, she's home. Pale and burning and happy. I didn't say hello. My fury returned. She had a big shoebox under her arm. She had returned with her boots. While she put them on, I continued trying to study. I didn't watch her, but I could tell she needed help. The boots were tight. After a while she managed to get them on by herself, then she walked up to my table and stood there, in blood-coloured legs, waiting for me to notice. I could feel her excitement. She was trembling with pleasure. I knew what expression was in her face. Every muscle working not to smile. She waited for me to look up, collapse with approval, to admit she was magnificent in those boots. But the blizzard was in my heart. I refused to look. Suddenly, my paper, books, slides, microscope—everything on the table was all over the kitchen floor. Nicki is strong. She plays tennis like a man. I jumped up. I felt I had been killed, wiped out of the world.

'She still claims, I hit her. I don't remember. I remember rushing out into the blizzard with no coat or hat. Why? To buy a gun. I didn't really know what I wanted until I happened to pass a pawnshop. I saw guns in the window. I had a pocket watch that my father gave me when I left for medical school. A Waltham Premier worth about two hundred dollars. Gold case. Gothic numericals. A classic watch. Also a heavy gold chain. In exchange for that watch I got a rifle. Then I asked the man for a bullet. I couldn't pay for it, but I told him the deal was off unless he gave me a bullet. He said. "One bullet?" I screamed, "Give me a bullet." He gave it to me. If I'd asked for a ton of bullets, he would have thought nothing. But ask for one bullet and there's trouble.'

'The police were waiting for you,' said Berliner, 'when you got home.'

'I noticed the police car in front of the house, its light blinking through the storm. So I entered an alley behind the house and went up to the roof and loaded the rifle. I intended to go to the flat and blow my brains out in front of Nicki.'

'I thought you were going to shoot her,' I said.

'Her? I'd never shoot her. I'm her slave. I wanted to make a point about our relationship. But the police were in the flat. I was on the roof with a loaded rifle, freezing in the storm. I aimed into the storm, toward the medical school, and fired. How could I shoot myself? I'd have been on that roof with a bullet in my head, covered by snow, and nobody would have found me until spring. What comes to mind when you commit suicide is amazing. Listen, I have a question. My story made me hungry. Is there anything to eat?'

Kramer rose from his pillow with a brooding face. 'Men,' he said 'Terry is hungry. I believe him because I too am hungry. I suppose all of us could use a little bite. Any other night I would suggest we send out for pizza. Or I myself would make us an omelette. But not tonight. You are lucky tonight. Very lucky. Tomorrow, in this room, Nancy is having a meeting of her women's group. So the refrigerator happens to be packed with good things. Let me itemize. In the refrigerator there is three different kinds of salad. There is big plates of chicken, turkey and salmon. There is also a pecan pie. I love pecan pie. There is two pecan pies and there is two lemon pies. There is a chocolate cake which, even as I speak of it, sucks at me. I am offering all this to you men. Wait, Berliner. I have one more thing to say, Berliner. In the alcove behind the kitchen, rests a case of zinfandel. It is good, good California. Men, I offer to you this zinfandel.'

Berliner was already in the kitchen. The rest of us stayed to cheer Kramer. Even I cheered. Despite his tattooed arms, which reminded me of snakes, I cheered. His magnanimity was unqualified. No smallest doubt or reluctance troubled his voice. Every face in the room became like his, an animal touched by glee. We were 'lucky', said Kramer. Lucky, maybe, to be men. Life is unfair business. Whoever said otherwise? It is a billion bad shows, low blows, and number one has more fun. Nancy's preparations for her women's group would feed our club. The idea of delicious food, taken this way, was thrilling. Had it been there for us, it would have been pleasant. But this was evil, like eating the other woman. We discovered Berliner on his knees before the refrigerator, door open, his head inside. We cheered again, crowding up behind him as he passed things out to us, first a long plate of salmon, the whole pink fish intact, then the chicken, then a salad bowl sealed with a plastic sheet through which we saw dazzling green life. It would be a major feast, a huge eating. To Cavanaugh, standing beside me, I said, 'I thought you had to leave early.' He didn't reply. He pulled his watch off, slipped it into his pocket, and shouted, 'I see pâté in there. I want that, too.'

The cheers came again. Some of the men had already started on the salmon, snatching pieces of it with their fingers. Kramer, who had gone to the alcove, reappeared with black bottles of zinfandel, two under his arms, two in his hands. He stopped, contemplated the scene in his kitchen, and his dark eyes glowed. His voice was all pleasure. 'This is a wonderful club. This is a wonderful club.'

1980
The End of the
English Novel

Bill Buford

The novel has always smacked of inadequacies. It is regularly less than what is expected of it. Or, worse, it is more. But rarely the thing we had in mind, never quite settling upon an identity that it is easy to be happy about. Fifty years ago Ortega y Gasset confidently pronounced it dying. Twenty years ago, Marshall McLuhan tried hard to demonstrate that it was already dead. It wasn't, and, for some reason, isn't, still very much available as an attractive even if expensive instance of Randall Jarrell's weak apology for it: 'A longish piece of prose with something wrong with it.'

Since the war, the British novel has developed its own indigenous difficulties, or, at least, its own vernacular of complaint. When Gore Vidal remarked at the recent Edinburgh Festival that there are only 'middle class novels for middle class readers with middle class problems' he was echoing a tired charge that has become as predictable as much of the writing occasioning it. For John Sutherland, the complaint was raised to its most explicit by the best-sellers list five years ago, dominated with eerie appropriateness by the publication of Jane Austen's unfinished novel *Sanditon*, inviting the observation that the books that are published and purchased still belong very much to that novel of sense and sensibility which has merely been written and rewritten for nearly two centuries. Bernard Bergonzi's dark phrase is, in this context, ominously emblematic: the novel is no longer novel.

This vocabulary of termination has suddenly acquired a significance which has authoritatively dropped it from the theoretical to the base, real court of the marketplace. The Current Crisis in Publishing is, we understand from the many articles it has generated, of unprecedented proportions, and is noisy with terrible doomsday pronouncements. But it is not, in the end, the book as object which is threatened—for more are appearing (even if briefly) than ever before, although their number and kind have enlarged the image of publishing to something uncomfortably akin to the fast food industry—but the book as fiction, as an instance of literature: not the things in the window or on the railway platform, but the stuff apparently too cumbersome to consume on the run.

The implications of the present Crisis are obvious. It's not simply that a literature exists which many find disappointing. It's that we are being told, from now on, it can be no other way. There are reasons for it—the rising costs of this or that, the 'pound', inflation, foreign markets—and the reasons are real in a simple pocketbook way. Faced with many English novels, I confess I'd rather watch television. Faced recently by their price, I see I have no choice.

In such a context, what a publisher says is important. Recently Robert McCrum, a young editor at Faber & Faber, offered his view of the Crisis in the *Bookseller*. A young editor at Faber is virtually a symbol, and when he enters the most prominent columns of the nation's trade magazine to say that the situation is hopeless, some scrutiny—of the Crisis and the institutions suffering from it—is not warranted. It is necessary.

McCrum's article is entitled 'Writing without Risk' and is written with terrible finality: current writing is bad because it is written by bad writers. Nothing could be simpler or more incontrovertible: publishers, after all, don't produce literature; they can only be ready for it when it arrives. I am starting to see matters from a vastly different perspective, and my view proceeds from a belief that since the war British publishing and bookselling have never been less ready for literature than they are today. The Current Crisis in Publishing I am suggesting is far worse than any of the daily newspapers are even beginning to describe.

McCrum has three complaints, the first of which is by now fairly familiar: British writers are lifeless and sapped, 'happier adding to the myths, writing about the world we have lost'. The complaint is familiar stuff: a revision of Vidal's grievance against the middle class, Sutherland's of the novel of sense and sensibility, or Bergonzi's of the dreadful droning sameness of the contemporary. The complaint, however, must be questioned. There are undeniably a great many gifted writers in Britain. There are arguably more gifted writers than in any other time in the twentieth century. But unlike most other historical periods, the problem is not simply one of number but of kind: today's interesting fiction has until recently exhibited little sense

29

of unity, except for the superficial unity of being uneasily different from the writing usually promulgated as English: that post-war, pre-modern variety of the middle-class monologue, with C. P. Snow on one side and perhaps Margaret Drabble and Melvyn Bragg on the other (Kingsley Amis will always be nearby providing vitriolic commentary). Now, unlike (I suspect) Robert McCrum, I have no quarrel with these writers or their readers who, for reasons still obscure to me, keep buying their books. My quarrel is with those responsible for allowing these books to crowd out the kinds of books I'd like to read.

And that grievance originates from the assumptions tucked, like bedsheets, around McCrum's second and most important complaint: 'British writing seems immune to the philosophical and intellectual fevers of the time, inoculated against innovation by its native pragmatism.' The healthy (and well founded) suggestion here is that serious modern writing should be defined as much by international concerns as local ones, and it is a great convenience that ideas, unlike kinds of humour and automobiles made in Japan, are not inhibited by national borders. In the twentieth century, moreover, ideas (largely because of the book) have become extremely portable, and observation full of implications that don't seem to have been understood: the philosophical and intellectual fevers of the time are not transmitted merely by contact or proximity; no metaphor, regardless of its power, will render ideas contagious: much of the time they have to be read, and this is where the trouble begins.

We are all familiar with the complaint that English writers are, in McCrum's phrase, artistically timid, and cannot seem to carry off what the Americans keep getting away with. But the English writer's timidity is partly predetermined. The American writer's sense of experiment is largely the consequence of participating in an international dialogue. 'There is a movement of younger writers,' Charles Newman, former Editor of *TriQuarterly* observed fourteen years ago,

> to learn unselfconsciously from national literatures other than their own. There are very few promising and/or young American

writers today who have not been more influenced by 'foreign' writing than by any of their immediate predecessors. And the genuine merit of 'national discoveries', such as those of the new French novelists, have only become ascertainable as writers of other cultures have adapted them to their own experience, without being committed to a programmatic defense of *la méthode*.

The four most influential writers on the American fiction 'renaissance' of the Sixties and Seventies were foreign: Joyce, Kafka, Nabokov, and especially Borges. In 1961 Borges shared the International Publishers' Prize with Beckett. In 1962 New Directions published the English translation of *Labyrinths*. In England, *no hardback publisher ever bought the rights*. The book appeared in 1970, eight years later, four years after Newman's article, and ten years after it was written, as a Penguin Modern Classic.

Two months ago, Picador bravely (even if recklessly) published G. Cabrera Infante's *Three Trapped Tigers*, remarkable for a formal inventiveness which invites comparisons with two other 'experimental' books published this year: John Barth's *LETTERS* and Gilbert Sorrentino's *Mulligan's Stew*. Difference: *Three Trapped Tigers* was written in 1965 and translated and published in America in 1970, most probably long before *LETTERS* or *Mulligan's Stew* existed as possible ideas. Is it really surprising that a book of this sort, written over fifteen years ago, should be dismissed here—when at last it does appear—as an oh-yes-another-one-of-those? Books, unlike the *Daily Mirror*, can confidently outlast the week, the month, or the year. But they, like the ideas they carry, must be remarkable indeed to endure the span of a decade and a half.

Translations into English are notorious money losers, but it is easy to see how the losses are continually of the publishers' own making. There can be no market for foreign literature if the books do not come out regularly enough to create it. Last spring I came across Sidgwick and Jackson's admirable publication of Mario Satz's *Sol*, the first novel of an intended trilogy. The book is big, interesting, and expensive, and arrives like a half-eaten piece of food from someone else's exotic feast. Is it worth buying this book when—with the resistance to foreign literature so strong—I am certain that it is mostly a gesture, and that the remaining two volumes of the trilogy will never appear? Exactly who, to use McCrum's phrase, is approaching his or her task without risk? In the most recent *Index Translatorium* I could locate (1977), I found very few countries that translated less than Britain (for instance, Iceland and Botswana and, possibly, Uruguay). In contrast to the 486 *literary* works translated here, 1,186 appeared in France and 3,389 in Germany.

Insulation generates insularity, and the barriers are not strictly linguistic. William Gass, an American, quite possibly the most exciting practitioner of the English language, has only one book in print here (an essay). William Gaddis has none. And John Hawkes's recent novel, *The Passion Artist*, has spent eighteen months circulating around London looking for a publisher. How, in such a context, can the British writer be anything but provincial? Where can one catch these 'intellectual fevers of our time'? Do publishers really believe that ideas are merely contagious? I'm afraid I'm highly suspicious of McCrum's confident assertion that 'the attics of London are not full of embryo Conrads'. If such an embryo Conrad existed would a publisher recognize him? Or worse, would a publisher encourage him to write like the *real* Conrad of nearly a hundred years ago? There are reasons why English writers demonstrate the nervous wish to be elsewhere.

Of course, it is a commonplace that what is published in the end is decided by the Great British Public. A mythic beast of extraordinary proportions—with puffy white arms, sustained by McVitie's chocolate biscuits and books about the Queen Mother—this Great Public has been elevated to virtually incontestable authority. The personality requires some scrutiny if only because it seems to be determining the shape of British literature so exclusively, especially now during the Great Crisis. Is this Public, I'm asking, a real entity of such an incontrovertible sway or is it merely a marvellous mythology of an industry sustaining a decisively archaic practice?

The book trade, like the items it sells, is one of the most enjoyable institutions to have survived the nineteenth-century English middle class. It was of course that great, liberal, and particular public—with its one language, one education, (usually) one sex, and its one overriding determination to know things comprehensively—which engendered and supported marvellous intellectual periodicals like the *Edinburgh Review* and the *Quarterly* (circulation at 14,000), the *Fortnightly Review* (25,000), the *Athenaeum* (18,000), or the *Cornhill* (in 1860, 110,000). That those periodicals do not exist today and, for some very important reasons, would never survive is probably the best indication of how we in 1980 are different.

It was also that great, liberal club—wanting to know its many things—which engendered and supported the commissioning book trade, whose function was simply to keep all newly published books in stock. The assortment was fairly consistent from one shop to the next. The reading public was, after all, the same throughout the country: it could be said that its members read in the same accent.

Today's British book trade is sweet, old-fashioned, and self-protected. It is also remarkable for the extent to which it has hardly developed throughout its history. Businesses, resisting specialization, have changed little, and the customer, pretty much like the novel he buys, is invited to remain the same. In Britain, I understand, there are roughly 2,500 bookshops. In Germany, there are 6,000. In the United States, where the population is only four times larger, there are 16,217. Something is wrong.

General bookshops sustained literary fiction because of the specific public with specifically general interests entering them. That public no longer exists, and there is no way that general bookshops can adequately sustain literary fiction today, but general bookshops unquestionably (and unquestioned) dominate. One of the many casualties has been the most ridiculous: the campus book trade. In the university town where this magazine is published, it is common for students, in numbers up to 300, to attend a lecture about a book which has sold out or was never available in the first place. The town's largest and most famous bookshop offers a window display which tacitly suggests that most of the university's students live and buy their books somewhere on the far side of the country. On the week I am writing this there was one work of fiction on display. Last week there was none.

In the United States, there are many reasons why there should be over 2,600 generically distinct campus bookshops. In Britain, there is absolutely no reason why there are not even enough to justify a statistic. I am not urging booksellers to create a 'market'. I'm saying that the market exists and has existed for some time: it's made of people not getting the books they need, and everybody—from author to reader—is suffering.

The significance of the success of Virago and the Picador series is that they have demonstrated how some publishers have been able to cultivate new markets from which, potentially, new kinds of writing—distinct from competitive market identities—can emerge. Though still terribly limited, this success (reinforced by Quartet and the Women's Press, and, in both hardback *and* paperback, by Writers and Readers, Allison and Busby, Carcanet, and others) suggests the extent to which the Great British Public takes on far too much blame far too often. It is time that publishers, distributors, and booksellers recognize that this Public is not one public, perversely homogeneous, but many publics with many needs to be served. If the adventurous novels are to be sustained—something other than the tired version of Covent Garden or the impoverished replication of *Lucky Jim* or yet another rendering of what it is like, man, to be an international television/film/journalist/playwriting/jet-setting/bed-hopping/continent jumping/Oxbridge Personality—then it is time to secure the audience (it's there, you don't have to look far) that will buy them.

The Current Crisis in Publishing is revealing just how anachronistic publishing and bookselling are and just how much this society is trying to sustain its creative artists and their achievements on a system regularly incapable of performing the task it is called upon to perform. Thirty years ago the official historian of the Longman publishing house proudly announced that nothing significant had changed in publishing since 1842.

His remarks today acquire a terrible pertinence: 'Those who have controlled the business during the last 107 years have provided no *new* answers. The interesting thing is that in themselves and in their policies, they have provided the old answers over and over again.' The interesting thing, now, is they continue to do so: the book, in more than one sense is a hand-made art in an economy no longer able to accommodate it.

Robert McCrum's article is, I'm sure, not representative of the person who wrote it, amounting to an instance of the high brutality of good intentions. The problem is derived from the position he argues from, a position which can only end up reinforcing the practices of an industry which is choking off the best examples of its product. And the problem is entirely unrelated to what I understand to be McCrum's central argument and third complaint—that writers and publishers take too much for granted, and are incapable of the determination and artistic integrity of those from politically repressed nations. The real censorship taking place is not political but economic, has little to do with writers and everything to do with the way their writing is produced, distributed and sold. Hardback publishers are this culture's most influential arbiters of taste: they determine what we value if only because they determine what we will have the opportunity to judge. It is urgent to distinguish the current state of publishing and bookselling from the actual state of fiction.

In *Fiction and the Fiction Industry*, John Sutherland suggests that the literary-publishing complex, by nature inert and backward-looking, requires complete destruction of old forms as a precondition of advance; such was the case with the three-decker novel in the nineteenth century. Is the present hysteria an intimation of another revolution? Can we really believe that most publishers are going to risk publishing another Borges or another Gass or another Márquez? And do we really believe they will spot the embryo Conrad? How are we to measure silent censorship, how can we take the dimensions of a nothing? The prospect is gloomy and irritating and angering, and invokes like a banner Lawrence's anarchic phrase quite importantly revised: surgery for the way novels are made—or a bomb.

What it means to put a text in print must change. The culture in which creative prose must now make its way is obviously developing into a novelty culture, to which the busy, busy book business appears as one of its most efficient contributors. Indeed, the Present Crisis should be, in the end, not a cause for despair but celebration. New outlets must be developed if creative prose is to find its readers, let alone be supported by them.

The most important reason why the *Edinburgh Review*, *Quarterly*, the *Fortnightly Review*, *Cornhill*, or *Athenaeum* do not exist today is because the public who purchased them is no longer around. The alternative, however, is not in the tired continuation or uninspired variation of their format: the crowd of exhausted reviews busy with a books-in-brief or a truncated fiction chronicle or current 'hit' list merely caters to the industry's mindless pace, generating mini-ideas which, like the books they're about, exist only to be pulped. It is obvious that a new publication must come into existence which relies upon a specific, even if narrow group of readers who care not to have their intelligence insulted every time they turn the page. It must be along the lines of Charles Newman's dreams—a publication that is independent and personal and notable for the quality of its sentences. But most importantly it would respond to the culture of its time by refusing to be an instance of its worst ways, dedicated, above all, to a collaboration of writer and producer and reader. The prospect, for instance, of the reader having a definable relationship to what he reads has only been tentatively explored. Imagine a reader commissioning a writer, in the same way and for the same reasons that one commissions a sculptor. Or a group of readers commissioning a whole issue or even a series of issues. The possibilities are endless.

Today's novel is in fact far more novel than it is commonly understood to be: it is not the novel which is dying, although it may well be the old ways of its production which are, a disjunction made particularly acute by the coincidence of this Great Publishing Crisis and the development of a new kind of fiction. What it means to tell a story has, virtually unnoticed, taken on a new set of meanings, even if the most obvious and unfortunate one of them is that the story may never appear in hardback or, worse, never reach its potential readers.

What it means to tell, to write, to narrate, to *make up* is changing, and it is a change significant enough to be distinguished from the aesthetic concerns which have dominated the last eighty years. The twentieth century—in its modernism or its postmodernism or its literature of exhaustion—has been grounded in an attitude of opposition which is too crude and too simple and too incomplete to be viable today. The modernist precepts of Ortega y Gasset, with its dialectical rejection of the nineteenth century, was a crucial response to an entrenched bourgeois culture which is no longer the enemy because it is no longer a presence in the same way. In the art dubiously and thanklessly entitled 'postmodernist', Ortega y Gasset's precepts are elevated to a creed. But postmodernism confronts not a nineteenth-century literature but a twentieth-century art, not a bourgeois society but the unwieldy anonymous mass-marketed twentieth-century mind. Modernism was the careful collision of the permanent and the new; postmodernism has inevitably become the reckless collusion of the new and the useless: it smells of literary leftovers, with thoughts, like food, not quite digested.

Postmodernist art is important because it invites us to recognize the particular brutal emptiness of the twentieth century. But in its laboured refutation of a tradition that is increasingly difficult to identify and in its persistent depictions of the passive, vacant mindlessness readily generated by the various media around us, it is conflated with the context of its making, not transcending the problem but being an instance of it. Debilitating deconstructions dissolving into pathetic patter.

Current fiction is remarkable for its detachment, its refusal to be affiliated, its suspicion of the old hierarchies and authorities. It is not modernist or pre-modernist or postmodernist or of that debate, but managing nevertheless to be both arriving and departing at once. If I am right that we are moving into a different period of creative prose, it is characterized by a writing which, freed from the middle-class monologue, is experimentation in the real sense, exploiting traditions and not being wasted by them. The writer today is managing to reassert the act of narration—the telling not simply of fictions but stories—not in deference to the referential workings of bourgeois realism but as an instance of the human imagination. In the work of many writers—Salman Rushdie is an outstanding example—we are moving closer to the fiction of Gabriel Márquez or Italo Calvino, a magic realism, rising out of an age of technical exhaustion, where telling is at the centre of our consciousness.

The old divisions and the old generalizations are no longer usable. The fiction of today is testimony to an invasion of outsiders, using a language much larger than the culture. The English novel has been characterized by the self-depictions of its maker's dominance: the novel of sense and sensibility is informed by the authority of belonging. Today, however, the imagination resides along the peripheries; it is spoken through a minority discourse, with the dominant tongue re-appropriated, re-commanded, and importantly re-invigorated. It is, at last, the end of the English novel and the beginning of the British one.

1981
Vitamins
Raymond Carver

I had a job and Patti didn't. I worked a few hours a night for the hospital. It was a nothing job. I did some work, signed the card for eight hours, went drinking with the nurses. After a while Patti wanted a job. She said she needed a job for her self-respect. So she started selling multiple vitamins and minerals door-to-door.

For a while she was just another girl who went up and down blocks in strange neighbourhoods knocking on doors. But she learned the ropes. She was quick and had excelled at things in school. She had personality. Pretty soon the company gave her a promotion. Some of the girls who weren't doing so hot were put to work under her. Before long she had herself a crew and a little office out in the mall. But the names and faces of the girls who worked for her were always changing. Some girls would quit after a few days, after a few hours sometimes. One or two of the girls were good at it. They could sell vitamins. These girls stuck with Patti. They formed the core of the crew. But there were girls who couldn't give away vitamins.

The girls who couldn't cut it would last a week or so and then quit. Just not show for work. If they had a phone they'd take it off the hook. They wouldn't answer their door. At first Patti took these losses to heart, like the girls were new converts who had lost their way. She blamed herself. But she got over that. Too many girls quit. Once in a while a girl would quit on her first day in the field. She'd freeze and not be able to push the doorbell. Or maybe she'd get to the door and something would happen to her voice. Or she'd get the opening remarks mixed up with something she shouldn't be saying until she got inside. Maybe it was then the girl would decide to bunch it, take the sample case, and head for the car where she hung around until Patti and the others had finished. There'd be a hasty one-on-one conference. Then they'd all ride back to the office. They'd say things to buck themselves up. 'When the going gets tough, the tough get going.' And, 'Do the right things and the right things will happen.' Stuff like that. Now and then a girl disappeared in the field, sample case and all. She'd hitch a ride into town, then beat it. Just disappear. But there were always girls to take their places. Girls were coming and going. Patti had a list. Every few weeks or so she ran a little ad in the Pennysaver and more girls showed up and another training session was in order. There was no end of girls.

The core group was made up of Patti, Donna, and Sheila. My Patti was a beauty. Donna and Sheila were medium-pretty. One night Sheila confessed to Patti that she loved her more than anything on earth. Patti told me she used those words. Patti had driven her home and they were sitting in front of Sheila's apartment. Patti said she loved her too. She loved all her friends. But not in the way Sheila had in mind. Then Sheila touched Patti's breast. She brushed the nipple through Patti's blouse. Patti took Sheila's hand and held it. She told her she didn't swing that way. Sheila didn't bat an eye. After a minute, she nodded. But she kept Patti's hand. She kissed it, then got out of the car.

That was around Christmas. The vitamin business was off, and we thought we'd have a party to cheer everybody up. It seemed like a good idea at the time. But Sheila got drunk early and passed out. She passed out on her feet, fell over, and didn't wake up for hours. One minute she was standing in the middle of the living room, laughing. Then her eyes closed, the legs buckled, and she went down with a glass in her hand. The hand holding the drink smacked the coffee table as she fell. She didn't make a sound otherwise. The drink poured into the rug. Patti and I and somebody else lugged her out to the back porch and put her down on a cot and tended to forget about her.

Everybody got drunk and went home. Patti went to bed. I wanted to keep on, so I sat at the table with a drink until it started to get light out. Then Sheila came in from the porch and began complaining. She said she had this headache that was so bad it was like somebody was sticking hot wires into her temples. It was such a headache, she said, she was afraid it might leave her with a permanent squint. And she was sure her little finger was broken. She showed it to me. It looked purple. She bitched that we'd let her sleep all night with her contacts in. She wanted to know didn't anybody give a shit. She brought the finger up close and looked at it. She shook her head. She held the finger as far away as she could and looked some more. It was as if she couldn't believe the things that must have happened

41

to her that night. Her face was puffy, and her hair was all over. She looked hateful and half-crazy. She ran cold water over her finger. 'God, oh God,' she said and cried some over the sink.

But she'd made a serious pass at Patti, a declaration of love, and I didn't have any sympathy.

I was drinking scotch and milk with a sliver of ice. Sheila leaned against the drainboard. She watched me from little slits of eyes. I took some of my drink. I didn't say anything. She went back to telling me how bad she felt. She said she needed to see a doctor. She said she was going to wake Patti. She said she was quitting, leaving the state, going to Portland, and she had to say goodbye to Patti. She kept on. She wanted Patti to drive her to the emergency room.

'I'll drive you,' I said. I didn't want to do it, but I would.

'I want Patti to drive me,' she said. She was holding the wrist of her bad hand with her good hand, the little finger as big as a pocket flashlight. 'Besides, we need to talk. I want to tell her I'm leaving. I need to tell her I'm going to Portland. I need to say goodbye.'

I said, 'I guess I'll have to tell her for you. She's asleep.'

She turned mean. 'We're *friends*,' she said. 'I have to talk to her. I have to tell her myself.'

I shook my head. 'She's asleep. I just said so.'

'We're friends and we love each other,' she said. 'I have to say goodbye to her.' She made to leave the kitchen.

I started to get up. I said, 'I told you I'll drive you.'

'You're drunk! You haven't even been to bed yet.' She looked at her finger again and said, 'Goddamn, why'd this have to happen?'

'Not too drunk to drive you to the hospital,' I said.

'I won't ride with you, you bastard!' Sheila yelled.

'Suit yourself. But you're not going to wake Patti. Lesbo bitch,' I said.

'Fucker bastard,' she said. She said that and then she went out of the kitchen and out the front door without using the bathroom or even washing her face. I got up and looked out the window. She was walking down the road toward Fulton Avenue. Nobody else was up. It was too early.

I finished my drink and thought about fixing another one. I fixed one.

Nobody saw any more of Sheila. None of us vitamin-related people anyway. She walked to Fulton Avenue and out of our lives. Later on that day Patti said, 'What happened to Sheila?' and I said, 'She went to Portland.' That was that. Patti didn't ask the details.

I had the hots for Donna, the other member of the core group. We'd danced to some Duke Ellington records that night. I'd held her pretty tight, smelled her hair, and kept a hand at the small of her back as I guided her over the rug. I got turned on dancing with her. I was the only guy at the party and there were six or seven girls dancing with each other. It was a turn-on to look around the living room. I was in the kitchen when Donna came in with her empty glass. We were alone for a minute. I got her into a little embrace. She hugged me back. We stood there and hugged.

Then she said, 'Don't. Not now.' When I heard that 'not now' I let go and figured it was money in the bank.

So I'd been at the table reconstructing that hug, Donna on my mind, when Sheila came in with her bum finger.

I thought some more on Donna. I finished the drink. I took the phone off the hook and headed for the bedroom. I took off my clothes and got in beside Patti. I lay for a minute, winding down. Then I started in. But she didn't wake up. Afterwards, I closed my eyes.

It was afternoon when I opened them again, and I was in bed alone. Rain was blowing against the window. A sugar doughnut lay on Patti's pillow, and a glass of old water sat on the nightstand. I was still drunk and couldn't figure anything out. I knew it was Sunday and close to Christmas. I ate the doughnut and drank the water. I went back to sleep until I heard Patti running the vacuum. She came into the bedroom and asked about Sheila. That's when I told her, said she'd gone to Portland.

A week or so into the New Year Patti and I were having a drink. She'd just come home from work. It wasn't so late, but it was dark and rainy. I was going to work in a couple of hours. But first we were having us some scotch and talking. Patti was tired. She was down in the dumps and on to her third drink. Nobody was buying vitamins. She was reduced to Donna, core, and Sandy, a semi-new girl and a kleptomaniac. We were talking about things like negative weather and the number of parking tickets Patti had accumulated and let go. Finally, how maybe we'd be better off if we moved to Arizona, some place like that.

I fixed us another one. I looked out the window. Arizona wasn't a bad idea.

Patti said, 'Vitamins.' She picked up her glass and swirled the ice. 'For shit sake! I mean, when I was a girl this is the last thing I ever saw myself doing. Jesus, I never thought I'd grow up to sell vitamins. Door-to-door vitamins. This beats everything. This blows my mind.'

'I never thought so either, honey,' I said.

'That's right,' she said. 'You said it in a nutshell.'

'Honey.'

'Don't honey me,' she said. 'This is hard, brother. This life is not easy, any way you cut it.'

She seemed to think things over for a minute. She shook her head. Then she finished her drink. She said, 'I even dream of vitamins when I'm asleep. I don't have any relief. There's no relief! At least you can walk away from your job after work and leave it behind. Forget about it. I'll bet you haven't had one dream about your job. You don't come home dead tired and fall asleep and dream you're waxing floors or whatever you do down there. Do you? After you've left the fucking place, you don't come home and dream about the fucking job!' she screamed.

I said, 'I can't remember what I dream. Maybe I don't dream. I don't remember anything when I wake up.' I shrugged. I didn't keep track of what went on in my head when I was asleep. I didn't care.

'You dream!' Patti said. 'Even if you don't remember. Everybody dreams. If you didn't dream, you'd go crazy. I read about it. It's an outlet. People dream when they're asleep. Or else they'd go nuts. But when I dream I dream of vitamins. Do

44

you see what I'm saying?' She had her eyes fixed on me.

'Yes and no,' I said. It wasn't a simple question.

'I dream I'm pitching vitamins,' she went on. 'I dream I've run out of vitamins and I have a dozen orders waiting to be written if I can just show them the fucking *product*. Understand? I'm selling vitamins day and night. Jesus, what a life,' she said. She finished her drink.

'How's Sandy doing? She still have sticky fingers?' I wanted to get us off this subject. But there wasn't anything else.

Patti said, 'Shit,' and shook her head as if I didn't know anything.

We listened to it rain.

'Nobody is selling vitamins,' Patti said. She picked up her glass. But it was empty. 'Nobody is buying vitamins. That's what I'm telling you. I just told you that. Didn't you hear me?'

I got up to fix us another one. 'Donna doing anything?' I read the label on the bottle and waited.

Patti said, 'She made a little sale a few days ago. That's all. That's all that's happened this week. It wouldn't surprise me if she quit. I wouldn't blame her,' Patti said. 'If I was in her place, I'd think of quitting. But if she quits, then what? Then I'm back at the start, that's what. Ground zero. The middle of winter, people sick all over the state, people dying, and nobody thinks they need vitamins. I'm sick as hell myself.'

'What's wrong, honey?' I put the drinks on the table and sat down. She went on as if I hadn't said anything. Maybe I hadn't.

'I'm my own best customer,' she said. 'I've taken so many vitamins I think they may be doing something to my skin. Does my skin look OK to you? Can a person OD on vitamins? I'm getting to where I can't even go to the bathroom like a normal person.'

'Honey,' I said.

Patti said, 'You don't care if I take vitamins or don't take vitamins. That's the point. You don't care. You don't care about anything. The windshield wiper quit this afternoon in the rain. I almost had a wreck. I came this close.'

We went on drinking and talking until it was time for me to go to work. Patti said she was going to soak in a hot tub, if she didn't fall asleep first. 'I'm asleep on my feet,' she said. She said, 'Vitamins, for shit's sake. That's all there is any more.' She looked around the kitchen. She looked at her empty glass. 'Why in hell aren't you rich?' She laughed. She was drunk. But she let me kiss her. Then I left for work.

There was a place I went to after work. I'd started going for the music and because I could get a drink there after closing hours. It was a place called the Off-Broadway. It was a spade place in a spade neighbourhood. It was run by a spade named Khaki and was patronized by spades, along with a few whites. People would show up after the other places in town had stopped serving. They'd ask for house specials—RC Colas with a belt of whisky—or else they'd bring their own stuff in under their coats or in the women's ditty bags, order RC and build their own. Musicians showed up to jam, and the drinkers who wanted to keep drinking came to drink and listen to the music. Sometimes people danced on the little dance floor. But usually they sat in the booths and drank and listened to the music.

Now and then a spade hit another spade in the head with a bottle. Once a story went around that somebody had followed another somebody into the Gents and cut the man's throat while he stood in front of the urinal. But I never saw any trouble. Nothing that Khaki couldn't handle. Khaki was a big spade with a bald head that gleamed under the fluorescents. He wore Hawaiian print shirts that hung over his pants. I think he carried a pistol inside his waistband. At least a sap. If somebody started to get out of line, Khaki would walk over to where it was beginning, some voice rising over the other voices and the music. He'd rest his big hand on the party's shoulder and say a few words and that was that. I'd been going there off and on for months. I was pleased that he'd say things to me like, 'How're you doing tonight, friend? 'Or, 'Friend, I haven't seen you for a spell. Glad to see you. We're here to have fun.'

The Off-Broadway is where I took Donna on our first and last date.

I walked out of the hospital just after midnight. It'd cleared up and stars were out. I still had this buzz from the scotch I'd had with Patti. But I was thinking to hit New Jimmy's for a quick one on the way home. Donna's car was parked in the space beside my car. Donna was inside the car. I remembered that hug we'd had in the kitchen. Not now, she'd said.

I walked over to her door. She rolled the window down and knocked ashes from her cigarette.

'I couldn't sleep,' she said. 'I have things on my mind, and I couldn't sleep.'

I said, 'Donna. Hey, I'm glad to see you.'

'I don't know what's wrong with me,' she said.

'You want to go some place for a drink? I could have been out of this place an hour ago,' I said.

'I haven't been here long. Anyway, I needed time to think. I guess one drink can't hurt. Patti's my friend,' she said. 'You know that.'

'She's my friend too,' I said. Then I said, 'Let's go.'

'Just so you know,' she said.

'There's this place. It's a spade place,' I said. 'They have music. We can get a drink, listen to some music.' 'You want to drive me?' Donna said.

'Scoot over.'

She started in about vitamins. Vitamins were in a skid, vitamins had taken a nosedive. The bottom had fallen out of the vitamin market.

Donna said, 'I hate to do this to Patti. She's my best friend, and she's trying to build things up for us. But I may have to quit. This is between us. Swear it! But I have to eat. I have to pay rent. I need new shoes and a new coat. Vitamins can't cut it,' she said. 'I don't think vitamins is where it's at any more. I haven't said anything to Patti. Like I said, I'm still just thinking about it.'

Donna's hand lay next to my leg. I reached down and squeezed her fingers. She squeezed back. Then she took her hand away and pushed in the lighter. After she had her cigarette going, she put the hand back on the seat next to my leg. 'Worse than anything, I hate to let Patti down. You know what I'm saying? We were a team.' She handed me her cigarette. 'I know it's a different brand,' she said, 'but try it, you might like it.'

I pulled into the lot for the Off-Broadway. Three spades leaned against an old Chrysler that had a cracked front windshield. They were just lounging, passing a bottle in a paper sack. They looked us over. I got out and went around to open the door for Donna. I checked the doors, took her arm, and we headed for the street. The spades watched but didn't say anything.

'You're not thinking about moving to Portland?' I said. We were on the sidewalk. I put my arm around her waist.

'I don't know anything about Portland. Portland hasn't once crossed my mind.'

The front half of the Off-Broadway was like a regular spade cafe and bar. A few spades sat at the counter and a few more worked over plates of food at tables covered with red oilcloth. We passed through the cafe and into a big room in back. There was a long counter with booths against the wall. But at the back of the room was a platform where musicians could set up. In front of the platform was something that could pass for a dance floor. Bars and nightclubs were still serving, so people hadn't turned up at the Off-Broadway in any large numbers yet. I helped Donna take off her coat. We settled ourselves in a booth and put our cigarettes on the table. The spade waitress named Hannah came over. Hannah and me nodded. She looked at Donna. I ordered us two RC Cola specials and decided to feel good about things.

After the drinks came and I'd paid and we'd each had a sip, we started hugging. We carried on lightly for a while, squeezing and patting, kissing each other's face. Every so often Donna would stop and draw back, push me away a little, then hold me by the wrists. She'd gaze into my eyes. Then her lids would close slowly and we'd fall to kissing again. Pretty soon the place began to fill. We stopped kissing. But I kept my arm around her. She ran her fingers up and down my thigh. A couple of spade horn players and a white drummer began fooling around with a piece. I figured Donna and me would have another drink and listen to the set. Then we'd leave and go to her place to finish what we'd started.

I'd just ordered two more from Hannah when this spade named Benny came over with this other spade, a big dressed-up spade. The big spade had little red eyes and was wearing a three-piece grey pinstripe that looked new but was tight in the shoulders, a rose-coloured shirt, a tie, topcoat, a fedora. All of it.

'How's my man?' said Benny. Benny stuck out his hand for a brother handshake. Benny and I had talked. He knew I liked jazz and he used to come over to the booth and talk whenever he and I were in the place at the same time. He liked to talk about Johnny Hodges, how he had played sax accompaniment for Johnny. He'd say things like, 'When Johnny and me had this gig in Mason City.'

'Hi, Benny,' I said.

'I want you to meet Nelson,' Benny said. 'He just back from Vietnam today. This morning. He here to listen to some of these good sounds. He got his dancing shoes on in case.' He looked at Nelson and nodded. 'This here is Nelson.'

I was looking at Nelson's shiny black shoes, and then I looked at Nelson. He seemed to want to place me from somewhere. He studied me. Then he let loose a rolling grin that showed his teeth. He looked down the booth.

'This is Donna,' I said. 'Donna, this is Benny, and this is Nelson. Nelson, this is Donna.'

'Hello, girl,' Nelson said and Donna said right back, 'Hello there, Nelson. Hello, Benny.'

'Maybe we'll just slide in and join you folks?' Benny said. 'OK?' I said, 'Sure.' But I was sorry they hadn't found some place else. 'We're not going to be here long,' I said. 'Long enough to finish this drink is all.'

'I know man, I know,' Benny said. He sat across from me after Nelson had let himself down into the booth. 'Things to do, places to go. Yes, sir, Benny knows,' he said and winked.

Nelson looked across the booth to Donna. He stared at her. Then he took off the hat. He seemed to be examining the brim as he turned the hat around in his big hands. He made room for the hat on the table. He looked up at Donna. He grinned and squared his shoulders. He had to square his shoulders every few minutes. It was like he was very tired. I wished they'd have landed some place else.

'You real good friends with him, I bet,' Nelson said to Donna, not wasting a minute.

'We're good friends,' Donna said.

Hannah came over. Benny asked for RC's. Hannah went away and Nelson worked a pint of whisky from his topcoat pocket.

'Good friends,' Nelson said. 'Real good friends.' He unscrewed the lid.

'Watch out, Nelson,' Benny said. 'Keep that bottle out of sight. Nelson just got off the plane from Vietnam,' Benny said.

Nelson raised the bottle and drank some of his whisky. He screwed the lid back, laid the bottle on the table, and tried to cover it with his hat. 'Real good friends,' he said.

Benny looked at me and rolled his eyes. But he was drunk too. 'I got to get into shape,' he said to me. He drank RC from both of their glasses and then held the glasses under the table and poured whisky. He put the bottle in his coat pocket. 'Man, I ain't put my lips to a reed for a month now. I got to get with it.'

We were bunched in the booth, glasses in front of us, Nelson's hat on the table. 'You,' Nelson said to me. 'You with somebody else, ain't you? This beautiful woman, she ain't your wife. I know that. But you real good friends with this woman. Ain't I right?'

I had some of my drink. I couldn't taste the whisky. I couldn't taste anything. I said, 'Is all that shit about Vietnam true we see on the TV?'

Nelson had his red eyes fixed on me. After a time he said, 'What I want to say is, Do you know where your wife is? Hah? I bet she's out with some dude and she be laying in his arms this minute. She be touching his nipples, pulling his pud for him while you sitting here big as life with your good friend. I bet she have herself a good friend too.'

'Nelson,' Benny said.

'Nelson nothing,' Nelson said.

Benny said, 'Nelson, let's leave these people be. There's somebody in that other booth. Somebody I told you about. Nelson just this morning got off a plane,' Benny said. 'Nelson—'

'I bet I know what you thinking,' Nelson said. He kept on with it. 'I bet you thinking, Now here's a big drunk nigger and what am I going to do with him? Maybe I have to whip his ass. Hah? That what you thinking?'

I looked around the room. I saw Khaki standing near the platform, the musicians working away behind him. Some couples were on the floor. People had piled into the booths and were listening to the music. I thought Khaki looked right at me, but if he did he looked away again.

'Ain't it your turn to talk now?' Nelson said. 'I just teasing you. I ain't done any teasing since I left Nam. I teased the gooks some.' He grinned again, his big lips rolling back. Then he stopped grinning and just stared.

'Show them that ear,' Benny said quickly. He put his empty glass on the table. 'Nelson got himself an ear off one of them little dudes,' Benny said. 'He carry it with him. Show them, Nelson.'

Nelson sat there. Then he started feeling the pockets of his topcoat. He took things out of the pockets. He took out a handkerchief, some keys, a box of cough drops.

Donna said, 'I don't want to see an old ear. Ugh. Double ugh. Jesus.' She looked at me.

'We have to go,' I said.

Nelson was still feeling in his pockets. He took a wallet from a pocket inside the suit coat and put it on the table. He patted the wallet. 'Five thousand dollars there. Listen here,' he said to Donna. 'I going to give you two bills. OK? Two one hundred dollar bills. I got fifty them. You with me? I give you two of them. Then I want you to French me. Just like his wife doing some other big fellow. You listening? You know goddamn well she got her lips around somebody's hammer this minute while he here with his hand up your skirt. Fair's fair. Two one hundreds. Here.' He pulled the corners of the bills from his wallet. 'Hell, here another hundred for your friend. So he won't feel left out. He don't have to do nothing. You don't have to do nothing,' Nelson said to me. 'You just sit here and drink your drink. Sit here and listen to the music. Good music. Me and this woman walk out together like good friends. And she walk back in by herself. Won't be long, she be back.'

'Nelson,' Benny said, 'this is no way to talk. Nelson, Nelson.'

Nelson grinned. 'I finished what I have to say.' Then he said,

'But I ain't joking.' He took the handkerchief and wiped his face. He turned to Benny.

'I always say my mind. Benny, you know me. You still my friend, Benny? Hell, we all good friends. But I want what I want,' Nelson said. 'And I willing to pay for it. Don't want something for nothing. I pay for it, or I take it. That simple.'

He found what he'd been feeling for. It was a silver cigarette case which he worked open. I looked at the ear inside. It lay on a piece of cotton. The ear was brown, like a dried mushroom. It was beginning to curl. But it was a real ear and it was attached to a key chain.

'God,' said Donna. 'Yuck.'

Benny and I looked at the ear.

'Something, hah?' Nelson said. He was watching Donna.

'I'm not going outside with you and that's that,' Donna said. 'No way. I'm not going and that's all there is to it.'

'Girl,' Nelson said.

'Nelson,' I said. And then Nelson fixed his red eyes on me. He pushed the hat and wallet and cigarette case out of his way.

'What you want?' Nelson said. 'I give you what you want.'

Benny closed his eyes and then he opened them and said, 'Thank heaven, here come Khaki. Nelson, Benny going to make a prediction. Benny predict that in thirty seconds Khaki going to be standing here asking if everything be all right, if everybody happy.'

Donna said, 'I'm not happy. I'm not one bit happy,' Donna said.

Khaki came over to the booth and put a hand on my shoulder and the other hand on Benny's shoulder. He leaned over the table, his head shining under the lights. 'How you folks? You all having fun?'

'Everything all right, Khaki,' Benny said. 'Everything A-OK. These people was just fixing to leave. Me and Nelson going to sit here and listen to the music makers.'

'That's good,' Khaki said. 'Folks be happy is my motto.' He looked around the booth. He looked at Nelson's wallet on the table and at the open cigarette case next to the wallet. He saw the ear.

'That a real ear?' he said.

Benny said, 'It is. Show him that ear, Nelson. Nelson just stepped off the plane from Vietnam with this ear. This ear has travelled halfway around the world to be on this table tonight. Nelson, show him,' Benny said.

Nelson handed the case over to Khaki.

Khaki examined the ear. He took up the chain and dangled the ear in front of his face. He looked at it. He let it swing back and forth on the chain. 'I heard about these dried-up ears and cocks and such things, but I ain't really believed it. Or I believed it, but I never really believed it till this minute.'

'I took it off one of them little gooks,' Nelson said. 'He couldn't hear nothing with it no more. I wanted me a keepsake.'

'My God,' said Khaki. He turned the car on its chain. 'I guess I seen everything.'

Donna and I began getting out of the booth.

'Girl, don't go,' Nelson said.

'Nelson,' Benny said.

Khaki was watching Nelson now. I stood beside the booth with Donna's coat. My legs were crazy.

Nelson raised his voice. He said, 'If you go with this fucker, let him put his face in your sweets, you going to fry in hell with him!'

We started to move away from the booth. People were looking.

'Nelson just got off the plane from Vietnam this morning,' I heard Benny say. 'We been drinking all day. This been the longest day on record. But me and him we going to be fine, Khaki.'

Nelson yelled something over the music. He yelled, 'You fixing to plow that, son of a bitch, but it ain't going to do no good! It ain't going to help none!' I heard him say that, and then I couldn't hear any more. The music stopped, and then it started again. We didn't look back. We kept going. We got out to the sidewalk.

I opened the door for her and went around to my side. I drove us back to the hospital. Donna stayed over on her side of the car. From time to time she'd use the lighter on a cigarette, but she wouldn't talk.

I tried to say something. I said, 'Maybe I should have taken *his* ear for a souvenir. Look, Donna, don't get on a downer because of this. I'm sorry it happened,' I said.

'Maybe I should have taken his money,' Donna said. 'That's what I was thinking.'

I kept driving and didn't look at her. I couldn't say anything that would help.

'It's true,' she said. 'Maybe I should've taken the money.' She shook her head. 'I don't know. I don't know what I'm saying. I just shouldn't have been there.' Donna began to cry. She put her chin down and cried.

'Don't cry,' I said. There was nothing else to say.

'I'm not going in to work tomorrow, today, whenever it is the alarm goes off,' she said. 'I'm not going in. I'm going to quit. I'm leaving town. I take what happened back there as a sign.' She pushed in the lighter and waited for it to pop out.

I pulled in beside my car and killed the engine. I scanned the rear-view, half expecting to see that old Chrysler drive into the lot with Nelson in the front seat. I kept my hands on the wheel for a minute, and then dropped them to my lap. I didn't want to touch Donna. She knew it. She didn't want to be touched either. The hug we'd given each other in my kitchen that night, the kissing we'd done at the Off-Broadway, it seemed to belong in somebody else's life now, not my life.

I said, 'What are you going to do?' But right then I didn't care. Right then she could have died of a heart attack and it wouldn't have meant anything.

'Maybe I could go up to Portland,' she said. 'There must be something in Portland. Portland is on everybody's mind these days. Portland's a drawing card. Portland this, Portland that. Portland's as good a place as any. It's all the same.'

'Donna,' I said. 'I'd better go.' I started to let myself out. I cracked the door and the overhead came on.

'For Christ's sake turn off that light!'

I got out in a hurry. 'Night, Donna,' I said.

She nodded.

I left her staring at the dash and went to my car. I saw her move over behind the wheel. Then she just sat there without doing anything. She looked at me. I waved. She didn't wave back. So I started the car and turned on the headlights. I slipped it in gear and fed it the gas. Donna would get herself home OK.

In the kitchen I poured scotch, drank some of it, and took the glass into the bathroom. I brushed my teeth. Then I pulled open a drawer. Patti yelled something from the bedroom that I couldn't understand. She opened the bathroom door. She was still dressed. She'd fallen asleep with her clothes on.

'What time is it?' she screamed. 'I've overslept! Jesus, oh my God! You've let me oversleep, goddamn you!'

She was wild. She stood in the doorway with her clothes on. She could have been fixing to go to work. But there was no sample case, no vitamins. She was having a bad dream, that's all. She began shaking her head back and forth.

I couldn't take any more tonight. 'Go back to sleep, honey. I'm looking for something,' I said. I knocked stuff out of the medicine cabinet. Things rolled into the sink. 'Where's the aspirin?' I said. I knocked down more things. I didn't care. 'Goddamn it,' I said. Things kept falling.

1982

A City of the Dead,
A City of the Living

Nadine Gordimer

*Y*ou only count the days if you are waiting to have a baby
or you are in prison. I've had my child but I'm counting the
days since he's been in this house.

The street delves down between two rows of houses like the
abandoned bed of a river that has changed course. The
shebeen-keeper who lives opposite has a car that sways and
churns its way to her fancy wrought-iron gate. Everyone else,
including shebeen customers, walks over the stones, sand and
gullies, home from the bus station. It's too far to bicycle to work
in town.

The house provides the sub-economic township planner's
usual two rooms and kitchen with a little yard at the back, into
which his maquette figures of the ideal family unit of four fitted
neatly. Like most of the houses in the street, it has been
arranged inside and out to hold the number of people the
ingenuity of necessity provides for. The garage is the home of
sub-tenants. (The shebeen-keeper, who knows everything about
everybody, might remember how the house came to have a
garage—perhaps a taxi owner once lived there.) The front door
of the house itself opens into a room that has been subdivided
by greenish brocade curtains whose colour had faded and
embossed pattern worn off before they were discarded in
another kind of house. On one side of the curtains is a living
room with just space enough to crate a plastic-covered sofa and
two chairs, a coffee table with crocheted cover, vase of dyed
feather flowers and oil lamp, and a radio-and-cassette-player
combination with home-built speakers. There is a large
varnished print of a horse with wild orange mane and flaring
nostrils on the wall. The floor is cement, shined with black
polish. On the other side of the curtains is a bed, a burglar-
proofed window, a small table with candle, bottle of anti-acid
tablets and alarm clock. During the day a frilly nylon night-
gown is laid out on the blankets. A woman's clothes are in a
box under the bed. In the dry-cleaner's plastic sheath, a man's
suit hangs from a nail.

A door, never closed, leads from the living room to the
kitchen. There is a sink, which is also the bathroom of the

house, a coal-burning stove finned with chrome like a 1940s car, a pearly blue formica dresser with glass doors that don't slide easily, a table and plastic chairs. The smell of cooking never varies: mealie-meal burning, curry overpowering the sweet reek of offal, sour porridge, onions. A small refrigerator, not connected, is used to store margarine, condensed milk, tinned pilchards; there is no electricity.

Another door, with a pebbled glass pane in its upper half, is always kept closed. It opens off the kitchen. Net curtains reinforce the privacy of the pebbled glass; the privacy of the tenant of the house, Samson Moreke, whose room is behind there, shared with his wife and baby and whichever of their older children spends time away from other relatives who take care of them in country villages. When all the children are in their parents' home at once, the sofa is a bed for two; others sleep on the floor in the kitchen. Sometimes the sofa is not available, since adult relatives who find jobs in the city need somewhere to live. Number 1907 Block C holds—has held— eleven people; how many it could hold is a matter of who else has nowhere to go. This reckoning includes the woman lodger and her respectable succession of lovers behind the green brocade curtain, but not the family lodging in the garage.

In the backyard, Samson Moreke, in whose name tenancy of Number 1907 Block C is registered by the authorities, has put up poles and chicken wire and planted Catawba grapevines that make a pleasant green arbour in summer. Underneath are three metal chairs and matching table, bearing traces of white paint, which—like the green brocade curtains, the picture of the horse with orange mane, the poles, chicken wire and vines—have been discarded by the various employers for whom Moreke works in the city as an itinerant gardener. The arbour is between the garage and the lavatory, which is shared by everyone on the property, both tenants and lodgers.

On Sundays Moreke sits under his grapevine and drinks a bottle of beer brought from the shebeen across the road. Even in winter he sits there; it is warmer out in the midday winter sun than in the house, the shadow of the vine merely a twisted rope—grapes eaten, roof of leaves fallen. Although the yard is behind the house and there is a yellow dog on guard tied to a packing-case shelter, there is not much privacy. A large portion of the space of the family living in the garage is taken up by a paraffin-powered refrigerator filled with soft-drink cans and pots of flavoured yogurt: a useful little business that serves the community and supplements the earnings of the breadwinner, a cleaner at the city slaughterhouse. The sliding metal shutter meant for the egress of a car from the garage is permanently bolted down. All day Sunday children come on errands to buy, knocking at the old kitchen door, salvaged from the city, that Moreke has set into the wall of the garage.

A street where there is a shebeen, a house opposite a shebeen cannot be private, anyway. All weekend drunks wander over the ruts that make the gait even of the sober seem drunken. The children playing in the street take no notice of men fuddled between song and argument, who talk to people who are not there.

As well as friends and relatives, acquaintances of Moreke—who have got to know where he lives through travelling with him on the buses to work—walk over from the shebeen and appear in the yard. Moreke is a man who always puts aside money to buy the Sunday newspaper; he has to fold away the paper and talk instead. The guests usually bring a cold quart or two with them (the shebeen, too, has a paraffin refrigerator, restaurant-size). Talk and laughter make the dog bark. Someone plays a transistor radio. The chairs are filled, and some comers stretch on the bit of tough grass. Most of the Sunday visitors are men but there are women, particularly young ones, who have gone with them to the shebeen or taken up with them there; these women are polite and deferent to Moreke's wife, Nanike, when she has time to join the gathering. Often they will hold her latest—fifth living—baby while she goes back into the kitchen to cook or hangs her washing on the fence. She takes a beer or two herself, but although she is in her early thirties and knows she is still pretty—except for a missing front tooth—she does not giggle or get flirtatious. She is content to sit with the new baby on her lap, in the sun, among men and women like herself, while her husband tells anecdotes which make them laugh or challenge him. He learns a lot from the newspapers.

Nanike was sitting in the yard with him and his friends the Sunday a cousin arrived with a couple of hangers-on. They didn't bring beer, but were given some. There were greetings, but who really hears names? One of the hangers-on fell asleep on the grass, a boy with a body like a baggy suit. The other had a yellow face, lighter than anyone else present, narrow as a trowel, and the irregular pockmarks of the pitted skin were flocked, round the area where men grow hair, with sparse tufts of black. She noticed he wore a gold earring in one ear. He had nothing to say but later took up a guitar belonging to someone else and played to himself. One of the people living in the garage, crossing the path of the group under the arbour on his way to the lavatory with his roll of toilet paper, paused to look or listen, but everyone else was talking too loudly to hear the soft plang-plang, and the after-buzz when the player's palm stilled the instrument's vibration.

Moreke went off with his friends when they left, and came back, not late. His wife had gone to bed. She was sleepy, feeding the baby. Because he stood there, at the foot of the bed, did not begin to undress, she understood someone must be with him.

'Mtembu's friend.' Her husband's head indicated the other side of the glass-paned door.

'What does he want here now?'

'I brought him. Mtembu asked.'

'What for?'

Moreke sat down on the bed. He spoke softly, mouthing at her face. 'He needs somewhere to stay.'

'Where was he before, then?'

Moreke lifted and dropped his elbows limply at a question not to be asked.

The baby lost the nipple and nuzzled furiously at air. She guided its mouth. 'Why can't he stay with Mtembu? You could have told Mtembu no.'

'He's your cousin.'

'Well, I will tell him no. If Mtembu needs somewhere to stay, I have to take him. But not anyone he brings from the street.'

Her husband yawned, straining every muscle in his face.

Suddenly he stopped and began putting together the sheets of his Sunday paper that were scattered on the floor. He folded them more or less in order, slapping and smoothing the creases.

'Well?'

He said nothing, walked out. She heard the voices in the kitchen, but not what was being said.

He opened their door again and shut it behind him. 'It's not a business of cousins. This one is in trouble. You don't read the papers…the blowing up of that police station…*you* know, last month? They didn't catch them all… It isn't safe for Mtembu to keep him any longer. He must keep moving.'

Her soft jowls stiffened.

Her husband assured her awkwardly. 'A few days. Only for a couple of days. Then'—a gesture—'out of the country.'

*H*e never takes off the gold earring, even when he sleeps. He sleeps on the sofa. He didn't bring a blanket, a towel, nothing—uses our things. I don't know what the earring means; when I was a child there were men who came to work on the mines who had earrings, but in both ears—country people. He's a town person; another one who reads newspapers. He tidies away the blankets I gave him and then he reads newspapers the whole day. He can't go out.*

T*he others at Number 1907 Block C were told the man was Nanike Moreke's cousin, had come to look for work, and had nowhere to stay. There are people in that position in every house. No one with a roof over his head can say 'no' to one of the same blood—everyone knows that; Moreke's wife had not denied that. But she wanted to know what to say if someone asked the man's name. He himself answered at once, his strong thin hand twisting the gold hoop in his ear like a girl. 'Shisonka. Tell them Shisonka.'

'And the other name?'

Her husband answered. 'That name is enough.'

Moreke and his wife didn't use the name among themselves. They referred to the man as 'he' and 'him'. Moreke addressed him as 'Mfo', brother; she called him simply 'you'. Moreke answered questions nobody asked. He said to his wife, in front of the man, 'What is the same blood? Here in this place? If you are not white, you are all the same blood, here.' She looked at her husband respectfully, as she did when he read to her out of his newspaper.

The woman lodger worked in the kitchen at a Kentucky Fried Chicken shop in the city, and like Moreke was out at work all day; at weekends she slept at her mother's place, where her children lived, so she did not know the man Shisonka never left the house to look for work or for any other reason. Her lover came to her room only to share the bed, creeping late past whatever sleeping form might be on the sofa, and leaving before first light to get to a factory in the white industrial area. The only problem was the family who lived in the garage. The man had to cross the yard to use the lavatory. The slaughterhouse cleaner's mother and wife would notice he was there, in the house; that he never went out. It was Moreke's wife who thought of this, and told the woman in the garage her cousin was sick; he had just been discharged from hospital. And indeed, they took care of him as if he had been—Moreke and his wife, Nanike. They did not have the money to eat meat often but on Tuesday Moreke bought a pluck from the butchery near the bus station in the city; the man sat down to eat with them. Moreke brought cigarettes home—the man paid him—it was clear he must have cigarettes, needed cigarettes more than food. And don't let him go out, don't ever let him go to the shop for cigarettes, or over to Ma Radebe for drink, Moreke told his wife; *you* go, if he needs anything, *you* just leave everything, shut the house—go.

I wash his clothes with our things. His shirt and pullover have labels in another language, come from some other country. Even the letters are different. I give him food in the middle of the day. I myself eat in the yard, with the baby. I told him he should play the music, in there, if he wants to. He listens to Samson's tapes. How could I keep my own sister out of the house? When she saw him I said he was a friend of Samson— a new friend. She likes light-skinned. But it means people notice you. It must be very hard to hide. He doesn't say so. He doesn't look afraid. The beard will hide him; but how long does it take for a beard to grow, how long, how long before he goes away?

Every night that week the two men talked. Not in the room with the sofa and radio-and-cassette-player, if the woman lodger was at home on the other side of the curtains, but in the room where the Morekes slept. The man had a kitchen chair Moreke brought in; there was just room for it between the big bed and the wardrobe. Moreke lay on the bed with a pillow stuffed under his nape. Sometimes his wife stayed in the kitchen, at other times she came in and sat with the baby on the bed. She could see Moreke's face and the back of the man's head in the panel mirror of the wardrobe while they talked. The shape of the head swelled up from the thin neck, a puffball of black kapok. Deep in, there was a small patch without hair, a skin infection or a healed wound. His front aspect—a narrow yellow face keenly attentive, cigarette wagging like a finger from the corner of his lips, loop of gold round the lobe of one of the alert pointed ears—seemed unaware of the blemish, something that attacked him unnoticed from behind.

They talked about the things that interested Moreke; the political meetings disguised as church services of which he read reports but did not attend. The man laughed, and argued with Moreke patiently. 'What's the use, man? If you don't stand there? Stand with your feet as well as agree with your head... Yes, go and get that head knocked if the dogs and the *kerries* come. Since '76, the kids've shown you how... You know now.'

Moreke wanted to tell the man what he thought of the Urban Councils the authorities wanted to set up, and the Committees people themselves had formed in opposition. As, when he found himself in the company of a sports promoter, he wanted to give his opinion of the state of soccer today. 'Those Council men are nothing to me. You understand? They only want big jobs and smart cars for themselves. I'm a poor man, I'll never have a car. But they say they're going to make this place like a white Jo'burg. Maybe the government listens to them... They say they can do it. The Committees—eh?—they say like I do, *those Council men are nothing*—but they themselves, what can they do? They know everything is no good here. They talk; they tell us about it; they go to jail. So what's the use? What can you do?'

The man did not tell what he had done. 'The police station' was there, ready in their minds, ready to their tongues; not spoken.

The man was smiling at Moreke, at something he had heard many times before and might be leaving behind for good, now. 'Your Council. Those dummies. You see this *donga* called a street, outside? This place without even electric light in the rooms? You dig beautiful gardens, the flowers smell nice...and how many people must shit in that stinking hovel in your yard? How much do you get for digging the ground white people own? You told me what you get. "Top wages": ten rand a day. Just enough for the rent in this place, and not even the shit-house belongs to you, not even the mud you bring in from the yard on your shoes...'

Moreke became released, excited. 'The bus fares went up last week. They say the rent is going up...'

'Those dummies, that's what they do for you. You see? But the Committee tells you they don't pay the rent, because you aren't paid enough to live in the "beautiful city" the dummies promise you. Isn't that the truth? Isn't the truth what you *know*? Don't you listen to the ones who speak the truth?'

Moreke's wife had had, for a few minutes, the expression of one waiting to interrupt. 'I'll go to Radebe and get a bottle of beer, if you want.'

The two men gave a flitting nod to one another in approval.

Moreke counted out the money. 'Don't let anybody come back with you.'

His wife took the coins without looking up. 'I'm not a fool.' The baby was asleep on the bed. She closed the door quietly behind her. The two men lost the thread of their talk for a moment; Moreke filled it: 'A good woman.'

We are alone together. The baby likes him. I don't give the breast every time, now; yesterday when I was fetching the coal he fed the bottle to her. I ask him what children he has?

He only smiles, shakes his head. I don't know if this means it was silly to ask, because everyone has children.

Perhaps it meant he doesn't know, pretends he doesn't know—thinks a lot of himself, smart young man with a gold ring in his ear has plenty of girlfriends to get babies with him.

The police station was never mentioned, but one of the nights the man spent describing to the Moreke couple foreign places he had been to—that must have been before the police station happened. He told about the oldest city on the African continent, so old it had a city of the dead as well as a city of the living—a whole city of tombs like houses. The religion there was the same as the religion of the Indian shopkeepers, here at home. Then he had lived in another kind of country, where there was snow for half the year or more. It was dark until ten in the morning and again from three o'clock in the afternoon. He described the clothes he had been given to protect him against the cold. 'Such people, I can tell you. You can't believe such white people exist. If our people turn up there...you get everything you need, they just give it... And there's a museum—it's out in the country—they have ships there their people sailed all over the world more than 2,000 years ago. They may even have come here... This pullover is still from them...full of holes now...'

'Look at that, *hai*!' Moreke admired the intricately worked bands of coloured wools in a design based upon natural features he did not recognize—dark frozen forms of fir forests and the molecular pattern of snow crystals. 'She'll mend it for you.'

His wife was willing but apprehensive. 'I'll try and get the same colours. I don't know if I can find them here.'

The man smiled at the kindness of his own people. 'She shouldn't take a lot of trouble. I won't need it, anyway.'

No one asked where it was that the pullover wouldn't be needed; what kind of place, what continent he would be going to when he got away.

After the man had retired to his sofa that night Moreke read the morning paper he had brought from an employer's kitchen in the city. He kept lowering the sheets slowly and looking around at the room, then returning to his reading. The baby was restless; but it was not that he commented on.

'It's better not to know too much about him.'

His wife turned the child on to its belly. 'Why?'

Her face was innocently before his like a mirror he didn't want to look into. He had kept encouraging the man to go on with his talk of living in foreign places.

The shadows thrown by the candle capered through the room, bending furniture and bodies, flying over the ceiling, quieting the baby with wonder. 'Because then...if they question us, we won't have anything to tell.'

He did bring something. A gun.

He comes into the kitchen, now, and helps me when I'm washing up. He came in, this morning, and put his hands in the soapy water, didn't say anything, started cleaning up. Our hands were in the grease and soap. I couldn't see his fingers but sometimes I felt them when they bumped mine. He scraped the pot and dried everything. I didn't say thanks. To say thank you to a man—it's not man's work, he might feel ashamed.

He stays in the kitchen—we stay in the kitchen with the baby most of the day. He doesn't sit in there, any more, listening to the tapes. I go in and turn on the machine loud enough for us to hear it well in the kitchen.

By Thursday the tufts of beard were thickening and knitting together on the man's face. Samson Moreke tried to find Mtembu to hear what plans had been made but Mtembu did not come in response to messages and was not anywhere Moreke looked for him. Moreke took the opportunity, while the woman in whose garden he worked on Thursdays was out, to telephone Mtembu's place of work from her house, but was told that workshop employees were not allowed to receive calls.

He brought home chicken feet for soup and a piece of beef shank. Figs had ripened in the Thursday garden and he'd been given some in a newspaper poke. He asked, 'When do you expect to hear from Mtembu?'

The man was reading the sheet of paper stained with milky

sap from the stems of figs. Samson Moreke had never really been in jail himself—only the usual short-term stays for pass offences—but he knew from people who had been inside a long time that there was this need to read every scrap of paper that might come your way from the outside world.

'—Well, it doesn't matter. You're all right here. We can just carry on. I suppose Mtembu will turn up this weekend.'

As if he heard in this resignation Moreke's anticipation of the usual Sunday beer in the yard, the man suddenly took charge of Moreke and his wife, crumpling the dirty newspaper and rubbing his palms together to rid them of stickiness. His narrow yellow face was set clear-cut in black hair all round now, like the framed face of the king in Moreke's pack of worn cards. The black eyes and earring were the same liquid-bright. The perfectly ironed shirt he wore was open at the breast in the manner of all attractive young men of his age. 'Look, nobody must come here. Saturday, Sunday. None of your friends. You must shut up this place. Keep them all away. Nobody walking into the yard from the shebeen. That's *out.*'

Moreke looked from the man to his wife; back to the man again. Moreke half coughed, half laughed. 'But how do I do that, man? How do I stop them? I can't put bars on my gate. There're the other people, in the garage. They sell things.'

'*You* stay inside. Here in this house, with the doors locked. There are too many people around at the weekend. Let them think you've gone away.'

Moreke still smiled, amazed, helpless. 'And the one in there, with her boyfriend? What's she going to think?'

Moreke's wife spoke swiftly. 'She'll be at her mother's house.'

And now the plan of action fell efficiently into place; each knew his part within it. 'Oh yes. Thank the Lord for that. Maybe I'll go over to Radebe's tonight and just say I'm not going to be here Sunday. And Saturday I'll say I'm going to the soccer.'

His wife shook her head. 'Not the soccer. Your friends will want to come and talk about it afterwards.'

'*Hai, mama!* All right, a funeral, far away...' Moreke laughed, and stopped himself with an embarrassed drawing of mucus back through the nose.

68

W*hile I'm ironing, he cleans the gun.*
I saw he needed another rag and I gave it to him.

He asked for oil, and I took cooking oil out of the cupboard, but then I saw in his face that was not what he wanted. I went to the garage and borrowed Three-in-One from Nchaba's wife.

He never takes out the gun when Samson's here. He knows only he and I know about it.

I said, what happened there, on your head at the back—that sore? His hand went to it, under the hair, he doesn't think it shows, I'll get him something for it, some ointment. If he's still here on Monday.

Perhaps he is cross because I spoke about it.

Then when I came back with the oil, he sat at the kitchen table laughing at me, smiling, as if I was a young girl. I forgot— I felt I was a girl. But I don't really like that kind of face, his face—light-skinned. You can never forget a face like that. If you are questioned, you can never say you don't remember what someone like that looks like.

He picks up the baby as if it belongs to him. To him as well, while we are in the kitchen together.

T*hat* night the two men didn't talk. They seemed to have nothing to say. Like prisoners who get their last mealie-pap of the day before being locked up for the night, Moreke's wife gave them their meal before dark. Then all three went from the kitchen to the Morekes' room, where any light that might shine from behind the curtains and give away a presence was directed only towards a blind: a high corrugated tin fence in a lane full of breast-high khakiweed. Moreke shared his newspaper. When the man had read it, he tossed through the third-hand adventure comics and sales promotion pamphlets given away in city supermarkets Nanike Moreke kept; he read the manual *Teach Yourself How to Sell Insurance* in which, at some stage, 'Samson Moreke' had been carefully written on the flyleaf.

There was no beer. Moreke's wife knew her way about her kitchen in the dark; she fetched the litre bottle of coke that was on the kitchen table and poured herself a glass. Her husband stayed the offer with a raised hand; the other man's inertia over the manual was overcome just enough to move his head in refusal. She had taken up again the cover for the bed she had begun when she had had some free time, waiting for this fifth child to be born. Crocheted roses, each caught in a squared web of a looser pattern, were worked separately and then joined to the whole they slowly extended. The tiny flash of her steel hook and the hair-thin gold in his ear signalled in candlelight. At about ten o'clock there was a knock at the front door. The internal walls of these houses are planned at minimum specification for cheapness and a blow on any part of the house reverberates through every room. The black-framed, bone-yellow face raised and held, absolutely still, above the manual. Moreke opened his mouth and, swinging his legs over the side, lifted himself from the bed. But his wife's hand on his shoulder made him subside again; only the bed creaked slightly. The slenderness of her body from the waist up was merely rooted in heavy maternal hips and thighs; with a movement soft as the breath she expelled, she leaned and blew out the candles.

A sensible precaution; someone might follow round the walls of the house looking for some sign of life. They sat in the dark. There was no bark from the dog in the yard. The knocking stopped. Moreke thought he heard laughter, and the gate twang. But the shebeen is noisy on a Friday; the sounds could have come from anywhere. 'Just someone who's had a few drinks. It often happens. Sometimes we don't even wake up, I suppose, ay, Nanike.' Moreke's hoarse whisper, strangely, woke the baby, who let out the thin wail that meets the spectre in a bad dream, breaks through into consciousness a response to a threat that can't be defeated in the conscious world. In the dark, they all went to bed.

A city of the dead, a city of the living. It was better when *Samson got him to talk about things like that. Things far away can't do any harm. We'll never have a car, like the Councillors, and we'll never have to run away to those far places, like him. Lucky to have this house; many, many people are jealous of that. I never knew, until this house was so quiet, how much noise people make at the weekend, I didn't hear the laughing, the talking in the street, Radebe's music going, the terrible screams of people fighting.*

On Saturday Moreke took his blue ruled pad and an envelope to the kitchen table. But his wife was peeling pumpkin and slicing onions; there was no space, so he went back to the room where the sofa was, and his radio-and-cassette-player. First he addressed the envelope to their twelve-year-old boy at mission school. It took him the whole morning to write a letter, although he could read so well. Once or twice he asked the man how to spell a word in English.

He lay smoking on his bed, the sofa. 'Why in English?'

'Rapula knows English very well... It helps him to get letters...'

'You shouldn't send him away from here, *baba*. You think it's safer, but you are wrong. It's like you and the meetings. The more you try to be safe, the worse it will be for your children.' He stared quietly at Moreke. 'And look, now I'm here.'

'Yes.'

'And you look after me.'

'Yes.'

'And you're not afraid.'

'Yes, we're afraid...but of many things... When I come home with money...three times *tsotsis* have hit me, taken everything. You see here where I was cut on the cheek. This arm was broken. I couldn't work. Not even push the lawnmower. I had to pay some young one to hold my jobs for me.'

The man smoked and smiled. 'I don't understand you. You see? I don't understand you. Bring your children home, man. We're shut up in the ghetto to kill each other. That's what they want, in their white city. So you send the children away; that's what they want, too. To get rid of us. We must all stick together. That's the only way to fight our way out.'

That night he asked if Moreke had a chess set.

Moreke giggled, gave clucks of embarrassment. 'That board with the little dolls? I'm not an educated man! I don't know those games!'

They played together the game that everybody knows, that

71

is, played on the pavements outside shops and in factory yards, with the board drawn on concrete or in dust, and bottle tops for counters. This time a handful of dried beans from the kitchen served, and a board drawn by Moreke on a box lid. He won game after game from the man. His wife had the Primus stove in the room, now, and she made tea. The game was not resumed. She had added three completed squares to her bed-cover in two nights; after the tea, she did not take it up again. They sat listening to Saturday night, all round them, pressing in upon the hollow cement units of which the house was built. Often trampling steps seemed just about to halt at the front or back door. The splintering of wood under a truncheon or the shatter of the windowpanes, thin ice under the weight of the roving dark outside, waited upon every second. The woman's eyelids slid down, fragile and faintly greasy, outlining intimately the aspect of the orbs beneath, in sleep. Her face became unguarded as the baby's. Every now and then she would start, come to herself again. But her husband and the man made no move to go to bed. The man picked up and ran the fine head of her crochet hook under the rind of each fingernail, again and again, until the tool had done the cleaning job to satisfaction.

When the man went to bed at last, by the light of the cigarette lighter he shielded in his hand to see his way to the sofa, he found she had put a plastic chamber pot on the floor. Probably the husband had thought of it.

All Sunday morning the two men worked together on a fault in Moreke's tape player, though they were unable to test it with the volume switched on. Moreke could not afford to take the player to a repair shop. The man seemed to think the fault a simple matter; like any other city youngster, he had grown up with such machines. Moreke's wife cooked mealie-rice and made a curry gravy for the Sunday meal. 'Should I go to Radebe and get beer?' She had followed her husband into their room to ask him alone.

'You want to advertise we are here? You know what he said.'

'Ask him if it matters, if I go—a woman.'

'I'm not going to ask. Did he say he wants beer? Did I?'

But in the afternoon she did ask something. She went straight to the man, not Moreke. 'I have to go out to the shop.' It was very hot in the closed house; the smell of curry mixed with the smell of the baby in the fug of its own warmth and wrappings. He wrinkled his face, exposed clenched teeth in a suppressed yawn; what shops—had she forgotten it was Sunday? She understood his reaction. But there were corner shops that sold essentials even on Sundays; he must know that. 'I have to get milk. Milk for the baby.'

She stood there, in her over-trodden slippers, her old skirt and cheap blouse—a woman not to be noticed among every other woman in the streets. He didn't refuse her. No need. Not after all this past week. Not for the baby. She was not like her husband, big-mouth, friendly with everyone. He nodded; it was a humble errand that wouldn't concern him.

She went out of the house just as she was, her money in her hand. Moreke and the baby were asleep in their room. The street looked new, bright, refreshing, after the dim house. A small boy with a toy machine gun covered her in his fire, chattering his little white teeth with rat-a-tat-tttt. Ma Radebe, the shebeen-keeper, her hair plaited with blue and red beads, her beautiful long red nails resting on the steering wheel, was backing her car out of her gateway. She braked to let her neighbour pass and leaned from the car window. 'My dear'— in English—'I was supposed to be gone from this place two hours ago. I'm due at a big wedding that will already be over... How are you? Didn't see your husband for a few days...nothing wrong across the road?'

Moreke's wife stood and shook her head. Radebe was not one who expected or waited for answers when she greeted anyone. When the car had driven off Moreke's wife went on down the street and down the next one, past the shop where young boys were gathered scuffling and dancing to the shop-keeper's radio, and on to the purplish brick building with the security fence round it and a flag flying. One of her own people was on guard outside leaning on a hand machine gun. She went up the steps and into the office, where there were more of her own people in uniform, but one of *them* in charge. She spoke in her own language to her own kind, but they seemed disbelieving. They repeated the name of that other police station, that was blown up, and asked her if she was sure? She said she was quite sure. Then they took her to the white officer and she told in English—'There, in my house, 1907 Block C. He has been there a week. He has a gun.'

I don't know why I did it. I get ready to say that to anyone who is going to ask me, but nobody in this house asks. The baby laughs at me while I wash him, stares up while we're alone in the house and he's feeding at the breast, and to him I say out loud: I don't know why.

A week after the man was taken away that Sunday by the security police, Ma Radebe again met Moreke's wife in their street. The shebeen-keeper gazed at her for a moment, and spat.

1983
Rock Springs

Richard Ford

Edna and I had started down from Kalispell heading for Tampa-St Pete, where I still had some friends from the old glory days who wouldn't turn me in to the police. I had managed to scrape with the law in Kalispell over several bad cheques—which is a prison crime in Montana. And I knew Edna was already looking at her cards and thinking about a move, since it wasn't the first time I'd been in law scrapes in my life. She herself had already had her own troubles, losing her kids and keeping her ex-husband, Danny, from breaking in her house and stealing her things while she was at work, which was really why I had moved in in the first place, that and needing to give my little daughter, Cheryl, a better shake in things.

I don't know what was between Edna and me, just beached by the same tides when you got down to it. Though love has been built on frailer ground than that, as I well know. And when I came in the house that afternoon, I just asked her if she wanted to go to Florida with me, leave things where they sat, and she said, 'Why not? My datebook's not that full.'

Edna and I had been a pair eight months, more or less man and wife, some of which time I had been out of work, and some when I'd worked at the dog track as a lead-out and could help with the rent and talk sense to Danny when he came around. Danny was afraid of me because Edna had told him I'd been in prison in Florida for killing a man once, though that wasn't true. I had once been in jail in Tallahassee for stealing tyres and had got into a fight on the county farm where a man had lost his eye. But I hadn't done the hurting, and Edna just wanted the story worse than it was so Danny wouldn't act crazy and make her have to take her kids back, since she had made a good adjustment to not having them, and I already had Cheryl with me. I'm not a violent person and would never put a man's eye out, much less kill someone. My former wife, Helen, would come all the way from Waikiki Beach to testify to that. We never had violence, and I believe in crossing the street to stay out of trouble's way. Though Danny didn't know that.

But we were half down through Wyoming, going toward Interstate 80 and feeling good about things, when the oil light flashed on in the car I'd stolen, a sign I knew to be a bad one.

I'd got us a good car, a cranberry Mercedes I'd stolen out of an ophthalmologist's lot in Whitefish, Montana. I stole it because I thought it would be comfortable over a long haul, because I thought it got good mileage, which it didn't, and because I'd never had a good car in my life, just old Chevy junkers and used trucks back from when I was a kid swamping citrus with Cubans.

The car made us all high that day. I ran the windows up and down, and Edna told us some jokes and made faces. She could be lively. Her features would light up like a beacon and you could see her beauty, which wasn't ordinary. It all made me giddy, and I drove clear down to Bozeman, then straight on through the park to Jackson Hole. I rented us the bridal suite in the Quality Court in Jackson and left Cheryl and her little dog, Duke, sleeping while Edna and I drove to a rib barn and drank beer and laughed till after midnight.

It felt like a whole new beginning for us, bad memories left behind and a new horizon to build on. I got so worked up, I had a tattoo done on my arm that said FAMOUS TIMES, and Edna bought a Bailey hat with an Indian feather band and a little turquoise-and-silver bracelet for Cheryl, and we made love on the seat of the car in the Quality Court parking lot just as the sun was burning up on the Snake River, and everything seemed then like the end of the rainbow.

It was that very enthusiasm, in fact, that made me keep the car one day longer instead of driving it into the river and stealing another one, like I should have done and *had* done before.

Where the car went bad there wasn't a town in sight or even a house, just some low mountains maybe fifty miles away or maybe a hundred, a barbed-wire fence in both directions, hardpan prairie, and some hawks sailing through the evening air seizing insects.

I got out to look at the motor, and Edna got out with Cheryl and the dog to let them have a pee by the car. I checked the water and checked the oil stick, and both of them said perfect.

'What's that light mean, Earl?' Edna said. She had come and stood by the car with her hat on. She was just sizing things up for herself.

'We shouldn't run it,' I said. 'Something's not right in the oil.'

She looked around at Cheryl and Little Duke, who were peeing on the hardtop side by side like two little dolls, then out at the mountains, which were becoming black and lost in the distance. 'What're we doing?' she said. She wasn't worried yet, but she wanted to know what I was thinking about.

'Let me try it again,' I said.

'That's a good idea,' she said, and we all got back in the car.

When I turned the motor over, it started right away and the red light stayed off and there weren't any noises to make you think something was wrong. I let it idle a minute, then pushed the accelerator down and watched the red bulb. But there wasn't any light on, and I started wondering if maybe I hadn't dreamed I saw it, or that it had been the sun catching an angle off the window chrome, or maybe I was scared of something and didn't know it.

'What's the matter with it, Daddy?' Cheryl said from the back seat. I looked back at her, and she had on her turquoise bracelet and Edna's hat set back on the back of her head and that little black-and-white Heinz dog on her lap. She looked like a little cowgirl in the movies.

'Nothing, honey, everything's fine now,' I said.

'Little Duke tinkled where I tinkled,' Cheryl said, and laughed.

'You're two of a kind,' Edna said, not looking back. Edna was usually good with Cheryl, but I knew she was tired now. We hadn't had much sleep, and she had a tendency to get cranky when she didn't sleep. 'We oughta ditch this damn car first chance we get,' she said.

'What's the first chance we got?' I said, because I knew she'd been at the map.

'Rock Springs, Wyoming,' Edna said with conviction. 'Thirty miles down this road.'

She pointed out ahead. I had wanted all along to drive the car into Florida like a big success story. But I knew Edna was right about it, that we shouldn't take crazy chances. I had kept thinking of it as my car and not the ophthalmologist's, and that was how you got caught in these things.

'Then my belief is we ought to go to Rock Springs and

negotiate ourselves a new car,' I said. I wanted to stay upbeat, like everything was panning out right.

'That's a great idea,' Edna said, and she leaned over and kissed me hard on the mouth.

'That's a great idea,' Cheryl said. 'Let's pull on out of here right now.'

The sunset that day I remember as being the prettiest I'd ever seen. Just as it touched the rim of the horizon, it all at once fired the air into jewels and red sequins the precise likes of which I had never seen before and haven't seen since. The West has it all over everywhere for sunsets, even Florida, where it's supposedly flat but where half the time trees block your view.

'It's cocktail hour,' Edna said after we'd driven a while. 'We ought to have a drink and celebrate something.' She felt better thinking we were going to get rid of the car. It certainly had dark troubles and was something you'd want to put behind you.

Edna had out a whiskey bottle and some plastic cups and was measuring levels on the glovebox lid. She liked drinking, and she liked drinking in the car, which was something you got used to in Montana, where it wasn't against the law, where, though, strangely enough, a bad cheque would land you in Deer Lodge Prison for a year.

'Did I ever tell you I once had a monkey?' Edna said, setting my drink on the dashboard where I could reach it when I was ready. Her spirits were already picked up. She was like that, up one minute and down the next.

'I don't think you ever did tell me that,' I said. 'Where were you then?'

'Missoula,' she said. She put her bare feet on the dash and rested the cup on her breasts. 'I was waitressing at the Amvets. It was before I met you. Some guy came in one day with a monkey. A spider monkey. And I said, just to be joking, "I'll roll you for that monkey." And the guy said, "Just one roll?" And I said, "Sure." He put the monkey down on the bar, picked up the cup, and rolled out boxcars. I picked it up and rolled out three fives. And I just stood there looking at the guy. He was just some guy passing through, I guess a vet. He got a strange look on his face—I'm sure not as strange as the one I had—but he looked kind of sad and surprised and satisfied all at once. I said, "We can roll again." But he said, "No, I never roll twice for anything." And he sat and drank a beer and talked about one thing and another for a while, about nuclear war and building a stronghold somewhere up in the Bitterroot, whatever it was, while I just watched the monkey, wondering what I was going to do with it when the guy left. And pretty soon he got up and said, "Well, goodbye, Chipper," that was this monkey's name, of course. And then he left before I could say anything. And the monkey just sat on the bar all that night. I don't know what made me think of that, Earl. Just something weird. I'm letting my mind wander.'

'That's perfectly fine,' I said. I took a drink of my drink. 'I'd never own a monkey,' I said after a minute. 'They're too nasty. I'm sure Cheryl would like a monkey, though, wouldn't you, honey?' Cheryl was down on the seat playing with Little Duke. She used to talk about monkeys all the time then. 'What'd you ever do with that monkey?' I said, watching the speedometer. We were having to go slower now because the red light kept fluttering on. And all I could do to keep it off was go slower. We were going maybe thirty-five and it was an hour before dark, and I was hoping Rock Springs wasn't far away.

'You really want to know?' Edna said. She gave me a quick, sharp glance, then looked back at the empty desert as if she was brooding over it.

'Sure,' I said. I was still upbeat. I figured *I* could worry about breaking down and let other people be happy for a change.

'I kept it a week,' she said. She seemed gloomy all of a sudden, as if she saw some aspect of the story she had never seen before. 'I took it home and back and forth to the Amvets on my shifts. And it didn't cause any trouble. I fixed a chair up for it to sit on, back of the bar, and people liked it. It made a nice little clicking noise. We changed its name to Mary because the bartender figured out it was a girl. Though I was never really comfortable with it at home. I felt like it watched me too much. Then one day a guy came in, some guy who'd been in Vietnam, still wore a fatigue coat. And he said to me, "Don't you know that a monkey'll kill you? It's got more strength in its fingers than you got in your whole body." He said people had been killed in Vietnam by monkeys, bunches of them marauding while you were asleep, killing you and covering you with leaves. I didn't believe a word of it, except that when I got home and got undressed I started looking over across the room at Mary on her chair in the dark watching me. And I got the creeps. And after a while I got up and went out to the car, got a length of clothesline wire, and came back in and wired her to the doorknob through her little silver collar, and went back and tried to sleep. And I guess I must've slept the sleep of the dead—though I don't remember it—because when I got up I found Mary had tupped off her chair back and hanged herself on the wire line. I'd made it too short.'

Edna seemed badly affected by that story and slid low in the seat so she couldn't see out over the dash. 'Isn't that a shameful story, Earl, what happened to that poor little monkey?'

'I see a town! I see a town!' Cheryl started yelling from the back seat, and right up Little Duke started yapping and the whole car fell into a racket. And sure enough she had seen something I hadn't, which was Rock Springs, Wyoming, at the bottom of a long hill, a little glowing jewel in the desert with Interstate 80 running on the north side and the black desert spread out behind.

'That's it, honey,' I said. 'That's where we're going. You saw it first.'

'We're hungry,' Cheryl said. 'Little Duke wants some fish, and I want spaghetti.' She put her arms around my neck and hugged me.

'Then you'll just get it,' I said. 'You can have anything you want. And so can Edna and so can Little Duke.' I looked over at Edna, smiling, but she was staring at me with eyes that were fierce with anger. 'What's wrong?' I said.

'Don't you care anything about that awful thing that happened to me?' she said. Her mouth was drawn tight, and her eyes kept cutting back at Cheryl and Little Duke, as if they had been tormenting her.

'Of course, I do,' I said. 'I thought that was an awful thing.'

I didn't want her to be unhappy. We were almost there, and pretty soon we could sit down and have a real meal without thinking somebody might be hunting us.

'You want to know what I did with that monkey?' Edna said.

'Sure I do,' I said.

She said, 'I put her in a green garbage bag, put it in the trunk of my car, drove to the dump, and threw her in the trash.' She was staring at me darkly, as if the story meant something to her that was real important but that only she could see and that the rest of the world was a fool for.

'Well, that's horrible,' I said. 'But I don't see what else you could do. You didn't mean to kill it. You'd have done it differently if you had. And then you had to get rid of it, and I don't know what else you could have done. Throwing it away might seem unsympathetic to somebody, probably, but not to me. Sometimes that's all you can do, and you can't worry about what somebody else thinks.' I tried to smile at her, but the red light was staying on if I pushed the accelerator at all, and I was trying to gauge if we could coast to Rock Springs before the car gave out completely. I looked at Edna again. 'What else can I say?' I said.

'Nothing,' she said, and stared back at the dark highway. 'I should've known that's what you'd think. You've got a character that leaves something out, Earl. I've known that a long time.'

'And yet here you are,' I said. 'And you're not doing so bad. Things could be a lot worse. At least we're all together here.'

'Things could always be worse,' Edna said. 'You could go to the electric chair tomorrow.'

'That's right,' I said. 'And somewhere somebody probably will. Only it won't be you.'

'I'm hungry,' said Cheryl. 'When're we gonna eat? Let's find a motel. I'm tired of this. Little Duke's tired of it too.'

Where the car stopped rolling was some distance from the town, though you could see the clear outline of the Interstate in the dark with Rock Springs lighting up the sky behind. You could hear the big tractors hitting the spacers in the overpass, revving up for the climb to the mountains.

I shut off the lights.

'What're we going to do now?' Edna said irritably, giving me a bitter look.

'I'm figuring it,' I said. 'It won't be hard, whatever it is. You won't have to do anything.'

'I'd hope not,' she said, and looked the other way.

Across the road and across a dry wash a hundred yards was what looked like a huge mobile-home town, with a factory or a refinery of some kind lit up behind it and in full swing. There were lights on in a lot of the mobile homes, and there were cars moving along an access road that ended near the freeway overpass a mile the other way. The lights in the mobile homes seemed friendly to me, and I knew right then what I should do.

'Get out,' I said, and opened my door.

'Are we walking?' Edna said.

'We're pushing,' I said.

'I'm not pushing,' Edna said, and reached up and locked her door. 'All right,' I said. 'Then you just steer.'

'You pushing us to Rock Springs, are you, Earl? It doesn't look like it's more than about three miles,' Edna said.

'I'll push,' Cheryl said from the back.

'No, hon. Daddy'll push. You just get out with Little Duke and move out of the way.'

Edna gave me a threatening look, just as if I'd tried to hit her. But when I got out she slid into my seat and took the wheel, staring angrily ahead straight into the cottonwood scrub.

'Edna can't drive that car,' Cheryl said from out in the dark. 'She'll run it in the ditch.'

'Yes, she can, hon. Edna can drive it as good as I can. Probably better.'

'No, she can't,' Cheryl said. 'No, she can't either.' And I thought she was about to cry, but she didn't.

I told Edna to keep the ignition on so it wouldn't lock up and to steer into the cottonwoods with the parking lights on so she could see. And when I started, she steered it straight off into the trees, and I kept pushing until we were twenty yards into the cover and the tyres sank in the soft sand and nothing at all could be seen from the road.

'Now where are we?' she said, sitting at the wheel. Her voice was tired and hard, and I knew she could have put a good meal to use. She had a sweet nature, and I recognized that this wasn't her fault but mine. Only I wished she could be more hopeful.

'You stay right here, and I'll go over to that trailer park and call us a cab,' I said.

'What cab?' Edna said, her mouth wrinkled as if she'd never heard anything like that in her life.

'There'll be cabs,' I said, and tried to smile at her. 'There's cabs everywhere.'

'What're you going to tell him when he gets here? Our stolen car broke down and we need a ride to where we can steal another one? That'll be a big hit, Earl.'

'I'll talk,' I said. 'You just listen to the radio for ten minutes and then walk on out to the shoulder like nothing was suspicious. And you and Cheryl act nice. She doesn't need to know about this car.'

'Like we're not suspicious enough already, right?' Edna looked up at me out of the lighted car. 'You don't think right, did you know that, Earl? You think the world's stupid and you're smart. But that's not how it is. I feel sorry for you. You might've *been* something, but things just went crazy some place.'

I had a thought about poor Danny. He was a vet and crazy as a shit-house mouse, and I was glad he wasn't in for all this. 'Just get the baby in the car,' I said, trying to be patient. 'I'm hungry like you are.'

'I'm tired of this,' Edna said. 'I wish I'd stayed in Montana.'

'Then you can go back in the morning,' I said. 'I'll buy the ticket and put you on the bus. But not till then.'

'Just get on with it, Earl,' she said, slumping down in the seat, turning off the parking lights with one foot and the radio on with the other.

The mobile-home community was as big as any I'd ever seen. It was attached in some way to the plant that was lighted up behind it, because I could see a car once in a while leave one of the trailer streets, turn in the direction of the plant, then go slowly into it. Everything in the plant was white, and you could see that all the trailers were painted white and looked exactly alike. A deep hum came out of the plant, and I thought as I got closer that it wouldn't be a location I'd ever want to work in.

I went right to the first trailer where there was a light and knocked on the metal door. Kids' toys were lying in the gravel around the little wood steps, and I could hear talking on TV that suddenly went off. I heard a woman's voice talking, and then the door opened wide.

A large Negro woman with a wide, friendly face stood in the doorway. She smiled at me and moved forward as if she was going to come out, but she stopped at the top step. There was a little Negro boy behind her peeping out from behind her legs, watching me with his eyes half closed. The trailer had that feeling that no one else was inside, which was a feeling I knew something about.

'I'm sorry to intrude,' I said. 'But I've run up on a little bad luck tonight. My name's Earl Middleton.'

The woman looked at me, then out into the night toward the freeway as if what I had said was something she was going to be able to see. 'What kind of bad luck?' she said, looking down at me again.

'My car broke down out on the highway,' I said. 'I can't fix it myself, and I wondered if I could use your phone to call for help.'

The woman smiled down at me knowingly. 'We can't live without cars, can we?'

'That's the honest truth,' I said.

'They're like our hearts,' she said firmly, her face shining in the little bulb light that burned beside the door. 'Where's your car situated?'

I turned and looked over into the dark, but I couldn't see anything because of where we'd put it. 'It's over there,' I said. 'You can't see it in the dark.'

'Who all's with you now?' the woman said. 'Have you got your wife with you?'

'She's with my little girl and our dog in the car,' I said. 'My daughter's asleep or I would have brought them.'

'They shouldn't be left in that dark by themselves,' the woman said, and frowned. 'There's too much unsavouriness out there.'

85

'The best I can do is hurry back,' I said. I tried to look sincere, since everything except Cheryl being asleep and Edna being my wife was the truth. The truth is meant to serve you if you'll let it, and I wanted it to serve me. 'I'll pay for the phone call,' I said. 'If you'll bring the phone to the door I'll call from right here.'

The woman looked at me again as if she was searching for a truth of her own, then back out into the night. She was maybe in her sixties but I couldn't say for sure. 'You're not going to rob me, are you, Mr Middleton?' she said, and smiled like it was a joke between us.

'Not tonight,' I said, and smiled a genuine smile. 'I'm not up to it tonight. Maybe another time.'

'Then I guess Terrel and I can let you use our phone with Daddy not here, can't we, Terrel? This is my grandson, Terrel Junior, Mr Middleton.' She put her hand on the boy's head and looked down at him. 'Terrel won't talk. Though if he did he'd tell you to use our phone. He's a sweet boy.' She opened the screen for me to come in.

The trailer was a big one with a new rug and a new couch and a living room that expanded to give the space of a real house. Something good and sweet was cooking in the kitchen, and the trailer felt like it was somebody's comfortable new home instead of just temporary. I've lived in trailers, but they were just snail backs with one room and no toilet, and they always felt cramped and unhappy—though I've thought maybe it might've been me that was unhappy in them.

There was a big Sony TV and a lot of kids' toys scattered on the floor. I recognized a Greyhound bus I'd got for Cheryl. The phone was beside a new leather recliner, and the Negro woman pointed for me to sit down and call and gave me the phone book. Terrel began fingering his toys, and the woman sat on the couch while I called, watching me and smiling.

There were three listings for cab companies, all with one number different. I called the numbers in order and didn't get an answer until the last one, which answered with the name of the second company. I said I was on the highway beyond the Interstate and that my wife and family needed to be taken to town and I would arrange for a tow later. While I was giving the location, I looked up the name of a tow service to tell the driver in case he asked.

When I hung up, the Negro woman was sitting looking at me with the same look she had been staring with into the dark, a look that seemed to want truth. She was smiling, though. Something pleased her and I reminded her of it.

'This is a very nice home,' I said, resting in the recliner, which felt like the driver's seat of the Mercedes and where I'd have been happy to stay.

'This isn't *our* house, Mr Middleton,' the Negro woman said. 'The company owns these. They give them to us for nothing. We have our own home in Rockford, Illinois.'

'That's wonderful,' I said.

'It's never wonderful when you have to be away from home, Mr Middleton, though we're only here three months, and it'll be easier when Terrel Junior begins his special school. You see, our son was killed in the war, and his wife ran off without Terrel Junior. Though you shouldn't worry. He can't understand us. His little feelings can't be hurt.' The woman folded her hands in her lap and smiled in a satisfied way. She was an attractive woman and had on a blue-and-pink floral dress that made her seem bigger than she could've been, just the right woman to sit on the couch she was sitting on. She was good nature's picture, and I was glad she could be, with her little brain-damaged boy, living in a place where no one in his right mind would want to live a minute. 'Where do *you* live, Mr Middleton?' she said politely, smiling in the same sympathetic way.

'My family and I are in transit,' I said. 'I'm an ophthalmologist, and we're moving back to Florida, where I'm from. I'm setting up practice in some little town where it's warm year-round. I haven't decided where.'

'Florida's a wonderful place,' the woman said. 'I think Terrel would like it there.'

'Could I ask you something?' I said.

'You certainly may,' the woman said. Terrel had begun pushing his Greyhound across the front of the TV screen, making a scratch that no one watching the set could miss. 'Stop that, Terrel Junior,' the woman said quietly. But Terrel kept pushing his bus on the glass, and she smiled at me again as if we both understood something sad. Except I knew Cheryl would never damage a television set. She had respect for nice things, and I was sorry for the lady that Terrel didn't. 'What did you want to ask?' the woman said.

'What goes on in that plant or whatever it is back there beyond these trailers, where all the lights are on?'

'Gold,' the woman said, and smiled.

'It's what?' I said.

'Gold,' the Negro woman said, smiling as she had for almost all the time I'd been there. 'It's a gold mine.'

'They're mining gold back there?' I said, pointing.

'Every night and every day,' she said, smiling in a pleased way.

'Does your husband work there?' I said.

'He's the assayer,' she said. 'He controls the quality. He works three months a year, and we live the rest of the time at home in Rockford. We've waited a long time for this. We've been happy to have our grandson, but I won't say I'll be sorry to have him go. We're ready to start our lives over.' She smiled broadly at me and then at Terrel, who was giving her a spiteful look from the floor. 'You said you had a daughter,' the Negro woman said. 'And what's her name?'

'Irma Cheryl,' I said. 'She's named for my mother.'

'That's nice,' she said. 'And she's healthy, too. I can see it in your face.' She looked at Terrel Junior with pity.

'I guess I'm lucky,' I said.

'So far you are,' she said. 'But children bring you grief, the same way they bring you joy. We were unhappy for a long time before my husband got his job in the gold mine. Now, when Terrel starts to school, we'll be kids again.' She stood up. 'You might miss your cab, Mr Middleton,' she said, walking toward the door, though not to be forcing me out. She was too polite. 'If *we* can't see your car, the cab surely won't be able to.'

'That's true,' I said, and got up off the recliner where I'd been so comfortable.

'None of us have eaten yet, and your food makes me know how hungry we probably all are.'

'There are fine restaurants in town, and you'll find them,' the Negro woman said. 'I'm sorry you didn't meet my husband. He's a wonderful man. He's everything to me.'

'Tell him I appreciate the phone,' I said. 'You saved me.'

'You weren't hard to save,' the woman said. 'Saving people is what we were all put on earth to do. I just passed you on to whatever's coming to you.'

'Let's hope it's good,' I said, stepping back into the dark.

'I'll be hoping, Mr Middleton. Terrel and I will both be hoping.'

I waved to her as I walked out into the darkness toward the car where it was hidden in the night.

The cab had already arrived when I got there. I could see its little red and green roof lights all the way across the dry wash, and it made me worry that Edna was already saying something to get us in trouble, something about the car or where we'd come from, something that would cast suspicion on us. I thought, then, how I never planned things well enough. There was always a gap between my plan and what happened, and I only responded to things as they came along and hoped I wouldn't get into trouble. I was an offender in the law's eyes. But I always *thought* differently, as if I weren't an offender and had no intention of being one, which was the truth. But as I read on a napkin once, between the idea and the act a whole kingdom lies. And I had a hard time with my acts, which were oftentimes offender's acts, and my ideas, which were as good as the gold they mined there where the bright lights were blazing.

'We're waiting for you, Daddy,' Cheryl said when I crossed the road. 'The taxicab's already here.'

'I see, hon,' I said, and gave Cheryl a big hug. The cab driver was sitting in the driver's seat having a smoke with the lights on inside. Edna was leaning against the back of the cab between the tail lights, wearing her Bailey hat. 'What'd you tell him?' I said when I got close.

'Nothin',' she said. 'What's there to tell?'

'Did he see the car?'

She glanced over in the direction of the trees where we had hid the Mercedes. Nothing was visible in the darkness, though I could hear Little Duke combing around in the underbrush tracking something, his little collar tinkling. 'Where're we going?' she said. 'I'm so hungry I could pass out.'

'Edna's in a terrible mood,' Cheryl said. 'She already snapped at me.'

'We're tired, honey,' I said. 'So try to be nicer.'

'She's never nice,' Cheryl said.

'Run go get Little Duke,' I said. 'And hurry back.'

'I guess *my* questions come last here, right?' Edna said.

I put my arm around her. 'That's not true,' I said.

'Did you find somebody over there in the trailers you'd rather stay with? You were gone long enough.'

'That's not a thing to say,' I said. 'I was just trying to make things look right, so we don't get put in jail.'

'So *you* don't, you mean,' Edna said and laughed a little laugh I didn't like hearing.

'That's right. So I don't,' I said. 'I'd be the one in Dutch.' I stared out at the big, lighted assemblage of white buildings and white lights beyond the trailer community, plumes of white smoke escaping up into the heartless Wyoming sky, the whole company of buildings looking like some unbelievable castle, humming away in a distorted dream. 'You know what all those buildings are there?' I said to Edna, who hadn't moved and who didn't really seem to care if she ever moved any more ever.

'No. But I can't say it matters, 'cause it isn't a motel and it isn't a restaurant,' she said.

'It's a gold mine,' I said, staring at the gold mine, which, I knew now from walking to the trailer, was a greater distance from us than it seemed, though it seemed huge and near, up against the cold sky. I thought there should've been a wall around it with guards instead of just the lights and no fence. It seemed as if anyone could go in and take what they wanted, just the way I had gone up to that woman's trailer and used the telephone, though that obviously wasn't true.

Edna began to laugh then. Not the mean laugh I didn't like, but a laugh that had something caring behind it, a full laugh that enjoyed a joke, a laugh she was laughing the first time I laid eyes on her, in Missoula in the Eastgate bar in 1979, a laugh we used to laugh together when Cheryl was still with her mother and I was working steady at the track and not stealing cars or passing bogus cheques to merchants. A better time all around. And for some reason it made me laugh just hearing her, and we both stood there behind the cab in the dark, laughing at the gold mine in the desert, me with my arm around her and Cheryl out rustling up Little Duke and the cab driver smoking in the cab and our stolen Mercedes-Benz, which I'd had such hopes for in Florida, stuck up to its axle in sand, where I'd never get to see it again.

'I always wondered what a gold mine would look like when I saw it,' Edna said, still laughing, wiping a tear from her eye.

'Me too,' I said. 'I was always curious about it.'

'We're a couple of fools, ain't we, Earl?' she said, unable to quit laughing completely. 'We're two of a kind.'

'It might be a good sign, though,' I said.

'How could it be?' she said. 'It's not our gold mine. There aren't any drive-up windows.' She was still laughing.

'We've seen it,' I said, pointing. 'That's it right there. It may mean we're getting closer. Some people never see it at all.'

'In a pig's eye, Earl,' she said. 'You and me see it in a pig's eye.'

And she turned and got into the cab to go.

The cab driver didn't ask anything about our car or where it was, to mean he'd noticed something queer. All of which made me feel like we had made a clean break from the car and couldn't be connected with it until it was too late, if ever. The driver told us a lot about Rock Springs while he drove, that because of the gold mine a lot of people had moved there in just six months, people from all over, including New York, and that most of them lived out in the trailers. Prostitutes from New York City, who he called 'B-girls', had come into town, he said, on the prosperity tide, and Cadillacs with New York plates cruised the little streets every night, full of Negroes with big hats who ran the women. He told us that everybody who got in his cab now wanted to know where the women were, and when he got our call he almost didn't come because some of the trailers were brothels operated by the mine for engineers and computer people away from home. He said he got tired of running back and forth out there just for vile business. He said that *60 Minutes* had even done a programme about Rock Springs and that a blow-up had resulted in Cheyenne, though nothing could be done unless the prosperity left town. 'It's prosperity's fruit,' the driver said. 'I'd rather be poor, which is lucky for me.'

He said all the motels were sky-high, but since we were a family he could show us a nice one that was affordable. But I told him we wanted a first-rate place where they took animals, and the money didn't matter because we had had a hard day and wanted to finish on a high note. I also knew that it was in the little nowhere places that the police look for you and find you. People I'd known were always being arrested in cheap hotels and tourist courts with names you'd never heard of before. Never in Holiday Inns or Travelodges.

I asked him to drive us to the middle of town and back out again so Cheryl could see the train station, and while we were there I saw a pink Cadillac with New York plates and a TV aerial being driven slowly by a Negro in a big hat down a narrow street where there were just bars and a Chinese restaurant. It was an odd sight, nothing you could ever expect.

'There's your pure criminal element,' the cab driver said, and seemed sad. 'I'm sorry for people like you to see a thing like that. We've got a nice town here, but there're some that want to ruin it for everybody. There used to be a way to deal with trash and criminals but those days are gone forever.'

'You said it,' Edna said.

'You shouldn't let it get *you* down,' I said to the cab driver. 'There's more of you than them. And there always will be. You're the best advertisement this town has. I know Cheryl will remember you and not *that* man, won't you, honey?' But Cheryl was asleep by then holding Little Duke in her arms on the taxi seat.

The driver took us to the Ramada Inn on the Interstate, not

far from where we'd broken down. I had a small pain of regret as we drove under the Ramada awning that we hadn't driven up in a cranberry-coloured Mercedes but instead in a beat-up old Chrysler taxi driven by an old man full of complaints. Though I knew it was for the best. We were better off without that car, better, really, in any other car but that one, where the signs had turned bad.

I registered under another name and paid for the room in cash so there wouldn't be any questions. On the line where it said 'Representing', I wrote 'ophthalmologist' and put 'MD' after the name. It had a nice look to it, even though it wasn't my name.

When we got to the room, which was in the back where I'd asked for it, I put Cheryl on one of the beds and Little Duke beside her so they'd sleep. She'd missed dinner, but it only meant she'd be hungry in the morning, when she could have anything she wanted. A few missed meals don't make a kid bad. I'd missed a lot of them myself and haven't turned out completely bad.

'Let's have some fried chicken,' I said to Edna when she came out of the bathroom. 'They have good fried chicken at the Ramadas, and I noticed the buffet was still up. Cheryl can stay right here, where it's safe, till we're back.'

'I guess I'm not hungry any more,' Edna said. She stood at the window staring out into the dark. I could see out the window past her some yellowish foggy glow in the sky. For a moment I thought it was the gold mine out in the distance lighting the night, though it was only the Interstate.

'We could order up,' I said. 'Whatever you want. There's a menu on the phone book. You could just have a salad.'

'You go ahead,' she said. 'I've lost my hungry spirit.' She sat on the bed beside Cheryl and Little Duke and looked at them in a sweet way and put her hand on Cheryl's cheek just as if she'd had a fever. 'Sweet little girl,' she said. 'Everybody loves you.'

'What do you want to do?' I said. 'I'd like to eat. Maybe I'll order up some chicken.'

'Why don't you do that?' she said. 'It's your favourite.' And she smiled at me from the bed.

I sat on the other bed and dialled room service. I asked for chicken, garden salad, potato and a roll, plus a piece of hot apple pie and ice tea. I realized I hadn't eaten all day. When I put down the phone I saw that Edna was watching me, not in a hateful way or a loving way, just in a way that seemed to say she didn't understand something and was going to ask me about it.

'When did watching me get so entertaining?' I said, and smiled at her. I was trying to be friendly. I knew how tired she must be. It was after nine o'clock.

'I was just thinking how much I hated being in a motel without a car that was mine to drive. Isn't that funny? I started feeling like that last night when that purple car wasn't mine. That purple car just gave me the willies, I guess, Earl.'

'One of those cars *outside* is yours,' I said. 'Just stand right there and pick it out.'

'I know,' she said. 'But that's different, isn't it?' She reached and got her blue Bailey hat, put it on her head, and set it way back like Dale Evans. She looked sweet. 'I used to like to go to motels, you know,' she said. 'There's something secret about them and free—I was never paying, of course. But you felt safe from everything and free to do what you wanted because you'd made the decision to be there and paid that price, and all the rest was the good part. Fucking and everything, you know.' She smiled at me in a good-natured way.

'Isn't that the way this is?' I said. I was sitting on the bed, watching her, not knowing what to expect her to say next.

'I don't guess it is, Earl,' she said, and stared out the window. 'I'm thirty-two and I'm going to have to give up on motels. I can't keep that fantasy going any more.'

'Don't you like this place?' I said, and looked around at the room. I appreciated the modern paintings and the lowboy bureau and the big TV. It seemed like a plenty nice enough place to me, considering where we'd been already.

'No, I don't,' Edna said with real conviction. 'There's no use in my getting mad at you about it. It isn't your fault. You do the best you can for everybody. But every trip teaches you something. And I've learned I need to give up on motels before some bad thing happens to me. I'm sorry.'

'What does that mean?' I said, because I really didn't know what she had in mind to do, though I should've guessed.

'I guess I'll take that ticket you mentioned,' she said, and got up and faced the window. 'Tomorrow's soon enough. We haven't got a car to take me anyhow.'

'Well, that's a fine thing,' I said, sitting on the bed, feeling like I was in a shock. I wanted to say something to her, to argue with her, but I couldn't think what to say that seemed right. I didn't want to be mad at her, but it made me mad.

'You've got a right to be mad at me, Earl,' she said, 'but I don't think you can really blame me.' She turned around and faced me and sat on the window sill, her hands on her knees. Someone knocked on the door. I just yelled for them to set the tray down and put it on the bill.

'I guess I *do* blame you,' I said. I was angry. I thought about how I could have disappeared into that trailer community and hadn't, had come back to keep things going, had tried to take control of things for everybody when they looked bad.

'Don't. I wish you wouldn't,' Edna said, and smiled at me like she wanted me to hug her. 'Anybody ought to have their choice in things if they can. Don't you believe that, Earl? Here I am out here in the desert where I don't know anything, in a stolen car, in a motel room under an assumed name, with no money of my own, a kid that's not mine, and the law after me. And I have a choice to get out of all of it by getting on a bus. What would you do? I know exactly what you'd do.'

'You think you do,' I said. But I didn't want to get into an argument about it and tell her all I could've done and didn't do. Because it wouldn't have done any good. When you get to the point of arguing, you're past the point of changing anybody's mind, even though it's supposed to be the other way, and maybe for some classes of people it is, just never mine.

Edna smiled at me and came across the room and put her arms around me where I was sitting on the bed. Cheryl rolled over and looked at us and smiled, then closed her eyes, and the room was quiet. I was beginning to think of Rock Springs in a way I knew I would always think of it, a low-down city full of crimes and whores and disappointments, a place where a woman left me, instead of a place where I got things on the straight track once and for all, a place I saw a gold mine.

'Eat your chicken, Earl,' Edna said, 'Then we can go to bed. I'm tired, but I'd like to make love to you anyway. None of this is a matter of not loving you, you know that.'

Sometime late in the night, after Edna was asleep, I got up and walked outside into the parking lot. It could've been any time because there was still the light from the Interstate frosting the low sky and the big red Ramada sign humming motionlessly in the night and no light at all in the east to indicate it might be morning. The lot was full of cars all nosed in, most of them with suitcases strapped to their roofs and their trunks weighed down with belongings the people were taking some place, to a new home or a vacation resort in the mountains. I had laid in bed a long time after Edna was asleep, watching the Atlanta Braves on cable television, trying to get my mind off how I'd feel when I saw that bus pull away the next day, and how I'd feel when I turned around and there stood Cheryl and Little Duke and no one to see about them but me alone, and that the first thing I had to do was get hold of some automobile and get the plates switched, then get them some breakfast and get us all on the road to Florida, all in the space of probably two hours, since that Mercedes would certainly look less hid in the daytime than the night, and word travels fast. I've always taken care of Cheryl myself as long as I've had her with me. None of the women ever did; most of them didn't even seem to like her, though they took care of me in a way so that I could take care of her. And I knew that once Edna left, all that was going to get harder. Though what I wanted most to do was not think about it just for a little while, try to let my mind go limp so it could be strong for the rest of what there was. I thought that the difference between a successful life and an unsuccessful one, between me at that moment and all the people who owned the cars that were nosed in to their proper places in the lot, maybe between me and that woman out in the trailers by the gold mine, was how well you were able to put things like this out of your mind and not be bothered by them, and maybe, too, by how many troubles like this one you had to face in a lifetime. Through luck or design they had all faced fewer troubles, and by their own characters, they forgot them faster. And that's what I wanted for me. Fewer troubles, fewer memories of trouble.

I walked over to a car, a Pontiac with Ohio tags, one of the ones with bundles and suitcases strapped to the top and a lot more in the trunk, by the way it was riding. I looked inside the driver's window. There were maps and paperback books and sunglasses and the little plastic holders for cans that hang on the window wells. And in the back there were kids' toys and some pillows and a cat box with a cat sitting in it staring up at me like I was the face of the moon. It all looked familiar to me, the very same things I would have in my car if I had a car. Nothing seemed surprising, nothing different. Though I had a funny sensation at that moment and turned and looked up at the windows along the back of the Ramada Inn. All were dark except two. Mine and another one. And I wondered, because it seemed funny, what would you think a man was doing if you saw him in the middle of the night looking in the windows of cars in the parking lot of the Ramada Inn? Would you think he was trying to get his head cleared? Would you think he was trying to get ready for a day when trouble would come down on him? Would you think his girlfriend was leaving him? Would you think he had a daughter? Would you think he was anybody like you?

1984
Jackdaw Cake
Norman Lewis

When I was first pushed by my mother into the presence of my Aunt Polly, the bandages had only been removed from her face a few days before. They had exposed a patchwork of skin—pink and white—glazed in some places, and matt-surfaced in others, dependent upon the area of thigh or buttock from which it had been stripped to cover her burns. She had difficulty in closing her eyes (sometimes while asleep the lids would snap open). The fire had reached every part of her and she spoke in a harsh whisper that I could hardly understand. It was impossible to judge whether or not I was welcome, because the grey stripe of mouth provided by plastic surgery in its infancy could hold no expression. She bent down stiffly to proffer a cheek and, prodded by my mother, I reached up to select a smooth surface among the puckerings, the ridges and the nests of tiny wrinkles, and touch it with my lips.

In the background the second aunt, Annie, wearing long white gloves, holding a fan like a white feather duster, and dressed as if for her wedding, waited smilingly. I was soon to learn that the smile was one that nothing could efface. Dodging in and out of a door at the back of the hallway, the third aunt, Li, seemed like a startled animal. She was weeping silently, and with these tears I would soon become familiar.

I was nine years of age, and the adults peopling my world seemed on the whole irrational, but it was an irrationality I had come to accept as the norm. My mother had brought me to this vast house and told me, without discussion, preparation or warning, that I was to live among these strangers—for whom I was to show respect, even love—for an unspecified period of time. The prospect troubled me, but like an Arab child resigned in his religion, I soon learned to accept this new twist in the direction of my life, and the sounds of incessant laughter and grief soon lost all significance, became commonplace and thus passed without notice.

My mother, bastion of wisdom and fountainhead of truth in my universe, had gone, her flexible maternal authority replaced by the disciplines of my fire-scarred Aunt Polly, an epileptic who had suffered at least one fit per day since the age of fourteen, in the course of which she had fallen once from a window, once into a river, and twice into a fire. Every day, usually in the afternoon, she staged an unconscious drama, when she rushed screaming from room to room, sometimes bloodied by a fall, and once leaving a menstrual splash on the highly polished floor. It was difficult to decide whether she liked or disliked me, because she extended a tyranny in small ways over all who had dealings with her. In my case she issued a stream of whispered edicts relating to such matters as politeness, punctuality and personal cleanliness, and by being scrupulous in their observance I found that we got along together fairly well. I scored marks with her by mastery of the tedious and lengthy collects I was obliged to learn for recitation at Sunday school. When I showed myself as word-perfect in one of these it was easy to believe that she was doing her best to smile, as she probably did also when I accompanied her in my thin and whining treble in one of her harmonium recitals of such favourite hymns as 'Through the Night of Doubt and Sorrow'.

Smiling Aunt Annie, who counted for very little in the household, and who seemed hardly to notice my presence, loved to dress up, and spent an hour or two every day doing this. Sometimes she would come on the scene attired like Queen Mary in a hat like a dragoon's shako, and at other times she would be a female cossack with cartridge pockets and high boots. Later when I went to school, and became very sensitive to the opinions of my school friends, she waylaid me once on my way home, to my consternation, got up as a Spanish dancer in a frilled blouse and skirt, with a high comb stuck into her untidy grey hair.

Li, youngest of the aunts, was poles apart from either sister. She and Polly had not spoken to each other for years, and occupied downstairs rooms at opposite ends of the house, while Annie made her headquarters in the room separating them, and when necessary transmitted curt messages from one to the other.

My grandfather, whom I saw only at weekends, filled every corner of the house with his deep, competitive voice, and a personality aromatic as cigar smoke. At this time he had been a widower for twenty-five years; a man with the face of his day—a prow of a nose, bulging eyes, and an Assyrian beard—who saw himself as close to God, and sometimes conversed with Him in a loud and familiar voice on business matters. A single magnificent coup had raised him to take his place among the eleven leading citizens of Carmarthen with a house in Wellfield Road. It was the purchase of a cargo of ruined tea from a ship sunk in Swansea harbour, which he laundered, packaged in bags dangerously imprinted with the Royal crest, and sold off at a profit of several thousand per cent to village shops and remote farming communities scattered through the hills.

This had bought him a house full of clocks and mirrors, with teak doors, a wine cellar, and a wide staircase garnished with wooden angels and lamps. After that he was to possess a French modiste as his mistress, the town's first Model T Ford, and a valuable grey parrot, named Prydeyn after a hero of *The Mabinogion*—too old by the time of my arrival to talk, but which could still, as it hung from a curtain rod in the drawing room, produce in its throat a passable imitation of a small, squeaking fart.

My grandfather had started life as plain David Lewis but, swept along on the tide of saline tea, he followed the example of the neighbours in his select street, and got himself a double-barrelled name, becoming David Warren Lewis. He put a crest on his notepaper, and worked steadily at his family tree, pushing the first of our ancestors back further and further into history until they became contemporary with King Howel Dda. For a brief moment the world was at his feet. He had even been invited to London to shake the flabby hand of Edward VII, but on the home front his life fell apart. The three daughters he had kept at home were dotty, a fourth got into trouble and had to be exported to Canada to marry a settler who had advertised for a wife, and the fifth, Lalla, an artist of sorts, who had escaped him to marry a schoolteacher called Bennett and settled in Cardiff, was spoken of as far from bright.

This was Welsh Wales, full of ugly chapels, of hidden money, psalm-singing and rain. The hills all around were striped and patched with small bleak fields, with sheep—seen from our house as small as lice—cropping the coarse grass, and seas of bracken pouring down the slopes to hurl themselves against the walls of the town. In autumn it rained every day. The water burst through the banks of the reservoir on top of Pen Lan and sent a wave full of fish down Wellfield Road, and then, spilling the fish all the way along Waterloo Terrace, as far as the market.

What impressed me most were the jackdaws, and the snails, on which the jackdaws largely lived. The snails were of every colour, curled and striped like little turbans in blue, pink, green and yellow, and it was hard to walk down the garden path without crushing them underfoot. There were thousands of jackdaws everywhere in the town, and our garden was always full of them. Sensing that my mad aunts presented no danger, they were completely tame. They would tap on the windows to be let into the house and go hopping from room to room in search of scraps.

Weekly the great ceremony took place of the baking of the jackdaw cake. For this, cooperation was forced upon my three aunts, for ingredients had to be decided upon, and bought: eggs, raisins, candied peel and sultanas, required to produce a cake of exceptional richness. Li did the shopping, because Polly was unable to leave the house, and Annie too confused to be able to buy what was necessary, put down her money, and pick up the change.

Each aunt took turns to bake and ice the cake. While they were kept busy doing this they seemed quite changed. Annie wore an ordinary dress and stopped laughing, Li didn't cry any more, and Polly's fits were quieter than on any other day. While the one whose turn it was did the baking, the others stood about in the kitchen and watched, and were for once quite easy to talk to.

On Saturday mornings at ten o'clock the cake was fed to the jackdaws. This had been happening for years, so that by half past nine the garden was full of birds, up to a hundred of them balancing and swinging with a tremendous gleeful outcry on the bushes and the low boughs of the trees. This was the great moment of the week for my aunts, and therefore for me. The cake would be cut into three sections and placed on separate plates on the kitchen table, and then at ten the kitchen windows were flung wide to admit the great black, squawking cataract of birds. For some hours after this weekly event the atmosphere was one of calm and contentment, and then the laughter and the weeping would start again.

Polly did all the cooking, and apart from that sat in the drawing room, watched over by the parrot Prydeyn, crocheting bedspreads with the stiff fingers that had not been spared by the fire. Li collected the instructions and the money left for her, and went out shopping, and Annie dressed up as a pirate, harlequin, clown, or whatever came into her head.

My grandfather worked in his tea-merchant's business in King Street, leaving the house early in the morning and returning as late at night as he decently could. On Sunday mornings, like all the rest of the community, he was hounded by his conscience to chapel, but in the afternoon he was accustomed to spend a little time with the Old English Game Fowl he bred, showed and—as the rumour went—had entered in secret cockfights in his disreputable youth. They were kept in wire pens in the back garden: each cockerel, or 'king' as it was known, separately with its hens. Show judges used to visit the house to test a contestant's ferocity by poking at it through the wire netting with a stick to which a coloured rag had been attached—any bird failing to attack being instantly disqualified.

The comb, wattles, ear lobes and any loose skin were removed from the head and neck of these birds, and there was frequently a little extra trimming-up to be done. Experience and skill were called for to catch and subdue a king in his prime and sometimes, like a Roman gladiator, my grandfather used a net. Once the bird was tied up and the head imprisoned in a wooden collar, he set to work in a leisurely fashion with a snip here and a snip there, using a specially designed variety of scissors known as a dubber.

The gamecocks often escaped from their pens and strutted about the back garden on the lookout for something to attack. My Aunt Li and I were usually chosen. They had enormously long legs—so long that they appeared to be walking on miniature stilts. My grandfather and my aunt Polly knew how to handle them and carried garden rakes to push them aside, but Li and I went in great fear of them. This they probably sensed, for any king that had managed to break out had the habit of lying in wait well out of sight until either of us came on the scene, when he would rush to the attack, leaping high into the air to strike at our faces with his spurs. In the end my aunt and I formed a defensive alliance, and this brought us closer together.

We based our strategy on cutting down the birds' numbers. Unlike normal chickens the game fowl laid only a few small eggs and had a short breeding season. Polly looked after the brooding hens and chicks, kept separate from the kings, and Li's method was to wait until her sister was out of the way, either having or recovering from a fit, then take several eggs from the clutch under a sitting hen and drop them into boiling water for a few seconds before putting them back. This promised to ease the situation in the coming year but did nothing to help us in our present trouble. My aunt bought a cat of a breed locally supposed to be descended from a pair of wild cats captured in Llandeilo forest about a hundred years ago. She brought it back in a sack one night, kept it in an outhouse without feeding it for three days, then let it loose in the garden. At this time there were two or three gamecocks at large, and the scuffle and outcry that followed raised our hopes; but in the morning the kings were still strutting through the flower beds ready for battle with all comers, and of the cat there was nothing to be seen.

As confidence and sympathy grew between us, my Aunt Li and I took to wandering round the countryside together. Li was a small woman, hardly bigger than me. She would wet me with her tears, and I would listen to her sad ravings and sometimes stroke her hand. One day she must have come to the grand decision to tell me what lay at the root of her sorrow. We climbed a stile and went into a field and, fixing her glistening eyes upon me she said, 'What I am going to tell you now you will remember every single day of your life.' But whatever she revealed must have been so startling that memory rejected it, for not a word of what was said remains in my mind.

The Towy River made and dominated Carmarthen, and it was always with us, whenever we went on our walks, throwing great, shining loops through the fields, doubling back on itself sometimes in a kind of afterthought, to encircle some riverside shack or a patch of sedge in which cows stood knee-deep to graze. In winter the whole valley filled up with floods, and people remembered nervously the prophecy of the enchanter Merlin that the floods would eventually engulf the town where he was buried. For my aunt these offered endless excitement, with drowning sheep and cattle being carried away on the yellow whiplash of the river's current, disappearing beneath the surface one after another as it swept them towards the sea, and the coracle men in their black, prehistoric boats spinning in whirlpools as they prodded at animals with their poles, trying to steer them to safety.

In summer the people of Carmarthen went on trips to the seaside at Llanstephan, at the river's mouth. There was no more beautiful, wilder or stranger place in the British Isles, but the local Welsh no longer saw its beauty, and familiarity and boredom drove all who could afford it further afield to Tenby, which was certainly larger and jollier. The Normans had built a castle in Llanstephan in about 1250, and there was an ancient church, and a few Victorian cottages, but apart from this handful of buildings little in the landscape had changed for thousands of years. Here the Towy finally unwound itself into the sea, its estuary enclosed in a great, silken spread of sand occupying a third of the horizon, to which our century had added not a single detail but the bones of two foundered ships in process of digestion by mud.

For the villagers a shadow hung over this scene. On fine Sundays and holidays throughout the summer, miners and their families would descend upon it. The train brought them from their hellish valleys to Ferryside across the estuary, and from Ferryside they would cross by boat to take joyous possession of the sands. At first warning of this invasion the people of Llanstephan made a bolt for their houses, slamming their doors behind them, drawing their curtains, keeping out of sight until six hours later the turn of the tide released them from their misery.

The miners were despised and hated by the villagers of Llanstephan in those days just as were field labourers in England by their more comfortable fellow-countrymen. To the villagers the miners were no better than foreigners, people whose habits were beyond their understanding—in particular the frantic pleasure they showed, and their noisily offensive good humour, when released in the calm and sober environment of Llanstephan on a Sunday afternoon. When I saw my first miners come ashore in Llanstephan I asked my aunt if they were dwarfs, so reduced in size had these Welshmen—identical in stock to those of Llanstephan—become after three generations of lives spent underground.

In Carmarthen and its surrounding villages people were obsessed with relationships, and practically everyone I met turned out to be a cousin four, five or even six times removed. Cousins who were old—say over thirty—were respectfully known as Aunties or Uncles, and one of the reasons for our trip to Llanstephan was to see an Auntie Williams who lived in the first of the line of cottages along the seafront. These were like little houses from a child's picture book, with old-fashioned gardens full of rosemary and honeysuckle, tabby cats everywhere, and fantail pigeons on the roofs.

Auntie Williams was a Welsh woman of the kind they still showed on picture postcards wearing black, steeple-crowned hats, and although the old witch's hat had gone she still wore in all weathers the shawl that went with it. She was famous for her early-red-apple tree—perhaps the last of its kind—which bore its ripe, brilliantly red fruit as early as August; and also for her husband, once a handsome man—as proved by the large coloured photograph in her front room, taken in uniform shortly before the Battle of the Somme, in which most of his lower jaw had been shot away. These days he wore a mask over the lower part of his face, and a tube protruding from his right nostril was fixed behind his ear. He was with us for lunch, dressed in a jaunty check jacket. Auntie Williams had boiled a sewin (a Welsh salmon); mixing a scrap of pink fish well-chewed by her into a bowl of gruel she fed her husband through the tube, and gently massaged his throat as it went down. Everybody in Llanstephan admired him for the cheerfulness with which he suffered his disability. He had published a little philosophical book designed to help others to bear such physical handicaps.

The finish of the meal, joined by two more neighbouring aunties, was spoiled by the arrival of the ferry boat, bringing the miners and their families. They came unexpectedly, as the jetty had been put out of action by the villagers in the preceding week; but the villagers had underestimated the miners' determination to enjoy themselves, which caused them to drag the heavy boat with tremendous effort clear of the water and on to the sand.

Until this calamity the three Llanstephan aunties, with their round country faces and polished cheeks, almost hard to tell apart, had been full of smiles, and by his gestures and noises Uncle Williams had seemed brimful of good humour. Aunt Li, whose vacant expression signified for me that she was not actually unhappy, was teasing a small crab she had found in a pool. Now suddenly, as the mining families climbed down from the boat and advanced towards us, a great change came over our family gathering. The miners' children, shrieking with delight, scampered ahead, and the miners and their wives trudged after them over the wet sand, carrying their boots and shoes, their little parcels of food, and two bulky packages. Watching this advance, the Llanstephan aunties' kindly, homely faces became different, barely recognizable. My Carmarthen relations laughed and wept in their meaningless way—or in the case of Polly were unable to produce a facial expression of any kind—but they had at least spared me the spectacle of anger, which was frighteningly new. The soft sing-song Welsh voices had lost their music and fallen flat as they talked of the wickedness of miners. It was a local theory, supported by the chapels, that poverty was the wage of sin—and the miners looked poor enough. Their women, who often worked alongside their men, were driven into the mines not by hunger, it was thought, but by shamelessness, and discussing this aspect of the mining life the Llanstephan aunties made the loading-up and manoeuvring of coal trucks in near-darkness 1,000 feet under the earth seem a carnal indulgence.

Mr Williams went into the house and came back with a placard which he fixed to a post by his wall. It said 'Remember the Sabbath Day, to keep it Holy', but the miners ignored it. Their children were everywhere, screaming with glee. They threw wet sand at each other, dug up cockles, dammed the little streams flowing on the beach, and even came to stare open-mouthed over the garden walls. When no one was watching I sneaked away to try to join them, but we did not easily mix. Immersed in their games, they ignored me, and I was too shy to speak.

Presently a miner beckoned to me. He and his wife were setting out their picnic on a cloth spread over the dry sand. The man was short but very strong-looking, with bow legs, and a snake tattooed on each forearm. He asked me my name, and I told him; his wife looked up and smiled and gave me a slice of cake. 'Sit you down,' she said, and I was just going to when Auntie Williams spotted me and let out a screech. 'Come you back by here.'

I went back and Auntie Williams said, 'What she give you, then?' I showed her the cake and she took it away and threw it to the pigeons. Wanting to get away from her I went over to Li, but she was no longer blank-faced as she had been when I left her, and that meant that something had upset her. She had lost her crab, and I thought it might be that. 'Like me to find you another crab, Auntie?' I asked, but she shook her head.

On the beach, sandwiches had been passed out to the children. The man who had spoken to me opened a bottle of beer. He drank from the neck, and passed it to his wife. The couple who had been carrying the two brown paper parcels untied the string and unwrapped them. One of the parcels held the box part of a gramophone, and the other the horn, and these they fixed together. We watched from our chairs under the apple tree while this was going on. No one spoke but I could feel the astonished horror. The people who had brought the gramophone wound it up and put on a record, and soon a thin, wheezing music reached us between the soft puffs of breeze and the squawking of the herring gulls flopping about overhead.

The people in the cottage next door had come out into the garden to watch what was going on, and one of them shouted a protest. Uncle Williams stood up, picked an apple and threw it in the direction of the couple with the gramophone, but with so little force that the apple hardly cleared our low wall. His example gave great encouragement to the others, though, and the man who had shouted from the garden next door threw a small stone. My feeling was that he never really intended to hit anything, and the stone splashed in a beach puddle, yards from the nearest of the miners, who gave no sign of realizing what was happening and went on eating their sandwiches and drinking their beer, never once looking in our direction. Next a bigger stone thudded on the sand, and there were more shouts from the cottages, and two or three children who had gone off to collect shells gave up and went back to join their parents.

More shouts and more stones followed—all the stones thrown by men whose aim was very bad, or who weren't trying. After a while the miners began to pack up, taking their time about it, and paying no attention at all to the villagers who were insulting them. The gramophone was taken apart and parcelled up as before, and everything they had brought with them packed away; then without looking back they began to move towards the ferry boat, and within half an hour they had managed to push the boat into the water; and that was the last of them.

Uncle Williams took down the placard and put it away, and his wife put on the kettle for tea. Nobody could find anything to say. The weather experts, who could tell by the look of the seaweed, had promised a fine afternoon, but the miners had ruined the day.

Li suddenly got up and said she was going home. 'We got two hours still to wait for the bus, Auntie,' I said. 'Never mind about the bus,' she said. 'I'm leaving now,' and she was off, marching down the path, and I could see by the way she was walking with her head thrown back and slightly to one side, that something had upset her, although there was no way of saying what. I'd seen enough of her by then to know that it wasn't the miners being there that bothered her—in which case it could only be something one of our Llanstephan relations had said or done. But what was it? I couldn't guess. There was no telling the way things took Aunt Li.

I ran to catch her up. It was six and a half miles to Carmarthen, but she was a fast walker, and I expected we'd beat the bus.

1985
Erotic Politicians
and Mullahs

Hanif Kureishi

The man had heard that I was interested in talking about his country, Pakistan, and that this was my first visit. He kindly kept trying to take me aside to talk. But I was already being talked at.

I was at another Karachi party, in a huge house, with a glass of whisky in one hand and a paper plate in the other. Casually I'd mentioned to a woman friend of the family that I wasn't against marriage. Now this friend was earnestly recommending to me a young woman who wanted to move to Britain with a husband. To my discomfort this go-between was trying to fix a time for the three of us to meet and negotiate.

I went to three parties a week in Karachi. This time I was with landowners, diplomats, businessmen and politicians: powerful people. This pleased me. They were people I wouldn't have been able to get at in England and I wanted to write about them. They were drinking heavily. Every liberal in England knows you can be lashed for drinking in Pakistan. But as far as I could tell, none of this English-speaking international bourgeoisie would be lashed for anything. They all had their trusted bootleggers who negotiated the potholes of Karachi at high speed on disintegrating motorcycles, the hooch stashed on the back. Bad bootleggers passed a hot needle through the neck of your bottle and drew your whisky out. I once walked into a host's bathroom to see the bath full of floating whisky bottles being soaked to remove the labels, a servant sitting on a stool serenely poking at them with a stick.

It was all as tricky and expensive as buying cocaine in London, with the advantage that as the hooch market was so competitive, the 'leggers delivered videotapes at the same time, dashing into the room towards the TV with hot copies of *The Jewel in the Crown*, *The Far Pavilions* and an especially popular programme called *Mind Your Language* which represented Indians and Pakistanis as ludicrous caricatures.

Everyone (except of course the mass of the population) had videos. And I could see why, since Pakistan TV was so peculiar. On my first day I turned it on and a cricket match was taking place. I settled in my chair. But the English players, who were on tour in Pakistan, were leaving the pitch. In fact Bob Willis and Ian Botham were running towards the dressing rooms surrounded by armed police, and this wasn't because Botham had made derogatory remarks about Pakistan. (He'd said it was a country to which he'd like to send his mother-in-law.) In the background a section of the crowd was being tear-gassed. Then the screen went black.

Stranger still and more significant, was the fact that the news was now being read in Arabic, a language few people in Pakistan understood. Someone explained to me that this was because the Koran was in Arabic, but everyone else said it was because General Zia wanted to kiss the arses of the Arabs.

I was having a little identity crisis. I'd been greeted so warmly in Pakistan, I felt so excited by what I saw and so at home with all my uncles, I wondered if I were not better off here than there. And when I said with a little unnoticed irony, that I was an Englishman, people fell about laughing. Why would anyone with a brown face, Muslim name and large well-known family in Pakistan want to lay claim to that cold decrepit little island off Europe where you always had to spell your name? Strangely, anti-British remarks made me feel patriotic, though I only felt patriotic when I was away from England.

But I couldn't allow myself to feel too Pakistani. I didn't want to give in to that falsity, that sentimentality. As someone said to me, provoked by the fact I was wearing jeans: we are Pakistanis, but you, you will always be a Paki—emphasizing the derogatory name the English used against Pakistanis, and therefore the fact that I couldn't rightfully lay claim to either place.

In England I was a playwright. In Karachi this meant little. There were no theatres; the arts were discouraged by the state—music and dancing are un-Islamic—and ignored by practically everyone else. As I wasn't a doctor, or businessman or military person, people suspected that this writing business I talked about was a complicated excuse for idleness, uselessness and general bumming around. In fact, as I proclaimed an interest in the entertainment business, and talked loudly about how integral the arts were to a society, moves were being made to set me up in the amusement arcade business, in Shepherd's Bush.

Finally the man got me on my own. His name was Rahman. He was a friend of my intellectual uncle. I had many uncles but Rahman preferred the intellectual one who understood Rahman's particular sorrow and like him considered himself to be a marginal man. In his fifties, a former Air Force officer, Rahman was liberal, well-travelled and married to an Englishwoman who now had a Pakistani accent.

He said to me: 'I tell you, this country is being sodomized by religion. It is even beginning to interfere with the making of money. And now we are embarked on this dynamic regression you must know, it is obvious, Pakistan has become a leading country to go away from. Our patriots are abroad. We despise and envy them. For the rest of us, our class, your family, we are in Hobbes's state of nature: insecure, frightened. We cling together out of necessity.' He became optimistic. 'We could be like Japan, a tragic oriental country that is now progressive, industrialized.' He laughed and then said, ambiguously: 'But only God keeps this country together. You must say this around the world: we are taking a great leap backwards.'

The bitterest blow for Rahman was the dancing. He liked to waltz and foxtrot. But now the expression of physical joy, of sensuality and rhythm, was banned. On TV you could see where it had been censored. When couples in Western programmes got up to dance there'd be a jerk in the film, and they'd be sitting down again. For Rahman it was inexplicable, an unnecessary cruelty that was almost more arbitrary than anything else.

Thus the despair of Rahman and my uncles' 'high and dry' generation. For them the new Islamization was the negation of their lives. It was a lament heard often; this was the story they told: Karachi was a goodish place in the Sixties and Seventies. Until about 1977 it was lively and vigorous. You could drink and dance in the Raj-style clubs (providing you were admitted) and the atmosphere was liberal—as long as you didn't meddle in politics, in which case you'd probably be imprisoned. Politically there was Bhutto: urbane, Oxford-educated, considering himself a poet and revolutionary, a veritable Chairman Mao of the subcontinent. He said he would fight obscurantism and illiteracy, ensure the equality of men and women, and increase access to education and medical care. The desert would bloom.

Later, in an attempt to save himself, appease the mullahs and rouse the dissatisfied masses behind him, he introduced various Koranic injunctions into the constitution and banned alcohol, gambling, horse racing. The Islamization had begun and was fervently continued after his execution.

Islamization built no hospitals, no schools, no houses; it cleaned no water and installed no electricity. But it was direction, identity. The country was to be in the hands of those who elected themselves to interpret the single divine purpose. Under the tyranny of the priesthood, with the cooperation of the army, Pakistan itself would embody Islam. There would now be no distinction between ethical and religious obligation; there would now be no areas in which it was possible to be wrong. The only possible incertitude was interpretation. The theory would be the eternal and universal principles which Allah created and made obligatory for men; the model would be the first three generations of Muslims; and the practice would be Pakistan.

This overemphasis on dogma and punishment strengthened the repressive, militaristic and rationalistically aggressive state seen all over the world in the authoritarian Eighties. With the added bonus that in Pakistan God was always on the side of the government.

But despite all the strident nationalism, as Rahman said, the patriots were abroad; people were going away: to the West, to Saudi Arabia, anywhere. Young people continually asked me about the possibility of getting into Britain and some thought of taking some smack with them to bankroll their establishment. They had what people called the Gulf Syndrome, a condition I recognized from my time living in the suburbs. It was a dangerous psychological cocktail consisting of ambition, suppressed excitement, bitterness and sexual longing.

Then a disturbing incident occurred which seemed to encapsulate the going-away fever. An eighteen-year-old girl from a village called Chakwal dreamed that the villagers walked across the Arabian Sea to Karbala, where they found work and money. Following this dream, people from the village set off one night for the beach, which happened to be near my uncle's house in fashionable Clifton. Here lived politicians and diplomats in LA-style white bungalows with sprinklers on the lawns, Mercedes in the drives and dogs and watchmen at the gates.

On the beach, the site of barbecues and late-night parties, the men of Chakwal packed their women and children into trunks and pushed them into the sea. Then they followed them into the water in the direction of Karbala. Soon all but twenty of the potential émigrés were drowned. The survivors were arrested and charged with illegal emigration.

It was the talk of Karachi. It caused much amusement but people like Rahman despaired of a society that could be so confused, so advanced in some aspects, so very naive in others.

About twelve people lived permanently in my uncle's house, plus servants who slept in sheds at the back just behind the chickens and dogs. Relatives sometimes came to stay for months, and new bits had to be built on to the house. All day there were visitors, in the evenings crowds of people came over; they were welcomed and they ate and watched videos and talked for hours. People weren't so protective of their privacy.

Strangely, bourgeois-bohemian life in London, in Notting Hill and Islington and Fulham, was far more formal. It was frozen dinner parties and the division of social life into the meeting of couples with other couples to discuss the lives of other coupling couples.

In Pakistan there was the continuity of the various families' knowledge of each other. People were easy to place; your grandparents and theirs were friends. When I went to the bank and showed the teller my passport, it turned out he knew several of my uncles, so I didn't receive the usual perfunctory treatment.

I compared the collective hierarchy of the family and the permanence of my family circle with my feckless, rootless life in London, in what was called the 'inner city'. There I lived alone, and lacked any long connection with anything. I'd hardly known anyone for more than eight years and certainly not their parents. People came and went. There was much false intimacy and forced friendship. People didn't take responsibility for each other. Many of my friends lived alone in London, especially the women. They wanted to be independent and to enter into relationships—as many as they liked, with whom they liked—out of choice. They didn't merely want to reproduce the old patterns of living. The future was to be determined by choice and reason, not by custom. The notions of duty and obligation barely had positive meaning for my friends: they were loaded, Victorian words, redolent of constraint and grandfather clocks, the antithesis of generosity in love, the new hugging, and the transcendence of the family. The ideal of the new relationship was no longer the S and M of the old marriage—it was F and C, freedom plus commitment.

In the large old families of Pakistan where there was nothing but old patterns disturbed only occasionally by new ways, this would have seemed a contrivance, a sort of immaturity, a failure to understand and accept the determinacies that life necessarily involved. So there was much pressure to conform, especially on the women.

'Let these women be warned,' said a mullah to the dissenting women of Rawalpindi. 'We will tear them to pieces. We will give them such terrible punishments that no one in future will dare to raise a voice against Islam.'

I remember a woman saying to me at dinner one night: 'We know at least one thing. God will never dare to show his face in this country—the women will tear him apart!'

In the Sixties of Enoch Powell and graffiti, the Black Muslims and Malcolm X gave needed strength to the descendants of slaves by 'taking the wraps off the white man'; Eldridge Cleaver was yet to be converted to Christianity and Huey P. Newton was toting his Army .45. A boy in a bedroom in a suburb, who had the King's Road constantly on his mind and who changed the pictures on his wall from week to week was unhappy, and separated from the Sixties as by a thick glass wall against which he could only press his face. But bits of the Sixties were still around in Pakistan: the liberation rhetoric, for example, the music, the clothes, the drugs, not as the way of life they were

119

originally intended to be, but as appendages to another, stronger tradition.

As my friends and I went into the Bara Market near Peshawar, close to the border of Afghanistan, in a rattling motorized rickshaw, I became apprehensive. There were large signs by the road telling foreigners that the police couldn't take responsibility for them: beyond this point the police would not go. Apparently the Pathans there, who were mostly refugees from Afghanistan, liked to kidnap foreigners. My friends, who were keen to buy opium which they'd give to the rickshaw driver to carry, told me everything was all right, because I wasn't a foreigner. I kept forgetting that.

The men of the north were tough, martial, insular and proud. They lived in mud houses and tin shacks built like forts for shooting from. Inevitably they were armed, with machine guns slung over their shoulders. In the street you wouldn't believe women existed here, except you knew they took care of the legions of young men in the area who'd fled from Afghanistan to avoid being conscripted by the Russians and sent to Moscow for re-education.

Ankle deep in mud, I went round the market. Pistols, knives, Russian-made rifles, hand grenades and large lumps of dope and opium were laid out on stalls like tomatoes and oranges. Everyone was selling heroin.

The Americans, who had much money invested in Pakistan, this compliant right-wing buffer zone between Afghanistan and India, were furious that their children were being destroyed by an illegal industry in a country they financed. But the Americans sent to Pakistan could do little about it. The heroin trade went right through Pakistani society: the police, judiciary, the army, landlords, customs officials were all involved. After all, there was nothing in the Koran about heroin. I was even told that its export made ideological sense. Heroin was anti-Western; addiction in Western children was what those godless societies with their moral vertigo deserved. It was a kind of colonial revenge. Reverse imperialism, the Karachi wits called it, inviting nemesis. The reverse imperialism was itself being reversed.

In a flat high above Karachi, an eighteen-year-old kid strung out on heroin danced cheerfully around the room in front of me pointing to his erection, which he referred to as his Imran Khan, the name of the handsome Pakistan cricket captain. More and more of the so-called multinational kids were taking heroin now. My friends who owned the flat, journalists on a weekly paper, were embarrassed.

But they always had dope to offer their friends. These laid-back people were mostly professionals: lawyers, an inspector in the police who smoked what he confiscated, a newspaper magnate and various other journalists. Heaven it was to smoke at midnight on the beach, as local fishermen, squatting respectfully behind you, fixed fat joints; the 'erotic politicians' themselves, The Doors, played from a portable stereo while the Arabian Sea rolled on to the beach. Oddly, heroin and dope were both indigenous to the country, but it took the West to make them popular in the East.

The colonized inevitably aspire to be like their colonizers—you wouldn't catch anyone of my uncle's generation with a joint in their mouth. It was infra dig, for peasants. They shadowed the British, they drank whisky and read *The Times*; they praised others by calling them 'gentlemen'; and their eyes filled with tears at old Vera Lynn records.

But the kids discussed yoga, you'd catch them standing on their heads. They even meditated. Though one boy who worked at the airport said it was too much of a Hindu thing for Muslims to be doing; if his parents caught him chanting a mantra he'd get a backhander across the chops. Mostly the kids listened to the Stones, Van Morrison and Bowie as they flew over ruined roads to the beach in bright red and yellow Japanese cars with quadrophonic speakers, past camels and acres of wasteland.

I often walked from my uncle's house several miles down a road towards the beach. Here, all along a railway track, the poor and diseased and hungry lived in shacks and huts; the filthy poor gathered around rusty standpipes to fetch water; or ingeniously they resurrected wrecked cars, usually Morris Minors; and here they slept in huge sewer pipes among buffalo, chickens and wild dogs. Here I met a policeman who I thought was on duty. But he lived here, and hanging on the wall of his falling-down shed was his spare white police uniform, which he'd had to buy himself.

A stout lawyer in his early thirties of immense charm—for him it was definitely the Eighties, not the Sixties. His father was a judge. He was intelligent, articulate and fiercely representative of the other 'new spirit' of Pakistan. He didn't drink, smoke or fuck. Out of choice. He prayed five times a day. He worked all the time. He was determined to be a good Muslim, since that was the whole point of the country existing at all. He wasn't indulgent, except religiously, and he lived in accordance with what he believed. I took to him immediately.

We had dinner in an expensive restaurant. It could have been in London or New York. The food was excellent, I said. The lawyer disagreed, with his mouth full, shaking his great head. It was definitely no good, it was definitely meretricious rubbish. But for ideological reasons only, since he ate with relish. He was only in the restaurant because of me, he said. There was better food in the villages. The masses had virtue, they knew how to eat, how to live. Those desiccated others, the marginal men I associated with and liked so much, were a plague class with no values. Perhaps, he suggested, this was why I liked them, being English. Their education, their intellectual snobbery, made them un-Islamic. They didn't understand the masses and they spoke in English to cut themselves off from the people. Didn't the best jobs go to those with a foreign education? He was tired of these Westernized elders denigrating their country and its religious nature.

The lawyer and I went out into the street. It was busy. There were dancing camels and a Pakistan trade exhibition. The exhibition was full of Pakistani imitations of Western goods: bathrooms in chocolate and strawberry, TVs with stereos attached; fans, air conditioners, heaters; and an arcade full of Space Invaders. The lawyer got agitated.

These were Western things, of no use to the masses. The masses wanted Islam, not strawberry bathrooms or...or elections. Are elections a Western thing? I asked. Don't they have them in India too? No—they're a Western thing, the lawyer said.

How could they be required under Islam? There need be only one party—the party of the righteous.

This energetic lawyer would have pleased and then disappointed Third World intellectuals and revolutionaries from an earlier era, people like Fanon and Guevara. This talk of liberation—at last the acknowledgement of the virtue of the toiling masses, the struggle against neocolonialism, its bourgeois stooges, and American interference—the entire recognizable rhetoric of freedom and struggle ends in the lawyer's mind with the country on its knees, at prayer. Having started to look for itself it finds itself in the eighth century.

I strode into a room in my uncle's house. Half-hidden by a curtain, on a veranda, was an aged woman servant wearing my cousin's old clothes, praying. I stopped and watched her. In the morning, as I lay in bed, she swept the floor of my room with some twigs bound together. She was at least sixty. Now, on the shabby prayer mat, she was tiny and around her the universe was endless, immense, but God was above her. I felt she was acknowledging that which was larger than she, knowing and feeling her own insignificance. It was not empty ritual. I wished I could do it.

I went with the lawyer to the mosque in Lahore, the largest in the world. I took off my shoes, padded across the immense courtyard with the other man—women were not allowed—and got on my knees, I banged my forehead on the marble floor. Beside me a man in a similar posture gave a world-consuming yawn. I waited but could not lose myself in prayer. I could only travesty the woman's prayer, to whom it had a world of meaning.

Did she want a society in which her particular moral and religious beliefs were mirrored, and no others, instead of some plural, liberal melange? A society in which her own cast of mind, her customs, way of life and obedience to God constituted authority? It wasn't as if anyone had asked her.

In Pakistan, England just wouldn't go away. Relics of the Raj were everywhere: buildings, monuments, Oxford accents, libraries full of English books, and newspapers. Many Pakistanis had relatives in England; thousands of Pakistani families depended on money sent from England. While visiting a village, a man told me that when his three grandchildren visited from Bradford, he had to hire an interpreter to speak to them. It was happening all the time—the closeness of the two societies, and the distance.

Although Pakistanis still wanted to escape to England, the old men in their clubs and the young eating their hamburgers took great pleasure in England's decline and decay. The great master was fallen. It was seen as strike-bound, drug-ridden, riot-torn, inefficient, disunited, a society which had moved too suddenly from puritanism to hedonism and now loathed itself. And the Karachi wits liked to ask me when I thought the Americans would decide the British were ready for self-government.

Yet people like Rahman still clung to what they called British ideals, maintaining that it is a society's ideals, its conception of human progress, that define the level of its civilization. They regretted, under the Islamization, the repudiation of the values which they said were the only positive aspect of Britain's legacy to the subcontinent. These were: the idea of secular institutions based on reason, not revelation or scripture; the idea that there were no final solutions to human problems; and the idea that the health and vigour of a society was bound up with its ability to tolerate and express a plurality of views on all issues, and that these views would be welcomed.

The English misunderstood the Pakistanis because they saw only the poor people, those from the villages, the illiterates, the peasants, the Pakistanis who didn't know how to use toilets, how to eat with knives and forks because they were poor. If the British could only see *them*, the rich, the educated, the sophisticated, they wouldn't be so hostile. They'd know what civilized people the Pakistanis really were. And then they'd like them.

1986
The Snap Election

James Fenton

The Project Is Thwarted

A man sets light to himself, promising his followers that he will rise again in three hours. When the time has elapsed, the police clear away the remains. Another man, a half-caste, has himself crucified every year—he has made a vow to do this until God puts him in touch with his American father. A third unfortunate, who has lost his mother, stands rigid at the gate of his house and has been there, the paper tells us, for the last fourteen years, 'gazing into an empty rubber plantation'.

I don't know when it was that I began noticing stories like these, or began to think that the Philippines must be a strange and fascinating place. Pirates came from there last year to attack a city in Borneo. Ships sank with catastrophic loss of lives. People came from all over the world to have psycho-surgeons rummage through their guts—their wounds opened and closed in a trice. There was a Holy War in Mindanao. There was a communist insurgency. Political dialogue was conducted by murderers. Manila was a brothel.

It was the Cuba of the future. It was going the way of Iran. It was another Nicaragua, another Cambodia, another Vietnam. But all these places, awesome in their histories, are so different from each other that one couldn't help thinking: this kind of talk was a shorthand for a confusion. All that was being said was that something was happening in the Philippines. Or more plausibly: a lot of different things were happening in the Philippines. And a lot of people were feeling obliged to speak out about it.

But still at this stage, although the tantalizing little items were appearing daily in the English press, I had not seen any very ambitious account of what was going on. This fact pleased me. I thought that if I planned well in advance, engineered a decent holiday and went off to Manila, I would have the place to myself, as it were. I would have leisure and space enough to work away at my own pace, not running after a story, not hunting with the pack of journalists. I would watch, and wait, and observe. I would control my project rather than have it control me.

But I had reckoned without the Reagan administration and the whims of a dictator. Washington began sending urgent and rather public envoys to Manila, calling for reforms and declaring that time was running out. There was something suspicious in all this. It looked as if they were trying to fix a deal with Marcos—for if they weren't trying to fix things the alternative view must be that they were destabilizing the dictatorship, and this seemed out of character. Then Marcos went on American television and announced a snap election. And this too smelled fishy. I couldn't imagine that he would have made such a move had he not been certain of the outcome. For a while it was uncertain whether the snap election could or would be held, for the terms which the dictator offered to his people appeared unconstitutional. The constitution required that Marcos resign before running again for office. But Marcos would not resign: he would offer a post-dated resignation letter only, and he would fight the presidential election in his role as president.

In other words, the deal was: Marcos would remain president but would hold a fair election to reassure his American critics that he still had the support of his people; if, by some fluke, it turned out that he did not have this support, the world had his word of honour that he would step down and let somebody else be president. And this somebody else, in all probability, would be the woman who was accusing Marcos of having murdered her husband. So if he stepped down, Marcos would very likely be tried for murder.

It didn't sound as if it was going to be much of an election. What's more, it was going to wreck my dream of having Manila all to myself. Indeed, my project was already in ruins. By now everybody in the world seemed to have noticed what an interesting place the Philippines was. There would be a massive press corps running after every politician and diplomat. There would be a deluge of background articles in the press. People would start getting sick of the subject well before I had had the chance to put pen to paper.

I toyed with the idea of ignoring the election altogether. It was a sham and a fake. It would be a 'breaking story'. If I stuck to my original plan, I would wait till Easter, which is when they normally hold the crucifixions. I wasn't going to be panicked into joining the herd.

Then I panicked and changed all my plans. Contrary to some

expectations, the opposition had united behind Corazón Aquino, the widow of the national hero Benigno 'Ninoy' Aquino. She was supposedly an unwilling candidate, and supposedly a completely inexperienced politician. But she was immensely popular—unwillingness and inexperience, it appeared, made a refreshing change. The assassination of her husband in 1983, as he stepped off the plane in Manila airport, was a matter that had never been cleared up. So there was a highly personal, as well as political, clash ahead.

(Not everybody believes, I was to discover, that President Marcos personally authorized the murder. At the time, one is assured, he was having one of his relapses. A man who was involved in the design of the presidential dentures told me, meaningly, that at the time of Ninoy's death Marcos's gums were very swollen—which was always a sign. And he added, intriguingly, that whenever Marcos's gums were swollen, the gums of General Ver, the Chief of Staff, swelled up in sympathy. Marcos was in the military hospital at the time, and I have it from someone who knew one of his nurses that, when he heard the news, Marcos threw his food tray at his wife, Imelda. Others say he slapped her, but I prefer the food tray version.)

In addition to the growing opposition to Marcos in the Philippines, there was the discrediting campaign in the United States, which began to come up with some interesting facts and theories. Marcos's vaunted war record had been faked. His medals were fakes. His property holdings overseas were vast. He was shifting huge sums of dollars back to the Philippines to finance the coming campaign. He was seriously ill from lupus erythematosus. He had had two kidney transplants, but whether he still had two kidneys was another matter. His supporters painted slogans around Manila: WE LOVE FM. His opponents, many of whom had a rough sense of humour, changed these to LUPUS LOVES FM.

At the outset of the campaign he was obviously very ill. One day his hands were mysteriously bleeding. Had he received the stigmata? He was carried into meetings on a chair. Perhaps he would be dead before the campaign was through.

Foreign observers had been invited to see fair play in the

elections. There was Senator Lugar and his American team, and there was an international team. Around 1,000 journalists arrived, plus other freelance observers. So that when I boarded my plane at Gatwick on January 30, it was with a sense of being stampeded into a story. I had no great hope of the elections. I was going just in case.

A Loyal Marcos Man

There's a special kind of vigilance in the foyer of a press hotel. The star TV correspondents move through, as film stars do, as if waiting to be recognized, spotted. When they come back sweating and covered with the dust of the road, they have a particular look which says: See, I have come back sweating, covered with the dust of the road. When they leave in a hurry on a hot news tip, they have a look which says: What? Me leave in a hurry on a hot news tip? No, I'm just sloping off to dinner. Everyone is alert to any sudden activity—the arrival of a quotable politician, the sudden disappearance of a rival crew, the hearty greetings of the old hands. When the foyer is full, it is like a stock exchange for news. When it is empty, you think: Where *are* they all? What's going on?

I was frisked at the door of the Manila Hotel. It was government-owned, and nobody was taking any chances. The bellboys came past wheeling massive displays of flowers. In the brown air beneath the chandeliers, obvious agents were keeping a track of events. The hotel telephone system was working to capacity, and there was trouble with crossed lines. But I finally got through to Helen, my main contact in Manila, and we agreed to meet in the Taproom.

Here the atmosphere was green from the glass reading lamps on the bar. A pale, shrunken face was knocking back some strong mixture. Hearing me order, the face approached me and made itself unavoidable. 'You're English, aren't you? You see? I can always tell. What you doing?'

'I'm a tourist.'

That made him laugh. 'Tourist? I bet you're MI 16.' I thought, if he wants me to be MI 16, that's fine by me. I stared into my whisky as if to confirm his analysis. By now he was rather close. I wondered how long it would take Helen to 'wash up and finish a few things'. My companion ordered another Brandy Alexander. He was going to get very drunk that night, he said, then he would get him a girlfriend.

He was English like me, he said, only he had been deported at the age of eight. Now his Filipina wife had left him, and at midnight it would be his birthday. Could he see my matches? Those were English matches, weren't they? I passed him the box. He was, he said, the only white man to have worn the uniform of Marcos's bodyguard.

Or maybe he said palace guard. He was wearing a *barong tagalog*, the Filipino shirt that you don't tuck in. He'd been at the palace that day—he'd just come from there—and he'd been in big trouble. Hadn't had the right clothes. Just look, he said, there are darns in my trousers. His wife had left him and she had taken all his clothes—everything. Now he was going to get drunk, get him a girl and go home at midnight.

Since it was my turn to talk, I suggested that he find the girl first, then go home.

'It's my *birthday*,' he said, staring at his watch under the reading lamp to see how long he had to drink till midnight. He had five hours in hand. His car was parked outside. I suggested he take a taxi home. He told me he had the biggest police car in Manila. I suggested he get a policeman to drive him home. He ordered another Brandy Alexander. The waiters smiled nervously at him and called him colonel. I began to think he might be for real.

He lurched forward confidentially. 'I'm a loyal Marcos man,' he said, 'but this election...' He shook his head. 'He'll win it,' he said, 'but it'll be a damn close thing. He'll lose in Metro Manila. Marcos is a great man, but it's the people around him. There's so much corruption at the palace. So many corrupt people...'

I didn't want any more of his confidences. I'd been here a couple of hours, and I wasn't going to be drawn. I said: 'Tell me about your ring.' It was as big as a stud box.

'Oh,' he said, 'it started off as a piece of jade, then I had my initials put on it, then the setting'—it seemed to include diamonds—'and then the stone fell out and I stuck it back with superglue.'

I thought it must be superglue, I said. In addition to the ring he had a heavy gold watch and an identity bracelet, all gross and sparkling.

'The Queen gave me a medal,' he said. 'And my wife threw it in the trash can! She threw it away! Look, she tied a knot in the ribbon!'

He fished the medal out of his trouser pocket. 'That's a George III medal,' he said. 'I'm English and proud of it. Any time I want, I can go back to Cheshire and eat kippers.'

Then he said: 'Would you do me a favour?'

I panicked a little.

'Those matches,' he said, 'English matches. Would you give them to me? You see, if I show these at the Palace, everyone'll be surprised. They won't know where I got them from. We don't have them here.'

I gave him the matches. 'What are you doing this evening?' he asked.

'I'm afraid I have a dinner appointment.'

He laughed at these little panics he knew how to create, and told me not to worry. He wasn't going to barge in on my night out. We returned to the subject of his wife. He produced a letter and told me to read it out loud.

It was very dark in the bar, so we had to huddle together by the reading light. The letter was from the Minister of Tourism: 'Dear —,' I read, 'Please remember that — is your husband and the father of your two children. Please give him back his clothes so that he can recover his self-respect.'

'Read it out,' said the colonel, 'read it out loud.'

Then he told me that Marcos could do nothing to help him. His wife had taken everything, the children, his clothes, the lot. The case was in a civil court and Marcos could do nothing about it.

This was the first time I had heard of a court beyond Marcos's control. I could see what the colonel meant about going back to Cheshire and eating kippers.

Pedro's Party

When Helen arrived the colonel looked startled and impressed.
I was impressed too. I hadn't expected Helen to look like Meryl
Streep. The colonel shot me a look and I shot one back. He
wanted to tell Helen about his wife. 'I'm sorry,' I said, 'but we're
late for our meeting.' Then I took the surprised Helen and
propelled her across the foyer.

'What's going on?' she said. I was just afraid we might be
landed with him all evening.

It turned out, though, that there was a meeting in hand. That
is, one of Helen's friends, Pedro, was giving a party, and if I
wanted to go, if I could stay awake after dinner, I was welcome.
Pedro's family were squatters, and I noticed—without realizing
how customary this was in the Philippines—that at the end of
the meal Helen and I had together, she packed up the remains
of our food and took it with us for Pedro's children.

I was impressed by Helen: she seemed to know everyone on
the street, and most of them by name. People greeted her from
the cafe as we passed, and the cigarette vendors called out to
us. We turned down a little alleyway and into a garden beneath
a mango tree. Pedro's hut consisted of a single room with a
covered extension. There was a large fridge outside, painted
green, with a 'Bad Bananas' sticker, and posters advertising a
performance of Antigone and a concert by an American pianist.
Helen disappeared indoors to talk to the women and children,
while the rest of us drank beer around a table. There were
reporters, photographers and theatre people, and members of
the foreign press corps, also friends of Helen. I was beginning
to get the idea. We were all friends of Helen. She had a whole
society of friends.

The great conversation topic was what had just happened in
the Manila Hotel. There had been a press conference. As
Marcos had been brought in, the *Paris-Match* photographer had
held his camera in the air to get a shot of him. Two of Marcos's
bodyguards had tried to snatch the camera, and the
photographer had tried to elbow them away. He had been
hustled out of the room and into the hotel kitchen, where the
bodyguards had taken turns beating him up. The chef who had

been passing was knocked over in the melee, and dropped the special cake he had prepared in Marcos's honour.

The party grew, and grew noisy. People taught me the political signs. The Laban sign was an L made with the thumb and first finger. That was the sign for Cory's campaign—'Laban' was Tagalog for 'fight'. The sign for the KBL, Marcos's party, was a V. If you turned your hand over and rubbed your thumb and fourth finger together, that was the sign for money, the bribe, the greasing of the machine. The boycott sign was an X, two fingers crossed, or two clenched fists across your chest. Many of the people present were solidly, and others liquidly, behind the election boycott. 'We're all partisans here!' shouted one guy. He was wearing a red baseball cap with a red star, and an embroidered badge saying DON'T SHOOT JOURNALISTS. No joke, that. Of the thirty journalists killed worldwide last year, half had been Filipinos. Several of the company were wearing the *tubao*, a purple and yellow kerchief which showed, if you wore it, you had probably been to 'the hell of Mindanao', one of the worst areas of the war.

Pedro moved among the guests, and plundered the crates of San Miguel beer. People tied their kerchiefs over their noses and made fearsome gestures, laughing hugely. A guitar was passed around and songs were sung from the war of independence against the Spanish. Helen sang too. She seemed to improvise a song in Tagalog, and this was doubly surprising because she had been complaining of laryngitis earlier in the evening. Now her voice had woken up for the occasion. It was deep and throaty. She was singing about the Mendiola Bridge, where all the big demonstrations ended up, and where the army or the police used to disperse the crowd with water cannon and tear gas.

There was another song about the Mendiola Bridge which went simply:

Mendiola Bridge is falling down
Falling down
Falling down
Mendiola Bridge is falling down
My First Lady

The First Lady being Imelda Marcos. I had heard she was very superstitious, always off to the soothsayer. One day she was told the three things that would happen before the Marcos regime fell: a major earthquake would destroy a church; a piece of earth would erupt after a long silence; and the opposition would cross Mendiola Bridge by force. Since that prophecy had been made, Marcos had spent 2.4 million dollars restoring a church in his native Ilocos Norte for his daughter Irene's wedding. A few weeks after the ceremony there had been an earthquake and the fault had run right through the church. Then the Mayon volcano had erupted after a long silence. As for the third condition, some people said it had already been fulfilled when some opposition people had been allowed across the bridge. But others said no: it must be crossed by force. The bridge was the point of defence along the road to the Malacañang Palace. I imagined that, to have achieved such a significance, it must be a great big handsome bridge. I certainly did not think that I should see the crowds swarm over it. But I was wrong on both counts.

The Americans at the party obviously shared Helen's love for the Filipinos, although they had not been here as long as she had. While I sat there blearily congratulating myself on having arrived and actually *met* people, they were thick in an involvement which I was yet to feel. I could see that they were really delighted to be at Pedro's house, a piece of somewhat haphazard carpentry. I too felt honoured. But I sensed in the Americans a feeling of guilt about the Filipinos, and when I asked one of them what was happening he said: 'It's all a sordid and disgusting deal. Marcos has everything on his side—the army, the police, the banking system, the whole apparatus. He's going to fix the election, and Washington is going to go along with it.'

Then he gave me a sharp look and said: 'You know what you're suffering from. You're suffering from jet-lag denial.' It was quite true. Pedro found me a taxi to the hotel.

My hotel, the Philippines Plaza, was a big mistake, perhaps my biggest mistake so far. When people heard I was staying there, they couldn't believe my bad judgement. The thing I couldn't explain to any of them was that I had needed the name of a hotel in order to tell the NPA where they could contact me. By coincidence, a friend from Ethiopia had been staying at this place and had dropped me a note. So now I was stuck in this isolated monstrosity, which I had known only by name, in the vain hope that I would receive some message. In order to deliver the message, the NPA would have to get past the matador on the front door. From what I knew of the NPA, that would be no problem. But what about me? I was a bad case of jet-lag denial. The matador, both of him, saluted and opened the taxi door. I paid my fare and stumbled out, at the height of his frogged breeches.

Among the Boycotters

Harry and Jojo picked me up the next morning. I felt fine, really fine. They, less so. Pedro's party had taken it out of them. Harry asked what I had expected of Manila. I paused. 'Probably from abroad you think there are killings going on all the time,' said Harry, 'but you know…they do the killings mostly at night.' And he laughed a good deal.

'Why are you laughing, Harry?' I said. 'I don't think that's funny at all.'

'You don't think it's funny. Europeans never think it's funny if someone's killed. But you know, we Filipinos, sometimes there are demonstrations where two or three people are killed, and immediately afterwards people are joking and fooling around. You have to joke in order to keep going. But I've noticed Europeans never joke about these things.'

He had been to Europe on business. Photography was only a sideline for him. He wanted me to know that the people we were about to see this morning, the Bayan marchers, were the most important people in the election. 'At the end,' said Harry, 'once the Cory supporters see that it has all been a fix, many of them will join Bayan, or return to its ranks.' The marches would go on, up and down the country. That was the important thing, and he insisted on the point throughout the day. Sometimes I would look at Harry and think: he's as proud of Bayan as if they were his sons and daughters, as if he were living through their achievements. At other times I felt I was being pressed for a response, a confidence. I couldn't reconcile my idea of Harry the owner of the small export business with Harry the admirer of the Left.

Bayan, the umbrella organization for the legal, 'cause-oriented' groups in the opposition, was said by some to be nothing but a Communist front. Others emphasized the diversity of political opinion within its ranks. I asked many people in subsequent weeks what the truth of the matter was. A Communist told me: 'It's not a Communist front—it *is* the Communists.' Others strongly rejected this. A Bayan member told me: 'It's like this. When the Communists speak, we listen to what they say. When Bayan speaks, they listen to us. We are neighbours. I never see my neighbour from one week to the next, but when he is cooking, I know what he'll be having for dinner.' It was an open secret, he said, that within four years the NPA would be marching through Manila. When that happened, Bayan would have helped them.

Harry said: 'Maybe there'll be some trouble today as the marchers come into the city. Maybe we'll see something.'

I said: 'I very much hope not.' I enjoyed disconcerting Harry with a resolutely anti-good-story line.

Harry said: 'You know, photographers—they love it when trouble begins.'

I wasn't looking for trouble.

We drove south on the highway, past small businesses, authorized dealers in this and that, scrappy banana palms, pawnshops, factories—some with their own housing estates adjacent—American-style eateries, posh condominiums and slums. As a first impression it offered nothing very shocking.

Just beyond Muntinlupa we met the marchers, about 1,000 of them with banners denouncing the US-Marcos dictatorship. Most of them were masked. They looked young, and I would have thought that they were students, but Harry insisted they were mainly peasants and workers. I was asked to sign a piece of paper explaining who I was. Most journalists, I realized, wore plasticated ID tags round their necks. In the absence of this, you were assumed to be from the American Embassy. A masked figure passed me with a megaphone, and shouted: 'Down with US imperialism.'

'They're very well organized,' said Harry. 'You'll see. They're ready for anything.' And it was true—they had their own first aid team and an ambulance. They quite expected to be shot. If Bayan was the legal arm of the people's struggle it was still organized like an army. The march was divided into units, and when they stopped at the Church of Our Lady you could see how the units stayed close together to avoid infiltration. As the march approached Manila they were expecting trouble from goons. It was clear that they were very experienced marchers and knew exactly how to maintain control of their numbers.

The people at the church had not made them welcome, but they took over the building nevertheless. Rice and vegetables were brought from the market, and they ate in groups, or rested in the cool of the building, under the crucified figure of the Black Nazarene, whose wavy brown wig reached down to his waist.

The marchers had seemed hostile at first, and I was in no hurry to talk to them if they didn't want to talk to me. Finally I met Chichoy, who was I suppose in his early twenties, and whose political work, he told me, was in educating peasants and workers towards a state of mind where they did not consider their grievances to be part of an inevitable order of things. It was good work and had produced gratifying results. But, as Chichoy said at one point, 'People like me do not live long. We are prepared to die at any time. The point is not to have a long life—a long life would be a good thing—the point is to have a meaningful life.' His way of speaking combined a serious firmness of tone with a deep sadness, as if his own death in the cause were something that he had often contemplated, very much regretted, but there it was.

Not all of the Bayan marchers struck me like this. Some of them seemed to relish the figures they cut, with their red flags and face masks, and their way of bringing drama on to the streets in the manner of the Peking ballet. Chichoy talked about how a fair election was an impossibility. He was adamant that the intention of the US was to support a dictatorship either way— if not Marcos, an alternative Marcos. If Ninoy Aquino had not been killed, maybe he would have become the alternative dictator. Firmly in his mind was the equation of the US with dictatorship. The Americans had to be overthrown. Their bases had to be closed down. The Philippines would become non-aligned, 'and that will be our contribution to world peace'.

The march moved off. It was one of a series converging on the city, and it joined with another group under the highway at Muntinlupa. People shouted: 'The Snap Election is a fake. So what. We're going to the mountains.' There were few police in sight, and nobody tried to stop the teams of girls with paint pots, who scrawled hurried slogans on the kerbs and walls. On a house which was decked with Marcos posters, I noticed a window full of boycott placards being waved wildly by unseen people. Bayan had its supporters—over a million of them in the country, it was said. But the crowds did not join in. It was as if these demonstrators were on a dangerous mission of their own. The people watched them and kept their own counsel.

We were marching underneath the raised highway, and the acoustics were tempting. When the firecrackers started exploding, the demonstrators cheered. For my part, I became extremely anxious. We had been expecting trouble, and I couldn't tell whether it was the demonstrators who were lobbing the firecrackers or the crowd. I didn't yet know that this was part of the Bayan style. I asked Harry, 'Who's throwing those things?'

'I don't know,' he said, clicking away. He hadn't caught the sense of my question.

The Bayan style was to make each demonstration look and sound as dangerous as possible. When the marches converged on Manila that evening, and the demonstrators sealed off roads by linking arms, the speed and drama with which they operated made it look as if a revolution was in the offing. The defiance of the slogans, the glamour of the torches, the burning tyres, the masked faces—it was a spectacular show. But the state was adopting an official policy of Maximum Tolerance, and the demonstrators had the streets to themselves.

The next day they came together and marched towards Malacañang. And so we arrived at the famed Mendiola Bridge, where the barricades were up, a massive press corps stood in waiting, and the military blocked the way. The bridge was insignificant enough: you wouldn't have noticed it if you had not been looking for it. On the side streets, US Embassy men with walkie-talkies were giving up-to-date accounts of the action. 'You ought to have a mask,' said Helen, 'there may be a dispersal.' But the tear gas was not used, and the water cannon was only there for display. They burned effigies of Reagan and Marcos at the foot of the barricade. Reagan caught alight easily, but Marcos was slow to burn.

Rival Rallies

I never found out whether it was actually true, but people said in a very confident way that Marcos had seeded the clouds in the hope of producing a downpour for Cory's *miting de avance*. If he did, it was another of his miscalculations—like the calling of the Snap Election. The Laban supporters had asked for the grandstand in Luneta Park, just by the Manila Hotel. They weren't allowed it, and were obliged to put up their own platform facing the opposite way. The park filled up. The grandstand itself filled up. The meeting overflowed. People tried to guess how many there were in the crowd—a million, two million? It was impossible to tell. It was the biggest rally I'd ever been in, and one of the friendliest and funniest.

I sat among the crowd just in front of the platform. We were jammed so tight that sitting itself was very difficult. But if we stood we got shouted at by the people behind us, whereas if we shouted at the people in front of us to sit down they literally could not do so. It was very painful, and went on for seven or eight hours. What a relief when the dancing girls came on, or when we all stood for a performance of 'Tie a Yellow Ribbon round the Old Oak Tree', Ninoy's old campaign song. The idiom of the rally was distinctly American, with extra-flash gestures, like the priest on the platform who ripped open his soutane to reveal a yellow Cory T-shirt, or Butz Aquino in his Texan hat, or the yellow-ribboned pigeons and the fireworks overhead.

It was not easy for a newcomer to tell the difference between the pop singers and professional crooners on the one hand, and the politicians and their wives and families on the other. Everyone sang—current hits, old favourites, I don't know what. The most electrifying speaker was undoubtedly Doy Laurel, although by the time he came on the anticipation was such that his work was easy. People had said Cory was not a professional politician. She was a professional something, though, taking the microphone and singing the Lord's Prayer. After the rabble-rousing of Laurel, the occasion had turned solemn and moving. When the crowd sang 'Bayan Ko', the national anthem of the Opposition, you felt all the accumulated laughter and cheering of the day turn into pure emotion. Religion and national feeling were at the heart of what Cory stood for.

The next day, Marcos had to do something about all this. The world's press had seen the great crowds. He had to come up with something equally impressive.

I sat on the balcony of my hotel room, with its view of Manila Bay. Helicopters were passing to and fro across the city. Ships arrived, laden down with people. Army trucks and coaches were busing in the Marcos supporters, who formed up in groups in the hotel forecourt, in order to march down to Luneta.

Helen arrived with Jojo and Bing, another of her gang. They'd come down from Quezon City, where the streets were alive with anger. The Marcos supporters were being stoned as they arrived from the boondocks. We went back to have a look.

The taxi man looked faintly nervous. He was carrying a Marcos flag—all the taxis at the Plaza did the same. He said: 'I think we may be stoned.'

I said: 'Wouldn't it be a good idea to remove that flag?' As soon as we were out of sight of the hotel, he did.

Along the road the 'noise barrage' had begun—long and short blasts on the horn, for Co-ry. Groups had gathered at street corners to jeer the buses as they passed. From the car in front of us people were handing out Marcos T-shirts to the other drivers. When a busload of Marcos supporters came past, we found they were all leaning out of the windows making the Laban sign and calling for Cory. Helen asked them what they were up to. Oh, they said, we're all Cory supporters here—we're only doing it for the money. And they laughed at us: we were going to have to pay for our taxi, they said, whereas they were being paid to ride in their bus. They all treated the occasion as a tremendous joke. It was worth their while attending a Marcos rally for a couple of dollars. Such sums were not easy to come by.

Bing and I were walking towards the meeting. An enormous number of people in T-shirts were already walking away from it. Bing asked them, straight-faced, 'Has Marcos spoken already?' No, they said. Then why were they leaving the meeting? They looked at him as if he were mad. They'd already had enough.

And now the clouds broke, and people really *had* had enough. As we ran for shelter in the Manila Hotel, the hired supporters (not one of whom would normally have been allowed to set foot in it) realized that they could hardly be turned away in their full Marcos paraphernalia. They stormed the foyer, pushing their way past the security guards and treating the whole occasion as a wonderful joke.

Marcos had been due to speak in the evening, but at this rate there wasn't going to be anybody left. So they brought him forward for an earlier rant.

And afterwards, no doubt, they called for the guy who had been told to seed the clouds, and gave him a very nasty time indeed.

Helen on Smoky Mountain

'Within that American body,' says Jojo, 'there's a Filipino soul struggling to escape.' Or another way of putting it was: 'Helen is the first victim of Filipino imperialism.' She has found herself in another language, and indeed she is in some danger of losing her American identity altogether. Among the circle of friends to whom she introduced me, she speaks English—when she speaks it—with a Filipino accent. Or perhaps it is more a matter of intonation. She will say: 'There's going to be viol*ence*.' She leans towards the end of the sentence. Instead of saying, 'They were *shooting* at me,' she says, 'They were shooting at *me*.' And she has forgotten the meaning of several English words.

English people sometimes find life relaxing in a foreign

language if it means that they can lose their class backgrounds. Americans, rather lacking this incentive, don't seem to like to unbend linguistically. Whenever I meet really good American linguists, I always assume they're on a journey away from something. I don't ask Helen very much about her past. It's not that I'm not impertinent. I pride myself on being just as impertinent as the next man. But whenever I garner little details about her past, it's so dramatic that I don't know what to say. If I said, 'So what does your little sister do now?' she would be bound to come up with something like, 'She was eaten by a school of barracudas.' And then I wouldn't know where to look.

She is essentially companionable and generous, and this leads her to do something I've never seen anybody do. She doesn't drink but she enjoys the company of drinkers, and, rather than lag behind as they get drunk, she gets mentally drunk first. One *calamansi* juice and she's slightly squiffy. After a couple of glasses of iced water she's well away.

Another unique feature: she's both a tomboy and a woman's woman. 'What do you mean by a woman's woman?' she said one day, bridling. Well, what I meant was that she's the kind of woman women like. She goes into a house and within seconds, it seems there are fascinating conversations taking place in the kitchen. Then suddenly all the women are going off to the cinema for a soppy movie in Tagalog. Helen has got them organized.

The tomboy side of Helen comes out in her professional life. The Filipino press corps is her gang, and she often says that it was a difficult gang to join, to be accepted by. There were suspicions. There were unkind rumours. She had to prove herself before she was considered one of the group. But by now the group in question is so large that going on a demonstration with Helen is like being taken to an enormous cocktail party which happens, for some reason, to be winding its way through the Manila streets towards the inevitable Mendiola Bridge. Hundreds and hundreds of introductions, slappings on the back, encounters with long-lost friends, wavings across a sea of heads.

Everything turns into a party around Helen. You suggest a working dinner *à deux*. By the evening in question it has turned into a feast *à huit*, with further complications about where to go afterwards, because another part of the party is waiting on the other side of the City, a third group is in the offing and there is even a chance that somebody she would like you to meet might turn up at a place which isn't exactly next door to where we are going but…

You have to consider this party as an event which is taking place all over Manila—like a demonstration.

One of the things that makes Helen really angry is the brothel aspect of Manila. The mere act of walking down certain Ermita streets is enough to send her into a passionate rage. She cannot relax among the sleaze—that would be a kind of connivance. If Helen's Filipino friends are rather curious to see the bars (which cater largely, it would appear, for Australians) she cannot follow them. Her rage would stand like a bouncer at the door, blocking her path.

She has a heroic conception of the Filipino people. The opposite conception—of an easy-going, lackadaisical, prostituted and eventually degraded nation—this she will fight against. You cannot help noticing that the struggle of the Filipino is carried on in the deepest recesses of her mind. Once she was saying, 'Anyway, even if Cory Aquino were to become President of the United States of America, that wouldn't change anything—'

'Helen, do you realize what you've just said? Cory isn't standing for President of the United States of America.'

'Is that what I said? Oh, so that's really Freudian, *huh*?'

'Yup.' The Filipino struggle is the missing radical wing of American politics. This is Helen's discovery.

The car stops at a red light and the pathetic moaning children beg for money.

'I'm not going to give money to you,' says Helen to a boy. 'You just give it to the police.'

The boy is scandalized and drops the moaning immediately. 'How do you know we give money to the police?'

'Everyone knows the police organize you kids. There's been gossip about it for years.'

'Well if you spread gossip like that, that means *you're* a

gossip,' he snaps. Helen laughs. It's obvious that the gossip is true. The police take a cut from the street urchins, just as they get money from the child prostitutes. Another Manila speciality.

Manila is a city of more than eight million, of whom three to four million live in the Tondo slums. And in some of these slums you see people who are barely managing to remain on the brink of existence. Smoky Mountain, one of the main garbage dumps of Metro Manila, is such a place. The people live from scavenging plastic or polythene which is then sold to dealers and recycled. The mountain itself provides a living for rival communities who take it in turns to go out and sift the garbage. Sometimes there are quarrels over the shifts, and the scavengers actually fight over the tip. The worst work is by night: it is said that the truck drivers pay no attention to the scavengers and drive over them.

Infant mortality among the scavengers is sixty-five to seventy per cent. The people live in huts at the foot of the tip, by the banks of the filthy Pasig River, a sewer in which they wash. It is here, by the bridge, that they sometimes find the mutilated victims of the latest 'salvaging'.

Coming here with Helen is like trailing in the wake of royalty. Word passes among the huts, the children swarm around her, they all know her by name, and she seems to know a great number of them. She loves making children laugh. She keeps a glove puppet in her camera bag for the purpose.

Up on the burning heap itself, I meet a boy who can say two sentences in English. 'I am a scabenger, I am a scabenger,' he repeats, and, 'This is garbage.' He makes me feel the top of his head, which has a perfectly round dent three inches across, where he was beaten up, and he opens his shirt to show me a scar running from his neck to his navel, a war wound from one of the scavengers' battles. In his hand he holds a piece of cloth, like a comforter. He is high on solvent.

He tells Helen of his desperation and asks for her help, but she is severe with him. She says she'll only help him if he gives up the solvent. He says he only takes it because life is so desperate. She says she knows all about that. She's been a drug addict herself. But addiction doesn't help any.

Helen is hard on herself. In work, she likes to push herself to the limit. All the day it's go, go, go until the point when she's about to keel over. At that moment, all other expressions leave her face and what you see is panic. When I catch her pushing herself to this point, I want to boss her about, like some Elder Brother from Outer Space.

But nobody bosses Helen about. She has her own destiny.

Election Eve: Davao

There is a way of seeing without seeming to see. Harry had it to a certain degree. An eyebrow moves. A quiet word alerts your attention to the fact that something is going on. But it is no use expecting to be able to follow the direction of a gaze, in order to work out what you are supposed to be taking in. The seer will not give himself away. He is entirely surreptitious.

I noticed it first with Harry among the boycotters in Muntinlupa. We were sitting in the car not far from a peanut stall. What Harry was watching, without seeming to watch, was the behaviour of the policemen standing by the stall, keeping an eye on the Bayan rally. Casually, as they talked, they were helping themselves to the peanuts. The stallholder made no protest. He was reading a comic. I suppose he too was seeing without seeming to see.

The policemen moved on. Then a plump figure in civilian clothes wandered past and the stallholder passed him some notes. 'What do you think he is?' I murmured to Harry.

'Looks like a gangster,' he said. The man had been collecting the protection money. A small sum, no doubt, and it wasn't as if the policemen had been stuffing their faces with the peanuts. It was just that these were the kind of overheads a peanut vendor had to allow for.

Davao was quiet on election eve. It felt almost as if a curfew was in force. The sale of alcohol was prohibited, and there was no life around the market. Our driver had told us that there were salvagings almost every day—meaning that bodies were found and the people knew from the state of their mutilations that this was the work of the military. The driver had his own odd code. He told us that he wouldn't go along a certain street because

145

there were a lot of dogs there and he couldn't stand dogs.

The eating place we found was open to the street, and the positioning of its television meant that the clientele sat facing the outside world, but with their heads tilted upwards. There was a programme of Sumo wrestling, with a commentary in Japanese. Even the adverts were in Japanese. The clientele were drinking soft drinks. Nobody was talking. Everyone was watching the wrestling.

It seemed a hostile sort of place. We chose our food from the counter, but the waitress was slow and indifferent. Behind her on the wall was a Marcos sticker and, for good measure, a Cory sticker. I sat with my back to the street. Jojo and Helen were facing outwards.

At first I didn't notice that Jojo had seen something. Then I turned round and scrutinized the darkened street. Two jeeps had drawn up. I could see a man with a rifle disappearing into a house. Then a confusion of figures coming back to the vehicles, which drove swiftly off. In short, nothing much.

'They're picking someone up,' said Jojo. 'There'll probably be a lot of that tonight.'

As far as I could tell, nobody else in the eating place had observed the little incident. They were all engrossed in the wrestling. Except I didn't know how many of them had this gift of seeing without seeming to see.

Voting Day in Mindanao

It wasn't hard to tell which areas were going to vote for Marcos and which for Cory. In the Cory areas people were out on the road, cheering and waving and making the Laban sign. In the Marcos areas there was an atmosphere of quiet tension. The crowd, such as it was, did not speak freely. There was a spokesman who explained calmly and simply that Marcos had done so much for this village that there was no support for the opposition. As we could see, the explanation continued, there was no intimidation or harrassment. People were voting according to their own free will. They all supported Marcos.

It was only out of earshot of this spokesman that members of my group were told *sotto voce* that they had been threatened with eviction if they voted the wrong way. Even so, some people said, they were not going to be coerced.

We drove to Tadeco, the huge banana plantation run by Antonio Florendo, one of the chief Marcos cronies. The Cory campaigners were hoping to get the votes from this area disqualified, as the register apparently featured far more names than Mr Florendo employed. He had something like 6,000 workers, many of whom were prisoners. But the register had been wildly padded.

The polling station was at the centre of Mr Florendo's domain. Rows and rows of trucks were lined up, and a vast crowd was milling around, waiting to vote. At the gates, a couple of disconsolate observers from NAMFREL, the National Movement for a Free Election, complained that they had been excluded from the station on the grounds that their papers lacked the requisite signatures. In fact the signatures were there and in order, but the people on the gate insisted this was not so. A sinister 'journalist' began inquiring who I was, and writing down my particulars. 'Oh, you come from England,' he said menacingly. 'Well, that may be useful if we all have to flee the country.' Whenever I tried to speak to somebody, this man shoved his microphone under my nose.

We asked to speak to Mr Florendo, and to our surprise he appeared, with an angry, wiry little lawyer at his side. The lawyer was trying to explain to us why the NAMFREL people should not be allowed in. He had a sheaf of papers to support his case. We introduced ourselves to Mr Florendo, who looked like a character from *Dynasty* or *Dallas*—Texan hat, distinguished white hair, all smiles and public relations. He was a model employer. Everything here was above board. No, the register had not been padded—we could come in and see for ourselves. We asked him why the NAMFREL people had been excluded. He turned to his lawyer and said: 'Is this so? Let them in, by all means.' The lawyer expostulated and pointed to his sheaf of papers. Mr Florendo waved him aside. Of course the NAMFREL people could come in. There was nothing to hide.

(One of the things they might have hidden better, which my companions noticed, was a group of voters lining up with ink on their fingers: they had already been through at least once.)

We asked if we could take Mr Florendo's picture. 'Oh,' he said, 'you must photograph my son, Tony-Boy—he's the handsome one.' And he called to Tony-Boy, a languid and peculiarly hideous youth. Mr Florendo thought that Tony-Boy could be a Hollywood star. I thought not. Mr Florendo invited us to lunch. I thought not again. Mr Florendo was overwhelming us with his honesty and generosity. He asked the crowd whether he was not a model employer, always available to his workers, and they all agreed that he was indeed a model employer.

In the early afternoon news came over the radio that the KBL had switched candidates, and that Imelda was now stepping in for her husband. 'But they can't do that,' I said. Oh yes they can, said the people in the car. For a while we believed the rumour. Jojo giggled helplessly. 'If Imelda gets in, there really will be panic buying. Only we've got no money to buy with. We'll just have to panic instead.' And he flopped into a panic as he contemplated the awesome prospect.

Now the returns began to be announced over the NAMFREL radio. The idea was to do a quick count, so that the possibilities of tampering would be kept to a minimum. In precinct after precinct the results were showing Cory winning by a landslide. Around Davao alone they had expected her to get seventy per cent of the vote. And this indeed seemed possible. It all depended on what went on in the outlying areas such as Mr Florendo's fief. NAMFREL could not observe everywhere. They simply didn't have enough people. But if they could monitor enough returns fast enough, they might be able to keep cheating to a minimum.

Davao, which features in stories as being one of the murder capitals of the world, had had a quiet day. I think only two people had been killed. The NPA-dominated quarter called Agpao, and nicknamed Nicaragpao, had voted for Cory, although it was plastered with boycott posters, including one which showed the people taking to the mountains.

As the radio continued to announce Cory wins, Jojo came up with an idea. The votes could be converted into different currencies. Cory gets ten million votes, and these are expressed as rupees. Marcos gets five million, but these are dollars. So Marcos wins after all.

Certainly some kind of device was going to be needed.

In the hotel lobby, a desk had been set up to coordinate the results. The blackboard showed Cory with a healthy lead.

On the television, it appeared that far fewer of the results had so far been added up. Marcos was doing OK.

The figures in the lobby came from NAMFREL, which was the citizens' arm of the official tabulating organization, COMELEC. In the end it would be the COMELEC figures which counted. But the sources of both figures were the same certified returns. Something very odd was happening.

The head of NAMFREL was called Joe Concepción. The head of COMELEC was Jaime Opinión. The television told us to trust Mr Opinión; the radio, Mr Concepción.

Late that night, the COMELEC count ground to a complete halt. Something had gone wrong—and it was perfectly obvious what.

The NAMFREL Struggle

There were several ways of fixing the election, all of which Marcos tried. The first was to strike names off the electoral register in areas of solid Cory support, and to pad out other registers with fictional names for the flying voters. You could bribe the voters with money and sacks of rice, or, above board and publicly, with election promises. You could intimidate the solid areas. You could bribe the tellers. You could have fake ballot papers (a franking machine for these had gone missing for a whole week before the election). You could put carbon paper under the ballot form, to make sure that an individual had voted the right way before you paid him off. You could print money for his pay-off, and if you printed the money with the same serial numbers there would be no record of how much you had printed. You could force the early closure of polling stations in hostile areas. You could do all these things and you might, if you were Marcos, get away with it.

But what if, after all that, the early returns made it plain that you still hadn't won?

Then you would have to start stealing the ballot boxes, faking the returns, losing the ballots, shaving off a bit here, padding a bit there and slowing down the returns so that, you hoped, once the initial wave of anger had subsided, you could eventually declare yourself the winner. To explain the delays in the counting of returns, there was a formula which never failed to unconvince. You could say over and over again on Channel Four, the government broadcasting station: 'What the foreign observers fail to realize is that the Philippines is a nation comprised of over 7,000 islands. It takes a long time to collect the ballot boxes. Some of them have to be brought by boat or by carabao from very remote areas.' But in the meantime votes would be taking a mysteriously long time to find their way from one side of Manila to the other.

This second phase of corruption was now beginning, and the people who stood against it were the NAMFREL volunteers and the Church. There was a great deal of overlap. Outside the town halls where the ballot boxes were kept and counted stood rows of nuns chanting Hail Marys, seminarians grouped under their processional crosses, Jesuits, priests and lay people. Outside Pasay Town Hall in Manila, the day after the election, I asked a Jesuit whether the whole of his order had taken to the streets in this way. He said that the only ones who hadn't were the foreigners, who didn't feel they could interfere. They were manning the telephones instead.

The Jesuit was a cheerful character. He told me that in the past members of his order used to go on retreat with Marcos once a year. He invited them down to a country residence of his in Bataan. They'd been very well catered for—food had come from a posh local restaurant. But Marcos himself had eaten very simply and kept retreat in the most pious manner. He had offered them the chance to go waterskiing, but the coastguard had said there were too many jellyfish.

'What would the Pope have said,' I asked him, 'if you'd gone waterskiing? Would he have approved?'

'Maybe not,' said the Jesuit. 'Skiing yes, waterskiing perhaps no.'

Anyway, these days of retreats with the Marcoses were now

over. Not only were the Jesuits out on the streets. There were all kinds of people. At the same place I talked at length to a police cadet who was an ardent NAMFREL supporter. There were poor people and there were extremely elegant ladies—but elegant in the Cory, not the Imelda, style. In the trouble spots, at Makati Town Hall and in the Tondo for instance, they had kept a vigil over the ballot boxes. They linked arms to protect them. They formed human chains to transport them. They all said, and they said it over and over again, that all they could do was protect the vote with their bodies. They were expecting harrassment and they got it. They were expecting to be beaten up. They were expecting martyrdom and they got that too.

The expression, 'the sanctity of the ballot', had been injected with real force, real meaning. It had been preached from every pulpit and it had sunk into every Catholic heart. The crony press was full of vituperation against the Church. It abominated Cardinal Sin. The Church that had once supported martial law, and had been courted by the Marcoses (Imelda was always swanning off to the Vatican), was now a public enemy. Paul's Epistle to the Romans was cited by the *Sunday Express* against the Church:

> Everyone must obey state authorities, because no authority exists without God's permission, and the existing authorities have been put there by God. Whoever opposes the existing authority opposes what God has ordered; and anyone who does so will bring judgment on himself.

But they did not continue with the next verse: 'For government, a terror to crime, has no terrors for good behaviour.' Which proves that Paul had not envisaged the Marcos dictatorship.

As the NAMFREL struggle continued, and behind the scenes the Marcos men were working out the best strategy for cooking the books, Marcos himself gave a press conference at Malacañang. You couldn't get near the palace by taxi. You had to stop at the beginning of a street called J. P. Laurel, then walk down past some old and rather beautiful houses in the Spanish colonial style. As you came through the gate, you found that the lawns had been turned over to the cultivation of vegetables in little parterres. I wondered whether these were siege rations. What were the Marcoses expecting? Beyond the vegetable garden lay a sculpture garden depicting mythological beings in concrete. It looked rather as if some member of the family had had a thing about being a sculptor, and been indulged in her illusions.

A further gate, a body search, and then you came to the grand staircase flanked by carved wooden figures, leading up to an ante-room where several grand ladies, Imelda-clones, sat chatting. The room's decorations were heavy. There was an arcaded gallery from which, I suppose, members of the Spanish governor's household would have looked down on the waiting petitioners. The ante-room led directly into a large and brightly lit hall, got up very much like a throne-room. Here the cameras were all set up, and Marcos was in the process of explaining that the delays of the night before had all been the fault of NAMFREL. They had refused to cooperate with COMELEC in what had been intended as a simultaneous and coordinated tabulation of results. However, that matter had all been cleared up earlier this morning. As far as the stopping of the count had been concerned, there had been no malicious, mischievous or illegal intent.

Marcos's eyes were lifeless. He could have been blind. Or perhaps he had only just been woken up. His mouth was an example of a thoroughly unattractive orifice.

He had his own set of figures, and he explained at great length how the arithmetic would work out. As he did so, his hand gestures were like those of a child imitating a plane taking off. He conceded he might have lost in Metro Manila. He conceded he had lost in Davao. But by moving his million and a half votes from the Solid North all round the shop, so that you could never tell quite what he had set them off against, he managed to arrive at a 'worst possible scenario' where he won by a million and a half votes.

I couldn't follow him. Imelda had slipped in at the side and was watching in admiration. Like any bad actress she had a way of telling you: this is what's going through my mind, this is what

I'm feeling. And the message she was putting across that day was: I've just slipped in, inconspicuously, to watch my husband brilliantly rebutting all the awful things that have been said about him by you foreign meddlers; look at him—isn't he wonderful?—*still*, at *his* age; how deeply I love him and how greatly I appreciate him, why is it that you lot can't see things the way I do? Don't look at me. I'm sitting here admiring my husband, plain little inconspicuous me.

And she shook her head very gently from side to side, unable to believe how great he was, and how lucky she had been.

The COMELEC Girls at Baclaran

The next evening I was sitting with some Americans in the foyer of the Manila Hotel, wondering whether perhaps we might not have preferred to be in Haiti. There was after all something gripping about the way the people there had dug up Papa Doc's bones and danced on them. And what would happen to all the dictators in exile? *Rolling Stone* suggested a Dictator Theme Park, where we could all go to visit them in natural surroundings.

A chap came up to our table, hovering about three inches off the floor, his eyes dilated. He had taken some high-quality something. 'Listen you guys, nobody move now because the opposition's watching. The COMELEC girls have walked out of the computer count, in protest at the cheating. The whole thing's fucked.'

We got up casually, one by one, and paid our bills. The 'opposition', the rival networks, were no doubt very far from deceived. At the door I bumped into Helen.

'Helen,' I said, 'be absolutely casual. Just turn round and come out with me. The COMELEC girls have walked out of the computer count. Let's get down there.'

But Helen was bursting for a pee. I swore her to secrecy and told her again to act natural. I knew, as I waited for her, that the chances of Helen crossing the foyer of the Manila Hotel without meeting a friend were zero. I dithered, frantic with casualness, by the door.

Helen kept her word, though, and only told one other journalist.

The COMELEC count was taking place in public, in a large conference centre which was one of the Marcoses' notorious extravagances. When we reached the auditorium there was nothing much to see. The girls, around thirty of them, had got up, taking their disks with them, and simply walked out of the building before anyone realized what was going on. The remaining operators were still in place, but because the girls who had walked out occupied a crucial part of the whole computer system, nothing could be done until they and their software were replaced.

A seething general, Remigio P. Octavio, was outside the auditorium. Helen asked him what had happened. Nothing had happened. 'Well, General, there seem to be quite a lot of operators missing.'

Nobody was missing, said Remigio. The girls had needed a rest. People in the gallery had been jeering at them, throwing stones and paper darts, and they'd gone outside for a rest. They were upset. The gallery had been full of Communists. And tomorrow, he said, he would make sure there were enough police down here to prevent a recurrence. He would bring in reinforcements.

'As for the girls,' said the General, 'they will be back again shortly.'

Helen wrote all this down on her pad. When she clicks into her reportorial mode and starts firing questions, it's an impressive sight. She laces her sentences with respectful language, and makes a great show of taking down every detail and improbability. But when somebody is lying to her in the way Remigio P. was, the effect of all this is mockery. I wondered whether the general would realize he was being sent up. If I had been him, I would have shot Helen.

The girls had taken refuge in Baclaran Church, and it was there the press corps tracked them down. By now they were said to be very scared at the consequences of their walkout. They needed all the protection the church could give them, but they also perhaps needed the protection of the press. Perhaps. Perhaps not. Members of the official teams of observers arrived. There was a great sense that these girls were in extreme danger.

It was the second time that day that I had been in Baclaran Church. In the afternoon it had been jam-packed as Cardinal Sin celebrated mass. Cory had attended. The crowds had spilled out into the churchyard and the street market nearby. Cardinal Sin had preached a sermon so emphatic in its praise of NAMFREL that he had made its members seem almost saints. Depending on your point of view, they were either heroes or villains. There was no middle ground.

Now the church was about a quarter full. Those who had heard about the walkout had come to express their support. To pass the time they sang 'Bayan Ko', and when the girls finally came out in front of the high altar the audience burst into applause.

The cameras had been set up long since and there were masses of photographers angling for a shot. The girls were sobbing and terrified. I could hardly bear to watch the grilling they got. Their spokeswoman said that they would not give their names, and that it was to be understood that what they had done was not political. They were not in fact (although we called them the COMELEC girls) officials of COMELEC. They were computer operators, highly qualified, who had been engaged to perform what they had taken to be a strictly professional job. All had gone well until the night before, when they began to be instructed not to feed in certain figures, so that the tally board giving the overall position was now at odds with what they knew to be the actual total so far.

I remember the word that was used. Discrepancies. Certain discrepancies had crept in, and the girls were worried by them. Finally they had decided that they were being asked to act unprofessionally. They had come out, and they had brought printouts and disks with them, in order to prove their case.

Earlier that evening the international team of observers had given a press conference at which John Hume, from Northern Ireland, had been the spokesman. He had been adamant that there had been cheating on the part of the KBL, but he had purposely left open the question of whether that cheating had been on such a scale as to alter the eventual result of the election. The reason he had done this was that people feared Marcos might declare the election null and void, using the evidence of the foreign observers. Marcos was still president. He hadn't needed to call the snap election. If he now annulled it he could, constitutionally, go on as if nothing had happened.

Now the COMELEC girls had come out with the most authoritative evidence of cheating so far. People had been killed for much, much smaller offences. The Americans could not possibly overlook this evidence, I thought. There would be no getting around it. That was why the girls were in such danger.

One of the American reporters said to the girls that of course they were entitled to withhold their names, but that if they did so Marcos would claim they had not come from COMELEC at all, that this was just black propaganda. For their sakes, they should tell us their names.

At which another pressman snapped, 'It's not for their sakes. You just want to get a good story.'

The press conference drew to a close. I was thinking: so many people have gone so far—they're so exposed—that the Cory campaign must move forward. If it grinds to a halt now, all these people are just going to be killed.

A figure came rushing into the church. It was the Jesuit from Pasay Town Hall, the one who had been so entertained by Marcos. He came up through the press. 'It's very important,' he said, 'it's very important. They *must* give their names. They *must* give their names.'

But the conference was already over, and the girls had gone into hiding.

This was the first part of James Fenton's three-part report on the fall of Marcos: 'The Snap Revolution', Granta 18.

1987
Weightless
Primo Levi

What I would like to experience most of all would be to find myself freed, even if only for a moment, from the weight of my body. I wouldn't want to overdo it—just to hang suspended for a reasonable period—and yet I feel intensely envious of those weightless astronauts whom we are permitted to see all too rarely on our TV screens. They seem as much at ease as fish in water: they move elegantly around their cockpit—these days quite spacious—propelling themselves forward by pushing gently off invisible walls, and sailing smoothly through the air to berth securely at their work place. At other times we have seen them conversing, as if it were the most natural thing—one of them 'the right way up', the other 'upside down' (but of course in orbit there is neither up nor down). Or we have seen them take turns to play childish games: one flicks a toffee with his thumbnail, and it flies slowly and in a perfectly straight line into the open mouth of his colleague. We have seen an astronaut squirt water from a plastic container into the air: the water does not fall or disperse but settles in a roundish mass which then, subject only to the weak forces of surface tension, lazily assumes the form of a sphere. What do they do with it then? It can't be easy to dispose of without damaging the delicate structures upholding its surface.

I wonder what it would take to make a documentary that would link together these visions, transmitted by some miracle from the satellites that flash past above our heads and above our atmosphere. A film like that, drawn from American and Soviet sources, and with an intelligent commentary, would teach everybody so much. It would certainly be more successful than the nonsense that is put out today, more successful too than porno movies.

I have also often wondered about the experiments, or more particularly the simulation courses which aspiring astronauts have to undergo and which journalists write about as if they were nothing out of the ordinary. What sense is there in them? And how is weightlessness simulated? The only technique imaginable would be to close the candidates in a vehicle in freefall: a plane or an elevator such as Einstein postulated for the experiment designed to illustrate the concept of special relativity. But a plane, even in a vertical fall, is braked by the resistance of the air, and a lift (or rather, a fall) has additional frictional forces acting on the cable. In both cases, weightlessness (or *abaria* to the die-hard classicists) would not be complete. And even in the best case— the quite terrifying scenario of a plane dropping like a stone from a height of five or ten or twenty miles, perhaps with an additional thrust from the engines in the final stages—the whole thing would last no more than a few tens of seconds: not enough time for any training or for measuring physiological data. And then there would be the question of stopping...

And yet almost all of us have experienced a 'simulation' of this decidedly non-terrestrial sensation. We have felt it in a childhood dream. In the most typical version, the dreamer becomes aware with joyous amazement that flying is as easy as walking or swimming. How could you have been so stupid as not to have thought of it before? You just scull with the palms of your hands and—hey presto—you take off from the floor, moving effortlessly; you turn around, avoiding the obstacles; you pass skilfully through doors and windows, and escape into the open air: not with the frenetic whirring of a sparrow's wings, not with the voracious, stridulant haste of a swallow, but with the silent majesty of the eagles and the clouds. Where does this presentiment of what is now a concrete reality come from? Perhaps it is a memory common to the species, inherited from our proto-bird-like aquatic reptiles. Or maybe this dream is a prelude to a future, as yet unclear, in which the umbilical cord which calls us back to mother earth will be superfluous and transparent: the advent of a new mode of locomotion, more noble even than our own complicated, unsteady, two-legged style with its internal inefficiencies and its need of external friction between the feet and the ground.

From this persistent dream of weightlessness, my mind returns to a well-known rendition of the Geryon episode in the seventeenth canto of the *Inferno*. The 'wild beast', reconstructed by Dante from classical sources and also from word-of-mouth accounts of the medieval bestiaries, is imaginary and at the same time splendidly real. It eludes the burden of weight. Waiting for its two strange passengers, only one of whom is subject to the laws of gravity, the wild beast rests on the bank with its forelegs, but its deadly tail floats 'in the void' like the stern-end of a Zeppelin moored to its pylon. At first, Dante was frightened by the creature, but then that magical descent to Malebolge captured the attention of the poet-scientist, paradoxically absorbed in the naturalistic study of his fictional beast whose monstrous and symbolic form he describes with precision. The brief description of the journey on the back of the beast is singularly accurate, down to the details as confirmed by the pilots of modern hang-gliders: the silent, gliding flight, where the passenger's perception of speed is not informed by the rhythm or the noise of the wings but only by the sensation of the air which is 'on their face and from below'. Perhaps Dante, too, was reproducing here unconsciously the universal dream of weightless flight, to which psychoanalysts attribute problematical and immodest significance.

The ease with which man adapts to weightlessness is a fascinating mystery. Considering that for many people travel by sea or even by car can cause bouts of nausea, one can't help feeling perplexed. During month-long spells in space the astronauts complained only of passing discomforts, and doctors who examined them afterwards discovered a light decalcification of the bones and a transitory atrophy of the heart muscles: the same effects, in other words, produced by a period of confinement to bed. Yet nothing in our long history of evolution could have prepared us for a condition as unnatural as non-gravity.

Thus we have vast and unforeseen margins of safety: the visionary idea of humanity migrating from star to star on vessels with huge sails driven by stellar light might have limits, but not that of weightlessness: our poor body, so vulnerable to swords, to guns and to viruses, is space-proof.

Translated from the Italian by Piers Spence

Primo Levi died on April 11, after a fall at his home in Turin. His death was reported by Italian newspapers as 'apparent suicide'.

1988
Among Chickens
Jonathan Miller

One

I never had a sense of humour. What started me in a theatrical direction was finding at a very early age that I had a talent. In fact, not so much a talent as a disability: I could impersonate chickens. I was a chicken. I said to people, I will imitate a chicken for you, and this pleased them. I don't know why. It did. Therefore I became extremely observant of the minute dialect of chickens.

For example, I became very interested in this double thing they have: it starts off with *'buk, buk, buk, buk'*, and then *'bacagh'* follows. I noticed that some of the cruder impersonators of chickens, and there were competitors at school, never understood that there was a rather subtle variation of *'buk, buk, buk'* for every *'bacagh'*. They used to think it was absolutely regular. But I noticed, and this was really a big breakthrough in chicken linguistics, that chickens liked to lead you up the garden path. They would lead you to expect that for every four or five *'buk'* there would be a *'bacagh'*; so people, the bad chicken impersonators, the unobservant ones, would go as follows: *'Buk, buk, buk, buk, bacagh, buk, buk, buk, buk, bacagh, buk, buk, buk, buk, buk, bacagh.'* What I noticed, after prolonged examination, was an entirely different pattern of chicken speech behaviour. Thus: *'Buk, buk, buk, buk, buk, buk, buk, buk, bacagh, buk, buk, buk, buk, buk, buk, buk, buk, buk...BACAGH, buk, buk...'*

I conducted this examination during the war, when food was short and we used to get food parcels from the United States, which for some reason always took the form of cling peaches. I don't know what the Americans thought we were suffering from—massive cling peach deficiency presumably. And one of the ways my own family was digging for victory was to rear chickens. We moved around a lot, following my father from one military hospital to another, not because he was a patient, but because he was a military psychiatrist and was often shifted from one nut-house to the next. Everywhere we went, we took a trailer behind the car, filled with hens. They would be kept in a camp at the bottom of the garden, like displaced persons. I watched these creatures for hours on end. They tormented me.

Two

I offer an example of humour from my professional experience. Recently, I directed a production of Eugene O'Neill's *Long Day's Journey into Night*. I wanted to see what would happen if I treated the play not as Greek tragedy, which is what O'Neill wanted, but as an orphan object that I had just found. And it struck me, as a foreigner, that it was a highly skilful version of a family squabble. Therefore, it seemed to me, it was necessary to get away from the usual incantatory manner of performing O'Neill and restore to the play the quality of conversation. In the process of making it like conversation something happened: it produced laughter. It was like moving a match over the abrasive surface on the box. If you move the match slowly, nothing happens, but if you strike at the right tempo—flames. There is the moment at the end of the play, when the mother comes downstairs in a demented state of morphine intoxication and the drunken elder brother turns and says, 'The mad scene, enter Ophelia.' The scene developed a momentum as we rehearsed, increasing in pace until the first preview the actor playing the part rose to his feet and said, at *terrific* speed, 'The mad scene, enter Ophelia,' and there was a roar of laughter from the audience. We had struck the match. The actor, afterwards, was devastated.

It was much earlier, in fact—while Peter Cook, Alan Bennett, Dudley Moore and myself were performing *Beyond the Fringe*—that I became very interested in what was happening up there on the stage, what it was that produced this strange respiratory convulsion. By the thousandth performance, it sounds like a sudden explosion, a noise from another planet. I became fascinated with laughter.

I had trained as a biologist and felt that if we do something from which we get acute pleasure, like laughter, it must have been planted in us, or else we acquired it, because it has powerful selective advantage. We wouldn't, that is, have the *experience* of pleasure unless there was, for the species, some sort of selective advantage in the *behaviour* that leads to it. Which immediately raises the question: what is it that nature gets out of the pleasure we take from laughter?

There are various theories. Henri Bergson thought it was the collective criticism of some anomalous and unfruitful behaviour on the part of one member of the herd. Freud saw it as the release of tension following the sudden introduction of forbidden material into consciousness.

I prefer to think something much more comprehensive is going on when we get pleasure out of, say, hearing a joke. Jokes are of course peculiar and rather limited examples, a subset of the large domain of humour. I think that jokes are a social lubricant—sometimes a highly formulaic one—that we use for the purposes of maintaining conviviality, especially among men. Men, as soon as they are in all-male company, start telling jokes like it was some sort of convulsion. In fact, one of the more trying features of being with lots of men is that jokes break out like an illness. It's a way of both keeping one's distance and registering membership of a group when there are no spontaneous grounds for shared membership. So-and-so says, 'Have you heard the one about bum bum bum bum?' and someone else says, 'That reminds me, did you hear the one about bum bum bum bum?' and before you know where you are there's a competitive fugue of joke-telling, like the Kwakiutl Indians who throw piles of blankets and copper shields into the sea in a demonstration of competitive hospitality. Jokes are a sign that you have in your pocket a social currency that allows you to join the game.

I'm fascinated by the ritual procedure of the exchange and also the obligatory response. In only one joke out of five is that response spontaneous laughter. The rest of the time the joke-hearers feel it incumbent on themselves to contribute a skilful impersonation of being killed with laughter. You hold your sides, you slap your thighs, you say, 'Doggone.' And this is simply to maintain the joke-teller's self-esteem. It is almost impossible, unless you are insensitive or almost pathologically sadistic, to withhold the impersonation of laughter from someone who has just told you a joke.

In fact, jokes have little to do with spontaneous humour. The teller has the same relationship to them that he or she might have to a Hertz Rent-a-Car. A joke is a hired object, with many previous users, and very often its ashtrays are filled with other people's cigarettes, and its gears are worn and slipping, because other people have driven this joke very badly before you got behind the wheel.

Jokes also conform to strict patterns, one of the most common being any one of a number of jocular trinities that cruise the world: 'There was this English fellow, an Irishman and a Jewish fellow.' They have a toy mechanism which is very simple and very conventional. It would not be difficult, I suspect, to produce a taxonomy of *all* jokes. There are not many types. There is the type about the deaf, blind or disabled; the type involving different nationalities; the type that works fine as long as you assume there are people who walk the street with names like 'Fuckarada'; and the type that, while still formulaic, draws on the news. For example: the *Challenger* jokes after the Shuttle disaster, the Chicken Kiev jokes after Chernobyl.

And when you laugh at any one of these various types you're really laughing at the predictable, or rather at the strange tension that exists between predictable generalization and a specific instance of it. Take the Jack Benny joke which was on one of his radio shows. We hear footsteps coming up behind Jack Benny, and a voice saying, 'Your money or your life.' There's silence. The voice repeats, 'Your money or your life.' And there's another long gap before Benny says, 'I'm thinking.' This is a pretty good joke; it relies on a generalization familiar to the audience—Jack Benny is very mean—and it works because it is a surprising way of reacquainting the audience with the generalization. When you laugh, you're laughing at the very specific way Jack Benny has characterized himself.

I remember a sketch in *Beyond the Fringe*. Peter Cook was a strange, rather withdrawn man in a shabby raincoat, sitting on a bench blankly asserting that he could have been a judge only he didn't have the Latin for the judging exams. He said, 'They're extremely rigorous, the judging exams, as compared to the mining exams which are extremely un-rigorous, see. They only ask you one question: "What is your name?" I got seventy-five per cent on that.'

For years I tried to work out precisely why this was funny. On one level it's obvious, but there is more to it than simply the obvious. It is an instance of what a philosopher would call a category mistake: it is in the nature of names that they are not something you can have seventy-five per cent knowledge of. You either know them or you don't. The sketch makes us conscious of something we know but don't generally think about, because it occurs at a pre-attentive level. You can only be examined on subjects in which there can be a scale of success. And knowing one's name is not, actually, one of those things. Another example: a cartoon in the *New Yorker* shows two explorers up to their neck in quicksand and there are these creepers hanging down; it's quite clear they are in difficulties, and the man behind is saying to the one in front, 'Quicksand or not, Barclay, I've half a mind to struggle.' Now it is in the nature of voluntary and involuntary action that they are distinct categories of thought. What this joke makes us aware of is that it's in the nature of struggling that you can't have half a mind to do it. You don't, as it were, say, 'Right, well, we've tried firing warning shots to alert the base camp, we've tried treading water, let's give struggling a chance.' Struggling, for example, could not feature as an Olympic event.

The joke makes us aware that we have complex notions about those things for which we can be praised and blamed, those things which could be said to be voluntary or involuntary, those things which we can do half-heartedly, those things which we do flat out and those things we can't help. The joke invites a readiness to re-perceive the world.

Three

Both my parents were Jewish. My mother was a reluctant and unwilling Jew, my father an embarrassed and guilty one. He was guilty because he had sprung away from his traditional orthodox ghetto background in the East End of London. His father had arrived in England in the 1870s and established a patriarchal Jewish household in Whitechapel. My father, contrary to what was expected of him, went to Cambridge University and became a doctor. Years later, after the Holocaust,

166

he came to feel guilt about this. He felt that he had gone too far from his roots and that he owed his people a debt. He tried to redeem that debt by seeing that his own children, who had not been raised as orthodox Jews, should begin to observe. For me, all this was improvised a bit hastily and a bit late. I was taken to Synagogue or Temple, and found myself puzzled by the fact that Jews had these peculiar books that were read backwards, written in a script that was unfamiliar. The books themselves resembled sheets of scorched matzo.

My father would create these Friday-night suppers with candles and an instant decor of Judaism. I had no interest in this whatsoever. I was told constantly by my father that I owed it to my people to identify with them. I didn't know how to, and didn't want to. I could feel Jewish only for anti-Semites, not for Jews. As a child I resented being Jewish: it seemed designed just to prevent me having fun. I spent the early part of my life dreaming, not of a white Christmas, but of a White Anglo-Saxon Protestant Christmas. There was this wonderful world of jolly people and Father Christmas in brilliant scarlet, a colour which never figured in Jewish life, with a white beard and jolly red cheeks, and I felt like one of those children in Hans Christian Andersen, with my nose pressed to the frosty pane. In a sense I felt myself neither fish nor fowl nor good red herring. Nor good salt herring, I'm afraid. (All of which reminds me of *The Merchant of Venice* which I directed with Lord Olivier, who arrived at one of the first rehearsals saying, 'My dear boy, as we are about to do this difficult and awful play, we must at all costs avoid offending the Hebrews, God I love them so.' And then he proceeded to bedeck himself with very complicated and offensive facial equipment. He had this nose made for himself that was like something out of *Die Sturmer*. And ringlets. And, finally, he spent £1,500 on a pair of dentures. I kept on saying, 'Larry, please don't do that, it's awful. Not many of us are like that really, and it will create an awfully offensive effect.' It took a long time to persuade him to drop this terrible equipment, but I never could get him to abandon the dentures.)

My mother was quite a bit different from my father. She was a writer, and had published her first novel when she was nineteen. She wrote all day and every day, and was rather intolerant of the noise made by her small children. She didn't like intrusions. She battered away on this funny little typewriter. She used the same one until she died. That was what she was like. She preserved in her life a scrupulous monotony. She rose at the same time every day, sent us to school and began to tap away at the typewriter, or else noted sentences, or fragments of sentences, on the slit-open envelopes of letters she'd received that morning, a habit encouraged by the paper shortage during the war. She would put away her typewriter at twelve-thirty prompt when we came back for lunch. This would be a rather glum meal of boiled chicken, not one of the chickens we kept, but another chicken, a chicken which looked as though it had never said a single *'bacagh'* in its entire life and had been simply tipped into hot water and come out with that awful goose-pimpled appearance that boiled chickens have. We ate the same meal every day. Boiled chicken, year in, year out.

My mother was an admirer of a little-known French writer whose name was Francis Ponge, a sort of parody name. Ponge was a man after my mother's own heart. Ponge wrote in minute detail about the appearance of such things as sand and mimosa and soap. Soap particularly fascinated him. Ponge wrote long essays on the appearance of soap, page after page of descriptions of soap. He wrote a novel titled *Soap*. My mother translated some of his poetry. This also concerned soap.

My mother taught me something of which I was very impatient at the time: the value of monotony. With hindsight I see that the imposition of her routine was in effect a spiritual exercise which has lasted the rest of my life. She saw epiphanies in the mundane.

Eventually I became fascinated by the appearance of the commonplace as well. I learned the pleasure of simply watching. I take enormous pleasure from watching, in restaurants, in railway carriages or on street corners. Anywhere. Elevators are good places. I like to see the way we handle social encounters at awkward moments. I like to see the little signs, the tiny

gestures, the twitches and grimaces of embarrassment. And it is here, amid the most minute detail of the commonplace and the ordinary and the mundane, that I find the greatest displays of humour.

Four

Finally, I also like to remember the noise of certain English steam trains. English steam trains which used to make a noise as they pulled out of smoky, bronchitic stations in North London. Hmmm. This is very long ago. I see myself in short trousers thinking about Betty Grable. First of all it was the whistle of the trains: 'Whooooooooooo.' Then: '*Chkuu, chkuu, ching, chkuu, chkuu, ching, chkuu, ching, chkuu, ching, chkuu, ching, chkuu, chkuu, ching, chkuu, chkuu* (faster and faster, softening to a gentle rhythm), *chkuu, ching, ching, chkuu, chkuu, ching, chkuu, ching, chkuu, chkuu, ching, ching, chkuu, chkuu, ching.*'

And so forth.

1989

6 March 1989

Salman Rushdie

Boy, yaar, they sure called me some good names of late:
e.g. opportunist (dangerous). E.g. full-of-hate,
self-aggrandizing, Satan, self-loathing and shrill,
the type it would clean up the planet to kill.
I justjust remember my own goodname still.

Damn, brother. You saw what they did to my face?
Poked out my eyes. Knocked teeth out of place,
stuck a dog's body under, hung same from a hook,
wrote what-all on my forehead! Wrote 'bastard'! Wrote 'crook'!
I justjust recall how my face used to look.

Now, misters and sisters, they've come for my voice.
If the Cat got my tongue, look who-who would rejoice—
muftis, politicos, 'my own people', hacks.
Still, nameless-and-faceless or not, here's my choice:
not to shut up. To sing on, in spite of attacks,
to sing (while my dreams are being murdered by facts)
praises of butterflies broken on racks.

1990

The State of Europe

Josef Škvorecký

George Steiner

Jurek Becker

Hans Magnus Enzensberger

Werner Krätschell

Isaiah Berlin

Abraham Brumberg

Günter Kunert

Ivan Klíma

Stephen Spender

Mircea Dinescu

On December 1, 1989, *Granta* asked a number of writers how they understood the events in Central and Eastern Europe. Change had come at an incomprehensible speed: the re-burying of Imre Nagy in Hungary, the opening of the borders there, the elections in Poland, the trains of immigrants into Germany, the resignation of Erich Honecker. It seemed impossible that change could come any faster, but it did, and in November events seemed to accelerate: on November 9, the Berlin Wall; sixteen days later, the resignation of Ladislav Adamec, the Czechoslovak prime minister. So many things in Europe would never, could never, be the same. Was it possible to record this particular moment, poised, as we felt we were at the beginning of December, between two histories: the one that existed before November 9, and that other one, still to be defined, already being debated, which we knew we were then entering?

This is what we asked of our writers. But, even in this, our judgement of the moment was premature. By the time the fifteen writers had received our letter (the weekend, it turned out, that Gorbachev and Bush were meeting in the Mediterranean), Erich Honecker was placed under house arrest; and by the time we received their answers Gustav Husák had resigned in Czechoslovakia. The week before Christmas, the last contribution to our forum arrived; it was written by the Romanian poet Mircea Dinescu, but it could not have been mailed by him. Since May, he has been under house arrest, under the surveillance, it is reported, of eighteen security officers. The day we received his translation, we also received the first reports from Timosoara in Romania. There were no Western journalists there; we had only unconfirmed reports of indiscriminate killings—the number of deaths being mentioned was terrible to contemplate. Dinescu's contribution—what should it be called? an essay? a polemic? a cry for help?—is a reminder of the utter and insistent and implacable seriousness of the issues underlying this debate.

Josef Škvorecký

These are days of understandable, and I hope not premature, jubilation in Czechoslovakia. The generation of twenty-year-olds who were bloodied by the police and went on to topple the power monopoly of the Communist Party, are experiencing pure bliss untainted by any—even tiny—drops of sadness. That's how it should be because it's natural. The twenty-year-olds have lost nothing yet, and only conditions of extreme severity can deprive a person of the happiness, eagerness and excitement that is youth. Difficulties, harassments, attempts to curb their freedom appear to young people as adventures, of which the regime has provided them with plenty, particularly in its lunatic campaigns against their favourite music. In these crusades the youngsters turned victorious, years before the present triumph. Nothing mars their euphoria now.

As one turns to the generation of their parents, now in their early forties, the picture changes. Two decades ago, when they were twenty themselves, this generation was as euphoric as their sons and daughters are today. But the Big Lie descended on Czechoslovakia and those who were starting adult life in 1968 lost their most creative, and potentially happiest, years to the abomination called *Realsozialismus*. There is sadness in their elation, but they still have a good reason to rejoice: at forty, one may still begin anew, and almost half of life lies ahead.

For the grandmothers and grandfathers, now in their sixties, the sadness changes to bitterness. They are the generation of the uranium mines, of the show trials, of the petty chicanery of security screenings; the closely watched generation for whom admission to universities was determined not by talent but by political reliability. Too many were never able to achieve what, at twenty, when life was hope and eagerness, they had thought they would. At sixty it's too late.

Of course everybody is glad that the bell tolls for the oppressive regimes that have been deforming human lives in Czechoslovakia since 1939—if this is indeed their definitive end. But those who have lived there cannot be blissfully unaware of what happened on the totalitarian 'road to socialism'. That road is literally paved with human skulls. Where did it lead? To the social security of the jail? In many lands it led not even to that, but rather to a society resembling a concentration camp.

It all appears to be a huge joke played on mankind by history.

The joke, however, is ebony black.

The days of the totalitarians may be numbered in most of Europe. Elsewhere they evidently are not; in some places they are just beginning. At universities in the West professors still preach the theory which was the backbone of the longer-lasting of the two deadening social experiments in our century. But Marx was right on one point: the only criterion of a theory's validity is the test of practice.

Let us rejoice by all means. I don't want to spoil the celebration. It's just that I've never been good at euphoria and I cannot purge my mind of some thoughts.

Sorry.

George Steiner

I am writing this note on December 5, 1989. It may be absurdly dated by the time it appears.

This is the obvious point. The speed of events in Eastern Europe, the hectic complexities of inward collapse and realignment are such as to make the morning papers obsolete before evening. There may have been comparable *accelarandos* before this: in France, from June to September 1789 (there is a haunting leap from that date to ours); or during those 'ten days that shook the world' in Lenin's Petrograd. But the geographical scale of the current earthquake, its ideological and ethnic diversity, the planetary interests which are implicated, do make it almost impossible to respond sensibly, let alone have any worthwhile foresight.

A touch of exultant irony is allowed in the face, precisely, of this triumph of the unexpected. No economist-pundit, no geopolitical strategist, no 'Kremlinologist' or socio-economic analyst foresaw what we are living through. There was, indeed, all manner of speculation on the decay of institutions and distributive means in the Soviet Union. Some sort of challenge in Poland was on the cards. But all the pretentious jargon, the econometric projection charts, the formalistic studies of international relations, have proved fatuous. We are back with Plutarch. The apocalypse of hope has been started by one man.

Historians will generate volumes of hindsight, sociologists

and economists will juggle determinants and predictable certainties. Eyewash. The fact is that we know next to nothing of the intuitive panic, the alarmed vision, the gambler's stab into the unknown which may or may not have brought on Gorbachev's hoisting of the old, sclerotic but certainly defensible order. If Plutarch won't do, we are back to the miraculous, to the tears of the Black Virgin over Poland, to the incensed saints and patriarchs who have taken to heart the long strangulation of Hungary, of Bulgaria. We are back to the enigmatic pulse-beat of the messianic.

Second gloss: the cardinal ambiguity in the role of the United States. That role is now almost surrealistically irrelevant. Bush bobbing on the waves of Malta is an apt picture. The US appears to be becoming a provincial colossus, ignorant of, indifferent towards Europe. It will have its heavy hands full with Latin and Central America, with the derisive patronage of Japan. Europe is again on its own.

On the other hand, the image, the 'symbol-news' of America has been decisive. The millions who poured westward through the broken Berlin Wall, the young of Budapest, Sofia, Prague or Moscow, are not inebriate with some abstract passion for freedom for social justice, for the flowering of culture. It is a TV-revolution we are witnessing, a rush towards the 'California-promise' that America has offered to the common man on this tired earth. American standards of dress, nourishment, locomotion, entertainment, housing are today the concrete utopia in revolutions. With *Dallas* being viewed east of the Wall, the dismemberment of the regime may have become inevitable. Video cassettes, porno cassettes, American-style cosmetics and fast foods, not editions of Mill, de Tocqueville or Solzhenitsyn, were the prizes snatched from every West Berlin shelf by the liberated. The new temples to liberty (the 1789 dream) will be McDonald's and Kentucky Fried Chicken.

Hence the paradox: as the US declines into its own 'pursuit of happiness', the packaged promise, the bright afterglow of that pursuit becomes essential in Eastern Europe and, very probably, in the post-medieval, Asiatic morass of the Soviet Union.

Everything can still go wrong. Gorbachev's survival seems to hang by a thread. Clearly, the old guard on the right is desperate, the new radicals on the left are crazily impatient. Slovak indifference chills the new Prague Spring. Can the lunatic and sadistic self-destruction of Romania be halted? What will happen if Yugoslavia splits? Not only in Peking are there large squares ideal for tanks. One prays and hopes and rejoices and rages at the tepid bureaucracies of the Common Market and the prim neoisolationism of Thatcherite Britain. Everywhere, we are witnessing an almost mad race between resurgent nationalism, ethnic hatreds and the counter-force of potential prosperity and free exchange.

The variant on Judaic-messianic idealism, on the prophetic vision of a kingdom of justice on earth, which we call Marxism, brought intolerable bestiality, suffering and practical failure to hundreds of millions of men and women. The lifting of that yoke is cause for utter gratitude and relief. But the source of the hideous misprision is not ignoble (as was that of Nazi racism): it lies in a terrible overestimate of man's capacities for altruism, for purity, for intellectual-philosophic sustenance. The theatres in East Berlin performed the classics when heavy metal and American musicals were wanted. The bookstores displayed Lessing and Goethe and Tolstoy, but Archer and Collins were dreamed of. The present collapse of Marxist-Leninist despotisms marks the vengeful termination of a compliment to man— probably illusory—but positive nonetheless.

What will step into the turbulent vacuum? Fundamentalist religion is clawing at our doors. And money shouts at us. The West inhabits a money-crazed amusement arcade. The scientific-technological pinball machines ring and glitter brilliantly. But the imperatives of privacy, of autonomous imagining, of tact and spirit and scruple in the face of non-utilitarian values, are dimmed. And we lay waste the natural world. Only an autistic mandarin would deny to the mass of his fellow men and women the improved living standards, the bread and circuses they are now fighting, emigrating or dreaming towards. But if one is possessed of the cancer of thought, of art, of utopian speculation, the shadows at the heart of the carnival are equally present.

The knout on the one hand; the cheeseburger on the other.

The Gulag of the old East, the insertion of pantyhose ads between gas-oven sequences of *Holocaust* on TV in the new West. That alternative *must* be proved false if man is to be man. Will the breaking of the walls make the choices more fruitful and meaningful, more attuned to human potential and limitation? Only a fool would prophesy.

P.S. December 11. Events have, in fact, accelerated during the past six days. The Prague secret police are now headed by a man who was their prisoner less than four weeks ago. There is no East German government. Bulgaria is swinging towards a multi party scheme. The Baltic republics are defying Moscow.

I can make more precise the notion of the Marxist overestimate of man. It was Moses' error all over again (remember his desperate rages and death short of the promised land), and Christ's illusion. As that error, and its savage cost, are once again made plain and amended, will Jew-hatred, in the persistent eschatological sense, smoulder into heat? Already there are ugly signals from Hungary and East Germany.

Jurek Becker

'Really existing socialism' is on the way out, no question. Good thing too, if you fix your mind on the true condition of life in the socialist states, and not the fictional version which their leaders have passed off as the truth. The West has won—and there's the rub.

Here in the West, we live in societies that have no particular goal or objective. If there is any guiding principle, it's consumerism. In theory, we can increase our consumption until the planet lies about us in ruins and, given current trends, that's precisely what will happen. In spite of everything we knew and understood about them, we had a hope that the socialist states might find a different path. That hope is gone. People there are desperate to adopt the principles of the West: the conversion of as many goods as possible into rubbish (which is what consumption means), and the free expression of all types of ideas (accompanied by a growing reluctance to think at all). Converts are liable to be especially strict and zealous in the observance of their new faith; I expect the same will apply to the people of these recently converted nations.

A few days ago, I was talking to a friend about the possibility of German reunification, the conversation that all Germans have been having these past days and weeks. He was in favour of it, I was against. After a while he lost his temper with me, and asked me how I could possibly justify the continued existence of the German Democratic Republic. I started thinking, and I'm still thinking now. If I can't think of any reasons, I shall have to change my mind and become a supporter of reunification. I shall have to be in favour of turning Eastern Europe into an extension of Western Europe.

The only argument I am able to come up with is perhaps more suitable for a poem than a political discussion: the most important thing about socialist states isn't any tangible achievements, but the fact that they give us a chance. Things are not cut and dried as they are here. The uncertainty there doesn't promise anything, of course, but it's our only hope for the continued existence of humanity. Eastern Europe looks to me like one last attempt. And when it's over, it'll be time to withdraw our money from the bank, and start hitting the bottle in earnest.

Translated from the German by Michael Hofmann

Hans Magnus Enzensberger

You find them in every European capital, in the centre of the city, where space is symbolic: corpulent centaurs, metal hermaphrodites, Roman emperors, Grand Dukes, eternally victorious generals. Under their hoofs, civil servants hurry to their ministries, or spectators into the opera, or believers to Mass. They represent the European hero, without whom the history of the continent is barely imaginable. But with the invention of the motor car, the spirit of the age dismounted—Lenin and Mussolini, Franco and Stalin, all managed without a whinnying undercarriage and the stockpiles of heroes in stone were shipped off to Caribbean islands or Siberian combines. Inflation and elephantiasis heralded the end of the hero whose principal preoccupations were conquest, triumph and delusions of grandeur.

Writers saw it coming. A hundred years ago literature waved goodbye to those larger-than-life characters whose very creation it had helped bring about. The victory song and the tales of derring-do belong now to prehistory. No one is interested in Augustus or Alexander; it is Bouvard and Pecuchet or Vladimir and Estragon. Frederick the Great and Napoleon have been relegated to the literary basement; as for those Hymns to Hitler and Odes to Stalin—they were destined for the scrap heap from the very start.

In the past few decades, a more significant protagonist has stepped forward: a hero of a new kind, representing not victory, conquest and triumph, but renunciation, reduction and dismantling. We have every reason to concern ourselves with these specialists in denial, for our continent depends on them if it is to survive.

It was Clausewitz, the doyen of strategic thinking, who showed that retreat is the most difficult of all operations. That applies in politics as well. The non plus ultra in the art of the possible consists of withdrawing from an untenable position. But if the stature of the hero is proportional to the difficulty of the task before him, then it follows that our concept of the heroic needs not only to be revised, but to be stood on its head. Any cretin can throw a bomb. It is a thousand times more difficult to defuse one.

Popular opinion, especially in Germany, holds to the traditional view. It demands steadfastness of purpose, insisting on a political morality which places single-mindedness and adherence to principle above all else, even, if it comes to it, above respect for human life. This unambiguity is not on offer from the heroes of retreat. Retreating from a position you have held involves not only surrendering the middle ground, but also giving up a part of yourself. Such a move cannot succeed without a separation of character and role. The expert dismantler shows his political mettle by taking this ambiguity on to himself.

The paradigm is particularly apparent in the wake of this century's totalitarian dictatorships. At first the significance of the pioneers of retreat was barely detectable. People still claim that

Nikita Khrushchev didn't know what he was doing, that he couldn't have guessed the implications of his actions; after all, he talked of perfecting communism, not of abolishing it. And yet, in his famous speech to the Twentieth Party Congress, he sowed more than the seeds of his own downfall. His intellectual horizons may have been narrow; his strategy clumsy and his manner arrogant, but he showed more courage in his own beliefs than almost any other politician of his generation. It was precisely the unsteady side to his character that suited him for his task. Today the subversive logic of his credentials as a hero lie open for all to see: the deconstruction of the Soviet empire began with him.

The internal contradictions of the historical demolition man were more starkly exposed in the career of János Kádár. This man who, a few months ago, was buried quietly and unobtrusively in Budapest, made a pact with the occupying forces after the failed uprising of 1956. It is rumoured that he was responsible for 800 death sentences. Hardly had the victims of his repression been buried than he got to work on the task that was to occupy him for the next thirty years: the patient undermining of the absolute dictatorship of the Communist Party. It is surprising that there was no serious disturbance; there were constant setbacks and shattered hopes, but through compromise and tactical manoeuvring Kádár's process moved inexorably forward. Without the Hungarian precedent it is hard to see how the dissolution of the Eastern Bloc would have begun; Kadar's trailblazing role in this is beyond dispute. It is equally clear that he was no match for the forces he helped to unleash. His was the archetypal fate of the historical demolition man: in doing his job he ended up undermining his own position. The dynamic he set in motion hurled him aside, and he was buried by his own successes.

Adolfo Suárez, General Secretary of the Spanish phalange, became prime minister after Franco's death. In a meticulously planned coup he did away with the regime, installed his own Unity Party in power and forced through a democratic constitution; the operation was delicate and dangerous. This was no vague hunch, like Khrushchev's; this was the work of an

182

intelligence at the height of its awareness: a military putsch would have led to bloody repression and perhaps a new civil war.

This course of action again is inconceivable from someone unable to differentiate beyond black sheep and white sheep. Suárez played a role in and gained advantage from the Franco regime. Had he not belonged to the innermost circles of power he would not have been in a position to abolish the dictatorship. At the same time, his past earned him the undying mistrust of all democrats. Indeed, Spain has not forgiven him to this day. In the eyes of his former comrades he was a traitor; those whose path he had cleared saw him as an opportunist. After abdicating his leading role in the period of transition he never found his feet again. His role in the party system of the republic has remained obscure. The hero of retreat can only be sure of one thing: the ingratitude of the fatherland.

The moral dilemma assumes almost tragic dimensions in the figure of Wojciech Jaruzelski. In 1981, he saved Poland from the inevitability of Soviet invasion. The price of salvation was the introduction of martial law and the internment of those very members of the unofficial opposition who today run the country under his presidency. The resounding success of his policies did not spare him the wrath of the Polish people, a large number of whom regard him to this day with utter hatred. No one cheers him; he will never escape the ghost of his past actions. Yet his moral strength lies in the fact that he knew from the very beginning that this is how it would turn out. No one has ever seen him smile. With his stiff, lifeless gestures and his eyes hidden behind dark sunglasses he personifies the patriot as martyr. This political Saint Sebastian is a figure of Shakespearean stature.

The same cannot be said of those who lagged behind him. Egon Krenz and Ladislav Adamec will in all probability merit only a footnote in history, the one as a burlesque, the other a petty bourgeois version of the heroic rearguard. But neither the grin of the German nor the fatherly countenance of the Czech should be allowed to obscure the importance of the part they played. The very agility we reproach them for has been their only service. In that paralysing stillness of the pregnant moment, when one side waits for the other to move and nothing happens, someone had to be the first to clear his throat, to utter the first half-choked whisper that started the avalanche. 'Someone,' a German social democrat once said, 'has to be the bloodhound.' Seventy years later someone had to spike the bloodhounds' guns, although as it turned out it was a communist Pulcinella who broke the deadly silence. No one will cherish his memory. This in itself makes him memorable.

The real hero of deconstruction, however, is himself the driving force. Mikhail Gorbachev is the initiator of a process with which others, willingly or unwillingly, can only struggle to keep up. His is—of this we can probably now be certain—a timeless figure. The sheer size of the task he has taken on is without precedent. He is attempting to dismantle the second to the last remaining monolithic empire of the twentieth century without the use of force, without panic, in peace. Whether he can succeed remains to be seen; he has already achieved what no one, even a few months ago, would have believed possible. It took long enough before the rest of the world began to understand what he was doing. The superior intelligence, the moral boldness, the far-reaching perspective of the man lay so far outside the horizons of the political elite, east and west, that no government dared take him at his word.

Gorbachev has no illusions about his popularity at home. The greatest proponent of the politics of doing without is confronted at every step with demands for something *positive*, as if it were enough simply to promise the people another golden future where everyone would receive free soap, rockets and brotherly affection, each according to his needs; as if there were any other way forward but by retreating; as if there were any other hope for the future but by disarming the Leviathan and searching for a way out of the nightmare and back to normality. It goes without saying that the protagonist risks his life with every step he takes on this path. He is surrounded on the right and on the left by enemies old and new, loud and silent. As befits the hero, Mikhail Gorbachev is a very lonely man.

Not that we should lionize these greater and lesser heroes of deconstruction; they are not asking for that. Any memorial would be superfluous. It is time, however, to take them seriously, to look more closely at what they have in common and how they differ. A political morality which recognizes only good and evil spirits will not be up to this task.

A German philosopher once said that by the end of the century the question would no longer be one of improving the world but of saving it, which applies not only to those dictatorships whose elaborate dismantling we have watched with our own eyes. The Western democracies are also facing an unprecedented dissolution. The military aspect is only one of many. We must also withdraw from our untenable position in the war of debt against the Third World, and the most difficult retreat of all will be in the war against the biosphere which we have been waging since the industrial revolution. It is time for our own diminutive statesmen to measure up to the demolition experts. An energy or transport policy worthy of the name will only come about through a strategic retreat. Certain large industries—ultimately no less threatening than one-party rule—will have to be broken up. The courage and conviction necessary to bring this about will hardly be greater than those the communist functionary had to summon up to do away with his party's monopoly.

But instead our political leadership senses victory, indulging in ridiculous posturing and self-satisfied lies. It gloats and it stonewalls, thinking it can master the future by sitting it out. It hasn't the slightest idea about the moral imperative of sacrifice. It knows nothing of the politics of retreat. It has a lot to learn.

Translated from the German by Piers Spence

Werner Krätschell
I think of three moments.

The first is on a Sunday, August 13, 1961: Lake Mälar in Sweden. One of the best summers of my life. I am in Finland with Albert, my favourite among eight brothers and sisters—he is twenty and I am twenty-one. We have left our parents' home in East Berlin and have set out 'illegally': we didn't get permission for our journey and so have committed a criminal offence. We flew from West Berlin to Hamburg, where we got West German passports, and continued our journey northwards, to the land of our dreams, as citizens of the Federal Republic.

Monday, August 14, 1961: The very next day the manager of the estate where we're staying comes rushing into the kitchen. We are eating breakfast, and he is shouting: 'It's all over, boys. You can't go back again. They've closed the borders.' He shows us the newspapers and the photos are upsetting.

In the evening we sit by the stove in our little guest house. It is built out over the lake and was once used by the washer-women for their hard work. We have a decision to make. Albert wants to stay. He is about to get his school diploma in West Berlin. I want to go back. I am studying theology and don't want to stop. Following an old family tradition, I want to become a minister, a minister 'in the East'. Every generation of our family has had one: I want to return to the parsonage, where, apart from my youngest sister, only my parents now remain. Mother has multiple sclerosis. That, too, is a reason.

November 9, 1989: In the evening, in the historic Friedrichstadt French church, I preside over one of the many recent and remarkable political meetings. I am joined by Manfred Stolpe, one of the leaders of the Protestant Church, and Lothar de Maizière, who, tomorrow, will be elected chairman of the Christian Democrats. All the guilty political parties have sent representatives to our meeting; we are witnessing a palace revolt amid members of this previously colourless, cowardly, corrupt Party. The Communist, Professor Döhle, speaks first. There is—because of the poor acoustics—laughter and spontaneous applause as I lead him to the front. For the first time in his life he now stands—irritated but happy—in a pulpit, with ecclesiastical permission, in the middle of the camp of the old 'class enemy', the Church. What an image, what emotion! Is it a foretaste of the night to come?

On leaving the church, a French journalist tells me a strange piece of news: Schabowski, the Communist Party boss in Berlin, and Egon Krenz, have hinted at the possibility that the border might be opened. I waste no time and drive quickly to Pankow. As I pass the Gethsemane church on Schönhauser Allee, I see images of the violence that occurred at the beginning of last month: once again, I see the police, the army, the 'Stasi' men, the armoured vehicles and shadowy figures wielding batons. I reach our home and find Konstanze, my twenty-year-old daughter and her friend Astrid, who is twenty-one. Rapidly we jump into the car and drive at great speed to the nearest border crossing: Bornholmer Strasse.

Dream and reality become confused. The guards let us through: the girls cry. They cling together tightly on the back seat, as if they're expecting an air raid. We are crossing the strip that for twenty-eight years has been a death zone. And suddenly we see West Berliners. They wave, cheer, shout. I drive down Osloer Strasse to my old school where I got my diploma in 1960. We don't stay long, however, and must return right away because there are still two younger children sleeping at home, and because Astrid is pregnant, and because I have to fly to London early in the morning. But, when we turn around, we see that we are not going to get through. We were among the very first to cross the border. Now the news has spread like wildfire. Hundreds, thousands block our way. There are people who recognize me and they pull open the car door: kisses and tears and we are all in a trance. Astrid, suddenly, tells me to stop the car at the next intersection. She wants only to put her foot down on the street just once. Touching the ground. Armstrong after the moon landing. She has never been in the West before.

All around us, people are beating their fists on my car with joy. The dents will remain, souvenirs of that night.

I hardly sleep and in the morning pass 'normally' through the Friedrichstrasse crossing point. Hundreds crowd through the narrow doors, which were, until yesterday, the 'gates of inhumanity'. My son Joachim stands on the other side. His 'summer at Lake Mälar' was in Hungary and was called 'Balaton'. There, also in August, he made his decision to leave his country and his parents' home. He was without hope. In May and June, he had demonstrated against both the rigging of the elections that had taken place earlier this year and the bloody suppression of the popular movement in China. The consequences were unpleasant. He attempted to escape, and, on his first attempt, he was caught by the Hungarian soldiers. He tried again, and, on his second attempt, he ran for his life. Now he's here. Weeks of pain—for him and for us—are over. His brother Johannes (thirteen) and sister Karoline (seven) don't yet understand the new possibilities. In August Joachim was still twenty-one. His decision was different from mine. Or was it just the same?

The twenty-eight years between: Not until I am on the plane on my way to London and I am alone, alone for the first time after all these dramatic weeks. What have these twenty-eight years meant to you?

Back then, at Lake Mälar in Sweden, I could not imagine that I would one day be married or that I would one day have children. Have they suffered? Yes: there have been hardships; no: there has been inner wealth. They grew up in a parsonage, where the beggar was as welcome as the diplomat, the worker as welcome as the poet. They have had music and Christmas, the landscape of the Mark Brandenburg and good friends. The friends came from the East and West and brought reports and thoughts which saved us from being provincial. And conversation: dense and full of passion. The way we were in those conversations, that's how we really were.

We lived in that other world made wretched by the Communists. We have known the broken and the damned and the ones deprived of their citizen rights. I am only realizing now how, for twenty-eight years, I got caught up again and again by their stories and by the need, therefore, to help them. So many times it had been necessary to get people 'to the West'—very often by difficult routes. They didn't want to live here, or they couldn't live here, or they weren't allowed to live here any more—it was always a question of life. But it was also necessary to protect the people who wanted or had to stay here, and who had fought back against the system of repression with their own small strength. I think of the groups that gathered in our churches and community centres since the beginning of the Eighties, made up of people who were discovering, without knowing it, the principle of non-violence, who were discovering as well that it was a political instrument, one that they then developed in themselves and for others, so that it became the hallmark of the changes.

What I can hear now, here and from the movements in Eastern Europe, is not only a cry for freedom and human dignity; I also hear an urgent plea to the community of Western Europe not to forget us. We want to be part of things when, in 1992, the Western European Community makes the leap into a better life. We don't want to become Europe's 'Third World'. I desire an end to the German as well as to the European division, in which the human dignity of the East Germans and the East Europeans is not damaged, but strengthened.

Translated from the German by Martin Chalmers

Isaiah Berlin

You ask me for a response to the events in Europe. I have nothing new to say: my reactions are similar to those of virtually everyone I know, or know of—astonishment, exhilaration, happiness. When men and women imprisoned for a long time by oppressive and brutal regimes are able to break free, at any rate from some of their chains, and after many years know even the beginnings of genuine freedom, how can anyone with the smallest spark of human feeling not be profoundly moved? One can only add, as Madame Bonaparte said when congratulated on the historically unique distinction of being mother to an emperor, three kings and a queen, *'Oui, pourvu que ça dure.'* If only we could be sure that there will not be a relapse, particularly in the Soviet Union, as some observers fear.

The obvious parallel, which must have struck everyone, is the similarity of these events to the revolutions of 1848–49, when a great upsurge of liberal and democratic feeling toppled governments in Paris, Rome, Venice, Berlin, Dresden, Vienna, Budapest. The late Sir Lewis Namier attributed the failure of these revolutions—for by 1850 they were all dead—to their having been, in his words, 'a Revolution of Intellectuals'.

189

However this may be, we also know that it was the forces unleashed against these revolutions—the armies of Prussia and Austria-Hungary, the southern Slav battalions, the agents of Napoleon III in France and Italy, and, above all, the Tsar's troops in Budapest—that crushed this movement and restored something like the status quo. Fortunately, the situation today does not look similar. The current movements have developed into genuine, spontaneous popular risings, which plainly embrace all classes. We can remain optimistic.

Apart from these general reflections, there is a particular thing which has struck me forcibly—the survival, against all odds, of the Russian intelligentsia. An intelligentsia is not identical with intellectuals. Intellectuals are persons who, as someone said, simply want ideas to be as interesting as possible. Intelligentsia, however, is a Russian word and a Russian phenomenon. Born in the second quarter of the nineteenth century, it was a movement of educated, morally sensitive Russians stirred to indignation by an obscurantist Church; by a brutally oppressive state indifferent to the squalor, poverty and illiteracy in which the great majority of the population lived; by a governing class which they saw as trampling on human rights and impeding moral and intellectual progress. They believed in personal and political liberty, in the removal of irrational social inequalities and in truth, which they identified to some degree with scientific progress. They held a view of enlightenment that they associated with Western liberalism and democracy.

The intelligentsia, for the most part, consisted of members of the professions. The best known were the writers—all the great names (even Dostoevsky in his younger days) were in various degrees and fashions engaged in the fight for freedom. It was the descendants of these people who were largely responsible for making the February Revolution of 1917. Some of its members who believed in extreme measures took part in the suppression of this revolution and the establishment of Soviet communism in Russia, and later elsewhere. In due course the intelligentsia was by degrees systematically destroyed, but it did not wholly perish.

When I was in the Soviet Union in 1945, I met not only two

great poets and their friends and allies who had grown to maturity before the Revolution, but also younger people, mostly children or grandchildren of academics, librarians, museum-keepers, translators and other members of the old intelligentsia, who had managed to survive in obscure corners of Soviet society. But there seemed to be not many of them left. There was, of course, a term 'Soviet intelligentsia', often used in state publications, and meaning members of the professions. But there was little evidence that this term was much more than a homonym, that they were in fact heirs of the intelligentsia in the older sense, men and women who pursued the ideals which I have mentioned. My impression was that what remained of the true intelligentsia was dying.

In the course of the last two years, I have discovered, to my great surprise and delight, that I was mistaken. I have met Soviet citizens, comparatively young, and clearly representative of a large number of similar people, who seemed to have retained the moral character, the intellectual integrity, the sensitive imagination and immense human attractiveness of the old intelligentsia. They are to be found mainly among writers, musicians, painters, artists in many spheres—the theatre and cinema—and, of course, among academics. The most famous among them, Andrei Dmitrievich Sakharov, would have been perfectly at home in the world of Turgenev, Herzen, Belinsky, Saltykov, Annenkov and their friends in the 1840s and 50s. Sakharov, whose untimely end I mourn as deeply as anyone, seems to me to belong heart and soul to this noble tradition. His scientific outlook, unbelievable courage, physical and moral, above all his unswerving dedication to truth, makes it impossible not to see him as the ideal representative, in our time, of all that was most pure-hearted and humane in the members of the intelligentsia, old and new. Moreover, like them, and I speak from personal acquaintance, he was civilized to his fingertips and possessed what I can only call great moral charm. His vigorous intellect and lively interest in books, ideas, people, political issues seemed to me, tired as he was, to have survived his terrible maltreatment. Nor was he alone. The survival of the entire culture to which he belonged underneath the ashes and

191

rubble of dreadful historical experience appears to me a miraculous fact. Surely this gives grounds for optimism. What is true of Russia may be even more true of the other peoples who are throwing off their shackles—where the oppressors have been in power for a shorter period and where civilized values and memories of past freedom are a living force in the still unexhausted survivors of an earlier time.

The study of the ideas and activities of the nineteenth-century Russian intelligentsia has occupied me for some years, and to find that, so far from being buried in the past, this movement—as it is still right to call it—has survived and is regaining its health and freedom, is a revelation and a source of great delight to me. The Russians are a great people, their creative powers are immense, and, once set free, there is no telling what they may give to the world. A new barbarism is always possible, but I see little prospect of it at present. That evils can, after all, be conquered, that the end of enslavement is in progress, are things of which men can be reasonably proud.

Abraham Brumberg

My grandfather, a prosperous merchant equally at home among cosmopolitan financiers and in the insular world of his native Lithuanian *shtetl*, lived and died in History. In 1918, he was stood up against a wall and shot, together with two of his sons, by Red Army conscripts. It was merely a chance historical moment that made my grandfather and his sons victims of the Bolshevik Revolution rather than of its enemies—or of local anti-Semitic cut-throats. But it cast a long shadow.

My father, a free-thinking socialist, was forced to flee the country in 1925. He had been involved in one of those student strikes which the Polish police, not keen on ideological distinctions, regarded as yet another 'Judaeo-Communist' plot. Nine years later, back in Poland as director of a children's sanatorium maintained by the Jewish socialist 'Bund', he used his revolver (the first and only time in his life) to fight off a group of communists bent on destroying this bastion of 'social fascism'. Another chance historical moment?

When the war broke out, my parents and I set off on a trek

that eventually took us from Warsaw to Soviet-occupied Vilna. Since the NKVD was combing the town for socialists, liberals, 'nationalists' and other enemies of the people, my father went into hiding, leaving my mother and me with local relatives. He surfaced several weeks later, when Vilna (now Vilnius) was turned over to Lithuania, only to disappear again when Soviet troops reoccupied Lithuania and the other two Baltic states.

For obvious reasons I, at the age of twelve, turned out to be the sole hold-out in my class against the allurements of revolutionary rhetoric All the others had joined the Red Pioneers. One day, we were reading aloud a hymn to Stalin written by Itzik Feffer, a Soviet Yiddish poet later executed as a spy. Each student was told to read one stanza. When it was my turn, I declaimed, though apparently without enough ardour:

He is deeper than the oceans,
He is higher than the peaks,
There is no one on this globe
Quite remotely like him.

Apparently, for my schoolmates, on the lookout for evidence of ideological turpitude, loudly demanded that the teacher force me to 'read the stanza again—with more feeling'. The teacher, not a Communist, looked sad—and complied. So did I, but the lesson sank in: terror needs no jails or bayonets to be effective.

My family managed to reach the United States in 1941. Wracked by questions, I began reading voraciously, seeking answers in works by eyewitnesses to history, erstwhile believers, anathemized enemies (for instance Leon Trotsky) and sympathetic but critical scholars such as Sidney Hook and William H. Chamberlin. I memorized entire chunks of the report by the Commission of Inquiry on the first two Moscow Trials (John Dewey, *Not Guilty*) and hurled them at my gauchist fellow students in New York's City College. We argued about the Communist coups in Eastern Europe, whether Tito was a fascist beast, and whether Stalin was the 'gravedigger of the

Revolution' or—in the words of Isaac Deutscher—the 'man who dragged Russia, screaming and kicking, into the twentieth century'.

And now, suddenly, there is change. In Czechoslovakia, the change was the death knell of the Communist Party, and it sounded when the workers laid down their tools on November 27. But in East Germany, the change came the moment that popular discontent turned to fury at the disclosures of massive corruption within the red bourgeoisie. The Germans, apparently, actually believed that Honecker et al lived as ascetically as Vladimir Ilich Lenin. Now they know otherwise. Will they still ask themselves how dedicated Communists who had spent years in Hitler's jails and camps had turned into sanctimonious revellers? Or will they conclude that Communists had always been, *au fond*, a pack of gangsters? In Poland, that seems to be the conclusion. 'Nothing but a pack of gangsters' is now the preferred sobriquet for all Communists, used indiscriminately even by Solidarity leaders whose past ties to the party were based on rather more than lust for power and privileges.

Questions: they generate more questions. Stalin was a monster, Lenin hardly a saint and Marx a prophet *manqué*; but have their mistakes, misdeeds and villainies sullied the goal of a just society? Did the path chosen by Lenin and the other founders of the Soviet state lead inevitably to Stalinism? Can we assume that all those questions that I and so many others agonized over have now, in these last months, been fully answered and disposed of?

Not likely.

In some countries, we now watch the discredited order and equally discredited myths giving way to virulent nationalism, ethnic hatreds and enthusiasm for unrestrained laissez-faire. I fear that the demise of Communism is to be accompanied not by the dispelling of the long shadow of history; it is to be accompanied by the erosion of tolerance and of historical memory.

I know that the current historical moment is as splendid as it is unique. But I am also aware of past moments. They include the death of Stalin, Khruschev's speech in 1956, the Hungarian insurrection, the outbreaks of unrest in East Germany and Poland, the Prague Spring, the birth of Solidarity in Poland, the rise of Gorbachev. Each of them was distinct, and each hastened the advent of the present Moment. And I am aware, too, of the deceits bred by faulty memory. Perhaps I owe this awareness to my father, whose bitter brushes with History taught him to suspect facile simplicities, to respect distinctions, and to ponder over unanswered questions. Like his own father, he lived his life in History. So have I. We all do, whether we know it or not.

Günter Kunert

At times of crisis in Germany there is talk of dreams, more so probably than in any other country in the world. Romanticism is a quintessentially German product, a museum piece that has taken on a new relevance with the Wall in Berlin fallen; writers from the East and West, falling suddenly into each other's arms appear to be as Romantic as their eighteenth- and nineteenth-century counterparts. At no time was this more apparent than on November 29, 1989 when a number of authors and intellectuals in East Berlin—among them, Stefan Heym, Volker Braun, Christa Wolf—published an appeal urging people to uphold the 'moral values' of the socialism of the German Democratic Republic and to bring into being a 'new', a 'true', a 'genuine' socialism.

We see today the crowds in Leipzig and East Berlin. They are raging at a system that has cheated them all their lives with its feudal structure of hierarchies. We see people whose most heartfelt desire is for an existence without fear or deprivation— a normal existence. And they are answered by writers and intellectuals who, having never known such deprivation, call for a purified, revitalized socialism.

What is going on in the heads of the authors of this declaration? Who are they? They seem to have set themselves up as the Praeceptor Germaniae, the old German head-teacher, lecturing the children as to what they should and should not do, and the role of lecturer, 'teacher', 'people's educator', is, of course, the favourite pose of the German poet and writer. What is this 'democratic socialism' and how is it supposed to inspire people who have been led around by the nose for forty years? It has little to do with them. Is it nothing more than the untested brainchild of an educated and domineering mentality? The authors of the declaration of November 29, 1989 set themselves up, once again, to dictate how life should be and how we should behave within their hypothetical construct, revealing, thus, their contempt for ordinary people. The ordinary people on the streets of East Germany have not the slightest interest in revitalizing socialism of any sort. They are not asking for a new system; they are asking, understandably, for a better life. And since no one has yet given them a concrete answer, they are now demanding the reunification of Germany as their last hope of rising out of the chaos of a state that has done nothing but exploit them. The intellectuals of course protest that reunification would mean 'selling out' East Germany, reducing it to a colony of the Federal Republic, but their protest hardly matters to the people on the streets. A better life is what matters to them, whatever the flag and whatever the government; no one wants to wait any longer. For forty years they have been fed on empty promises: why should a promise of 'democratic socialism' suddenly satisfy them?

Socialism is finished as an alternative to other systems of society, and it is disappearing from history. It is not yet clear what will take its place. This uncertainty is profoundly disturbing to East German intellectuals, who have always sought to shore themselves up with certainties and absolutes, however fictitious. The German intellectual, one could say in a variation on one of Brecht's Keuner stories, needs a God. He cannot exist without 'isms'. So he shuts his eyes to the facts and clings to a *fata morgana* made of paper untainted by the filth and blood of reality.

Translated from the German by Harriet Goodman

Ivan Klíma

The first pictures of the Prague demonstration of November 17 were of young girls placing flowers on shields held by riot police. Later the police got rough, but their furious brutality failed to provoke a single violent response. Not one car was damaged, not one window smashed during daily demonstrations by hundreds of thousands of people. Posters stuck up on the walls of houses, in metro stations, on shop windows and in trams by the striking students called for peaceful protest. Flowers became the symbol of Civic Forum.

It is only recently that we have seen the fragility of totalitarian power. Is it really possible that a few days of protest—unique in the history of revolutions for their peacefulness—could topple a regime which had harassed our citizens for four decades?

The rest of the world had all but forgotten the 1968 invasion of Czechoslovakia by the armies of five countries. Even now, our nation has barely recovered from that invasion; what did not recover was the leading force in the country, the Communist Party. By subsequently making approval of the invasion and the occupation a condition of membership, the Party deprived itself of almost all patriotic and worthy members, becoming for the rest of the nation a symbol of moral decay and betrayal. The government, then stripped of its authority and its intelligence, went on to devastate the country culturally, morally and materially. An economically mature country fell back among the developing countries, while achieving a notable success in atmospheric pollution, incidence of malignant tumours and short life expectancy.

Unrestrained power breeds arrogance. And arrogance threatens not only the subject but also the ruler. In Czechoslovakia the ruling party, deprived of an elite and of any outstanding personalities, combined arrogance with provocative stupidity. It persisted obstinately in defending the occupation of Czechoslovakia, indeed as an act of deliverance at a time when even the invaders themselves were re-examining their past. The government actually went so far as to suggest that the apologies offered by the Polish and Hungarian governments for their role in the invasion constituted interference in the internal affairs of the country. How could the nation consider such a government as its own?

The months leading up to the events of November, however static they may have seemed compared with the agitation in the neighbouring countries, were in fact a period of waiting for circumstances for change. The regime, unable to discern its utter isolation, in relation to both its own nation and the community of nations, reacted in its usual manner to a peaceful demonstration to commemorate the death of a student murdered by the Nazis fifty years ago. It could not have picked a worse moment—the patience of the silent nation had snapped; the circumstances had finally changed.

We, who had consistently tried to show the bankruptcy of the regime, were surprised at how quickly it collapsed under the blows of that one weapon, truth, voiced by demonstrators—students and actors who immediately went to the country to win over people—and then spread by a media no longer willing to serve a mendacious and brutal regime. As such non-violence was the only weapon we needed to use against violent power. Will those who were robbed, harassed and humiliated continue to be so magnanimous? As long as they can be they have in their power to realize the idea of a democratic Europe, a Europe for the next millennium, a Europe of nations living in mutual domestic peace.

Translated from the Czech by Daphne Dorrell

Stephen Spender

Perhaps because I am eighty what is happening today in the Soviet Union, East Germany, Czechoslovakia, Hungary and Bulgaria has the effect of making me feel that I am witnessing apocalyptic events out of the Book of Revelation. I do not apologize for beginning on this personal note. For the collapse of the totalitarian regimes in the Soviet Union and Eastern Europe is something that I had given up hope of witnessing in my lifetime. I was sure that it would happen eventually but that it would be perpetually postponed to the next century, after the millennium. I now have the almost biblical sense of being privileged to witness a miracle.

Perhaps some young people have the same kind of feeling. A historic event may seem to contemporaries part of a larger impersonal history being unfolded before their eyes, and yet at the same time strike each separately as being his or her intensely felt personal experience. The assassination of President Kennedy had this effect on thousands of people who, notoriously almost, remember what they were doing at the moment when they heard the news of Kennedy's death.

Judging from the newspapers, many people in the West— especially conservative politicians—take what they call 'the end of Communism' to signify the defeat of the evil Communist Satan and the triumph of the Capitalist God in a Manichean struggle between the forces of Good (Capitalism) and of Evil (Communism). This seems to me a dangerously false reading of recent events. What has triumphed is Democracy, the will of the people, and in a very unideological, politically scarcely realized, form. And this is not because socialism ('Communism with a human face') has failed but because Marxist ideology, tied to the concept of 'the dictatorship of the proletariat', has broken down.

The evil of Communism is that Marxist leaders, beginning with Lenin, believed that any means justified the end of overcoming capitalism. Communist leaders everywhere became corrupt as a consequence of their having absolute power. But today, when the corruption of the older generation of Communist leaders in East Germany is exposed, it is perhaps salutary to remember that in their youth many of these leaders were heroic idealists (though preaching 'historical materialism'). They were opponents of Hitler, and several were killed or imprisoned, ending their lives in concentration camps. Ernst Thaelmann, the German Communist leader, murdered by the Nazis in Buchenwald concentration camp in August 1944, would almost certainly be in the same position as his follower Erich Honecker, if he were alive today.

Perhaps it is too simple to read these events in terms of the political divisions which have dominated nations in the twentieth century. Of course resurgent nationalism and shortage of consumer goods help produce a revolutionary situation, but there is a historically unprecedented negative factor which seems to me tremendously important, especially among students and intellectuals. This might be called 'the boredom factor'. Life under a dictatorship of old-style ideologists, whether in Russia,

Eastern Europe or China, is extremely boring. Moreover, owing to modern systems of communication people living under dictatorships are made aware of the boredom of the system: the flow of information from the outside is unstoppable. The Berlin Wall may have prevented East Berliners reaching the West, but it was leaped over and penetrated at a million points by TV and radio bringing East Berliners news and images of the lifestyle, vitality and competitiveness of the West.

Commentators have had difficulty defining, in political terms of left or right, the changes taking place in the Communist world today. Apart from nationalism and very pressing economic problems the movement is perhaps more a cultural than a clearly definable political revolution. It is led by intellectuals and students who know what they want—freedom of self-expression and removal of the dead weight of censorship and Party dogma—better than they know the politics which they wish to see replace Communism.

The crowds of rejoicing young people who have got rid of their Communist Party leaders have streamed across the TV screens of Western Europe. Mass demonstrations proved their point when they were seen by a world in moving photographs. Violence had become superfluous and unnecessary. No one needed to be killed, and no Bastilles stormed. This theatre is the living truth of the liberation movements. It is significant that Václav Havel is a playwright. His Civic Forum has the look of characters in search of a party and a policy. What we see may show that we have moved beyond the nineteenth- and twentieth-century cycle of revolutions—murder followed by counter-revolutions, also murderous—to a period when great political-cultural changes are acts of recognition of changed states of consciousness among people, made apparent as *faits accomplis* by the mass media.

But that is to look far beyond the present, into the twenty-first century. Many things may go wrong. Gorbachev may fail and be succeeded by the military. Problems caused by mass starvation may supersede all others and may produce widespread death and violence. Nevertheless the recent events have shown that dictatorial regimes are incapable of replacing an old leadership with youthful leaders without the regimes and their ideology crumbling. There were signs of this in 1968 when the movement forward in Communist societies was reversed in Czechoslovakia by Soviet troops. It is difficult to believe that a reversal, if it happens, will be as effective—not even in China. If the present revolution is stopped in any one place, to be superseded by dictatorship, the media will assure that the consciousness of a democratic world, flooding in, will sooner or later break down the prison walls of the dictatorship.

Mircea Dinescu

Not long ago, in the icy Siberian plains, a few hard-frozen mammoths were discovered. The discoverers were astonished to find camomile flowers inside their bellies. I recalled the incident when I came upon an article in the Western press entitled 'Last Stalinist mammoth left in Romania'. I greatly fear that, when the social climate in Romania does change, we will not find any camomile flowers inside the belly of our Stalinist beast, but several dead bodies. People from the Jiu valley, from Barsov, Timisoara, Cluj, Iasi, Tirgu Mures and Bucharest have been and are still being swallowed alive. They are people about whom little, or even nothing at all, is known, who were courageous enough to vent their exasperation, even if only within their communities.

Who will intervene in Romania? God does not get involved in politics. I hope I will be forgiven for saying that our daily prayer does not seem to have been heard. Our priests have been forced into becoming trade unionists in cassocks. The 'accidental' deaths of a few troublesome priests, as well as the 'lay' pressure applied by the civilian representatives of the Secu Monastery to the more talkative members of the clergy, have introduced permanent terror into the holy orders. There are no Polish-style Catholic shipyards or factories in our country. There is no militant church, no icon to work miracles like the one in Czestochowa. Our icons are of the president; our factories are run by soldiers; and our churches have, in the winter, the highest number of funerals in the world.

Where can we go now that the Berlin Wall is being preserved, brick by brick, and transported to the Romanian border? Who will come to our defence? The lawyers, the men who studied the force and superiority of the 'Romanian Left' over the 'Roman Right' at the Law Faculty, are reduced to a state of powerlessness and obedience. They are so afraid of losing their jobs that they have come to consider the Romanian constitution as a mere propaganda instrument, a tool of the devil which cannot, therefore, really help you when it comes down to it. In a moment of desperation and rebellion, a former school friend pasted up a few anti-president notices at Bucharest's main railway station, and was condemned to five years' imprisonment. The worst attack against him was made, during the closed trial, by his defence lawyer.

Can we appeal to the popular militia? The strong, ruddy-cheeked lads stand in their fine uniforms at every ten metres on the streets of Bucharest. As they stare at the population they seem to be looking at a flock of helpless sheep. During their brief training, they have learned that anyone moving after ten at night, when the street lights go off, and when the cinemas, the restaurants and the theatres close—the hour, that is, when Romanian towns die—must be a criminal, or at the very least an evil pyromaniac, about to set fire to Lenin's statue, which was in fact burned last year.

Can we look to the members of the press for support—those apostles of the personality cult? For twenty years our newspapers have been reusing the same poorly reprinted photographs and the same meaningless sentences. The only space which provides any real information is the obituaries. In any case, it seems that the good journalists died with everyone else in the Second World War.

What about glasnost? Will anything come of Soviet openness? I do not know why it should be, but the window through which the Moscow press views Romania is quite hazy. Like an eclipse you cannot actually see anything through it. I have the impression that it is through General Jaruzelski's black glasses that Gorbachev is looking at Romania.

What of the dissidents? You do hear the odd squeak from them now and then, but so seldom that it makes you wonder if Romanians—there would appear to be only one dissident for every two million inhabitants here—are by nature more silent than the Germans, the Hungarians or the Poles. I have been preoccupied recently by another thought, though: that, paradoxically, the regime may be keeping our extremely small number of dissidents alive for propaganda purposes. Now that the Western press and human rights organizations have realized that the dissidents exist, it is too late to get rid of them. But this isn't the case. In actual fact there are twenty million protesters in Romania, unpublicized dissidents who live their lives gagged. I never heard about any anti-fascist demonstrations on the streets of Berlin in the 1940s. In the streets there was order and discipline; it was only in their homes that people whispered.

In our country political trials are not possible for the simple reason that it is written clearly in the constitution that a citizen has the right to freedom of opinions. Furthermore, a Party statute specifies that any member of the Party may criticize anyone else—even the General Secretary. A repressive organization operates undercover. Once marked as protester, you must learn to be careful—not to walk alone in town, for instance, or to let your children play outside. You must take care to disinfect your door handle thoroughly; it may be poisoned.

The situation in our country cannot be compared with anywhere in the world. When I heard that Václav Havel had a television and word processor in his Prague prison, I thought it was a joke. In Romania a writer is not allowed to have a typewriter in his own home without permission from the police. A Romanian dissident, a poet, was given the choice between three months in prison, spent in the company of hardened criminals waiting for some young lads to come along, or emigration. The writer chose exile.

How were most writers corrupted? In the 1950s a privileged elite emerged. With one poem published on the front page of the Party newspaper, you could buy an English-made overcoat and eat in the best restaurant in Bucharest for a whole month. What glorious times! 'Pelisor', once the luxurious residence of King Carol, became known as the 'House of Creators' for all those rolling off the conveyer belt of the new writing factories. History was standing on its head: the proletarian-culture poets were sprawling on what was once Queen Maria's bed, composing illiterate but enthusiastic 'revolutionary' poems. With a 'heigh-ho' and a 'praise Stalin' vineyards were sold off and some people got very rich. Millionaires appeared from the ranks of the Party writers. Ever since then it has been this kind of literary activist, buckled under the weight of so many privileges, who has been chosen to lead the artists and be their spokesman.

In the 1960s, the censors relaxed for a short time. In the years that followed, however, at a time when writers were not showing much enthusiasm for the new cultural revolution, imported from China, the confiscations and repressions began. Pelisor was once more turned into the new princes' summer residence; poems regained their symbolic value. Authors' photographs were removed from the covers of their books for fear of encouraging—God forbid—a personality cult. At the same time it was argued that the Writers' Union should be disbanded as it was a relic from the old system, an organization based on the Soviet model. Everything else, our transport system, our food packaging, was built on Japanese, American or French models.

Writers briefly manifested a sign of life in 1981, when, at a national conference, many of their voices sounded a little out of key from the tune the central authorities were singing. But their Union has long been undermined by the ineffective, passive resistance of some of its most prominent members, and by the vacuum left by the mass emigration of disillusioned writers. It has metamorphosed into a sort of cooperative making completely alien products.

Although the spectre of poverty hovers over the majority of Romanian writers today—even while the number of lucrative homages to the state have been increasing every month—a general strike is what is called for. A general strike of all writers would be the easiest solution for saving the face of Romanian culture. If they were to all speak with one voice, the mammoths of today would feed on camomile and perish.

Translated from the Romanian by Fiona Tupper-Carey

1991
Bears in Mourning
Adam Mars-Jones

When I think about it, it was terrible the way we behaved when Victor died. We behaved as if we were ashamed of him, or angry. It didn't show us at our best—we didn't cope at all well. We all knew Victor was 'ill', obviously, but none of us really took on board how bad things had got.

He was in the middle of our little group, our sect, but somehow he got lost all the same. I suppose each of us paid him some token attention—his conversation tended to go round in circles, particularly with the drink—and then left it to somebody else to do the real work: supporting him and talking him through the dark days. He was our brother Bear, but the fraternity didn't do well by him.

We Bears are a varied crowd. There's an organist, a social worker, a travel agent, an osteopath. That's not the full list, of course, that's off the top of my head. If it wasn't for membership of the Bear nation we would have nothing in common. Somehow we always thought that would be enough.

It's amazing that Victor was able to hold down his job for as long as he did, but then he'd done it for a long time. He was working with friends, people who would make allowances. In any case there was a structure set up, and within limits it ran itself. Every few months Victor, or rather the company that employed him, put out the first issue of a magazine devoted to some sure-fire subject—French cookery, classic cars, Sixties pop. When I say the first issue, I mean of course Parts One and Two, Part Two coming free.

It doesn't take long, with a halfway decent picture researcher, to get enough stuff from reference books to fill a few magazine pages. Tasters for future issues take care of the rest. Part Three never arrives, and maybe people wonder why not. Maybe they think, shame nobody bought Parts One and Two—it was such a good idea. Pity it didn't catch on.

I used to wonder what would have happened if one of Victor's magazines had really taken off, had sold and sold off the news-stands. Would there have come a time when Part Three became inevitable? I don't think so. I think Victor's employers would have carried on repackaging their little stack of ideas for ever. With a little redesign, they could put out the same Parts

One and Two every two years or so. Which they did.

Victor was prime Bear, Bear absolute. I know I haven't explained just what a Bear is, and it's not an easy thing to define. There have always been tubby men, but I can't think they ever formed a little self-conscious tribe before. *Tubby* isn't even the right word, but at least it's better than *chubby*. *Chubby* is hopeless, and *chubby-chaser* is a joke category.

To be a Bear you need, let's see, two essential characteristics, a beard and a bit of flesh to spare, preferably some body hair. But it's a more mysterious business than that. Some men will never be Bears however hairy they are, however much surplus weight they carry. They just look like hairy thin guys who've let themselves run to seed, thin men who could stand to lose a few pounds. A true Bear has a wholeness you can't miss—at least if you're looking for it.

It's a great thing to watch a Bear become aware of himself. All his life he's been made to feel like a lump, and then he meets a person, and then a whole group, that thinks he's heaven on legs. On tree-trunk legs. He's been struggling all his life against his body, and suddenly it's perfect. There have been quite a few lapsed health-club memberships in our little circle, I can tell you.

One of them was mine. I remember the first time I was hugged by a Bear, as a Bear. We were Bear to Bear. I remember how his hand squeezed my tummy—*tummy*'s a childish word but the others are worse—and I realized I didn't need to hold it in. He wasn't looking for a washboard stomach, the sort you can see in the magazines. He was happy with a wash-tub stomach like mine. He liked me just the way I was.

And Aids, Aids. Where does Aids come into this?

All of us were involved in the epidemic in some way, socially, politically, rattling collection buckets at benefit shows if nothing else. And of course we were all terrified of getting sick. But that's not what I'm getting at.

Aids is like the weather. It doesn't cause everything, but the things it doesn't cause it causes the causes of. So, yes, you'd think there'd be a link between a group of men who like their lovers to have a bit of meat on their bones, who like men with curves, and a disease that makes people shrivel away into a straight line up and down.

But I don't really think so. The Bear idea would have happened with or without Aids. The English language had a hand in it, by putting the words *bear* and *beard* so close to each other in the dictionary. Perhaps it's a sexual style that works differently in other languages. Has anyone in history ever really enjoyed beards, let alone based a little erotic religion around them? I suppose Victorian wives were the people in history most exposed to facial hair, and they weren't in much of a position to shop around or compare notes.

The beard is a mystery worn on the face. There are beards of silk and beards of wire, each with its charge of static, and it isn't easy to tell them apart without a nuzzle, or at least a touch of the hand.

We in our group are great observers of the way a beard shows up different pigments from the rest of the head hair. Ginger tints are common; less often, we see magical combinations of darkness and blondness. Beards age unpredictably, sometimes greying before the head hair, sometimes retaining a strong shade when all colour has drained from the scalp. The first frost may appear evenly across the beard, or locally in the sideboards, or on the chin, or at the corners of the mouth.

We in our group are tolerant of tufty beards, wispy beards, beards with asymmetrical holes. There are beards that Nature more or less insists on, to cover up her botches. Only a few bearers of the beard, we feel, positively bring it into disrepute, usually by reason of fancy razorwork. The beard to us is more than a sexual trigger, not far short of a sexual organ. Some of us even defend jazzman beards, goatees, beards that look like a few eyebrows stuck together. As a group, we particularly admire a beard that rides high on the cheeks, or one that runs down the neck unshaven.

Bears don't discriminate against age. It's just the other way about. We often say that someone is too young for his beard—he'll have to grow into it.

A man with a pure-white beard can expect as many looks of appreciation, still tinged with lust, as someone twenty, thirty years younger. There are many couples in our group, though few of them even try to be monogamous, and some of them are made up of figures who we might describe as Bear and Cub, Daddy Bear and Baby Bear—but even they don't take their roles very seriously. Neither of them tries too hard to play the grown-up.

It's as if in every generation of boy children there are a few who put their fingers in their ears during tellings of *Goldilocks*, filtering out the female elements in the story, until what they are left with is a fuzzy fable of furry sleepers, of rumpled beds and porridge.

Every happy period is a sort of childhood, and the last ten years have been a happy period for the Bears, in spite of everything.

So when I say that Victor was an absolute Bear, I mean that he had pale skin, heavy eyebrows and a startlingly dark beard, full but trimmed. No human hair is black, even Chinese or Japanese, and Raven Black hair dye is sold as a cruel joke to people who know no better, but Victor's came close. He was forty-two or three then, I suppose, and five foot eight, ideal Bear height. He pointed his feet out a bit, as if his tummy was a new thing and needed a new arrangement of posture to balance it.

We met in a bar. Under artificial light the drama of his colouring wasn't immediately obvious, and I mistook him for a German who had been rude to me in another bar a couple of months before. I suppose my body language expressed a pre-emptive rejection, which in the event Victor found attractive. After a while he came over to me and said, 'You win. You've stared me down. Let me buy you a drink.'

I went home with him in his old Rover to Bromley, an unexpectedly long journey, and a suburban setting that didn't seem to fit with the man who took me there. Later I learned that this had been his childhood home. When his mother died, Victor had let go a West End flat so as to keep his father company. It was a doomed gesture, as things turned out—one of a series—because his father soon found some company of his own. The companion may in fact have dated back to days before Victor's mother died.

It was late when we arrived at Bromley. I assumed we were alone in the house, in which case Victor's father was stopping out with his lady friend, but perhaps he was asleep in a bedroom I didn't see. If so, he slept soundly, and got up either before or after we did.

The bedroom was in chaos, but not knowing Victor it didn't occur to me to wonder whether it was an ebullient chaos or a despairing one. There was a big bulletin board on the mantelpiece, with photographs, letters and business cards pinned up on it, but there was still an overflow of paper and magazines. There was the inevitable shelf of Paddingtons, Poohs and koalas, and a single Snoopy to show breadth of mind.

Victor wanted first to be hugged and then fucked. He mentioned that this second desire was a rarity with him, and I could believe him. He was vague about the location of condoms. Eventually I found a single protective in a bedside drawer, of an unfamiliar brand (the writing on the packet seemed to be Dutch) and elderly appearance. I could find no lubricant that wouldn't dissolve it. I put it on anyway, to show willing, and lay down on top of Victor. I enjoyed the heat and mass of the man beneath me; I made only the most tentative pelvic movements, just vigorous enough to tear the dry condom. Then Victor remembered that he had some lubricant after all, under the bed.

Victor was apologetic about the confusion of our sexual transaction, but looking back I find it appropriate. He was both in and out of the world, even then, and he could summon up separately the elements of love-making, desire, caution, tenderness, but not string them together.

At some stage I noticed he was crying, and he went on for over an hour before he stopped. I hugged him some more, but I can't say that I took his distress very seriously. I didn't make anything of the fact that we didn't have a particularly good time in bed. Good sex isn't very Bear, somehow. I was already well used to awkwardness, lapses of concentration, sudden emotional outpourings. What could be more Bear than a fatherly man on a crying jag?

Bears are never far from tears, or wild laughter come to that. I have seen Bears cry just as hard as Victor did that night, beards matted with their tears, and be cheered up by a bowl of cereal or a cartoon on television. But of course Victor only stopped crying when he fell asleep. The curtains were open, and it was already beginning to get light. I hate sleeping like that—this Bear likes his cave dark—but I didn't stay awake long enough to do anything about it.

That was my only intimate contact with Victor, but the Bear community continued to revolve in its eccentric orbit around him. Everybody I met seemed to know him, and I ended up keeping track of him without making any great effort. Victor's father died a few months after we met, which I think was the great event in Victor's life. After that he had a succession of room-mates at the house—Bears, inevitably. They didn't stay long. Victor was hard going by then, even for Bears. But while they stayed, and while he stayed coherent, Victor took a fatherly interest in them, and would try to fix them up with compatible Bruins. That's a nice characteristic—that's a good thing to remember.

I invited Victor to dinner once about that time, and he phoned me on the evening arranged to warn me he'd be late. He never arrived. From friends on the Bear grapevine I learned that this pattern was typical.

After Victor died, the room-mate at the time wanted everything of Victor's, everything that was even reminiscent of Victor, cleared away at once. He wasn't being heartless, he just couldn't cope with a dead man's presence being imprinted so strongly on the rooms. I went along to help out, but it wasn't as straightforward a job as I had thought when we started. Apparently neutral objects kept leaping into hurtful life.

It turned out that Victor used to offer himself as a photographic model for his magazines and their stable-mates. Surprising that a man with low self-esteem should so much enjoy being photographed. But apparently he used to tease the company's photographic editor about the scarcity of bearded images in the media, and offered himself to make good the lack. So as we cleared the room we found that the slippered individual on the cover of a mid-Seventies hi-fi magazine, head cocked while he stroked a spaniel and listened to a hulking array of quadrophonic speakers, was a mid-Seventies Victor. The genial chef on another cover, stirring a golden sauce in a kitchen hung with gleaming copper pans, was also Victor. Victor was even a tasteful Adam on the cover of a pop-psychology mag, Parts One and Two, receiving a glossy apple from an Eve with scheming eyes. Finally all the traces of Victor's presence were gone, stuffed under beds or bundled into bin bags.

The worst part of the visit, though, was finding in Victor's wastepaper basket something that was like the opposite of a suicide note. It was the note he would have left for his room-mate if Victor had managed to decide to go on living. *Dear Bear*, it started, and it said

> Sorry I've been so hard to be around lately, that's the last thing you need. Thanks for bearing it anyway (bad joke), and I think I've turned the corner. I'll leave the car tomorrow—no point in taking it—and I'll see you in the p.m. Don't chuck the *Guardian*, there may be some jobs in it.
> Love Victor.

I had known that Victor was due to appear in court the next day for drunk driving (not his first offence) and was certain to lose his licence. I hadn't heard that he had also lost his job, which was probably because of his general unreliability, although the pretext had to do with fiddling expenses or paying somebody who was already on the staff to do piecework under another name.

Instead of turning up in court, and instead of leaving the note, which he crumpled up and threw in the wastepaper basket, Victor took the car and drove down to the country, Kent somewhere, I'm afraid I've blotted out the details. I think it was where his parents met, or had their first date, or went on their honeymoon. It had a private significance, but I've forgotten exactly what. I imagine it was a beauty spot, and that he reached it in the early hours. He must have waited a bit, after he arrived, for the crumbling exhaust pipe of the old Rover to cool down from the journey. He wouldn't have wanted to burn his hands or melt the hose. Perhaps he waited again afterwards, before he restarted the engine.

He didn't leave a note, but he hardly needed to. For weeks he had been sitting around drinking and listening to a record— the first single he had bought for years, I dare say. It was called *The Living Years* by Mike and the Mechanics, and by bad luck it was at number one. For a few weeks it was impossible to avoid it on the radio. It was all about not telling your father you loved him while he was alive, and Victor played it over and over again. Mike of the Mechanics is one of the very few beards in pop music, but I don't think that had anything to do with it. Far too lanky to be a Bear.

Victor had a little bag of runes, a sort of Celtic *I Ching*, given him by an Irish Bear who used them to make every decision, and he would draw a rune from the bag every now and then when he was drinking. He seemed to draw the blank tile rather a lot, or so I heard, from the black suede drawstring bag. The drawstring bag of fate. The blank rune means death, according to the little booklet that comes with the set, but I hope he read a little further and learned that it could also mean the absolute end of something. The blank tile can actually be a positive sign: new beginning. Still, I don't expect it would have mattered what tile he drew, or what he thought it meant.

I don't expect it occurred to Victor to think of that old magazine cover, with a younger and hopeful-looking him patting a dog and listening with an expression of neutral pleasure to an unspecified music. But I find myself thinking, as I didn't when Victor's death was fresh, of the two images, the one of posed contentment, and the other of real-life squalor and misery—a middle-aged man letting a pretentious pop single contain and enlarge all his sense of failure.

Suicide rates go down in wartime. Isn't that a fascinating fact? Except that I can never work out what it means. Does it mean that people with a self-destructive streak volunteer for dangerous jobs or missions, so they don't need to go to the trouble of topping themselves—they're either killed or cured? Or does it mean that people forget to be self-obsessed when there's a genuine crisis out there in the world?

You'd think there'd be a lot of Aids-related suicides, but there aren't. It can't just be a matter of being British, not wanting to make a fuss, all that. There must be a few people who freak out when they're diagnosed HIV-positive out of a clear blue sky; they're the most likely to lay hands on themselves. But anyone who's already shown symptoms must at least have considered the possibility. Knowing the worst can even calm people down in a certain sense.

It's different for people who are really sick. They're faced with a series of days only fractionally better or worse than the one before, and suicide is such an all-or-nothing business. It's really tricky deciding what individual trial finally tips a life over into being not worth the living, and then sticking to your decision. It's like a problem in algebra. What is x, such that x *plus 1* is unbearable?

But how do the survivors feel if someone does commit suicide in the middle of a war? That was the problem for the Bears— that was what we were dropped in. We knew damn well that Victor wasn't physically sick. He couldn't have taken an HIV test without our knowing. It seemed to us that he'd just thrown away a body that any of our sick friends, any dwindling Bear, would have jumped at. OK, so Victor was short of puff, no great shakes when it came to running up stairs. There are plenty of skinny people who could have learned to put up with that.

We were angry. Didn't Victor know there was a war on? We Bears had given bouquets that had appeared at the graveside stripped of their messages. We had laboured to clean the bathrooms of the dead, so that their heirs found nothing so much as a stain to alarm them—and had had our names forgotten however many times we were introduced to them. We had held our candles high at Trafalgar Square vigils, year after year, forming helpful compositional groups on cue, for press photographs that never got published. And there was Victor beautiful in his coffin, plump in his coffin, his poison-blued face hardly presenting a challenge to the undertaker's cosmetician.

Everywhere we look we see Aids. We can be driving along, not thinking of anything. We stop at the traffic lights and there's a cyclist waiting there too, foot flexed on the pedal, ready to shoot off first. The picture of health. Except that he's wearing a mask to filter the city air that makes us think of an oxygen mask, and there's a personal stereo fastened by a strap to his bicep that reminds us of a drip feed—as if he was taking music intravenously.

So how could Victor see anything but Aids? What gave him the right to follow his obsession with his father so far? Somehow while we were all busy he found the time to invent his own illness. Wasn't Aids good enough for him? We loved his flesh, but it was unnatural that he died with it unmelted. Dying fat is an obscenity, these days. You're not supposed to be able to take it with you.

These days I understand Victor a little better. His anti-suicide note has made me understand suicide in a way that no suicide note could ever do. His father dying made his failure final. When we finally worked out the access code for his home computer, we found it was full of rambling journal entries saying so. But in another way he must have been relieved. With both his parents dead, he didn't need to resist the temptation of suicide any more, for their sake. He had no loyalty to life. He felt no patriotism for the mortal country.

I realize now that Victor's life only amounted to a little loop of track, like a child's first model railway layout. There was only one set of points in the whole circuit, and every time Victor passed it he had to decide whether to commit himself to going round again. But even if he did, he knew that he'd be passing the points again soon. Sooner or later he was bound to make the other choice.

He didn't steer the way we do. He wasn't affected by our weather. His despair was a gyroscope. But any other time, we would have grieved for him.

I didn't go to the memorial service, though I know that one or two of the Bears did, along with a couple of colleagues from work. But all the Bears turned up to a funeral feast at the Bromley house. We had a sort of picnic, but there was an ugly feeling behind it all, a resentment we didn't quite come out with. Most of us got a little drunk, which didn't help. I remember wandering through the house, looking for signs of Victor, even though I had helped so recently to clear such things away. I found a photo of him in a drawer, and slipped it into a pocket. Then a little later, someone dragged out the bin bags of Victor's papers and possessions, and a little after that we made a bonfire.

1992

Ohne Mich: Why I Shall Never Return to Germany

Martha Gellhorn

I have been totting up the times that I swore never to return to Germany.

The first was in the summer of 1936 when I saw only a bit of the surface scum, but it was enough. A bunch of youngish beer bellies in brown shirts surrounded an old man and woman, poor people from my quick glance at them, who were on their hands and knees. I thought, but could not believe, that they were scrubbing the pavement. Whatever they were doing was hard and wrong, and these louts were jeering at them.

I was using the *Weltkriegsbibliothek* in Stuttgart for research. The librarian, a thin grey-faced woman, spoke in whispers, saying that they had a new director; she did not know how long the library would stay open. The library documented the Great War of 1914–18, hardly a popular subject, a record of defeat. One afternoon the new director arrived on horseback. He was young, blond and handsome in his brownshirt uniform. He galloped through the trees and untended high grass, and swung from his horse into an open French window. The building was an elegant old house in its own small park. He made a lot of noise in that silent place. The librarian listened with a strange expression; I was unused to the look of fear. Then he rode off, laughing. Though he had gone, the librarian would not answer questions about him or the former director.

I read the newspapers, coarse and belligerent in tone, which is how I learned of the war in Spain, described as the revolt of a rabble of 'Red Swine Dogs'. Those few weeks turned me into a devout anti-fascist. I had not grasped a tenth of the ugliness that pervaded Germany but decided, from disgust, that the country was now worthless. I was never coming back.

But I did, trailing after the soldiery across the bridge at Remagen in March 1945. From then until the end of the war in Europe I saw a lot of Germany. My private war aim was the liberation of the concentration camp at Dachau, the first Hitler had built in 1933. Dachau was a permanent atrocity, far worse than anything I had seen in war. A prisoner skeleton shuffled into the infirmary where I was listening to Polish doctor prisoners and announced the German surrender. The same day, in a fever of horror and loathing, I fled Dachau and cadged a lift on a plane ferrying American prisoners of war out of the accursed land. In our different ways, we all swore never to set foot again on German soil; nor were we apt to forget and forgive.

> I have not talked about how it was the day the American Army arrived, though the prisoners told me. In their joy to be free, and longing to see their friends who had come at last, many prisoners rushed to the fence and died electrocuted. There were those who died cheering, because that effort of happiness was more than their bodies could endure. There were those who died because now they had food, and they ate before they could be stopped, and it killed them. I do not know words to describe the men who have survived this horror for years, three years, five years, ten years, and whose minds are as clear and unafraid as the day they entered.
>
> …Dachau seemed to me the most suitable place in Europe to hear the news of victory. For surely this war was made to abolish Dachau, and all the other places like Dachau, and everything that Dachau stood for, and to abolish it forever.
>
> Martha Gellhorn, 'Dachau', May 1945
> from *The Face of War*

Then, in September 1946, after the Nuremberg War Crimes Trial had been going on for ten months, I finally felt some sort of duty to witness and report on it. Every day in that courtroom was a soul-sickening history lesson. No one alone could have known the whole story of Hitler's reign. The detail and the scale as pieced together from innumerable witnesses and innumerable documents truly disturbed the balance of one's mind. Meantime the citizens of Nuremberg, looking remarkably fit, kept saying that the concentration camp photographs, plastered over the town for their education, were Russian propaganda, probably pictures of German prisoners of war. And furthermore since we won the war, we could do anything we wanted, so why not shoot Goering and the other Nazi leaders instead of going on with this boring trial. Besides Jews were coming back and actually claiming their old homes and putting German families into the street and, of course, operating the black market. I thought this place and these people were poisonous; the air could not be breathed. Let the Germans rot in their rotten country; nothing would ever bring me here again.

A row of German women sat outside the white tape which marked off the military zone. They were watching their houses. No roof or window remains and often there is not a wall left either and almost everything in those houses has been blown about thoroughly by high explosives, but there they sat and kept mournful guard on their possessions. When asked why they did this, they started to weep. We have all seen such beastly and fantastic suffering accepted in silence that we do not react very well to weeping. And we certainly do not react well to people weeping over furniture. I remember Oradour in France, where the Germans locked every man, woman and child of the village into the church and set the church afire, and after the people were burned, they burned the village. This is an extremely drastic way to destroy property, and it is only one of many such instances. The Germans themselves have taught all the people of Europe not to waste time weeping over anything easy like furniture.

Martha Gellhorn, 'Des Deutsche Volk', April 1945
from *The Face of War*

Sixteen years passed. West Germany was now the favourite ally of the United States government and always referred to as 'the new Germany'. I became curious about the new Germans, those who were innocent of any involvement in the war, so in November and December 1962 I made a long tour of German universities from Hamburg to Munich, listening to students and sitting in on university seminars. With very few exceptions, the young Germans struck me as dismal. Their education was totally dismal. They were taught to learn by heart, to obey not think, and they had learned their lessons well: democracy and anti-communism, which went together, were good; it was necessary to please the great United States, Germany's powerful sponsor. Everyone must work hard and make money for themselves and the prosperity of the state. They were defensive about their parents (none of whom had been

Nazis) and humourless; dutiful children reciting the approved ideas. They weren't going to threaten the world, but, dear God, you could perish of boredom here. I escape from boredom wherever I find it; I need never come back to this chastened, respectable, supremely dull country.

In my opinion there is no New Germany, only another Germany. Germany needs a revolution which it has not had and shows no signs of having; not a bloody, old-fashioned revolution, with firing squads and prisons, ending in one more dictatorship, but an interior revolution of the mind, the conscience. Obedience is a German sin. Possibly the greatest German sin. Cruelty and bullying are the reverse side of this disciplined obedience. And Germans have been taught obedience systematically, as if it were the highest virtue, for as long as they have been taught anything... Twice their victors have imposed 'democracy' on a people who never fought for it themselves. Democracy may not be the most perfect form of government, but it is the best we have yet found, because it implies that the citizen has private duties of conscience, judgement and action. The citizen who says Yes to the state, no matter what, is a traitor to his country; but citizens have to learn how to say No and why to say No. Germans are still trained as before in their old authoritarian way; the young are not rebels either. At their best they are deeply troubled by their state and suspicious of it; at their worst they are indistinguishable from their ancestors—the interests of the state come first—and they are potentially dangerous sheep.
Martha Gellhorn, 'Is There a New Germany?', February 1964
from *The View from the Ground*

Nothing would have brought me back except that I worried about the European Community whose full flowering I will surely not live to see but I invest my faith in it. Germany, already the richest European country and, now, reunited, the strongest, began to alarm me: not that I imagined Germany again setting out to conquer Europe by force of arms but that I think Germans collectively are unsound. I think they have a gene loose, though I don't know what the gene is. The present generation of university students, forty-five years after the war, must be truly new Germans and I wanted to look at them, for they would be the future leaders of their own country and possibly of Europe. In November and December 1990, just over a year after the Wall came down, I repeated my 1962 method of touring universities.

They were certainly the best lot of Germans I have ever met. Their education had completely changed and now they were cajoled to think for themselves and speak their own ideas. Young women, for the first time in my experience, were naturally and unaffectedly equal, ready with their opinions. The atmosphere among them was friendly and informal, which was new. The students in East Germany were thrilled that they would be able to travel freely at last, but neither they nor the West German students were excited about reunited Germany. No *Deutschland über Alles* mentality except for a few freaks, regarded as freaks, in Heidelberg. It was odd that none of the young West Germans had foreign friends, though there were foreigners in all their universities; nor did the foreign students I spoke to seem charmed by Germans or eager to know them. The young West Germans assured me that only skinheads and such minor riff-raff were racist about the Turks, and that only nasty housewives took against 'the dirty Poles' who arrived in Berlin in rickety cars, made a lot of noise and litter and bought out the supermarkets, taking the food back for sale in Poland. There is no anti-Semitism in Germany, they said, because they did not feel that hating emotion. I missed irony, of which there were only rare sparks, but that's a fact of German life. They're good, decent kids, I concluded with relief; they will make good Europeans.

And then, from this summer onwards, the same kind of young thugs who were Hitler's Brownshirts began to spring from the paving stones and attacked, in the accepted style, the helpless and weak: refugees. Not Turkish men, who are tough and know how to defend themselves. The German government sat on its hands, while parades, rallies, stonings, hostel burnings proceeded in East Germany. I suspect that this revolting variation on the old Nazi themes may have suited the government as an excuse to change Germany's immigration laws. Those laws were formulated as penance for Germany's Nazi past: having uprooted and destroyed millions, this open-arms policy was a form of apology.

The slowness of the German government to take punitive action and the months of delay before mass public protests are a German problem. But where were the students, where were those good kids? Why weren't their universities alive and fierce with outrage rallies, why weren't they converging on Bonn to demand an end to Hitlerian terrorizing of non-Aryans? Hope deferred maketh the heart sick, as we know. I shall now definitely never go back to Germany, due to hope deferred.

A Turk drove my taxi to the Berlin airport. He was the only Turk I met, though they are so much spoken of. He was very big with a rough voice and threatening moustache. He had been driving a taxi in West Berlin for thirteen years. I asked why he didn't take out German citizenship, wouldn't that make life easier? He said, 'I do not wish to be German.'

1993
Dancing in Cambodia

Amitav Ghosh

Amitav Ghosh

One

On May 10, 1906, at two in the afternoon, a French liner called the *Amiral-Kersaint* set off from Saigon carrying a troupe of nearly a hundred classical dancers and musicians from the royal palace at Phnom Penh. The ship was bound for Marseille, where the dancers were to perform at a great colonial exhibition. It would be the first time Cambodian classical dance was performed in Europe.

Also travelling on the *Amiral-Kersaint* was the sixty-six-year-old ruler of Cambodia, King Sisowath, along with his entourage of several dozen princes, courtiers and officials. The King, who had been crowned two years before, had often spoken of his desire to visit France, and for him the voyage was the fulfilment of a lifelong dream.

The *Amiral-Kersaint* docked in Marseilles on the morning of June 11. The port was packed with curious onlookers; the city's trams had been busy since seven, transporting people to the vast, covered quay where the King and his entourage were to be received. The crowd was so large that two brigades of gendarmes and a detachment of mounted police had to be deployed to hold it back.

The crowd had its first, brief glimpse of the dancers when the *Amiral-Kersaint* loomed out of the fog shortly after nine and drew alongside the quay. A number of young women were spotted on the bridge and on the upper decks, flitting between portholes and clutching each other in what appeared to be surprise and astonishment.

Within minutes a gangplank decorated with tricoloured bunting had been thrown up to the ship. Soon the King himself appeared on deck, a good-humoured, smiling man, dressed in a tailcoat, a jewel-encrusted felt hat and a dhoti-like Cambodian *sampot* made of black silk. The King seemed alert, even jaunty, to those privileged to observe him at close range: a man of medium height, he had large, expressive eyes and a heavy-lipped mouth topped by a thin moustache.

King Sisowath walked down the gangplank with three pages following close behind him; one bore a ceremonial gold cigarette case, another a gold lamp with a lighted wick, and a third a gold spittoon in the shape of an open lotus. The King was an instant favourite with the Marseillais crowd. The port resounded with claps and cheers as he was driven away in a ceremonial landau; he was applauded all the way to his specially appointed apartments at the city's Préfecture.

In the meanwhile, within minutes of the King's departure from the port, a section of the crowd had rushed up the gangplank of the *Amiral-Kersaint* to see the dancers at first hand. For weeks now the Marseilles newspapers had been full of tantalizing snippets of information: it was said that the dancers entered the palace as children and spent their lives in seclusion ever afterwards: that their lives revolved entirely around the royal family; that several were the King's mistresses and had even borne him children; that some of them had never stepped out of the palace grounds until this trip to France. European travellers went to great lengths to procure invitations to see these fabulous recluses performing in the palace at Phnom Penh: now here they were, in Marseilles, visiting Europe for the very first time.

The dancers were on the ship's first-class deck; they seemed to be everywhere, running about, hopping, skipping, playing excitedly, feet skimming across the polished wood. The whole deck was a blur of legs, girls' legs, women's legs, 'fine, elegant legs', for all the dancers were dressed in colourful *sampots* which ended shortly below the knee.

The onlookers were taken by surprise. They had expected perhaps a troupe of heavily veiled, voluptuous Salomes; they were not quite prepared for the lithe, athletic women they encountered on the *Amiral-Kersaint*; nor, indeed, was the rest of Europe. An observer wrote later: 'With their hard and close-cropped hair, their figures like those of striplings, their thin, muscular legs like those of young boys, their arms and hands like those of little girls they seem to belong to no definite sex. They have something of the child about them, something of the young warrior of antiquity and something of the woman.'

Sitting regally among the dancers, alternately stern and indulgent, affectionate and severe, was the slight fine-boned figure of the King's eldest daughter, Princess Soumphady. Dressed in a gold-brown *sampot* and a tunic of mauve silk, this redoubtable woman had an electrifying effect on the Marseillais crowd. They drank in every aspect of her appearance: her betel-stained teeth, her chestful of medals, her gold-embroidered shoes, her diamond brooches and her black silk stockings. Her manner, remarked one journalist, was at once haughty and childlike, her gaze direct and good-natured; she was amused by everything and nothing; she crossed her legs and clasped her shins just like a man: indeed, except for her dress she was very much like one man in particular—the romantic and whimsical Duke of Reichstadt, *l'Aiglon*, Napoleon's tubercular son.

Suddenly to the crowd's delight, the Princess's composure dissolved. A group of local women appeared on deck, accompanied by a ten-year-old boy, and along with all the other dancers, the Princess rushed over, admiring their clothes and exclaiming over the little boy.

The journalists were quick to seize this opportunity. 'Do you like French women?' they asked the Princess.

'Oh! Pretty, so pretty…' she replied.

'And their clothes, their hats?'

'Just as pretty as they are themselves.'

'Would Your Highness like to wear clothes like those?'

'No!' the Princess said after a moment's reflection. 'No! I am not used to them and perhaps would not know how to wear them. But they are still pretty…oh! Yes…'

And with that she sank into what seemed to be an attitude of sombre and melancholy longing.

Two

The only person I ever met who knew both Princess Soumphady and King Sisowath was a dancer named Chea Samy. She was said to be one of Cambodia's greatest dancers, a national treasure. She was also Pol Pot's sister-in-law.

She was first pointed out to me at the School of Fine Arts in Phnom Penh—a rambling complex of buildings not far from the Wat Phnom where the United Nation's 20,000-strong peacekeeping force has its headquarters. It was January, only four months before country-wide elections were to be held under the auspices of Untac, as the UN's Transitional Authority in

Cambodia is universally known. Phnom Penh had temporarily become one of the most cosmopolitan towns in the world, its streets a traffic nightmare, with Untac's white Landcruisers cutting through shoals of careering scooters, mopeds and *cyclopousses*, like whales cruising through drifting plankton.

The School of Fine Arts was hidden from this multinational traffic by piles of uncleared refuse and a string of shacks and shanties. Its walled compound was oddly self-contained and its cavernous halls and half-finished classrooms were filled with the self-sustaining, honeycomb bustle of a huge television studio.

I had only recently arrived in Phnom Penh when I first met Chea Samy. She was sitting on a bench in the school's vast training hall: a small woman with the kind of poise that goes with the confidence of great beauty. She was dressed in an ankle-length skirt, and her grey hair was cut short. She was presiding over a class of about forty boys and girls, watching them go through their exercises, her gentle, rounded face tense with concentration. Occasionally she would spring off the bench and bend back a dancer's arm or push in a waist, working as a sculptor does, by touch, moulding their limbs like clay.

At the time I had no idea whether Chea Samy had known Princess Soumphady or not. I had become curious about the Princess and her father, King Sisowath, after learning of their journey to Europe in 1906, and I wanted to know more about them.

Chea Samy's eyes widened when I asked her about Princess Soumphady at the end of her class. She looked from me to the student who was interpreting for us as though she couldn't quite believe she had heard the name right. I reassured her: yes, I really did mean Princess Soumphady, Princess Sisowath Soumphady.

She smiled in the indulgent, misty way in which people recall a favourite aunt. Yes, of course she had known Princess Soumphady, she said. As a little girl, when she first went into the palace to learn dance, it was Princess Soumphady who had been in charge of the dancers: for a while the Princess had brought her up...

The second time I met Chea Samy was at her house. She lives a few miles from Pochentong airport, on Phnom Penh's rapidly expanding frontier, in an area that is largely farm land, with a few houses strung along a dirt road. The friend whom I had persuaded to come along with me to translate took an immediate dislike to the place. It was already late afternoon, and she did not relish the thought of driving back through those roads in the dark.

My friend, Molyka, was a mid-level civil servant, a poised attractive woman in her early thirties, painfully soft-spoken, in the Khmer way. She had spent a short while studying in Australia on a government scholarship, and spoke English with a better feeling for nuance and idiom than any of the professional interpreters I had met. If I was to visit Chea Samy, I had decided, it would be with her. But Molyka proved hard to persuade: she had become frightened of venturing out of the centre of the city.

Not long ago she had been out driving with a friend of hers, the wife of an Untac official, when her car was stopped at a busy roundabout by a couple of soldiers. They were wearing the uniform of the 'State of Cambodia', the faction that currently governs most of the country. 'I work for the government too,' she told them, 'in an important ministry.' They ignored her; they wanted money. She didn't have much, only a couple of thousand riels. They asked for cigarettes; she didn't have any. They told her to get out of the car and accompany them into a building. They were about to take her away when her friend interceded. They let her go eventually: they left UN people alone on the whole. But as she drove away they had shouted after her: 'We're going to be looking out for you: you won't always have an Untac in the car.'

Molyka was scared, and she had reason to be. The government's underpaid (often unpaid) soldiers and policemen were increasingly given to banditry and bouts of inexplicable violence. Not long before, I had gone to visit a hospital in an area where there were frequent hostilities between State troops and the Khmer Rouge. I had expected that the patients in the casualty ward would be principally victims of mines and Khmer Rouge shellfire. Instead I found a group of half a dozen women, some with children, lying on grimy mats, their faces and bodies pitted and torn with black shrapnel wounds. They had been travelling in a pickup truck to sell vegetables at a nearby market when they were stopped by a couple of State soldiers. The soldiers asked for money; the women handed out some but the soldiers wanted more. The women had no more to give and told them so. The soldiers let the truck pass but stopped it again that evening, on its way back. They didn't ask for anything this time; they simply detonated a fragmentation mine.

A couple of weeks after that visit I was travelling in a taxi with four Cambodians along a dusty, potholed road in a sparsely inhabited region in the north-west of the country. I had dozed off in the front seat when I was woken by the rattle of gunfire. I looked up and saw a State soldier standing in the middle of the dirt road, directly ahead. He was in his teens, like most uniformed Cambodians; he was wearing round, wire-rimmed sunglasses and his pelvis was thrust out, MTV-style. But instead of a guitar he had an AK-47 in his hands and he was spraying the ground in front of us with bullets, creating a delicate tracery of dust.

The taxi jolted to a halt; the driver thrust an arm out of the window and waved his wallet. The soldier did not seem to notice; he was grinning and swaying, probably drunk. When I sat up in the front seat, the barrel of his gun rose slowly until it was pointing directly at my forehead. Looking into the unblinking eye of that AK-47, two slogans unaccountably flashed through my mind; they were scrawled all over the walls of Calcutta when I was the same age as that soldier. One was 'Power comes from the barrel of a gun' and the other 'You can't make an omelette without breaking eggs'. It turned out he only had the first in mind.

Molyka had heard stories like these, but living in Phnom Penh, working as a civil servant, she had been relatively sheltered until that day when her car was stopped. The incident frightened her in ways she couldn't quite articulate; it reawakened a host of long-dormant fears. Molyka was only thirteen in 1975, when the Khmer Rouge took Phnom Penh. She was evacuated with her whole extended family, fourteen people in all, to a labour camp in the province of Kompong Thom. A few months later she was separated from the others and sent to work in a fishing village on Cambodia's immense freshwater lake, the Tonlé Sap. For the next three years she worked as a servant and nursemaid for a family of fisherfolk.

She only saw her parents once in that time. One day she was sent to a village near Kompong Thom with a group of girls. While sitting by the roadside she happened to look up from her basket of fish and saw her mother walking towards her. Her first instinct was to turn away; every detail matched those of her most frequently recurring dream: the parched countryside, the ragged palms, her mother coming out of the red dust of the road, walking straight towards her...

She didn't see her mother again until 1979, when she came back to Phnom Penh after the Vietnamese invasion. She managed to locate her as well as two of her brothers after months of searching. Of the fourteen people who had walked out of her house three and a half years before, ten were dead, including her father, two brothers and a sister. Her mother had become an abject, terrified creature after her father was called away into the fields one night, never to return. One of her brothers was too young to work; the other had willed himself into a state of guilt-stricken paralysis after revealing their father's identity to the Khmer Rouge in a moment of inattention—he now held himself responsible for his father's death.

Their family was from the social group that was hardest hit by the revolution: the urban middle classes. City people by definition, they were herded into rural work camps; the institutions and forms of knowledge that sustained them were destroyed—the judicial system was dismantled, the practice of formal medicine was discontinued; schools and colleges were shut down; banks and credit were done away with; indeed the very institution of money was abolished. Cambodia's was not a civil war in the same sense as Somalia's or the former Yugoslavia's, fought over the fetishism of small differences: it was a war on history itself, an experiment in the reinvention of society. No regime in history had ever before made so systematic and sustained an attack on the middle class. Yet, if the experiment was proof of anything at all, it was ultimately of the indestructibility of the middle class, of its extraordinary tenacity and resilience; its capacity to preserve its forms of knowledge and expression through the most extreme kinds of adversity.

Molyka was only seventeen then but she was the one who had to cope because no one else in the family could. She took a job in the army and put herself and her brothers through school and college; later she acquired a house and a car; she adopted a child and—like so many people in Phnom Penh—she took in and supported about half a dozen complete strangers. In one way or another she was responsible for supporting a dozen lives.

Yet now Molyka, who at the age of thirty-one had already lived through several lifetimes, was afraid of driving into the outskirts of the city. Over the last year the edges of the life she had put together were beginning to look frayed. Paradoxically, at precisely the moment when the world had ordained peace and democracy for Cambodia, uncertainty had reached its peak within the country. Nobody knew who would come to power after the UN-sponsored elections, or what would happen when they did. Her colleagues had all become desperate to make some provision for the future—by buying, stealing, selling whatever was at hand. Those two soldiers who had stopped her car were no exception. Everyone she knew was a little like that now—ministers, bureaucrats, policemen: they were all people who saw themselves faced with yet another beginning.

Now Molyka was driving out to meet Pol Pot's brother and sister-in-law: relatives of a man whose name was indelibly associated with the deaths of her own father and nine other members of her family. She had gasped in disbelief when I first asked her to accompany me: to her, as to most people in Cambodia, the name 'Pol Pot' was an abstraction; it referred to a time, an organization, a form of terror—it was almost impossible to associate it with a mere human being, one that had brothers, relatives, sisters-in-law. But she was curious too, and in the end, overcoming her fear of the neighbourhood, she drove me out in her own car, into the newly colonized farmland near Pochentong airport.

The house, when we found it, proved to be a comfortable

wooden structure, built in the traditional Khmer style, with its details picked out in bright blue. Like all such houses it was supported on stilts, and as we walked in, a figure detached itself from the shadows beneath the house and came towards us: a tall vigorous-looking man dressed in a sarong. He had a broad, pleasant face and short, spiky grey hair. The resemblance to Pol Pot was startling.

I glanced at Molyka: she bowed, joining her hands, as he welcomed us in, and they exchanged a few friendly words of greeting. His wife was waiting upstairs, he said, and led us up a wooden staircase to a large, airy room with a few photographs on the bare walls: portraits of relatives and ancestors, of the kind that hang in every Khmer house. Chea Samy was sitting on a couch at the far end of the room: she waved us in and her husband took his leave of us, smiling, hands folded.

'I wanted to attack him when I first saw him,' Molyka told me later. 'But then I thought—it's not his fault. What has he ever done to me?'

Three

Chea Samy was taken into the palace in Phnom Penh in 1925, as a child of six, to begin her training in classical dance. She was chosen after an audition in which thousands of children participated. Her parents were delighted: dance was one of the few means by which a commoner could gain entry into the palace in those days, and to have a child accepted often meant preferment for the whole family.

King Sisowath was in his eighties when she went into the palace. He had spent most of his life waiting in the wings, wearing the pinched footwear of a Crown Prince while his half-brother Norodom ruled centre stage. The two princes held dramatically different political views: Norodom was bitterly opposed to the French, while Sisowath was a passionate Francophile. It was because of French support that Sisowath was eventually able to succeed to the throne, in preference to his half-brother's innumerable sons.

Something of an eccentric all his life, King Sisowath kept no fixed hours and spent a good deal of his time smoking opium with his sons and advisers. During his visit to France the authorities even improvised a small opium den in his apartments at the Préfecture in Marseilles. '*Voilà!*' cried the newspapers, 'An opium den in the Préfecture! There's no justice left!' But it was the French who kept the King supplied with opium in Cambodia, and they could hardly do otherwise when he was a state guest in France.

By the time Chea Samy entered the palace in 1925 King Sisowath's behaviour had become erratic in the extreme. He would wander nearly naked around the grounds of the palace wearing nothing but a *kramar*, a length of chequered cloth knotted loosely around his waist. It was Princess Soumphady who was the central figure in the lives of the children of the dance troupe: she was a surrogate mother who tempered the rigours of their training with a good deal of kindly indulgence, making sure they were well fed and clothed.

On King Sisowath's death in 1927, his son Monivong succeeded to the throne, and soon the regime in the palace underwent a change. The new King's favourite mistress was a talented dancer called Luk Khun Meak, and she now gradually took over Princess Soumphady's role as 'the lady in charge of the women'. Luk Khun Meak made use of her influence to introduce several members of her family into the palace. Among them were a few relatives from a small village in the province of Kompong Thom. One—later to become Chea Samy's husband—was given a job as a clerk at the palace. He in turn brought two of his brothers with him, so they could go to school in Phnom Penh. The youngest of the two was a boy of six called Saloth Sar—it was he who was later to take the *nom de guerre*, Pol Pot.

Chea Samy made a respectful gesture at a picture on the wall behind her, and I looked up to find myself transfixed by Luk Khun Meak's stern, frowning gaze. 'She was killed by Pol Pot,' said Chea Samy, using the generic phrase with which Cambodians refer to the deaths of that time. The distinguished old dancer, mistress of King Monivong, died of starvation after the revolution. One of her daughters was apprehended by the Khmer Rouge while trying to buy rice with a little bit of gold.

Her breasts were sliced off, and she was left to bleed to death.

'What was Pol Pot like as a boy?' I asked, inevitably.

Chea Samy hesitated for a moment: it was easy to see that she had often been asked the question before and had thought about it at some length. 'He was a very good boy,' she said at last, emphatically. 'In all the years he lived with me, he never gave me any trouble at all.'

Then, with a despairing gesture, she said, 'I have been married to his brother for fifty years now, and I can tell you that my husband is a good man, a kind man. He doesn't drink, doesn't smoke, has never made trouble between friends, never hit his nephews, never made difficulties for his children...'

She gave up; her hands flipped over in a flutter of bewilderment and fell limp into her lap.

The young Saloth Sar's palace connection ensured places for him at some of the country's better-known schools. In 1949 he was awarded a scholarship to study electronics in Paris. When he returned to Cambodia, three years later, he began working in secret for the Indochina Communist Party. Neither Chea Samy nor her husband saw much of him, and he told them very little of what he was doing. Then in 1963 he disappeared; they learned later that he had fled into the jungle along with several well-known leftists and Communists. That was the last they heard of Saloth Sar.

In 1975 when the Khmer Rouge seized power, Chea Samy and her husband were evacuated like everyone else. They were sent off to a village of 'old people', long-time Khmer Rouge sympathizers and, along with all the other 'new people', were made to work in the rice fields. For the next couple of years there was a complete news blackout, and they knew nothing of what had happened: it was a part of the Khmer Rouge's mechanics of terror to deprive the population of knowledge. They first began to hear the words 'Pol Pot' in 1978 when the regime tried to create a personality cult around its leader in an attempt to stave off imminent collapse.

Chea Samy was working in a communal kitchen at the time, cooking and washing dishes. Late that year some Party workers stuck a poster on the walls of the kitchen: they said it was a picture of their leader, Pol Pot. She knew who it was the moment she set eyes on the picture.

That was how she discovered that the leader of Angkar, the terrifying, inscrutable 'Organization' that ruled over their lives, was none other than little Saloth Sar.

Four

A few months later, in January 1979, the Vietnamese 'broke' Cambodia—as the Khmer phrase has it—and the regime collapsed. Shortly afterwards Chea Samy and her husband, like all the other evacuees, began to drift out of the villages in which they had been imprisoned. Carrying nothing but a few cupfuls of dry rice, barefoot, half-starved and dressed in rags, they began to find their way back towards the places they had once known, where they had once had friends and relatives.

Walking down the dusty country roads, encountering others like themselves, the bands of 'new people' slowly began to rediscover the exhilaration of speech. For more than three years now they had not been able to speak freely to anyone with confidence, not even their own children. Many had reinvented their lives in order to protect themselves from the obsessive biographical curiosity of Angkar's cadres. Now, talking on the roads, they slowly began to shed their assumed personae; they began to mine their memories for information about the people they had met and heard of over the last few years, the names of the living and the dead.

It was the strangest of times.

The American Quaker, Eva Mysliwiec, arrived in the country in 1980; she was one of the first foreign relief workers to come to Cambodia and is now a legend in Phnom Penh. Some of her most vivid memories of that period are of the volcanic outbursts of speech that erupted everywhere at unexpected moments. Friends and acquaintances would suddenly begin to describe what they had lived through and seen, what had happened to them and their families and how they had managed to survive. Often people would wake up looking drained and haggard; they would see things at night, in their dreams, all those things they had tried to put out of their minds when they were happening because they would have gone mad if they'd stopped to think about them—a brother called away in the dark; an infant battered against a tree; children starving to death. When you saw them in the morning and asked what had happened during the night, they would make a circular gesture, as though the past had been unfolding before them like a turning reel, and they would say, simply, 'Camera.'

Eventually, after weeks of wandering, Chea Samy and her husband reached the western outskirts of Phnom Penh. There, one day, entirely by accident, she ran into a girl who had studied dance with her before the revolution. The girl cried, 'Teacher! Where have you been? They've been looking for you everywhere.'

There was no real administration in those days. Many of the resistance leaders who had come back to Cambodia with the Vietnamese had never held administrative positions before: for the most part they were breakaway members of the Khmer Rouge who had been opposed to the policies of Pol Pot and his group. They had to learn on the job when they returned, and for a long time there was nothing like a real government in Cambodia. The country was like a shattered slate: before you could think of drawing lines on it, you had to find the pieces and fit them together

But already the fledgling Ministry of Culture had launched an effort to locate the classical dancers and teachers who had survived. Its officials were overjoyed to find Chea Samy. They quickly arranged for her to travel through the country to look for other teachers and for young people with talent and potential.

'It was very difficult,' said Chea Samy. 'I did not know where to go, where to start. Most of the teachers had been killed or maimed, and the others were in no state to begin teaching again. Anyway there was no one to teach: so many of the children were orphans, half-starved. They had no idea of dance; they had never seen Khmer dance. It seemed impossible; there was no place to begin.'

Her voice was quiet and matter of fact but there was a quality of muted exhilaration in it too. I recognized that note at once for I had heard it before: in Molyka's voice, for example, when she spoke of the first years after the 'Pol-Pot-time', when slowly, patiently, she had picked through the rubble around her, building a life for herself and her family. I was to hear it again and again in Cambodia—most often in the voices of women. They had lived through an experience very nearly unique in human history: they had found themselves adrift in the ruins of a society which had collapsed into a formless heap, its scaffolding systematically dismantled, picked apart with the tools of a murderously rational form of social science. At a time when there was widespread fear and uncertainty about the intentions of the Vietnamese, they had had to start from the beginning, literally, like ragpickers, piecing their families, their homes, their lives together from the little that was left.

Like everyone around her, Chea Samy too had started all over again—at the age of sixty, with her health shattered by the years of famine and hard labour. Working with quiet, dogged persistence, she and a handful of other dancers and musicians slowly brought together a ragged, half-starved bunch of orphans and castaways, and with the discipline of their long, rigorous years of training they began to resurrect the art that Princess Soumphady and Luk Khun Meak had passed on to them in that long-ago world when King Sisowath reigned. Out of the ruins around them they began to forge the means of denying Pol Pot his victory.

Five

Everywhere he went on his tour of France, King Sisowath was accompanied by his Palace Minister, an official who bore the simple name of Thiounn (pronounced *Choun*). For all his Francophilia, King Sisowath spoke no French, and it was Minister Thiounn who served as his interpreter.

Minister Thiounn was widely acknowledged to be one of the most remarkable men in Cambodia: his career was without precedent in the aristocratic, rigidly hierarchical world of Cambodian officialdom. Starting as an interpreter for the French at the age of nineteen, he had overcome the twin disadvantages of modest birth and a mixed Khmer-Vietnamese ancestry to become the most powerful official at the court of

Phnom Penh: the Minister, simultaneously, of Finance, Fine Arts and Palace Affairs.

This spectacular rise owed a great deal to the French, to whom he had been of considerable assistance in their decades-long struggle with Cambodia's ruling family. His role had earned him the bitter contempt of certain members of the royal family, and a famous prince had even denounced the 'boy-interpreter' as a French collaborator. But with French dominance in Cambodia already assured, there was little that any Cambodian prince could do to check the growing influence of Minister Thiounn. Norodom Sihanouk, King Sisowath's great-grandson, spent several of his early years on the throne smarting under Minister Thiounn's tutelage: he was to describe him later as a 'veritable little king…as powerful as the French *Résidents-Supérieurs* of the period.'

The trip to France was to become something of a personal triumph for Minister Thiounn, earning him compliments from a number of French ministers and politicians. But it also served a more practical function, for travelling on the *Amiral-Kersaint*, along with the dancers and the rest of the royal entourage, was the Minister's son, Thiounn Hol. In the course of his stay in France the Minister succeeded in entering him as a student in the Ecole Coloniale. He was the only Cambodian commoner to be accepted: the three other Cambodians who were admitted at the same time were all members of the royal family.

Not unpredictably the Minister's son proved to be a far better student than the princelings and went on to become the first Cambodian to earn university qualifications in France. Later, the Minister's grandsons, scions of what was by then the second most powerful family in Cambodia, were to make the same journey out to France.

One of those grandsons, Thiounn Mumm, acquired a doctorate in applied science and became the first Cambodian to graduate from the exalted Ecole Polytechnique. In the process he also became a central figure within the small circle of Cambodians in France: the story goes that he made a point of befriending every student from his country and even went to the airport to receive newcomers.

Thiounn Mumm was, in other words, part mentor, part older brother and part leader: a figure immediately recognizable to anyone who has ever inhabited the turbulent limbo of the Asian or African student in Europe—that curious circumstance of social dislocation and emotional turmoil that for more than a century now has provided the site for some of the globe's most explosive political encounters. And Thiounn Mumm was no ordinary student mentor for he was also a member of a political dynasty—the Cambodian equivalent of the Nehrus or the Bhuttos.

Among Thiounn Mumm's many protégés was the young Pol Pot, then still known as Saloth Sar. It is generally believed that it was Thiounn Mumm who was responsible for his induction into the French Communist Party in 1952. Those Parisian loyalties have proved unshakeable: Thiounn Mumm and two of his brothers have been members of Pol Pot's innermost clique ever since.

That this ultra-radical clique should be so intimately linked with the palace and with colonial officialdom is not particularly a matter of surprise in Cambodia. 'Revolutions and coups d'état always start in the courtyards of the palace,' a well-known political figure in Phnom Penh told me. 'It's the people within who realize that the King is ordinary, while everyone else takes him for a god.'

In this case, the proximity of the Thiounns and Pol Pot to the elitist racially exclusive culture of the court may have had a formative influence on some aspects of their political vision: it may even have been responsible, as the historian Ben Kiernan has suggested, for the powerful strain of 'national and racial grandiosity' in the ideology of their clique. That strain has eventually proved dominant: the Khmer Rouge's programme now consists largely of an undisguisedly racist nationalism, whose principal targets, for the time being, are Vietnam and Cambodia's own Vietnamese minority.

A recent defector, describing his political training with the Khmer Rouge, told UN officials that: 'As far as the Vietnamese are concerned, whenever we meet them we must kill them, whether they are militaries or civilians, because they are not ordinary civilians but soldiers disguised as civilians. We must kill them whether they are men, women or children, there is no distinction, they are enemies. Children are not militaries but if they are born or grow up in Cambodia, when they will be adult, they will consider Cambodian land as theirs. So we make no distinction. As to women, they give birth to Vietnamese children.'

Shortly before the elections, in a sudden enlargement of its racist vocabulary, the Khmer Rouge also began to incite violence against 'white-skinned, point-nosed Untac soldiers'.

Six

The more I learned of Pol Pot's journey to France, and of the other journeys that had preceded it, the more curious I became about his origins. One day, late in January, I decided to go looking for his ancestral village in the province of Kompong Thom.

Kompong Thom has great military importance, for it straddles the vital middle section of Cambodia, the strategic heart of the country. The town of Kompong Thom is very small: a string of houses that grows suddenly into a bullet-riddled marketplace, a school, a hospital, a few roads that extend all of a hundred yards, a bridge across the Sen river, a tall, freshly painted Wat, a few outcrops of blue-signposted Untac-land and then, the countryside again, flat and dusty, clumps of palms leaning raggedly over the earth, fading into the horizon in a dull grey-green patina, like mould upon a copper tray.

Two of the country's most important roadways intersect to the north of the little town. One leads directly to Thailand and the Khmer Rouge controls large chunks of territory on either side of it. This road is one of the most hotly contested in Cambodia and there are daily exchanges of shells and gunfire between Khmer Rouge guerrillas and the State of Cambodia troops who are posted along it.

The point where the two roads meet is guarded by an old army encampment, now controlled by the State. Its perimeter is heavily mined: the mines are reputed to have been laid by the State itself—partly to keep the Khmer Rouge out, but also to keep its own none-too-willing soldiers in.

Here, in this strategic hub, this centre of centres, looking for

Pol Pot's ancestral home, inevitably I came across someone from mine. He was a Bangladeshi sergeant, a large, friendly man with a bushy moustache: we had an ancestral district in common, in Bangladesh, and the unexpectedness of this discovery—at the edge of a Cambodian minefield—linked us immediately in a ridiculously intimate kind of bonhomie.

The sergeant and his colleagues were teaching a group of Cambodian soldiers professional de-mining techniques. They were themselves trained sappers and engineers, but as it happened none of them had ever seen or worked in a minefield that had been laid with intent to kill, so to speak. For their Cambodian charges, on the other hand, mines were a hazard of everyday life, like snakes or spiders.

This irony was not lost on the Bangladeshi sergeant. 'They think nothing of laying mines,' he said, in trenchant Bengali. 'They scatter them about like popped rice. Often they mine their own doorstep before going to bed, to keep thieves out. They mine their cars, their television sets, even their vegetable patches. They don't care who gets killed; life really has no value here.'

He shook his head in perplexity, looking at his young Cambodian charges: they were working in teams of two on the minefield—an expanse of scrub and grass that had been divided into narrow strips with tape. The teams were inching along their strips, one man scanning the ground ahead with a mine detector, the other lying flat, armed with a probe and trowel, ready to dig for mines. By this slow, painstaking method, the team had cleared a couple of acres in a month. This was considered good progress, and the sergeant had reason to be pleased with the job he and his unit had done.

In the course of their work, the sergeant and his colleagues had become friends with several Cambodian members of their team. But the better they got to know them and the better they liked them, the more feckless they seemed and the more hopeless the country's situation. This despite the fact that Cambodians in general have a standard of living that would be considered enviable by most people in Bangladesh or India; despite the fact that Kompong Thom—for all that it has been on the front line for decades—is better-ordered than any provincial town in the subcontinent; and despite the fact that the sergeant was himself from a country that had suffered the ravages of a bloody civil war in the early Seventies.

'They're working hard here because they're getting paid in dollars,' the sergeant said. 'For them it's all dollars, dollars, dollars. Sometimes, at the end of the day, we have to hand out a couple of dollars from our own pockets to get them to finish the day's work.'

He laughed. 'It's their own country, and we have to pay them to make it safe. What I wonder is: what will they do when we're gone?'

I told him what a long-time foreign resident of Phnom Penh had said to me: that Cambodia was actually only fifteen years old: that it had managed remarkably well considering it had been built up almost from scratch after the fall of the Pol Pot regime in 1979; and that this had been achieved in a situation of near-complete international isolation. Europe and Japan had received massive amounts of aid after the Second World War, but Cambodia, which had been subjected to one of the heaviest bombings in the history of war, had got virtually nothing. Yet Cambodians had made do with what they had.

But the sergeant was looking for large-scale proofs of progress—roads, a functioning postal system, Projects, Schemes, Plans—and their lack rendered meaningless those tiny, cumulative efforts by which individuals and families reclaim their lives—a shutter repaired, a class taught, a palm tree tended—which are no longer noticeable once they are done since they sink into the order of normalcy, where they belong, and cease to be acts of affirmation and hope. He was the smallest of cogs in the vast machinery of the UN, but, no less than the international bureaucrats and experts in Phnom Penh, his vision of the country was organized around his part in saving it from itself.

'What Cambodians are good at is destruction,' he said. 'They know nothing about building—about putting things up and carrying on.'

He waved good-naturedly at the Cambodians, and they waved back, bobbing their heads, smiling and bowing. Both sides were working hard at their jobs, the expert and the amateur, the feckless and the responsible: doughty rescuer and hapless rescued were both taking their jobs equally seriously.

Seven

I got blank stares when I asked where Pol Pot's village was. Pol Pot had villages on either side of Route 12, people said, dozens of them, nobody could get to them, they were in the forest surrounded by minefields. I might as well have asked where the State of Cambodia was. Nor did it help to ask about 'Saloth Sar': nobody seemed ever to have heard of that name.

One of the people I asked, a young Cambodian called Sros, offered to help, although he was just as puzzled by the question as everybody else. He worked for a relief agency and had spent a lot of time in Kompong Thom. He had never heard anybody mention Pol Pot's village and would have been sceptical if he had. But I persuaded him that Pol Pot was really called Saloth Sar and had been born near the town: I'd forgotten the name of the village but I had seen it mentioned in books and knew it was close by.

He was intrigued. He borrowed a scooter, and we drove down the main street in Kompong Thom, stopping passers-by and asking respectfully: 'Bong, do you know where Pol Pot's village is?'

They looked at us in disbelief and hurried away: either they didn't know or they weren't saying. Then Sros stopped to ask a local district official, a bowed, earnest-looking man with a twitch that ran all the way down the right side of his face. The moment I saw him, I was sure he would know. He did. He lowered his voice and whispered quickly into Sros's ear: the village was called Sbauv, and to get to it we had to go past the hospital and follow the dirt road along the River Sen. He stopped to look over his shoulder and pointed down the road.

There was perhaps an hour of sunlight left, and it wasn't safe to be out after dark. But Sros was undeterred; the thought that we were near Pol Pot's birthplace had a galvanic effect on him. He was determined to get there as soon as possible.

Sros had spent almost his entire adult life behind barbed wire, one and a half miles of it, in a refugee camp on the Thai border.

He had entered it at the age of thirteen and had come to manhood circling around and around the perimeter, month after month, year after year, waiting to see who got out, who got a visa, who went mad, who got raped, who got shot by the Thai guards. He was twenty-five now, diminutive but wiry, very slight of build. He had converted to Christianity at the camp, and there was an earnestness behind his ready smile and easy-going manners that hinted at a deeply felt piety.

Sros was too young to recall much of the 'Pol-Pot-time', but he remembered vividly his journey to the Thai border with his parents. They left in 1982, three years after the Vietnamese invasion. Things were hard where they were, and they'd heard from Western radio broadcasts that there were camps on the border where they would be looked after and fed.

Things hadn't turned out quite as they had imagined: they ended up in a camp run by a conservative Cambodian political faction, a kind of living hell. But they bribed a 'guide' to get them across to a UN-run camp, Khao I Dang, where the conditions were better. Sros went to school and learned English and after years of waiting, fruitlessly, for a visa to the West, he took the plunge and crossed over into Cambodia. That was a year ago. With his education and his knowledge of English he had found a job without difficulty, but he was still keeping his name on the rosters of the UN High Commission for Refugees.

'My father says to me, there will be peace in your lifetime and you will be happy,' he told me. 'My grandfather used to tell my father the same thing, and now I say the same thing to my nephews and nieces. It's always the same.'

We left Kompong Thom behind almost before we knew it. A dirt road snaked away from the edge of the city, shaded by trees and clumps of bamboo. The road was an estuary of deep red dust: the wheels of the ox carts that came rumbling towards us churned up crimson waves that billowed outwards and up into the sky. The dust hung above the road far into the distance, like spray above a rocky coastline, glowing red in the sunset.

Flanking the road on one side were shanties and small dwellings, the poorest I had yet seen in Cambodia: some of them no more than frames stuck into the ground and covered with plaited palm leaves. Even the larger houses seemed little more than shanties on stilts. On the other side of the road the ground dropped away sharply to the River Sen: a shrunken stream now, in the dry season, flowing sluggishly along at the bottom of its steep-sided channel.

It was impossible to tell where one village ended and another began. We stopped to ask a couple of times, the last time at a stall where a woman was selling cigarettes and fruit. She pointed over her shoulder: one of Pol Pot's brothers lived in the house behind the stall, she said, and another in a palm-thatch shanty in the adjacent yard.

We drove into the yard and looked up at the house: it was large compared to those around it, a typical wooden Khmer house on stilts, with chickens roosting underneath and clothes drying between the pillars. It had clearly seen much better days and was badly in need of repairs.

The decaying house and the dilapidated, palm-thatched shanty in the yard took me by surprise. I remembered having read that Pol Pot's father was a well-to-do farmer and had expected something less humble. Sros was even more surprised: perhaps he had assumed that the relatives of politicians always got rich, one way or another. There was an augury of something unfamiliar here—a man of power who had done nothing to help his own kin. It was a reminder that we were confronting a phenomenon that was completely at odds with quotidian expectation.

Then an elderly woman with close-cropped white hair appeared on the veranda of the house. Sros said a few words to her and she immediately invited us up. Greeting us with folded hands, she asked us to seat ourselves on a mat while she went inside to find her husband. Like many Khmer dwellings the house was sparsely furnished, the walls bare except for a few religious pictures and images of the Buddha.

The woman returned followed by a tall gaunt man dressed in a faded sarong. He did not look as much like Pol Pot as the brother I had met briefly in Phnom Penh, but the resemblance was still unmistakable.

His name was Loth Sieri, he said, seating himself beside us, and he was the second oldest of the brothers. Saloth Sar had gone away to Phnom Penh while he was still quite young, and after that they had not seen very much of him. He had gone from school to college in Phnom Penh, and then finally to Paris. He smiled ruefully. 'It was the knowledge he got in Paris that made him what he is,' he said.

He had visited them a few times after returning to Cambodia but then he had disappeared and they had never seen him again: it was more than twenty years now since he, Loth Sieri, had set eyes on him. They had been treated no differently from anyone else during the Pol-Pot-time; they had not had the remotest idea that 'Pol Pot' was their brother Sar, born in their house. They only found out afterwards.

Was Saloth Sar born in this very house? I asked. Yes, they said, in the room beside us, right next to the veranda.

When he came back from France, I asked, had he ever talked about his life in Paris—what he'd done, who his friends were, what the city was like?

At that moment, with cows lowing in the gathering darkness, the journey to Paris from that village on the Sen River seemed an extraordinary odyssey. I found myself very curious to know how he and his brothers had imagined Paris, and their own brother in it. But no. The old man shook his head: Saloth Sar had never talked about France after he came back. Maybe he had shown them some pictures—Loth Sieri couldn't recall.

I remembered, from David Chandler's biography, that Pol Pot was very well read as a young man, and knew large tracts of Rimbaud and Verlaine by heart. But I was not surprised to discover that he had never allowed his family the privilege of imagining.

Just before getting up, I asked if he remembered his relative, the dancer Luk Khun Meak, who had first introduced his family into the royal palace. He nodded and I asked, 'Did you ever see her dance?'

He smiled and shook his head; no, he had never seen any 'royal' dancing, except in pictures.

It was almost dark now; somewhere in the north, near the minefield, there was the sound of gunfire. We got up to go, and the whole family walked down with us. After I had said goodbye and was about to climb on to the scooter, Sros whispered in my ear that it might be a good idea to give the old man some money. I had not thought of it; I took some money out of my pocket and put it in his hands.

He made a gesture of acknowledgement, and as we were about to leave he said a few words to Sros.

'What did he say?' I asked Sros when we were back on the road.

Shouting above the wind, Sros said: 'He asked me: "Do you think there will be peace now?"'

'And what did you tell him?' I said.

'I told him, "I wish I could say yes."'

Eight

On July 10, 1906, one month after their arrival in France, the dancers performed at a reception given by the Minister of Colonies in the Bois du Boulogne in Paris. 'Never has there been a more brilliant Parisian fête,' said *Le Figaro*, 'nor one with such novel charm.' Invitations were much sought after, and on the night of the performance cars and illuminated carriages invaded the park like an 'army of fireflies'.

While the performance was in progress a correspondent spotted the most celebrated Parisian of all in the audience, the bearded Mosaic figure of 'the great Rodin [going] into ecstasies over the little virgins of Phnom Penh, whose immaterial silhouettes he drew with infinite love'.

Rodin, now at the age of sixty-six, France's acknowledged apostle of the arts, fell immediately captive: in Princess Soumphady's young charges he discovered the infancy of Europe. 'These Cambodians have shown us everything that antiquity could have contained,' he wrote soon afterwards. 'It is impossible to think of anyone wearing human nature to such perfection; except them and the Greeks.'

Two days after the performance Rodin presented himself at the dancers' Paris lodgings in the Avenue Malakoff with a sketchbook under his arm. The dancers were packing their belongings in preparation for their return to Marseilles, but

Rodin was admitted to the grounds of the mansion and given leave to do what he pleased. He executed several celebrated sketches that day, including a few of King Sisowath.

By the end of the day the artist was so smitten with the dancers that he accompanied them to the station, bought a ticket and travelled to Marseilles on the same train. He had packed neither clothes nor materials and, according to one account, upon arriving in Marseilles and finding that he was out of paper, he had to buy brown paper bags from a grocery store.

Over the next few days, sketching feverishly in the gardens of the villa where the dancers were now lodged, Rodin seemed to lose thirty years. The effort involved in sketching his favourite models, three restless fourteen-year-olds called Sap, Soun and Yem, appeared to rejuvenate the artist. A French official saw him placing a sheet of white paper on his knee one morning. 'He said to the little Sap: "Put your foot on this," and then drew the outline of her foot with a pencil, saying "Tomorrow you'll have your shoes, but now pose a little more for me!" Sap, having tired of atomizer bottles and cardboard cats, had asked her "papa" for a pair of pumps. Every evening—ardent, happy but exhausted—Rodin would return to his hotel with his hands full of sketches and collect his thoughts.'

Photographs from the time show Rodin seated on a garden bench, sketching under the watchful eyes of the policemen who had been posted at the dancers' villa to ensure their safety. Rodin was oblivious: 'The friezes of Angkor were coming to life before my very eyes. I loved these Cambodian girls so much that I didn't know how to express my gratitude for the royal honour they had shown me in dancing and posing for me. I went to the Nouvelles Galeries to buy a basket of toys for them, and these divine children who dance for the gods hardly knew how to repay me for the happiness I had given them. They even talked about taking me with them.'

On their last day in France, hours before they boarded the ship that was to take them back to Cambodia, the dancers were taken to the celebrated photographer Baudouin. On the way, passing through a muddy alley, Princess Soumphady happened to step on a pat of cow dung. Horrified she raised her arms to the heavens and flung herself, wailing, upon the dust, oblivious of her splendid costume. The rest of the troupe immediately followed suit; within moments the alley was full of prostrate Cambodian dancers, dressed in full performance regalia.

'What an emptiness they left for me!' wrote Rodin. 'When they left I thought they had taken away the beauty of the world. I followed them to Marseilles; I would have followed them as far as Cairo.'

His sentiments were exactly mirrored by King Sisowath. 'I am deeply saddened to be leaving France,' the King said on the eve of his departure, 'in this beautiful country I shall leave behind a piece of my heart.'

Nine

The trip to France evidently cast King Sisowath's mind into the same kind of turmoil, the same tumult that has provoked generations of displaced students—the Gandhis, the Kenyattas, the Chou en Lais, among thousands of their less illustrious countrymen—to reflect upon the unfamiliar, wintry worlds beyond the doors of their rented lodgings.

On September 12, 1906, shortly after their return to Cambodia, the King and his ministers published their reflections in a short but poignant document. Cast in the guise of a Royal Proclamation, it was, in fact, a venture into a kind of travel writing. It began: 'The visits that His Majesty made to the great cities of France, his rapid examination of the institutions of that country, the organization of the different services that are to be found there, astonished him and led him to think of France as a paradise.'

Emulation, they concluded, was 'the only means of turning resolutely to the path of progress'.

Over the brief space of a couple of thousand words the King and his ministers summed up their views on the lessons that France had to offer Cambodia. Most of these had to do with what later came to be called 'development': communications had to be improved, new land cleared for agriculture; peasants had to increase their production, raise more animals, exploit their forests and fisheries more systematically, familiarize themselves with modern machinery and so on. A generation later, Cambodian political luminaries, such as Khieu Samphan, writing their theses in Paris, were to arrive at oddly similar conclusions, although by an entirely different route.

But it was on the subject of the ideal relationship between the state and its people, that the King and his ministers were at their most prescient: it was here, they thought, that Europe's most important lessons lay. 'None should hesitate to sacrifice his life,' they wrote, 'when it is a matter of the divinity of the King or of the country. The obligation to serve the country should be accepted without a murmur by the inhabitants of the kingdom; it is glorious to defend one's country. Are Europeans not constrained by the same obligation, without distinction either of rank or of family?'

Alas for poor King Sisowath, he was soon to learn that travel writing was an expensive indulgence for those who fell on his side of the colonial divide. In 1910 the Colonial Ministry in Paris wrote asking the King to reimburse the French government for certain expenses incurred during his trip to France. As it happened Cambodia's budget had paid for the entire trip, including the dancers' performance at the Bois du Boulogne. In addition, the King, who was ruinously generous by nature, had personally handed out tips and gifts worth several thousands of francs. In return he and his entourage had received a few presents from French officials. Amongst these were a set of uniforms given by the Minister of Colonies and some rose bushes that had been presented to the King personally at the Elysée Palace by none other than the President of the Republic, Armand Fallières. The French government now wanted to reclaim the price of the uniforms and the rose bushes from the Cambodians.

For once, the obsequious Minister Thiounn took the King's side. He wrote back indignantly refusing to pay for gifts that had been accepted in good faith.

The royal voyage to France found its most celebrated memorial in Rodin's sketches. The sketches were received with acclaim when they went on exhibition in 1907. After seeing them, the German poet Rilke wrote to the master to say, 'For me, these sketches were amongst the most profound of revelations.'

The revelation Rilke had in mind was of 'the mystery of Cambodian dance'. But it was probably the sculptor rather than the poet who sensed the real revelation of the encounter: of the power of Cambodia's involvement in the culture and politics of modernism, in all its promise and horror.

Ten

As for King Sisowath, the most significant thing he ever did was to authorize the founding of a high school where Cambodians could be educated on the French pattern. Known initially as the Collège du Protectorat, the school was renamed the Lycée Sisowath some years after the King's death.

The Lycée Sisowath was to become the crucible for Cambodia's remaking. A large number of the students who were radicalized in Paris in the Fifties were graduates of the Lycée. Pol Pot himself was never a student there but he was closely linked with it and several of his nearest associates were Sisowath alumni including his first wife, Khieu Ponnary, and his brother-in-law and long-time deputy, Ieng Sary.

Among the most prominent members of that group was Khieu Samphan, one-time President of Pol Pot's Democratic Kampuchea and now the best known of the Khmer Rouge's spokesmen. Through the Sixties and early Seventies Khieu Samphan was one of the pre-eminent political figures in Cambodia. He was renowned throughout the country as an incorruptible idealist: stories about his refusal to take bribes, even when begged by his impoverished mother, have passed into popular mythology. He was also an important economic thinker and theorist; his doctoral thesis on Cambodia's economy, written at the Sorbonne in the Fifties, is still highly regarded. He vanished in 1967 and lived in the jungle through the long years of the Khmer Rouge's grim struggle, first against Prince Sihanouk, then against the rightist regime of General Lon Nol, when American planes subjected the countryside to saturation bombing.

Khieu Samphan surfaced again after the 1975 revolution as

President of Pol Pot's Democratic Kampuchea. When the regime was driven out of power by the Vietnamese invasion of 1979, he fled with the rest of the ruling group to a stronghold on the Thai border.

As the Khmer Rouge's chief public spokesman and emissary he played a prominent part in the UN-sponsored peace negotiations from 1988 onwards. Later, in the months before this year's elections, it was he who was the Khmer Rouge's mouthpiece as it reneged on the peace agreements, while launching ever more vituperative attacks on the UN. The Khmer Rouge's manoeuvres did not come as a surprise to anyone who had ever dealt with its leadership: the surprise lay rather in the extent to which Untac was willing to go on appeasing them. Effectively, the Khmer Rouge succeeded in taking advantage of the UN's presence to augment its own military position while sabotaging the peace process.

In 1991 and 1992, when Khieu Samphan was travelling around the world, making headlines, there was perhaps only a single soul in Phnom Penh who followed his activities with an interest that was not wholly political: his forty-nine-year-old younger brother, Khieu Seng Kim.

I met Khieu Seng Kim one morning, standing by the entrance to the school of classical dance. A tall man, with a cast in one eye and untidy grizzled hair, he was immediately friendly, eager both to talk about his family and to speak French. Within minutes of our meeting we were sitting in his small apartment, on opposite sides of a desk, surrounded by neat piles of French textbooks and dog-eared copies of *Paris-Match*.

The brick wall behind Khieu Seng Kim was papered over with pictures of relatives and dead ancestors. The largest was a glossy magazine picture of his brother Khieu Samphan, taken soon after the signing of the peace accords in 1991. He is standing beside the assembled leaders of all the major Cambodian factions: Prince Sihanouk, Son Sann of the centrist Khmer People's National Liberation Front and Hun Sen of the 'State of Cambodia'. In the picture everybody exudes a sense of relief, bonhomie and optimism; everyone is smiling, but no one more than Khieu Samphan.

Khieu Seng Kim was a child in 1950, when his brother, recently graduated from the Lycée Sisowath, left for Paris on a scholarship. By the time he returned with his doctorate from the Sorbonne, eight years later, Khieu Seng Kim was fourteen, and the memory of going to Pochentong airport to receive his older brother stayed fresh in his mind. 'We were very poor then,' he said, 'and we couldn't afford to greet him with garlands and a crown of flowers, like well-off people do. We just embraced and hugged and all of us had tears flowing down our cheeks.'

In those days, in Cambodia, a doctorate from France was a guarantee of a high-level job in the government, a means of ensuring entry into the country's privileged classes. Their mother would accept nothing less for herself and her family. She had struggled against poverty most of her life; her husband, a magistrate, had died early, leaving her five children to bring up on her own. But when, despite her entreaties, her son refused to accept any of the lucrative offers that came his way, once again she had to start selling vegetables to keep the family going. Khieu Seng Kim remembers seeing his adored brother—the brilliant economist with his degree from the Sorbonne—sitting beside his mother, helping her with her roadside stall.

In the meanwhile, Khieu Samphan also taught in a school, founded an influential left-wing journal and gradually rose to political prominence. He even served in Sihanouk's cabinet for a while, and with his success the family's situation eased a little.

And then came the day in 1967 when he melted into the jungle.

Khieu Seng Kim remembers the day well: it was Monday, April 24, 1967. His mother served dinner at seven-thirty and the two of them sat at the dining table and waited for Khieu Samphan to arrive: he always came home at about that time. They stayed there till eleven, without eating, listening for every footstep and every sound; then his mother broke down and began to cry. She cried all night, 'like a child who has lost its mother'.

At first they thought that Khieu Samphan had been arrested. They had good reason to, for Prince Sihanouk had made a speech two days before, denouncing Khieu Samphan and two close friends of his, the brothers Hu Nim and Hou Yuon. But no arrest was announced, and nor was there any other news the next day.

Khieu Seng Kim became a man possessed: he could not believe that the brother he worshipped would abandon his family; at that time he was their only means of support. He travelled all over the country, visiting friends and relatives, asking if they had any news of his brother. Nobody could tell him anything: it was only much later that he learned that Khieu Samphan had been smuggled out of the city in a farmer's cart the evening he failed to show up for dinner.

Eight years later, in 1975, when the first Khmer Rouge cadres marched into Phnom Penh, Khieu Seng Kim went rushing out into the streets and threw himself upon them, crying: 'My brother is Khieu Samphan, my brother is your leader.' They looked at him as though he were insane. 'The Revolution doesn't recognize families,' they said, brushing him off. He was driven out of the city with his wife and children and made to march to a work site just like everybody else.

Like most other evacuees Khieu Seng Kim drifted back towards Phnom Penh in 1979, after the Pol Pot regime had been overthrown by the Vietnamese invasion. He began working in a factory, but within a few months it emerged that he knew French and had worked as a journalist before the Revolution. The new government contacted him and invited him to take up a job as a journalist. He refused; he didn't want to be compromised or associate himself with the government in any way. Instead, he worked with the Department of Archaeology for a while as a restorer, and then took a teaching job at the School of Fine Arts.

'For that they're still suspicious of me,' he said, with a wry smile. 'Even now. That's why I live in a place like this, while everyone in the country is getting rich.'

He smiled and lit a cigarette; he seemed obscurely pleased at the thought of being excluded and pushed on to the edges of the wilderness that had claimed his brother decades ago. It never seemed to have occurred to him to reflect that there was probably no other country on earth where the brother of a man who had headed a genocidal regime would actually be invited to accept a job by the government that followed.

I liked Khieu Seng Kim, I liked his quirky younger-brotherishness. For his sake I wished his mother were still alive—that indomitable old woman who had spread out her mat and started selling vegetables on the street when she realized that her eldest son would have no qualms about sacrificing his entire family on the altar of his idealism. She would have reminded Khieu Seng Kim of a few home truths.

Eleven

Khieu Samphan talked very little about his student days upon his return from France. He did however tell one story that imprinted itself vividly on his younger brother's mind. It had to do with an old friend, Hou Yuon.

Hou Yuon was initiated into radical politics at about the same time as Khieu Samphan and Pol Pot; they all attended the same study groups in Paris; they did Party work together in Phnom Penh in the Sixties, and all through the desperate years of the early Seventies they fought together, shoulder to shoulder, in conditions of the most extreme hardship, with thousands of tons of bombs crashing down around them. So closely were Khieu Samphan and Hou Yuon linked, that along with a third friend, Hu Nim, they became a collective legend, known as the 'Three Ghosts'.

Once, at a Cambodian gathering in Paris, Hou Yuon made a speech criticizing the corruption and venality of Prince Sihanouk's regime. He was overheard by an official and soon afterwards his government scholarship was suspended for a year. Khieu Samphan's scholarship was suspended too as he was known to be Hou Yuon's particular friend.

To support themselves the two men began to sell bread. They would study during the day, and at night they would walk around the city hawking long loaves of French bread. With the money they earned, they paid for their upkeep and bought books; the loaves they couldn't sell they ate. It was a hard way to earn money, Khieu Samphan told his brother, but at the same time it was oddly exhilarating. Walking down those lamplit streets late at night, talking to each other, he and Hou Yuon somehow managed to leave behind the night-time of the spirit that had befallen them in Paris. They would walk all night long, with the fragrant, crusty loaves over their shoulders, looking into the windows of cafes and restaurants, talking about their lives and about the future.

When the revolution began, Hou Yuon was one of the first to die. His moderate views were sharply at odds with the ultra-radical, collectivist ideology of the ruling group. In August 1975, a few months after the Khmer Rouge took power, he addressed a crowd and vehemently criticized the policy of evacuating the cities. He is said to have been assassinated as he left the meeting, on the orders of the party's leadership. Hu Nim served for a while as Minister of Information. Then on April 10, 1977 he and his wife were taken into 'Interrogation Centre S-21'— the torture chambers at Tuol Sleng in Phnom Penh. He was executed several months later, after having confessed to being everything from a CIA agent to a Vietnamese spy.

Khieu Samphan was then head of state. He is believed to have played an important role in planning the mass purges of that period.

For Khieu Samphan and Pol Pot, the deaths of Hou Yuon, Hu Nim and the thousands of others who were executed in torture chambers and execution grounds were not a contradiction but rather a proof of their own idealism and ideological purity. Terror was essential to their exercise of power. It was an integral part not merely of their coercive machinery, but of the moral order on which they built their regime; a part whose best description still lies in the line that Büchner, most prescient of playwrights, gave to Robespierre (a particular hero of Pol Pot's)—'Virtue is terror, and terror virtue'—words that might well serve as an epitaph for the twentieth century.

Twelve

Those who were there then say there was a moment of epiphany in Phnom Penh in 1980. It occurred at a quiet, relatively obscure event: a festival at which classical Cambodian music and dance were performed for the first time since the revolution.

Dancers and musicians from all over the country travelled to Phnom Penh for the festival. Proeung Chhieng, one of the best-known dancers and choreographers in the country, was one of those who made the journey: he came to Phnom Penh from Kompong Thom where he had helped assemble a small troupe of dancers after the fall of Democratic Kampuchea. He himself had trained at the palace since his childhood, specializing in the role of Hanuman, the monkey-god of the Ramayana epic, a part that is one of the glories of Khmer dance. This training proved instrumental in Proeung Chhieng's survival: his expertise in clowning and mime helped him persuade the interrogators at his labour camp that he was an illiterate lunatic.

At the festival he met many fellow students and teachers for the first time since the revolution: 'We cried and laughed while we looked around to see who were the others who had survived. We would shout with joy: "You are still alive!" and then we would cry thinking of someone who had died.'

The performers were dismayed when they began preparing for the performance: large quantities of musical instruments, costumes and masks had been destroyed over the last few years. They had to improvise new costumes to perform in; instead of rich silks and brocades they used thin calico, produced by a government textile factory. The theatre was in relatively good shape, but there was an electricity crisis at the time, and the lighting was dim and unreliable.

But people flocked to the theatre the day the festival began. Onesta Carpene, a Catholic relief worker from Italy, was one of the handful of foreigners then living in Phnom Penh. She was astonished at the response: the city was in a shambles; there was debris everywhere, spilling out of the houses, on to the pavements; the streets were jammed with pillaged cars; there was no money and very little food—'I could not believe that in a situation like that people would be thinking of music and dance.' But still they came pouring in, and the theatre was filled far beyond its capacity. It was very hot inside.

Eva Mysliwiec, who had arrived recently to set up a Quaker relief mission, was at that first performance. When the first

259

musicians came onstage she heard sobs all around her. Then, when the dancers appeared in their shabby, hastily made costumes, suddenly, everyone was crying: old people, young people, soldiers, children—'You could have sailed out of there in a boat.'

The people who were sitting next to her said: 'We thought everything was lost, that we would never hear our music again, never see our dance.' They could not stop crying; people wept through the entire performance.

It was a kind of rebirth: a moment when the grief of survival became indistinguishable from the joy of living.

Parts of this article are based on reports in 1906 editions of Le Petit Provençal, Le Petit Marseillais *and* Le Figaro, *and on the letters and documents in the following files in the Archives d'Outre-Mer at Aix-en-Provence: GGI 2576, 5822, 6643 and 15606. GGI 5822 contains a French translation of the royal proclamation on the king's voyage to France. The quotations in sections one and eight are from* Rodin et l'Extrême Orient, *(Paris, 1979) and from Frederic V. Grunefeld,* Rodin: A Biography *(New York, 1987).*

1994
Ghost Story

Seamus Deane

Katie had always told us bedtime stories when we were younger, with good and bad fairies, mothers whose children had been taken by the fairies but were always restored, haunted houses, men who escaped from danger and got back to their families, stolen gold, unhappy rich people and their lonely children, houses becoming safe and secure after overcoming threats from evicting landlords and police, saints burned alive who felt no pain, devils smooth and sophisticated who always wore fine clothes and talked in la-di-da accents. She had so many accents and so many voices that it hardly mattered to us if we got mixed up in the always labyrinthine plot. Now that we were growing up, all that had stopped. But she would still tell stories of a different kind, downstairs in the kitchen, if we got her in the mood and if my parents were not there. I always felt their presence was a kind of censorship on what Katie would say, especially now.

'There was this young woman called Brigid McLaughlin,' she told Eilis and me one afternoon, after we had helped her with a big laundering of clothes and were all sitting about the kitchen, Katie in the armchair with her back to the window and her feet up on a pile of cushions. My mother was asleep upstairs. 'Mind you, this was long before my time. I heard it from your great-uncle Constantine's mother, God be good to them both but better to him for he's in more need of it, the aul' heathen.' She laughed at that and fell to brooding for a while. We didn't stir. This was her way of telling a story. If you hurried her up, she cut it short, and it lost all its wonder.

Brigid had been hired by a private arrangement to look after two children, two orphans, a boy and a girl, who lived away down in the southern part of Donegal where they still spoke Irish, but an Irish that was so old that many other Irish speakers couldn't follow it. Brigid had been brought up there before coming up here to Derry, so the language was no problem to her. Anyway, the children's uncle was going away to foreign parts and he wanted someone to look after them and educate them a bit. Now one of the odd things about these children was their names. The boy was called Francis, and the girl was called

Frances. Even in Irish you couldn't tell the names apart, except in writing. No one knows why their parents christened them so. The parents themselves, they had been carried off by the cholera during the Great Famine, though they were well enough off themselves and had never starved. Anyway, however it was, this young woman—Brigid—was sent down there to look after them. She had a year's contract, signed in her father's house. But she was not, for all of that year, to leave the children out of her charge and was never to take them away from the house itself. Everything she needed would be supplied, on the uncle's arrangement, by the shopkeepers in the village a couple of miles away. So off she went to this big farmhouse in the middle of nowhere to look after Frances, the girl, who was nine, and Francis, the boy, who was seven.

She wrote home to her father for the first few months, and all seemed to be well. But then the letters stopped. It was only after it was all over that people found out what had happened.

The children were beautiful, especially the girl. She was dark. The boy was fair. They spoke Irish only. Brigid taught them all she knew, every morning for two hours, every afternoon for one hour. But they had this habit, they told Brigid, that they had promised each other never to break. Every day they would go to the field behind the house, where their parents were buried, and put flowers on the grave and sit there for a long time. They always asked her to leave them alone to do this; she could watch them, they said, from an upstairs window. So Brigid did that. And all was well. But after some time had passed, and summer had waned, Brigid tried to discourage them more strongly, for it was often wet and beginning to get cold. Still, the children insisted. On one particularly bad day in the autumn, when the rain was coming down in sheets, and the wind was howling, she stopped them going. She wouldn't give in. And they, in turn, insisted. Finally, she put them in their rooms and told them that was the end of it. They could visit their parents' grave in decent weather, but she wasn't going to have them falling ill by doing so in such conditions, no more than their parents would want her to, or want them to insist on doing. After a big quarrel, the first they ever had, the children went to their rooms and, after a bit, when it was dark, Brigid went to bed. Now, would you believe this? It's the God's truth. The next morning, when she went to their rooms, what did she find? She found the boy was now dark-haired, as his sister had been, and the girl was fair-haired, as her brother had been. And they didn't seem to notice! They told her they had always been like that, that she was imagining things. You can imagine! Poor Brigid! She thought she was going out of her mind. She examined them all over, she questioned them, she threatened not to give them any meals until they told her the truth. But they just sat there and told her she was the one who had got everything wrong.

Right, says Brigid, we'll see who's imagining things. We'll go into the village. We'll go to the priest. We'll go to anyone we meet and we'll put the question to them. The children agreed and off they went to the parochial house and found the priest in and waited in the drawing room to meet him. Brigid sat down and then got up and sat down again while the children, polite and well-mannered as they usually were, sat before her on straight-backed chairs, quiet and as assured as any two grown-ups would have been. When the priest came in, Brigid went straight to him and said, 'Father, Father, for the love of God, look at these two children, Francis and Frances, and tell me what has happened, for I don't know if they're in the hands of the devil or what it could be.' And the priest, very surprised and shocked, looked at her, looked at them, caught her by the wrist and sat her down, shaking his head and asking her what did she mean, to take it slowly, tell him again. But the children, she cried at him, look at the children, they've changed, they've switched colours. Look! She pointed at them and there they were, looking at her and the priest, and they were the colour and complexion they had always been, the girl dark, and the boy fair. We told her, they said to the priest, we had always been like this, but she says we changed colour and she frightened us. Both of them began to cry, and Brigid began to wail, and the priest ran between them like a scalded cat for a while before he could calm things down.

Poor Brigid! She knew the priest thought she was going strange, and the children were so loud in their protests and so genuinely upset that she began to wonder herself. Especially as the children kept their complexions just as they had been for days and days after and during that time.

No matter what the weather, Brigid let them visit their parents' graves and watched them from the upstairs window and saw nothing wrong. But she couldn't sleep at night, for she knew, she knew, she knew that she had not been mistaken. She could clearly remember examining them—running her hands up the back of their hair, seeing the boy's skin that shade darker, the girl's skin the white and pink that had been the boy's. She knew she had not imagined this, and yet there it was! She lay in the bed clutching her rosary beads and telling her prayers and every so often shaking with a fit of the weeps, for she knew either she was mad, or there was something very strange in that house and very frightening about those children.

With all this sleeplessness she took to walking about her room and now and again she would pull back the curtain to look outside, over to the left, to the field where the grave lay. It was no more than a week after she had gone to the priest that she looked out one night and saw to her terror that there was a kind of greenish light swimming above the grave, and in that light she could see the children standing there, hand in hand, staring down at the ground from which the light seemed to be welling up. She was so terrified that when she tried to cry out, she could not; when she wanted to move, she was paralysed; when she wanted to cry, her eyes were dry-dead in her head. She didn't know how long she stood like that but eventually she moved and forced herself out the door and as she did she began to wail their names—Francis, Frances, Frances, Francis—over and over as she rushed along the corridor. With that, she heard them, in their bedrooms, crying out, and went in to find them wakened and terrified, still warm and dry, both of them, still with sleep in their eyes. She brought them to her room and put them in her bed, shook holy water over them, told them to pray, told them not to be frightened, made herself go to the window again and look, and all was dark—no greenish light, no figures of children at the grave.

The night passed somehow. The children slept. She lay in the bed alongside them and held them as close as she dared without wakening them. But when they woke and asked her for breakfast and what had happened, she went cold all over. For now their voices were changed. The boy had the girl's voice, and the girl had the boy's voice. She put her hands over her ears. She shut her eyes. Then she said she became calm for a moment. She knew she had to see. So she asked the children to come with her to the bathroom to wash before they ate. She helped them undress, even though they usually undressed themselves. And sure enough, their sexes had changed too. The boy was a girl, and the girl was a boy. And they paid no notice! They washed themselves and said nothing. She made them breakfast, she gave them lessons, she let them out to play under the apple trees in the front garden. She knew, she said, that if she brought them to the priest or the doctor, the same thing would happen; they would change back and leave her looking like a lunatic. She knew, too, that if she left the house—even if she could find a way of doing so, for there was little or no transport to be had and certainly none to take them as far north as Derry, and there was nowhere else she could think of—something terrible would happen. She knew now she was being challenged by evil, and the children were being stolen from her by whatever was in that grave out the back. Oh, she knew without knowing how she knew it. There was no question.

Katie paused for a long time. The clock on the mantelpiece ticked. Eilis was bending down in her chair, her fair hair falling over her face. I wanted to peep in the shaving mirror on the wall to make sure my hair was still dark. Katie went on brooding. A coal in the fire cracked, and little blue flames began to hiss. There was no sound from upstairs. Some families, Katie told us, are devil-haunted; it's a curse a family can never shake off. Maybe it's something terrible in the family history, some terrible deed that was done in the past, and it just spreads and it spreads down the generations like a shout down a tunnel that echoes and echoes and never really stops.

Now I wanted her to stop, but she went on. I wished my mother would come awake or that someone would come in and interrupt. But everyone seemed to have gone. In an hour, the house would be alive with people, Katie would rush to get the dinner ready, I would scrub down the deal table, Eilis would start clattering the knives and forks. My father would arrive, my mother would appear, people would be chattering about this and that, the radio would be turned on for the news.

Anyway, anyway, Katie continued, passing her hand over her broad, kind face in a circular, washing movement, there the poor girl was, locked in with something terrible, and the two strange children changing over from one to another before her very eyes. She wrote down in a notebook all the changes there were, changes from boy to girl, changes back to what they had been when she first came. Some of the changes were smaller than others. One day it would be the colour of their eyes. The girl's would be blue, although she was still dark-haired and olivy-skinned; the boy's would be brown. Another day it would be their height. The girl was a little taller, normally, but one day she was the boy's height, and he hers. One day, she swears, their teeth changed. She had his smile, he had hers. Another day, it was their ears. Another day, their hands. On and on, for thirty-two days she watched all these changes. The children continued to sleep in her room, and on seven of the nights throughout those thirty-two days she saw the greenish light on the grave and the figures of the children standing there, hand in hand, even while they were lying asleep in her bed in the room with her. By now, it was deep into November. She was living as if she would explode at any minute but she kept her panic down. When anyone came to visit—the priest, the doctor, a tradesman—the children were always as they should be. No matter how she watched, she never saw the moment of change from one condition to the next. Then suddenly, everything got worse.

She was brushing Frances's hair in front of a long, free-standing mirror that you could adjust to whatever angle you liked. It had a wooden frame, a mix she said of two woods: one was called bird's-eye maple and the other rosewood. She wouldn't have known this, but the children told her. They knew every detail of every article of furniture, every piece of china, every item of cutlery, every floor-covering and wall-hanging, every picture and clock, in the house. They knew the names of the local people to whom the farmland had been rented out for pasture, they knew the conditions of the rental, they knew the grazing in the different fields—everything! She had just finished brushing the girl's hair and was giving it a final stroke or two when she looked and saw herself in the mirror, standing there with the brush in one hand and the other cupped in mid-air, as though holding something. But the girl wasn't there, wasn't in the mirror, although Brigid was touching her, holding the strands of the child's hair in her hand. She stood there, stock-still, wanting to fall to the ground, keeping herself upright by dint of her will. The boy was in the room at the time and he came over, asking her to hurry up and finish brushing for he wanted to go downstairs and play with his sister. He moved into the frame of the mirror and he too disappeared. Brigid asked them to look, and they did, and she asked them, could they see themselves? And they said yes, of course they could, and laughed, but uneasily. And they could see her too, they said. The grandfather clock in the bedroom corridor struck at that moment, ten strokes. She remembered that. She counted them. It was ten o'clock in the morning of November 21. And that clock never moved a solitary inch thereafter. It stopped and it never started again.

Now she didn't know it at the time, but that was the very hour and day the parents of those children had died, five years before. They both died at the same time. And it was then that the children stopped going out to the grave every day. It was then they stopped the changes. It was then, she said, that she knew the two people in the grave outside had finally come into the house. She went to the priest and asked him to come and bless the house. He did. He walked all through it, bearing the host with him, saying the Latin prayers, throwing the dashes of holy water on all the doors, all the exits and entrances. When he had done, he asked Brigid why she had covered up all the mirrors in the house. She told him. He commanded her then to bring the children to him in front of the big mirror in the bedroom and he took off the velveteen cloth she had draped over it and stood them in front of him before it. And there they were, just as normal. He would have to do something about this, he said; he would write to the uncle and see what could be done. The doctor would call and see her, and his housekeeper would come in now and then to help her. At least January wasn't far off, and then she could go back home, for the uncle would have returned by then. So, all this was done. But when Brigid was left alone, as she had to be, she felt the presence of the dead parents all over again; the house was colder, and every so often she would see the greenish light under the door of one of the rooms that had been closed up, or fading away at the end of the upstairs corridor, or thinning out to a mossy line in the frame of a window as she entered a room.

Then one night, she said, they came for the children, who were in her bed as usual. They lay there awake, unable to sleep, and the little girl began to sing a song Brigid had never heard before in a language that was not Irish or English, and the little boy joined in. Brigid stood before them, a crucifix in her hand, praying, praying, with the flesh prickling all over her. Those children lay there, she said, their voices in unison, singing this sad, slow air, and all the changes she had seen before passing over them, one by one, faster and faster, until she didn't know which was the boy, which the girl. The whole house was booming, as with the sound of heavy feet on the wooden stair. The greenish light came into the room in mid-air and spread all over it, and with that came this whispering of voices, a man's and a woman's, whispering, whispering, furious, almost as if they were spitting in anger except that the voices were dry, whipped up like swirlings of dust in a wind. The children stopped their singing and sat up in the bed, their eyes standing in their heads, their mouths open but without sound, their arms outstretched to Brigid. She opened her arms to them, dropping the crucifix on the bed, and she says she felt them, their hands and their arms, felt her own hands touching their shoulders, and with that, the greenish light disappeared, the whispering stopped and the children were gone. All that was left was the warmth of the bed, the dents in the pillows, the wind whistling outside.

She got the priest out of his bed in the middle of that night and he came with her, hurrying down the road, buttoning his long coat, telling her she should not have left the children, that this was the last straw, she'd have to go home. But when they got to the empty house and searched it and found no children, he began to accuse her of having made off with them and was going to get the doctor, who had a pony and trap, to go to the next town for the police. Oh Father, she said, do that. Do what you must. But before you do, come out the back with me. She led him to the grave, and there they saw, the both of them, the greenish light wavering over the mound of earth and, clear as a lark-song, heard the voices of the two children, coming from the heart of the light, singing, singing their strange song. The priest blessed himself and fell on his knees, as did Brigid with him, and they stayed there in the wind and the rain until morning when the greenish light faded and the voices with it.

The children were never seen again.

All the mirrors in the house had shattered, all the clocks stopped at the hour of ten, only the children's clothes were left to show that they had once been there. God knows what the uncle thought when he came back. Brigid was taken home, the uncle came to see her, she talked to him, she talked to everyone who would listen for maybe six months after her return, she went completely strange in the head and people used to bless themselves when she appeared and hurry away. Then Brigid stopped talking. Until the day she died she never spoke again, would never leave her room, would never have a mirror near her. Only every year, on November 21, you could hear her up in her room, singing this song, in words none could understand, a song no one had ever heard, that must have been the song the children sang that night long ago, in south Donegal, only five years after the Famine. And the blight's on that family to this very day.

At last, my mother moved upstairs, the bells of the cathedral began to ring, and the noises of the world outside came dappling in as Katie blessed herself, laughed and shook her head at something, and told me to get the scrubbing brush and warm water for the table. Eilis sat there, her hair falling fair over her obscured face.

270

1995
Girls

Harold Pinter

Iread this short story in a magazine where a girl student goes into her professor's office and sits at his desk and passes him a note which he opens and which reads: 'Girls like to be spanked.' But I've lost it. I've lost the magazine. I can't find it. And I can't remember what happened next. I don't even know whether the story was fiction or fact. It may have been an autobiographical fragment. But from whose point of view was the story told? The professor's or the girl's? I don't know. I can't remember. The blinding ignorance I am now experiencing is the clearest and cleanest road to madness. What I want to know is quite simple. Was she spanked? If, that is, she was including herself in her all-embracing proposition. If she was including herself in her all-embracing proposition, did she, personally, benefit from it? Was she, not to put too fine a point on it, one of those girls? Was she, or is she, one of those girls who, according to her account, like to be spanked? If that was the case, did it happen? Did it happen in the professor's office, on the professor's desk? Or not? And what about the professor? What did he make of it all? What kind of professor was he, anyway? What was his discipline? Did he subject the assertion (girls like to be spanked) to serious critical scrutiny? Did he find it a dubious generalization or, at any rate, did he set out to verify it? Did he, in other words, put it to the test? Did he, for example, in other words, say: 'OK. Lie on my desk, bottom up, face averted, and let us both determine whether there is substance to this assertion or not'? Or did he simply warn the student, in the interests of science, to tread warily for evermore, in the perilous field of assertion?

The trouble is, I can't find the magazine. I've lost it. And I've no idea how the story—or the autobiographical fragment—developed. Did they fall in love? Did they marry? Did they give birth to lots of little animals?

A man or woman or both must have written this piece about a girl who walks into her professor's office and sits at his desk and passes him a note which he opens and which reads: 'Girls like to be spanked.' But I don't know his or her name; I don't know the author's identity. And I simply don't know whether the girl was in fact spanked, there and then, without further ado, in the professor's office, on his desk, or at any other time, on someone else's desk, here, there, everywhere, all the time, on the hour, religiously, tenderly, fervently, ceaselessly, forever and forever and forever. But it's also possible that she wasn't talking about herself. She might not necessarily have meant that *she* liked to be spanked. She may just have been talking about other girls, girls she didn't even know, millions of girls she hadn't even met, would never meet, millions of girls she hadn't in fact ever actually heard of, millions and billions of girls on the other side of the world who, in her view, liked, simply, without beating about the bush, to be spanked. Or on the other hand she may have been talking about other girls, girls born at Cockfosters or studying American Literature at the University of East Anglia, who had actually told her personally, in breathtaking spasms of spectacular candour, that they, when all was said but nothing yet done, liked, when the chips were down, nothing better than to be spanked. In other words, her assertion (girls like to be spanked) might have been the climax of a long, deep, thoroughly researched course of study she had undertaken honourably and had honourably concluded.

I love her. I love her so much. I think she's a wonderful woman. I saw her once. She turned and smiled. She looked at me and smiled. Then she wiggled to a cab in the cab rank. She gave instructions to the cab driver, opened the door, got in, closed the door, glanced at me for the last time through the window and the cab drove off and I never saw her again.

1996
Agnes of Iowa

Lorrie Moore

Her mother had given her the name Agnes, believing that a good-looking woman was even more striking when her name was a homely one. Her mother was named Cyrena and was beautiful to match but had always imagined her life would have been more interesting, that she herself would have had a more dramatic, arresting effect on the world and not ended up in Cassell, Iowa, if she had been named Enid or Hagar or Maude. And so she named her first daughter Agnes, and when Agnes turned out not to be attractive at all but puffy and prone to a rash between her eyebrows, her hair a flat and bilious hue, her mother back-pedalled and named her second daughter Linnea Elise (who turned out to be a lovely, sleepy child with excellent bones, a sweet, full mouth and a rubbery mole above her lip which later in life could be removed without difficulty, everyone was sure).

Agnes herself had always been a bit at odds with her name. There was a brief period in her life, in her mid-twenties, when she had tried to pass it off as French—she had put in the *accent grave* and encouraged people to call her 'On-yez'. This was when she was living in New York City and often getting together with her cousin, a painter who took her to parties in TriBeCa lofts or at beach houses or at mansions on lakes upstate. She would meet a lot of not very bright rich people who found the pronunciation of her name intriguing. It was the rest of her they were unclear on. 'On-yez, where are you from, dear?' asked a black-slacked, frosted-haired woman whose skin was papery and melanomic with suntan. 'Originally.' She eyed Agnes's outfit as if it might be what in fact it was: a couple of blue things purchased in a department store in Cedar Rapids.

'Where am I from?' Agnes said it softly. 'Iowa.' She had a tendency not to speak up.

'Where?' the woman scowled, bewildered.

'Iowa,' Agnes repeated loudly.

The woman in black touched Agnes's wrist and leaned in confidentially. She moved her mouth in a concerned and exaggerated way, like an exercise. 'No, dear,' she said. '*Here* we say O-*hi*-o.'

That had been in Agnes's mishmash decade, after college. She had lived improvisationally then, getting this job or that, in restaurants or offices, taking a class or two, not thinking too far ahead, negotiating the precariousness and subway flus and scrimping for an occasional facial or a play. Such a life required much expendable self-esteem. It engaged gross quantities of hope and despair and set them wildly side by side, like a Third World country of the heart. Her days grew messy with contradictions. When she went for walks, for her health, cinders would spot her cheeks, and soot would settle in the furled leaf of each ear. Her shoes became unspeakable. Her blouses darkened in a breeze, and a blast of bus exhaust might linger in her hair for hours. Finally her old asthma returned and, with a hacking, incessant cough, she gave up. 'I feel like I've got five years to live,' she told people, 'so I'm moving back to Iowa so that it'll feel like fifty.'

When she packed up to leave she knew she was saying goodbye to something important, which was not that bad in a way because it meant that at least you had said hello to it to begin with, which most people in Cassell, Iowa could not claim to have done.

A year later she married a boyish man twelve years her senior, a Cassell realtor named Joe, and together they bought a house on a little street called Birch Court. She taught a night class at the Arts Hall and did volunteer work on the Transportation Commission in town. It was life like a glass of water: half-full, half-empty, half-full; oops, half-empty. Over the next six years she and Joe tried to have a baby, but one night at dinner, looking at each other in a lonely way over the meat loaf, they realized with a shock that they probably never would. Nonetheless they still tried, vandalizing what romance was left in their marriage.

'Honey,' she would whisper at night when he was reading under the reading lamp, and she had already put her book away and curled toward him, wanting to place the red scarf over the lampshade but knowing it would annoy him and so not doing it. 'Do you want to make love? It would be a good time of month.'

And Joe would groan. Or he would yawn. Or he would

277

already be asleep. Once, after a long hard day, he said, 'I'm sorry, Agnes. I'm just not in the mood.'

She grew exasperated. 'You think *I'm* in the mood?' she said. 'I don't want to do this any more than you do.' He looked at her in a disgusted way, and it was two weeks after that they had the identical sad dawning over the meat loaf.

At the Arts Hall, formerly the Grange Hall, Agnes taught the Great Books class but taught it loosely, with cookies. She let her students turn in poems and plays and stories that they themselves had written; she let them use the class as their own little time to be creative. Someone once even brought in a sculpture: an electric one with blinking lights.

After class she sometimes met with students individually. She recommended things for them to write about or read or consider in their next project. She smiled and asked if things were going well in their lives. She took an interest.

'You should be stricter,' said Willard Stauffbacher, the head of the Instruction Department. He was a short, balding musician who taped to his door pictures of famous people he thought he looked like. Every third Monday he conducted the monthly departmental meeting—aptly named, Agnes liked to joke, since she did indeed depart mental. 'Just because it's a night course doesn't mean you shouldn't impart standards,' Stauffbacher said in a scolding way. 'If it's piffle, use the word *piffle*. It's meaningless? Write *meaningless* at the top of every page.' He had once taught at an elementary school and once at a prison. 'I feel like I do all the real work around here,' he added. He had posted near his office a sign that read:

RULES FOR THE MUSIC ROOM

I WILL STAY IN MY SEAT UNLESS [*sic*] PERMISSION TO MOVE
I WILL SIT UP STRAIGHT
I WILL LISTEN TO DIRECTIONS
I WILL NOT BOTHER MY NEIGHBOUR
I WILL NOT TALK WHEN MR STAUFFBACHER IS TALKING
I WILL BE POLITE TO OTHERS
I WILL SING AS WELL AS I CAN

Agnes stayed after one night with Christa, the only black student in her class. She liked Christa a lot—Christa was smart and funny, and Agnes would sometimes stay late with her to chat. Tonight Agnes had decided to talk Christa out of writing about vampires all the time.

'Why don't you write about that thing you told me about that time?' Agnes suggested.

Christa looked at her sceptically. 'What thing?'

'The time in your childhood, during the Chicago riots, walking with your mother through the police barricades.'

'Man, I lived that. Why should I want to write about it?'

Agnes sighed. Maybe Christa had a point. 'It's just I'm no help to you with this vampire stuff,' Agnes said. 'It's formulaic genre fiction.'

'You would be of more help to me with my *childhood*?'

'Well, with more serious stories, yes.'

Christa stood up, perturbed. She grabbed her paperback. 'You with all your Alice Walker and Zora Hurston. I'm not interested in that any more. I've done that already. I read those books years ago.'

'Christa, please don't be annoyed.' *Please do not talk when Mr Stauffbacher is talking.*

'You've got this agenda for me.'

'Really, I don't at all,' said Agnes. 'It's just that—you know what it is? It's that I'm sick of these vampires. They're so roaming and repeating.'

'If you were black, what you're saying might have a different spin. But the fact is you're not,' Christa said, and picked up her coat and strode out—though ten seconds later she gamely stuck her head back in and said, 'See you next week.'

'We need a visiting writer who's black,' Agnes said in the next depart mental meeting. 'We've never had one.'

They were looking at their budget, and the readings this year were pitted against Dance Instruction, a programme headed up by a redhead named Evergreen.

'The Joffrey is just so much central casting,' said Evergreen, apropos of nothing. As a vacuum cleaner can start to pull up the actual thread of a carpet, her brains had been sucked dry by too much yoga. No one paid much attention to her.

'Perhaps we can get Harold Raferson in Chicago,' Agnes suggested.

'We've already got somebody for the visiting writer slot,' said Stauffbacher coyly. 'An Afrikaner from Johannesburg.'

'What?' said Agnes. Was he serious? Even Evergreen barked out a laugh.

'W. S. Beyerbach. The university's bringing him in. We pay our four hundred dollars and we get him out here for a day and a half.'

'Who?' asked Evergreen.

'This has already been decided?' asked Agnes.

'Yup.' Stauffbacher looked accusingly at Agnes. 'I've done a lot of work to arrange for this. *I've* done all the work!'

'Do less,' said Evergreen.

When Agnes had first met Joe, they'd fallen madly upon each other. They'd kissed in restaurants; they'd groped under coats at the movies. At his little house they'd made love on the porch, or the landing of the staircase, against the wall in the hall, by the door to the attic, filled with too much desire to make their way to a real room.

Now they struggled self-consciously for atmosphere, something they'd never needed before. She prepared the bedroom carefully. She played quiet music and concentrated. She lit candles—as if she were in church praying for the deceased. She donned a filmy gown. She took hot baths and entered the bedroom in nothing but a towel, a wild fish-like creature of moist, perfumed heat. In the nightstand drawer she still kept the charts a doctor once told her to keep, still placed an X on any date she and Joe actually had sex. But she could never show these to her doctor, not now. It pained Agnes to see them. She and Joe looked like worse than bad shots. She and Joe looked like idiots. She and Joe looked dead.

Frantic candlelight flickered on the ceiling like a puppet show. While she waited for Joe to come out of the bathroom, Agnes lay back on the bed and thought about her week, the stupid politics of it—the Arts Hall, the Transportation Commission, all those loud, smacking collisions of public good and private power. She was not very good at politics. Once, before he was elected, she had gone to a rally for Bill Clinton, but when he was late and had kept the crowd waiting for over an hour, and when the sun got hot and bees began landing on people's heads, when everyone's feet hurt, and tiny children began to cry, and a state assemblyman stepped forward to announce that Clinton had stopped at a Dairy Queen in Des Moines and that was why he was late—Dairy Queen!—she had grown angry and resentful and apolitical in her own sweet-starved thirst and she'd joined in with some other people who had started to chant, 'Do us a favour, tell us the flavour.'

Through college she had been a feminist—more or less. She shaved her legs, *but just not often enough*, she liked to say. She signed day-care petitions and petitions for Planned Parenthood. And although she had never been very socially aggressive with men, she felt strongly that she knew the difference between feminism and Sadie Hawkins Day—which some people, she believed, did not.

'Agnes, are we out of toothpaste or is this it?—Oh, OK, I see.'

And once, in New York, she had quixotically organized the ladies'-room line at the Brooks Atkinson Theater. Because the play was going to start any minute, and the line was still twenty women long, she had got six women to walk across the lobby with her to the men's room. 'Everybody out of there?' she'd called in timidly, allowing the men to finish up first, which took a while, especially with other men coming up impatiently and cutting ahead in line. Later at intermission, she saw how it should have been done. Two elderly black women, with greater expertise in civil rights, stepped very confidently into the men's room and called out, 'Don't mind us, boys. We're coming on in. Don't mind us.'

'Are you OK?' asked Joe, smiling. He was already beside her. He smelled sweet, of soap and minty teeth, like a child.

'I think so,' she said and turned toward him in the bordello light of their room. He had never acquired the look of maturity-anchored-in-sorrow that burnished so many men's faces. His own sadnesses in life—a childhood of beatings, a dying mother—were like quicksand, and he had to stay away from them entirely. He permitted no unhappy memories spoken aloud. He stuck with the same mild cheerfulness he'd honed successfully as a boy, and it made him seem fatuous—even, she knew, to himself. Probably it hurt his business a little.

'Your mind's wandering,' he said, letting his own eyes close.

'I know.' She yawned, moved her legs on to his for warmth, and in this way, with the candles burning into their tins, she and Joe fell asleep.

Spring arrived, cool and humid. Bulbs cracked and sprouted, shot up their green periscopes, and on April 1 the Arts Hall offered a joke lecture by T. S. Eliot, visiting scholar. 'The Cruellest Month', it was called. 'You don't find it funny?' asked Stauffbacher.

April fourth was the reception for W. S. Beyerbach. There was to be a dinner afterward, and then Beyerbach was to visit Agnes's Great Books class. She had assigned his second collection of sonnets, which were spare and elegant, with sighing and diaphanous politics. The next afternoon there was to be a reading.

Agnes had not been invited to the dinner, and when she asked about this, in a mildly forlorn way, Stauffbacher shrugged as if it were totally out of his hands. 'I'm a *published poet*,' Agnes wanted to say. She had had a poem published once—in the *Gizzard Review*, but still!

'It was Edie Canterton's list,' Stauffbacher said. 'I had nothing to do with it.'

She went to the reception anyway, annoyed, and when she planted herself like a splayed and storm-torn tree near the cheese, she could feel the crackers she was eating forming a bad paste in her mouth and she became afraid to smile. When she finally introduced herself to W. S. Beyerbach, she stumbled on her own name and actually pronounced it 'On-yez'.

'On-yez,' repeated Beyerbach in a quiet Englishy voice. Condescending, she thought. His hair was blond and white, like a palomino, and his eyes were blue and scornful as mints. She could see he was a withheld man; although some might say *shy*, she decided it was *withheld*: a lack of generosity. Passive-aggressive. It was causing the people around him to squirm and nervously improvise remarks. He would simply nod, the smile on his face faint and vaguely pharmaceutical. Everything about him was tight and coiled as a door-spring. From living in *that country*, thought Agnes. How could he live in that country?

Stauffbacher was trying to talk heartily about the mayor. Something about his old progressive ideas and the forthcoming convention centre. Agnes thought of her own meetings on the Transportation Commission, of the mayor's leash law for cats, of his new squadron of meter maids and bicycle police, of a councilman the mayor once slugged in a bar. 'Now, of course, the mayor's become a fascist,' said Agnes in a voice that sounded strangely loud, bright with anger.

Silence fell in the room. Edie Canterton stopped stirring the punch. Agnes looked around. 'Oh,' she said. 'Are we not supposed to used *that word* in this room?' Beyerbach's expression went blank. Agnes's face burned in confusion.

Stauffbacher looked pained, then stricken. 'More cheese, anyone?' he asked, holding up the silver tray.

After everyone left for dinner, she went by herself to the Dunk 'N Dine across the street. She ordered a California BLT and a cup of coffee, and looked over Beyerbach's work again: dozens of images of broken, rotten bodies, of the body's mutinies and betrayals, of the body's strange housekeeping and illicit pets. At the front of the book was a dedication—*To D. F. B. (1970–1989)*. Who could that be? A political activist maybe, 'a woman who had thrown aside the unseasonal dress of hope' only to look for it again 'in the blood-blooming shrubs'. Perhaps if Agnes got a chance, she would ask him. Why not? A book was a public thing, and its dedication was part of it. If it was too personal a question for him, tough. She would find the right time, she decided, paying the cheque and putting on her jacket, crossing the street to the Hall. She would wait for the moment, then seize it.

He was already at the front door when she arrived. He greeted her with a stiff smile and a soft 'Hello, On-yez'. His accent made her own voice ring coarse and country-western.

She smiled and then blurted, 'I have a question to ask you.'
Her voice sounded like Johnny Cash's.

Beyerbach said nothing, only held the door open for her and
then followed her into the building.

She continued as they stepped slowly up the stairs. 'May I
ask you who your book is dedicated to?'

At the top of the stairs they turned left down the long
corridor. She could feel his steely reserve, his lip-biting, his
shyness no doubt garbed and rationalized with snobbery, but
so much snobbery to handle all that shyness that he could not
possibly be a meaningful critic of his country. She was angry
with him. *How can you live in that country?* she wanted again
to say, although she remembered when someone once said that
to her—a Danish man, on Agnes's senior trip abroad to
Copenhagen. It was during the Vietnam War, and the man had
stared meanly, righteously. 'The United States: how can you live
in that country?' the man had asked. Agnes had shrugged. 'A
lot of my stuff is there,' she said, and it was only then that she
first felt all the dark love and shame that came from the pure
accident of home, the deep and arbitrary place that happened
to be yours.

'It's dedicated to my son,' Beyerbach said finally.

He would not look at her, but stared straight ahead along
the corridor floor. Now Agnes's shoes sounded very loud.

'You lost a son,' she said.

'Yes,' he said. He looked away, at the passing wall, past
Stauffbacher's bulletin board, past the men's room, the women's
room, some sternness in him broken, and when he turned back
she could see his eyes filling with water, his face reddened with
unbearable pressure.

'I'm so sorry,' Agnes said.

They walked side by side, their footsteps echoing down the
corridor toward her classroom. All the anxieties she felt with
this mournfully quiet man now mimicked the anxieties of love.
What should she say? It must be the most unendurable thing
to lose a child. Shouldn't he say something of this? It was his
turn to say something.

But he would not. And when they finally reached the

284

classroom, she turned to him in the doorway and, taking a package from her purse, said simply, in a reassuring way, 'We always have cookies in class.'

Now he beamed at her with such relief that she knew she had for once said the right thing. It filled her with affection for him—perhaps, she thought, that's where affection begins: in an unlikely phrase, in a moment of someone's having unexpectedly but at last said the right thing. *We always have cookies in class*.

She introduced him with a bit of flourish and biography. Positions held, universities attended. The students raised their hands and asked him about apartheid, about shanty towns and homelands, and he answered succinctly, after long sniffs and pauses, only once referring to a question as 'unanswerably fey', causing the student to squirm and fish around in her purse for something, nothing, Kleenex perhaps. Beyerbach did not seem to notice. He went on, speaking of censorship: how a person must work hard not to internalize a government's programme of censorship, since what a government would like best is for you to do it yourself; how he himself was not sure he had not succumbed. Afterward, a few students stayed and shook his hand, formally, awkwardly, then left. Christa was the last. She too shook his hand and then started chatting amiably. They knew someone in common—Harold Raferson in Chicago!—and as Agnes quickly wiped the seminar table to clear it of cookie crumbs, she tried to listen but couldn't really hear. She made a small pile of crumbs and swept them into one hand.

'Goodnight,' sang out Christa when she left.

'Goodnight, Christa,' said Agnes, brushing the crumbs off her hand and into the wastebasket.

She straightened and stood with Beyerbach in the empty classroom. 'Thank you so much,' she said, finally, in a hushed way. 'I'm sure they all got quite a lot out of that. I'm very sure they did.'

He said nothing but smiled at her gently.

She shifted her weight from one leg to the other. 'Would you like to go somewhere and get a drink?' she asked. She was standing close to him, looking up into his face. He was tall, she saw now. His shoulders weren't broad, but he had a youthful straightness to his carriage. She briefly touched his sleeve. His suit coat was corduroy and bore a faint odour of clove. This was the first time in her life that she had ever asked a man out for a drink.

He made no move to step away from her; he actually seemed to lean toward her a bit. She could feel his dry breath, see up close the variously hued spokes of his irises, the greys and yellows in the blue. There was a sprinkling of small freckles near his hairline. He smiled, then looked at the clock on the wall. 'I would love to, really, but I have to get back to the hotel to make a phone call at ten-fifteen.' He looked a little disappointed—not a lot, thought Agnes, but certainly a *little*. She would have bet money on it.

'Oh, well,' she said. She flicked off the lights, and in the dark he carefully helped her on with her jacket. They stepped out of the room and walked together in silence, back down the corridor to the front entrance of the Hall. Outside on the steps the night was balmy and scented with rain. 'Will you be all right walking back to your hotel?' she asked. 'Or—'

'Oh, yes, thank you. It's just around the corner.'

'Right. That's right. Well, my car's parked way over there. So, I guess I'll see you tomorrow afternoon at your reading.'

'Yes,' he said. 'I shall look forward to that.'

'Yes,' she said. 'So shall I.'

T he reading was in the large meeting room at the Arts Hall and was from the sonnet book she had already read, but it was nice to hear the poems again in his hushed, pained tenor. She sat in the back row, her green raincoat sprawled beneath her on the seat like a large leaf. She leaned forward on to the seat ahead of her, her back an angled stem, her chin on double fists, and she listened like that for some time. At one point she closed her eyes, but the image of him before her, standing straight as a compass needle, remained caught there beneath her lids, like a burn or a speck or a message from the mind.

Afterward, moving away from the lectern, Beyerbach spotted her and waved, but Stauffbacher, like a tugboat with a task, took his arm and steered him elsewhere, over toward the side table with the little plastic cups and warm Pepsi. *We are both men,* the gesture seemed to say. *We both have bach in our names.* Agnes put on her green coat. She went over toward the Pepsi table and stood. She drank a warm Pepsi, then placed the empty cup back on the table. Beyerbach finally turned toward her and smiled familiarly. She thrust out her hand. 'It was a wonderful reading,' she said. 'I'm very glad I got the chance to meet you.' She gripped his long, slender palm and locked thumbs. She could feel the bones in him.

'Thank you,' he said. He looked at her coat in a worried way. 'You're leaving?'

She looked down at her coat. 'I'm afraid I have to get going home.' She wasn't sure whether she really had to or not. But she'd put on her coat, and it now seemed an awkward thing to take it off.

'Oh,' he murmured, gazing at her intently. 'Well, all best wishes to you, On-yez.'

'Excuse me?' There was some clattering near the lectern.

'All best to you,' he said, something retreating in his expression.

Stauffbacher suddenly appeared at her side, scowling at her green coat, as if it were incomprehensible.

'Yes,' said Agnes, stepping backward, then forward again to shake Beyerbach's hand once more; it was a beautiful hand, like an old and expensive piece of wood. 'Same to you,' she said. Then she turned and fled.

For several nights she did not sleep well. She placed her face directly into her pillow, then turned it for some air, then flipped over to her back and opened her eyes, staring past the stark angle of the door frame at the far end of the room toward the tiny light from the bathroom which illuminated the hallway, faintly, as if someone had just been there.

For several days she thought perhaps he might have left her a note with the secretary, or that he might send her one from an airport somewhere. She thought that the inadequacy of their goodbye would haunt him too, and that he might send her a postcard as elaboration.

But he did not. Briefly she thought about writing him a letter, on Arts Hall stationery, which for money reasons was no longer the stationery but photocopies of the stationery. She knew he had flown to the West Coast, then off to Tokyo, then Sydney, then back to Johannesburg, and if she posted it now, perhaps he would receive it when he arrived. She could tell him once more how interesting it had been to meet him. She could enclose her poem from the *Gizzard Review*. She had read in the newspaper an article about bereavement—and if she were her own mother she would have sent him that too.

Thank God, thank God, she was not her mother.

May settled firmly into Cassell with a spate of thunder showers. The perennials—the myrtle and grape hyacinths—blossomed around the town in a kind of civic blue, and the warming air brought forth an occasional mosquito or fly. The Transportation Commission meetings were dreary and long, too often held during the dinner hour, and when Agnes got home she would replay them for Joe, weeping about the photo radar and the widening interstate.

When her mother called, Agnes got off the phone fast. When her sister, Linnea, now in Minneapolis, called about their mother, Agnes got off the phone even faster. Joe rubbed her shoulders and spoke to her of carports, of kerb appeal, of mortgage rates and asbestos-wrapped pipes.

At the Arts Hall she taught and fretted and continued to receive the usual memos from the secretary, written on the usual scrap paper—except that the scrap paper, for a while, consisted of the extra posters for the Beyerbach reading. She would get a long disquisition on policies and procedures concerning summer registration and she would turn it over, and there would be his face—sad and pompous in the photograph. She would get a simple phone message—'Your husband called. Please call him at the office'—and on the back would be the ripped centre of Beyerbach's nose, one minty eye, an elbowish chin. Eventually there were no more, and the scrap paper moved on to old contest announcements, grant deadlines, Easter concert notices.

At night she and Joe did yoga to a yoga show on TV. It was part of their effort not to become their parents, though marriage, they knew, held that hazard. The functional disenchantment, the sweet habit of each other, had begun to put lines around her mouth, lines that looked like quotation marks—as if everything she said had already been said before. Sometimes their old cat, Madeline, a fat and pampered calico reaping the benefits of life with a childless couple during their childbearing years, came and plopped herself down with them, between them. She was accustomed to much nestling and appreciation and drips from the faucet, though sometimes she would vanish outside, and they would not see her for days, only to spy her later, in the yard, dirty and matted, chomping a vole or eating old snow.

For Memorial Day weekend Agnes flew with Joe to New York, to show him the city for the first time. 'A place,' she said, 'where if you're not white or not born there, it's no big deal. You're not automatically a story.' She had grown annoyed with Iowa, the pathetic, third-hand manner in which the large issues and conversations of the world were encountered there. The oblique and tired way history obligingly insinuated itself. If ever. She longed to be a citizen of the globe!

They roller skated in Central Park. They looked in the Lord & Taylor windows. They went to the Joffrey. They went to a hair salon on Fifty-seventh Street, and there she had her hair dyed a vibrant red. They sat in the window booth of a coffee shop and got coffee refills and ate pie.

'So much seems the same,' she said to Joe. 'When I lived here, everyone was hustling for money. The rich were. The poor were. But everyone tried hard to be funny. Everywhere you went—a store, a facial place—someone was telling a joke. A good one.' She remembered it had made any given day seem bearable, that impulse toward a joke. It had been a determined sort of humour, an intensity mirroring the intensity of the city, and it seemed to embrace and alleviate the hard sadness of people using each other and marring the earth the way they did. 'It was like brains having sex. It was like every brain was a sex maniac.' She looked down at her pie. 'People really worked at it, the laughing,' she said. 'People need to laugh.'

'They do,' said Joe. He took a swig of coffee, his lips out over the cup in a fleshy flower. He was afraid she might cry—she was getting that look again—and if she did, he would feel guilty and lost and sorry for her that her life was not here any more but in a far and boring place with him. He set the cup down and tried to smile. 'They sure do,' he said. And he looked out the window at the rickety taxis, the oystery garbage and tubercular air, seven pounds of chicken giblets dumped on the kerb in front of the coffee shop where they were. He turned back to her and made the face of a clown.

'What are you doing?' she asked.

'It's a clown face.'

'What do you mean, a clown face?' Someone behind her was singing 'I Love New York', and for the first time she noticed the strange irresolution of the tune.

'A regular clown face is what I mean.'

'It didn't look like that.'

'No? What did it look like?'

'You want me to do the face?'

'Yeah, do the face.'

She looked at Joe. Every arrangement in life carried with it the sadness, the sentimental shadow, of its not being something else but only itself. She attempted the face—a look of such monstrous emptiness and stupidity that Joe burst into a howling sort of laughter, like a dog, and then so did she, air exploding through her nose in a snort, her head thrown forward, then back, then forward again, setting loose a fit of coughing.

'Are you OK?' asked Joe, and she nodded. Out of politeness he looked away, outside, where it had suddenly started to rain. Across the street two people had planted themselves under the window ledge of a Gap store, trying to stay dry, waiting out the downpour, their figures dark and scarecrowish against the lit window display. When he turned back to his wife—oh, his sad, young wife—to point this out to her, to show her what was funny to a man firmly in the grip of middle age, she was still bent sideways in her seat so that her face fell below the line of the table, and he could only see the curve of her heaving back, the fuzzy penumbra of her thin spring sweater, and the garish top of her bright, new and terrible hair.

1997
Are We Related?
Linda Grant

My mother and I are going shopping, as we have done all our lives. 'Now Mum,' I tell her, 'don't start looking at the prices on everything. I'm paying. If you see something you like, try it on. You are the mother of the bride, after all.' At long last one of her two daughters (not me) is getting married.

In recent years my mother has become a poverty shopper; she haunts jumble sales looking for other people's cast-offs. I don't like to think of her trying on someone else's shoes which she does not because she is very poor but because footwear is fixed in her mind at 1970s prices. Everything she sees in the shops seems to cost a fortune. 'You paid £49.99 for a pair of shoes?' she would cry. 'They saw you coming.'

'But Mu-um, that's how much shoes cost these days.'

'Yes, but where do you go looking?'

In my childhood, my mother had aspired far beyond her station to be a world-class shopper. Her role models were Grace Kelly and Princess Margaret, Ava Gardner and Elizabeth Taylor. She acquired crocodile shoes and mink stoles, an eternity ring encrusted with diamonds, handbags in burnished patent leather. In her shut-up flat in Bournemouth were three wardrobes full of beautiful, expensive garments all on wooden or satin hangers, many in their own protective linen bags—a little imitation Chanel suit from the Sixties that came back into fashion every few years; her black Persian broadtail coat with its white mink collar and her initials, RG, sewn in blue silk thread in an italic script on to the hem of the black satin lining, surrounded by a sprig of embroidered roses; her brown mink hat for high days and holidays.

And so today I want the best for her, as she and my father had always wanted the best for us. 'The best that money can buy,' my father always boasted when he bought anything. 'Only show me the best,' he told shopkeepers.

'So we're looking for a dress?' A nice dress. The sales are still raging through the summer's heat, hot shoppers toiling up and down Oxford Street. We should, I think, find something for £60 or £70. 'John Lewis is full of them,' a friend has said. She has an idea of the kind of dress someone's mother would wear, an old biddy's frock, a shapeless floral sack.

'I don't think that's her kind of thing,' I had told her, doubtfully. But then who knew what was left? Could my mother's fashion sense be so far eroded that she would have lost altogether those modes of judgement that saw that something was classic and something else merely frumpy?

'I'm not having a dress, I want a suit,' my mother says as the doors part automatically to admit the three of us, for tagging along is my nephew, her grandson, who also likes to shop.

'OK. A suit. Whatever you like.'

And now we're in the department store, our idea of a second home. My mother has never been much of a nature lover, an outdoors girl. We used to leave the city once, years ago, when we motored out of town in the Humber Hawk, parked in a lay-by, ate cold roast chicken from silver foil, then drove home early so my father could watch the racing and my mother refold her clothes. By the Sixties we considered a day out to be a drive to the new service station on the M6 where we enjoyed a cup of tea as the cars sped along to London below. My mother has never got her hands dirty in wellingtons, bending down among the flower beds to plant her summer perennials. Or put her hands to the oars of a boat or tramped across a ploughed field in the morning frost or breasted any icy waves. She shrinks in fear from sloppy-mouthed dogs and fawning kittens. But show her new improved tights with Lycra! They never had that in my day, she says admiringly on an excursion to Sainsbury's, looking at dose-ball washing liquid.

And no outing can offer more escape from the nightmare of her present reality than shopping for clothes, the easiest means we know of becoming our fantasies and generally cheering ourselves up all round. Who needs the psychiatrist's couch when you have shopping? Who needs Prozac?

Through the handbags, gloves and scarves and utilitarian umbrellas. Not a glance at fabrics and patterns for neither my mother nor I have ever run up our own frocks at the sewing machine, shop-bought *always* being superior to home-made in our book. Why do an amateur job when you could get in a professional?

Up the escalators to the first floor where the land of dreams lies all around us, suits and dresses and coats and skirts and jackets. And where to begin? How to start? But my mother has started already.

At once a sale rack has caught her eye with three or four short navy wool crêpe jackets with nipped-in waists, the lapels and slanted pockets edged in white, three mock mother-of-pearl buttons to do it up. My mother says she thinks she is a size twelve. She tries the jacket on right then and there and it takes fifty years off her. She stands in front of the mirror as Forties Miss, dashing about London in the Blitz, on her way to her job in Top Ops. She turns to us, radiant. 'What do you think?'

'Perfect.' The sleeves are too long, but this is a small matter. We will summon the seamstress and she will take them up, her mouth full of pins. As my mother folds the sleeves under I steal a covert look at the price tag. The jacket is reduced to £49.99, and this, in anybody's book, is a bargain.

'Now I need a skirt and blouse. I've got to match the navy.'

She disappears between the rails and I am anxious for it is not hard to lose sight of her, she has shrunk so in recent years. Five feet two all my life but I doubt if she is that now; perhaps she is under five feet. Her only grandson, the one whose mother is belatedly marrying at long last, doing the decent thing by her mother, at eleven is taller than her. How long will it be before he can lean his chin on the top of her head?

She's back quickly with her selection. The navy of the skirt and blouse she has chosen match each other and the jacket exactly, which isn't the easiest thing in the world to do so that I know that her perception of colour is quite unaltered and whatever else is wrong with her, there is nothing the matter with her eyes. I take the garments from her as we walk to the changing rooms, for everything apart from the smallest and lightest of handbags is too heavy for her now. A full mug of tea is too heavy for her to pick up. In cafes where they serve coffee in those large green and gold cups from France, she is stymied, remains thirsty.

What she gives me to hold is a Karl Lagerfeld skirt and a Jaeger blouse, both substantially reduced, at £89.99 and £69.99, but not within the £60 budget I had estimated when the old biddy dress came to mind, like those which hang from rails ignored by my mother. She has obeyed my instruction. She has not looked at the prices. Half-submerged in whatever part of the brain contains our capacity to make aesthetic judgements, her old good taste is buried and my injunction to ignore the prices has been the key that released it. A young woman of twenty-five could attend a job interview in the outfit she has put together.

In the changing room, she undresses. I remember the body I had seen in the bath when I was growing up, the convex belly that my sister used to think was like a washing-up bowl from two Caesarean births. The one that I have now, myself. She used to hold hers in under her clothes by that rubberized garment called a roll-on, a set of sturdy elasticized knickers. She had been six and a half stone when she got married which rose to ten stone after bearing her daughters, and she would spend twenty years adhering to the rules of Weightwatchers without ever noticeably losing a pound. She more or less stopped eating when my father died, apart from cakes and sweets and toast with low calorie marge, on which regimen she shed two stone and twice was admitted to hospital suffering from dehydration.

As she removes her skirt, I turn my head away. It is enough to bear witness to the pornography of her left arm, a swollen sausage encased in a beige rubber bandage, the legacy of a pioneering mid-Eighties operation for breast cancer which removed her lymph glands. The armpit is hollow.

The ensemble is in place when I look back. The pencil skirt, a size ten, is an exact fit but the blouse (also a ten) is a little too big, billowing round her hips, which is a shame for it is beautiful, in heavy matte silk with white overstitching along the button closings.

And now my mother turns to me in rage, no longer placid and obedient, not the sweet little old-age pensioner that shop assistants smile at to see her delight in her new jacket.

Fury devours her. 'I will not wear this blouse, you will not make me wear this blouse.' She bangs her fist against the wall and (she is the only person I have ever seen do this) she stamps her foot, just like a character from one of my childhood comics or a bad actress in an amateur production.

'What's the matter with it?'

She points to the collar. 'I'm not having anyone see me in this. It shows up my neck.'

I understand for the first time why, on this warm July day as well as every other, she is wearing a scarf knotted beneath her chin. I had thought her old bones were cold, but it is vanity. My mother was seventy-eight the previous week. 'Go and see if they've got it in a smaller size,' she orders.

My patient nephew is sitting beneath a mannequin outside watching the women come and go. There are very few eleven-year-old boys in the world who would spend a day of the school holidays traipsing around John Lewis with their aunt and their senile gran looking for clothes but let's face it, he has inherited the shopping gene. He's quite happy there, sizing up the grown ladies coming out of the changing rooms to say to their friends, 'What do you think? Is it too dressy?' or 'I wonder what Ray's sister will be wearing. I'll kill her if it's cream.'

'Are you all right?' He gives me the thumbs-up sign.

There is no size eight on the rack and I return empty-handed. My mother is standing in front of the mirror regarding herself: her fine grey hair, her hazel eyes, her obstinate chin, the illusory remains of girlish prettiness, not ruined or faded or decayed but withered. Some people never seem to look like grown-ups but retain their childish faces all their lives and just resemble elderly infants. My mother did become an adult once but then she went back to being young again; young with lines and grey hair. Yet when I look at her I don't see any of it. She's just my mother, unchanging, the person who tells you what to do.

'Where've you been?' she asks, turning to me. 'This blouse is too big round the neck. Go and see if they've got it in a smaller size.'

'That's what I've been doing. They haven't.'

'Oh.'

So we continue to admire the skirt and the jacket and wait for the seamstress to arrive, shut up together in our little cubicle where once, long ago, my mother would say to me: 'You're not having it and that's final. I wouldn't be seen dead with you wearing something like that. I don't care if it's all the rage. I don't care if everyone else has got one. You can't.'

My mother fingers the collar on the blouse. 'I'm not wearing this, you know. You can't make me wear it. I'm not going to the wedding if I've got to wear this blouse.'

'Nobody's going to make you wear it. We'll look for something else.'

'I've got an idea. Why don't you see if they have it in a smaller size.'

'I've looked already. There isn't one. This is the last...'

'No, I must interrupt you. I've just thought, do you think they've got it in a smaller size?'

'That's what I'm trying to tell you. They haven't got one.'

Her shoulders sag in disappointment. 'Anyway,' I say, to distract her, 'the seamstress will be along in a minute to take up the sleeves.'

She looks down at her arms. 'Why? They aren't too long.'

'That's because you folded them up.'

She holds the cuffs between her fingers. 'Oh, that's right.' She looks back at herself in the mirror, smiling. 'I love this jacket. But I don't like the blouse. Well, I do like it but it's too big round the neck. Why don't you nip outside and see if they've got a smaller one?'

'I've been. They haven't. I've told you already.'

'Did you? I don't remember. Have I ever told you that I've been diagnosed as having a memory loss?'

'Yes.'

Now the seamstress has come. My mother shows her the blouse. 'It's too big round the neck,' she tells her. 'Can you take it in?'

'No, Mum, she's here to alter the jacket.'

'Why? There's nothing the matter with it.'

'Yes there is. The sleeves are too long.'

'No they aren't.'

'That's because you've turned them up.'

'Well, never mind that. Go and see if they've got this blouse in a smaller size.'

And so it goes, like Alice in the garden, on the path where whatever she does always leads straight back to where she started. We are through the looking glass now, my mother and I, where we wander in that terrible wilderness without landmarks, nothing to tell you that you passed here only moments before.

We pay for the jacket and the skirt which are wrapped, the jacket remaining, ready to be collected absolutely no later than the day before the wedding, which is cutting it a bit fine but what can you do? We leave John Lewis and walk a few yards to the next store which is D. H. Evans.

Up the escalator to the dress department and on a sale rack is the very Jaeger blouse! And there are plenty of them and right at the front what is there but an eight.

'Look!' I cry. 'Look what they've got and in your size.'

My mother runs towards me, she really does pick up her legs and break into a trot. '*Well*, they didn't have that in John Lewis.'

'They did but it was too big and they didn't have a smaller one.'

'Did they? I don't remember.'

She tries the blouse on in the changing rooms. The fit is much better. She looks at the label. 'Jaguar. I've never heard of them.' Her eyes, which could match navy, sometimes jumbled up letters.

'Not jaguar, Jaeger.'

'Jaeger! I've never had Jaeger in my life before.'

'You must be joking. You've got a wardrobe full of it.'

'Have I? I don't remember. Have I told you I've been diagnosed with a memory loss?'

'Yes,' I say. 'You've told me.'

'And now,' my mother announces, 'I need a jacket and a skirt.'

'We've bought those already.'

'Where are they then?'

'The skirt is in this bag and the jacket is being altered.'

'Are you sure?'

'Positive.'

'What colour are they?'

'Navy.'

'Well, that's lucky,' she says pointing triumphantly to the blouse, 'because this is navy.'

My mother wants to take the tube home (or rather to the Home in which we have incarcerated her) for a taxi is an unnecessary extravagance. 'I'm fresh,' she says. But I am not. A moment always comes, towards the end of these outings, when I want to go into a bar and have a drink, when I wish I carried a hip flask of innocuous vodka to sip, sip, sip at throughout the day. Most of all I want it to stop, our excursion. I can't put up with any more and I fall into cruel, monosyllabic communication. 'Yes, Mum.' 'No, Mum.' 'That's right.' 'Mmm.'

Here is a taxi and do not think for a moment, Madam, that despite the many burdens of your shopping, however swollen your feet or fractious your child, that you are going to take this cab before me.

'Get in,' I order. As we drive off up Portland Place I am calculating how much her old biddy outfit has cost. It has come to £209.97 which is more than I have paid for mine and has beaten out all of us, including the bride herself, on designer labels.

My mother holds on to her two purchases, from which floral prints have been rigorously excluded.

She looks at us both, her daughter and grandson. She's puzzled about something. She has a question she needs to ask. 'Just remind me,' she says. 'How am I related to you?'

What is wrong with her? It isn't Alzheimer's disease but something called Multi-Infarct Dementia or MID. Tiny, silent strokes had been occurring in her brain, mowing down her recollections of what she had said half a minute ago. They were not the kind of strokes that paralysed or blurred her speech, far from it. She isn't confined to a chair but can walk for miles.

'Why do we have to go back now?' she complains. 'I'm still fresh. You know I've always been a walker.'

Apart from the physical wasting, she looks normal—she looks like a sweet little old lady—and people start up conversations with her which proceed as they expected until a question answered a moment before would be asked again—'No, I must interrupt, you haven't told me yet where you live.'

'As I just said, Birmingham.'

And then asked and asked and asked until you lost your patience because you thought you had been entering a dialogue which had its rules of exchange, and it turned out that what you were really talking to was an animate brick wall. Questions asked over and over again not because she couldn't remember the reply but because a very short tape playing in her head had reached its end and wound itself back to the beginning to start afresh. She knows the conventions of conversation—these have not deserted her—but she cannot recall what she has said herself a few moments before.

Sometimes the question is repeated before the person she is asking has finished getting through their response. There are little holes in her brain, real holes in the grey matter, where the memory of her life used to be and what she has done half an hour or even a few minutes ago.

She has no sense at all of the progress of her memory's ebb. I do. She does not know what lies ahead and I'm not going to tell her. Soon, she will no longer recognize me, her own daughter, and if her disease progresses as Alzheimer's does, her muscles will eventually forget to stay closed against the involuntary release of waste products. She will forget to speak and one day even her heart will lose its memory and forget to beat and she will die.

'Does she know you?' people ask, with that concerned, sympathetic tone in their voices. There is this thing which everyone can tell you about senile dementia, that after a while the most extraordinary event occurs—sufferers no longer recognize their closest relatives and believe that a wife of fifty years is an impostor and a beloved son changing his mother's sheets is a burglar who has entered the house to steal her valuables. When people ask me in that particular way, 'Does she know you?' what they imagine is a vacant drooling wreck in a chair from whom the last vestige of personality has fled, or perhaps a desolate wandering soul in house slippers condemned until death to walk the halls of the asylum, mumbling. Not a screaming harridan with eyes sharp for matching navy.

When did it begin, this business with my mother? Where was the start of it? Even now, when we have tests and diagnoses and medical records, I still feel that who my mother was once and who she is now are bound up together. Where did her personality end and where did the dementia begin? There is another aspect of her condition; it is called by doctors emotional incontinence. It causes her to come out with the most surprising things—rages, tears, but also information that she has suppressed for the whole of her life.

Whenever I asked her what her father did for a living she said, 'He was a cobbler.'

I assumed he had a shop. I always thought that.

'And what did your father do?' someone asked her recently. My mother replied at once: 'He went round the houses where someone had died and bought their shoes then he did them up and my mother sold them on a stall at Bootle market.' She'd kept that quiet for nearly eighty years.

When I sent away for her birth certificate (because she had given her mother's maiden name as a password for a bank account and couldn't remember it any more) I saw that her father signed it with a cross. He lived, it seemed, the most scavenging of lives, a poor illiterate who in another country would have crawled across refuse dumps to find something he could sell. I come, after all, from a family with a dodgy memory, one which mythologized its own past to fill in the gaps it either did not want to tell us about, or didn't know itself.

'I don't remember' was the answer to so many of my insistent questions. And whenever they told me they didn't remember, I always assumed they had something interesting to hide: like the repressed existence of my older half-sister Sonia, whose phone call to the house when I was ten and picked up the phone before anyone else and said in my best telephone voice, 'Who's speaking please?' was the first, rude intimation that I was a middle, not an oldest child.

Or why there was an eight-year gap between my younger sister and me. Or what my father's name was when he came from Poland, or why the family later changed the one they took when they arrived. Did they drop Ginsberg after I was born, landing me with two complicated birth certificates, because my father had been called guinea pig when he was at school? Or was it that letter from Mosley's resurgent post-war fascists promising the extermination of my Daddy and all his line? I still don't know.

When I think about my mother's loss of memory I understand that remembering things implies continuity, but my grandparents on both sides had, nearly a hundred years ago, become immigrants, stepped off the edge of the known world into England and the twentieth century, the century in which my family was to all intents born. She was the last of her line, my mum, the youngest of six who married one of six and all the brothers and sisters now dead and their husbands and wives. The world of my forefathers was locked up in her brain which, in certain places, had been turned off at the mains, so to speak.

On the day she revealed my grandfather's true occupation we were looking at old photographs and she began to talk about how her mother and father had come from Russia and how her father had said he would have stayed if only he could have got his hands on a gun to defend himself and 'your father told me that when he was a little boy he overheard *his* father talking— in Yiddish, you understand—and there was a girl and they came one night, and they came back every night and she went mad in the end and when it was born they killed it.'

'What are you talking about? Who came? Who was the girl?'

'What girl?'

'The one you were just talking about.'

'What was I saying? I can't remember.'

It was so ironic that Jews, who insist on forgetting nothing, should wind up, in my mother's case, remembering nothing.

If there was a beginning, I can't place a marker on it now. There is only the chronology of that year in which she went from being an independent widow in her own flat to her first involuntary steps through the doors of the Home, where she was living in the summer of 1996, the day of the shopping trip.

Whenever she had another stroke, she moved further down the stair into the dark cellar of her life. We got the diagnosis in April 1993 when we paid £60 to a man in Harley Street to tell us what was wrong. But the year which began for us at Christmas 1994 was the one in which great tracts of memory started to disappear in quick succession. And it was not just a matter of blouses, for the disease began to turn its malign attention to the very heart of her, her own identity.

We had always regarded Christmas as an entirely commercial festival, editing out the Infant Jesus and the manger and the carols and Midnight Mass. So when I invited my mother and sister and brother-in-law and nephew to my new flat for Christmas what we all anticipated was a good meal and the exchange of gifts.

They arrived on Christmas Eve and we sent her to bed in my room while I slept on an inflatable mattress in my study below. Michele said the next morning, 'I was up with Mum all night.'

'Why?'

'She kept getting up every five minutes and trying to leave because she thought she was in the wrong house. She didn't recognize the bedroom. I wrote out THIS IS LINDA'S NEW HOUSE. YOU ARE IN THE RIGHT ROOM on a piece of paper and propped it on the chest of drawers but she folded it up and put it in the drawer for safe keeping. I found all the keys to the front door in her handbag.'

My mother came down for breakfast: 'I've had a terrible night. I thought I was in the wrong flat and someone would come in and say "What are YOU doing in MY room?"' She said it in the tone of Father Bear asking Goldilocks, 'Who's been sleeping in MY bed?'

She and Michele had gone out to buy me a house-warming present, a radio for the kitchen as I had requested which I had opened with delight and mock surprise. 'Ooh, a radio! *Just* what I wanted. I can listen to music now when I cook.'

Several times as I was preparing lunch she pulled me away from the stove. 'Now this is important. I haven't bought you a house-warming present so I want you to take some money and get it yourself.'

'You've already bought me a house-warming present.'

'Have I? What is it?'

'A radio. Look, there it is.'

She examined it with uncertain eyes. 'I don't remember buying it. Are you sure?'

'Positive.'

After lunch, which was surprisingly good given the circumstances, my mother said, 'I'll wash up.'

'Fine with me.' It would get her out of the way for three quarters of an hour.

She came back a few minutes later. 'Linda, do you know you've got no sink in your kitchen?'

'What do you mean, no sink?'

'Come and have a look.'

She gestured round the room. 'Where is it?'

'There.'

'Oh, yes. I see it now.'

The following morning, taking a few glasses from the living room to the kitchen, I fell down a flight of stairs. Bruises blossomed across my back and legs. The pain was frightful. When I picked myself up and crawled to a chair Michele appeared. 'I've got the most stinking cold,' she said.

A summit conference was held. 'I vote we abandon Christmas,' I proposed. 'Let's just forget all about it.'

Mark said, 'The presents were lovely, the tree was lovely, the meal was lovely, the only problem was the people.'

We needed one of those smart weapons that would have vaporized the guests but left the trappings of Christmas intact.

'I want to go home,' my mother said. 'I don't like it here.'

Michele made a pretence of ringing the station to enquire about train times, though we had no intention of allowing her to travel home alone. 'There aren't any trains to Bournemouth on Boxing Day,' she said.

'Any to Liverpool?'

'But you don't live in Liverpool.'

'Don't I?'

'No.'

'Do I have a home any more?'

'Of course you do.'

'Where is it, because I can't remember.'

'It's in Bournemouth, where you moved with Dad.'

'Oh, yes, that's right. But sometimes, you know, I look round when I'm in my flat and I don't recognize where I am. Sometimes I start crying and I can't remember what I'm crying about.'

She began another sentence then broke off. 'I don't remember what I was talking about.' She cried again, easy tears that stopped as easily, for like cigarette smoke, the memory of her sorrow had disappeared without trace into the air.

Mark drove Michele and Ben back to Oxford, then my mother to Bournemouth and then back to Oxford. He spent the whole of Boxing Day on motorways, but that was better than spending it *en famille* Grant, he said.

April 1995. I went to Capri and stayed in a terracotta-coloured hotel built on the spot where the Emperor Tiberius once hurled his victims into the sea. Every morning I went to the deserted dining room for breakfast, came back and worked on my novel, and in the afternoon I ascended by the funicular railway to the town. The island was quiet; it was the week before Easter and the first tourist arrivals from the mainland were due but they weren't there yet. I did circular walks on paved paths in suede shoes and a pale lilac silk jacket and whatever fork I took, my wanderings always ended among the smartest of shops. One early afternoon I had a manicure. I bought my mother a musical box of inlaid wood which played ''Twas on the Isle of Capri that I met her'. Some friends who had driven from Rome to Naples took the boat over to spend the day with me. We had lunch overlooking a gorge and the blue Mediterranean spread itself in front of us, like the best kind of dress. This was what living was cracked up to be, privileged, effortless, exquisite. I was cut off from tragedy and tears. I dwelt that week in fairyland.

At home the new flat was full of plaster dust and builder's rubble, squalor on the grand scale. My mother rang me promptly the morning after my return.

'What are we doing for Pesach? You aren't going to leave me on my own in this flat with a box of matzo are you?'

'What would you like to do? Michele and Mark and Ben are in San Francisco but I could come to you.'

'I'm not staying here. I'm the only one who never goes away. I'm always here on my own.'

Later, searching through her things, I found a scrap of paper. On it she had written: <u>People</u> TAKe <u>STRAN</u>geares IN FOR <u>YONTIF</u> I HAVe <u>NOT</u> Bean <u>OUT</u>.

'That's not true,' I said. 'You were here at Christmas.'

'Was I? I don't remember.'

'Should I come and pick you up on the train?'

'Rubbish. I can manage on my own.'

But I didn't think that she could. She did not know any longer that Waterloo was the terminus station. 'Why isn't it called London?' she had asked me. This was the mother who when we took our annual Christmas trips to London confidently navigated buses and tubes and taxis. We went to the Tower of London and Kensington Palace, to little shops on Bond Street she had read about in a magazine at the hairdresser's, to the East End for Jewish food at Blooms. There were photos of me with pigeons on my head in Trafalgar Square, an outstretched hand filled with corn. Now she moved in a restricted universe, frightened of venturing beyond certain well-known routes near her own home.

So I took the train to Bournemouth and walked along the road from the station to her flat, in the bosky south coast air of a spring morning to the avenue lined with pine trees that were deceptively similar to the ones in Capri. I rang her entryphone buzzer and she let me in. I passed through the large empty lobby with chairs that no one sat in, vases with dusty silk flower arrangements which no one admired, came up in the small wood-panelled lift to her silent floor with its four flats. Her door was ajar.

I walked in. I called out, 'Where are you, Mum?'

'Here.'

The worst of her illness for me then and now was seeing her, sitting on the toilet, crying, struggling to put on her tights.

'I don't think I can handle myself any more.' She wept. 'Sometimes I think I'm so brave, what I manage to do. Do you think I'm ready?'

'Ready for what?'

'To go somewhere else.'

'What sort of place are you thinking of?'

'Somewhere they'll look after me.'

'Yes,' I said. 'I think you're ready.'

I saw her loneliness, her isolation from the world, the battle to make it through every day without major mishap, without getting lost or burning herself or falling in the bath or forgetting to take her tablets or turn the gas off or pay her phone bill or eat. I saw the programmes marked with a cross on the television pages of her *Daily Mail*, the programmes which were her only company day after day, her television friends. The casts of all her soap operas were the ones who said goodnight to her and the presenters of the breakfast shows said good morning. They smiled at her and spoke to her as if she had no memory loss at all, never irritated, never complaining. They did her the honour of assuming she had as much sense in her head as they had.

As if she lived in a house that was falling down, she ran hither and thither trying to repair her roof or mend her floor, anything to stop the place from tumbling down around her ears for she fought not just to manage her everyday life but to maintain her existence as a human being, a social animal with rights and responsibilities and likes and dislikes.

I could see now that my family had by necessity reconstructed itself and its past for the life it would live in a new land. Cut off from the previous century, from its own line of continuity with its memory of itself, it made itself up. All the lies and evasions and tall stories are what you must have when you are inventing yourself. Now my mother was bent on a similar task, that of continuously inventing for *herself* (and the rest of the world) a coherent identity and daily history. For a lifetime of practising deceit had only prepared her for her greatest role, dementia, in which she did everything she could to pretend to the world that she was right as rain and could not stop to talk if she saw someone in the street for really, she had to dash, she was meeting a friend for morning coffee. Her neighbours told me that, later. They suspected that there was no date. Instead of cakes and gossip she would return to her empty flat, with neither husband nor children nor grandchildren, to cry her eyes out. Yet she went on presenting a bold facade, a fictitious person for inspection, hoping it would pass muster.

This was a battle which called up everything she had in her. It was her capacity for deception that armed her against the destruction of her self. Only to me, for a moment, who saw her alone and vulnerable, sitting on the toilet trying to dress, did she reveal the bruising exhaustion of that daily combat.

We took the train to London. 'Would you like to live in London or Bournemouth?'

'London. Definitely. You're not making me stay in Bournemouth.'

I knew why. Because of the humiliation; she who had once been a helper would now be the helped. She who had once held the hands of her old dears at the day centre, where she volunteered with other active Jewish ladies, would have her own clutched by her former equals.

There was no trouble that night remembering where she was but the next morning I found all my drawers and cupboards immaculately tidied. In her case, beautifully folded, were some of my clothes.

I raised again the matter of her moving on.

'I will have my own kitchen will I, because I'm not eating other people's food?'

'No, I don't think you would have your own kitchen.'

'I'm not going then.'

'But it's not like you cook much anyway.'

'Yes, but if I didn't have a kitchen I'd feel like I was in a home.'

'What sort of place would you like to move to?'

'Where they have a warden.'

'You mean sheltered housing.'

'That's right, sheltered housing.'

'I'm not sure if that's the right place for you.'

'Well I'm not going into a home and that's the end of it.'

Walking along the street she suddenly exploded like a match thrown into a box of fireworks, remembering an old grudge she bears against my sister.

'You're taking her side, are you? You're no better than her. Where's the bus? I'm going. I'm getting the bus home.'

'Well you can't. You can't get a bus from here to Bournemouth.'

She began to sob. 'I want to go home, I want to go home. I'll get a taxi, then, you can't stop me.'

We reached my house and she went and sat down and cried. I left the room. I came in ten minutes later. 'Do you want a cup of tea?'

'Yes. But tell me. Have I had a row with someone? I think I've had a row but I can't remember who with. Was it Michele? I don't remember.' It was an excellent new tactic this. Whatever was upsetting her, if you left her alone for a few minutes she couldn't remember it.

The next day I mentioned Michele.

'Michele. Who's Michele?'

'Your daughter.'

'I've got a daughter called Michele.'

'Who lives in Oxford.'

'Who lives in Oxford.'

We were at Piccadilly Circus. 'Where are we, Mum?' I asked her. She looked around. 'Bournemouth.'

Like Michele at Christmas I developed a violent, atrocious cold, the kind where you feel nauseous and dizzy if you stand up. How could I take her to Bournemouth and come back in one very long afternoon? We went by taxi to Waterloo and I put her on the train in the care of another passenger. I went home and as soon as I thought she might have returned I rang. She answered the phone without concern.

'Was the journey all right?'

'Yes. Why shouldn't it be?'

The following day she rang me. 'You've left me like a dog all over Pesach. I haven't budged from this flat for a week. I've been all alone with just a box of matzo. What kind of daughter are you to do this to your own mother?'

'Mum, you were here, yesterday. You've been in London.'

'Don't you lie to me, you liar. I've not been out the door.'

'Don't you remember being in London? At my flat. You stayed here.'

'In Brixton?'

'No, the new flat.'

'When did you move?'

309

'In December.'

'And you've never bleddy invited me for a cup of tea.'

'You were here. You stayed here. You've only just got back.'

'I'm not listening to you another minute. You're telling me I'm mad.' The phone slammed down at the other end.

I rang her back at once. She was crying her eyes out. 'You bitch,' she screamed and the phone went down again. This went on for the next hour.

I rang her the next morning. 'What's new?' she enquired in a calm, bright voice. 'I haven't spoken to you for ages.'

She wanted me to do something. When she asked me if she was ready, she knew she was but she could not accept responsibility for making the decision for herself. She wanted to rest now, to let go of all the burden of her life, but she needed someone to make her. So she could say, 'I was advised to. I wanted to stay in my own home but they wouldn't let me.' A member of that superior breed, the 'specialist', would be called in and then pride could be satisfied and indignity stared out.

But Michele and I were too taken in by the current fashion in social work and the advice columns: respect the rights of the elderly; consult them; do not force them to do what they do not want. Michele had already rung the Help the Aged helpline. The thinking went like this: old people with dementia were best left to stay in familiar surroundings for as long as possible, where they were habitualized. It was moving that caused crises, where they would have to deal with unaccustomed rooms and would not have, secure in an undamaged portion of their minds, the routes to and from home. When they were taken away, like dogs they tried to find their way back. Then they were locked in, the keys and the bolts got heavier until in the end only a secure mental institution could hold them. Better to keep her where she was. And anyway she had rights. We could not put her away just to suit us, we were told. My mother's rights allowed her to spend twenty-three hours alone, crying, overdosed or under-medicated because fifteen minutes after her taking her tablets she couldn't remember if she had swallowed them or not. Her nightmare went on and on.

I read these sentences from other people's lives: 'Just because

I'm old doesn't mean I'm stupid.'

'Just because I'm old doesn't mean I don't see, don't understand.'

So for several more months my mother was treated like an adult, like a fully-paid-up member of the human race.

October 1995. Yom Kippur, the Day of Atonement, the most important day in the Jewish year when even the least observant Jew makes their way to the synagogue.

Yom Kippur is also a day of remembrance. It is the day when we say the prayer of Yiskor that offers up our words to God for the souls of the dead. Children are ushered out and adults whose parents are both still living leave voluntarily. First there are spoken the names of the congregants who have passed away in the last twelve months. Then come the prayers for the dead whose relatives in the congregation have offered money to charity to hear their names uttered aloud. Then there is our public memory of the nameless dead of the Holocaust.

Those who remain offer their own individual prayer for their dead relatives, their mother or father, husband or wife. So we cast our chain of memory down through the generations and link ourselves with all the forgotten ones of the past who have nobody left to mourn them. The synagogue is at its fullest. The old and the sick and frail stumble there any way they can to say Yiskor. To do less is to have done nothing.

This was the most important day of the year, when my mother would pray for the souls of her dead parents, and for her brothers Abe and Harry and her sisters Miriam and Gertie, and Gertie's only child, Martin, who died of leukaemia when he was only twenty-six, and for her own husband. But I thought she was too confused to travel to London and that it would be best if I came to her.

'I will not, I will not stay in Bournemouth,' she shouted at me down the phone. 'This place reminds me too much of your father at this time of year. I want to come to London.'

'I'll come and get you on the train.'

In fact it was all to the good that she had decided that London was the place to be because my long-lost cousin Sefton,

311

who had lived in Israel for the past twenty-five years, was back in town and so I invited him to come and see my mother. 'Sefton!' she cried. 'My favourite nephew.' She remembered everything about him, who his wife was and how they had married and when he had gone abroad.

I rang her just before I left the house to remind her what time my train arrived. I explained that if she was there to meet me with her small suitcase we would only have a brief wait until the return journey.

'Yes,' she said. 'Don't worry. I've got it written down.'

I did not know if she would be there but she was, only a few minutes late, standing without any luggage. 'I've got to buy my ticket,' she said. 'I've been to the bank.' She no longer kept money in a purse or wallet but in a small plastic bag.

'Mum, where's your case?'

She looked around. 'Where's my case. Bugger it, I don't need any clothes.'

'Of course you do. What have you brought with you?'

'Nothing.'

'Have you got your pills?'

'Yes, they're in my bag.'

'Show me.'

'Bugger off. I've got them.'

'I want to see.'

Meekly, she gave me her small handbag, the lightest of all those she owned and held across her shoulder by its strap. She was so little now. Little and old and confused. A mugger's ideal target.

There were no pills.

'We're going to go back now and pack properly.'

'Oh, do we have to?'

'Yes.'

We walked along the road to the flat. She let us in and sat down for a few minutes with her eyes closed, exhausted, in what used to be my father's chair. Then she opened them and said: 'Well, I'm delighted you've come for the weekend. How long are you staying?'

'I'm not staying. I've come to pick you up. You're coming to London.'

She burst into tears. 'Now you tell me. Do we have to?'

'But it was you who insisted. You said you wouldn't stay here.'

Her mood changed like a radio clicking to another station, from sobbing violins to angry drums.

'You're not going to make me stay in Bournemouth. I'll cut my throat if I've got to stay here.'

'Well that's good, because Sefton is coming to see us in London.'

'Who's Sefton?'

'Uncle Louis's son.'

'No, doesn't ring a bell.'

I watched her pack, a few things that didn't belong to each other thrown into a small case.

'Underwear, Mum.'

'I don't need that, do I?'

We went back to the station and caught the train. The orange signal lights inside the tunnel at Waterloo caught her eye as we approached the platform. 'Ooh,' she said. 'Isn't it beautiful, like fairyland.'

As we went towards the tube I saw a newspaper placard announcing that O. J. Simpson had been found guilty. 'I'm just stopping to buy the *Evening Standard*, Mum.'

'Why, anything interesting in it?'

'The verdict on O. J. Simpson,' I told her. Of course she would not know what I was talking about.

'Well, I think he did it, don't you? I've been addicted to the trial.' Thus my mother, who did not know what day of the week it was, what was up and what was down, had for many months been following one of the most complex criminal cases of the century.

I went in to see her as she was getting ready for bed. She was standing with her nightdress on over her clothes.

'Mum! What are you dressed like that for? Are you cold?'

'No. Why?'

'You've got your nightie over your clothes. You don't do that.'

She looked down, uncertainly. 'Don't you?'

The following morning we went in the rain by taxi to the synagogue at Muswell Hill. She gave out little cries and ran to embrace people, complete strangers as it turned out. They saw my embarrassment. I saw the look of pitying understanding in their eyes. She did not follow the service.

On each seat was the congregation's community magazine. It contained an article about a nursing home adjacent to the synagogue. It was called Charles Clore House after the famous Jewish philanthropist who had once owned Selfridges, exactly the kind of man my parents admired and longed to be like themselves.

She read it over and over again. 'Do you think I'm ready?' she asked.

'Shush. Don't talk so loud. Whisper. Remember where you are.'

'Why? Where am I?'

My mother's diabetes ruled out fasting so I took her for lunch in a cafe where she had a bowl of soup and a sandwich. Someone I knew came in and I saw him start to come over to speak to us but I shook my head. Her voice was so loud though she wasn't deaf, she smiled so brightly at people she did not know and they all, without exception, said, 'Oh, she's so sweet.'

'I must give you some money,' she offered.

'What for?'

'For the pictures.'

'What pictures?'

'Where we've just been. We've been to the pictures. I can't remember what the film was but I know we've been. Have I told you I've been diagnosed with a memory loss?'

And it was then that I thought, 'That's it. This has gone far enough. She's got to go into a home whether she likes it or not. I must *do* something.'

I saw that the mother, who for so long I thought had made my life such a misery, was gone. That I was never going to win the great argument with her about the kind of daughter she expected me to be for my adversary had left the field. In her place was a bewildered infant whom the world insisted on treating as an adult with no one to protect her. My mother, my child.

After half a lifetime of being an inadequate, undutiful daughter, now I was to take on a role I had refused elsewhere, that of a parent. It was up to me to do what I thought was best for her, to tell her how she could and could not behave, to protect her from danger, make sure she was properly housed and fed, to find her the best attention money could buy. Like many women of my generation, I thought I had won freedom and independence. I hadn't of course. Now I was to become my mother's guardian, as tied to her as if she were my baby.

My cousin Sefton came for lunch and as soon as he walked into the room my mother ran to greet him. After an absence of a quarter of a century the visual recognition portion of her brain was intact.

'You're as handsome as you ever were,' she told him. 'My favourite nephew.'

We looked at old photographs.

'Who's that?' she asked, pointing to a picture of his father.

'That's my father.'

'Who is your father?'

'Louis.'

'But you're Louis.'

'No, I'm Sefton.'

'How am I related to you?'

'I'm your nephew.'

'So who is your father?'

'Louis.'

'That's right. How's your wife? She was very beautiful, you know. She used to be a beauty queen.' It was true, she had been.

Why could she remember Anne, met perhaps two or three times and not since the 1960s? Why could she whisper to me when he was out of the room, 'His wife isn't Jewish, you know'?

And why was it, as we waved goodbye to Sefton, that she turned to me and smiled and said, 'He's lovely. Who is he?'

I took her back to Bournemouth on a packed train. I watched her lips moving as she tried to capture the thoughts that drifted through her mind like fast clouds. A woman opposite us was watching her too. She looked at her in pity. She looked at me and I saw in her face what she thought, 'The poor bloody daughter, having to look after her.' Perhaps she thought I was one of those selfless, dedicated women who loved their mothers so much they would never put her in a home. I stared back at her, eyeball to eyeball. I sent out a telepathic message. I'm not what you think. This situation is not as you imagine. I *am* going to put her in a home.

'Mum,' I said. 'Show me your chequebook.' She handed it over. On the day she left Bournemouth she had withdrawn two lots of £30. She only had £30 when she met me at the station. Thumbing back through the stubs, I saw that on various days she had withdrawn multiple amounts of money. I imagined that she had gone to the bank, written a cheque, then forgotten later that she had been.

She rang me the next morning. She was crying.

'I've left my chequebook at your house. Will you send it back to me.'

'No, you definitely haven't left it here because I was looking at it on the train and you put it back in your bag yourself.'

'I *haven't* got it. Why won't you listen to me?'

'Honestly, Mum, I promise you that you have got your chequebook. It is there.'

'It *isn't*. Why are you doing this to me? I've got no money for food. I'm hungry and I've got no money. Please, please send me my chequebook.'

'I can't because I haven't got it.'

The familiar routine began. The phone slammed down then a minute or two later rang again.

'Linda, it's Mum. I can't find my chequebook. Have you got it?'

'No, we just had this conversation.'

'When?'

'Two minutes ago.'

'We didn't.'

'Yes, we did.'

'Well never mind that. I want you to send me my chequebook.'

'I can't. I haven't got it.'

'Please, please, I'm so hungry.'

It went on for two days. The phone calls every hour or so as if they had never occurred before. I went out for a while. My cleaner said, 'Linda, I was cleaning your office and there was the most terrible message on the answering machine. Whoever it was was in the most awful distress. I didn't know what to do. It was something about a chequebook.' The last call came at twenty past midnight on Saturday, the latest my mother had ever phoned me. The first began at ten to eight the next morning.

In the evening people were coming to dinner. It was early October and unusually warm. The last of the first phase of redecorating was over and I was free to entertain, to be gracious, to lay my marble table with my canteen of cutlery and place there the squat, cut-glass tumblers that I had stolen from my father's cocktail cabinet. To be on the safe side I put the answering machine on. The phone rang and everyone went quiet as my mother's demented voice formed a faint but audible backdrop to the Delia Smith beef casserole which we ate in defiance of threats to our own future sanity, just before the BSE scare went ballistic. 'I'm hungry, I've got no money for food. Why won't you help me?'

First thing on Monday morning I rang my mother's bank. I don't think anyone has been so pleased to hear my voice as that young clerk who, it turned out, dealt with my mother's account.

And that phone call, followed by others to social workers and doctors and matrons of homes, marked the end of my mother's adult life. From that day on, she was to be my dependant. When she went into the Home we took her money away from her, her door keys, her chequebook, her credit card, her kitchen, her cupboard with its boxes of dinner services for best, her furniture. We left her in a small room with some photographs and a fraction of her once-fabulous wardrobe. The jewels were gone already, stolen down the years by window cleaners and home helps.

The actual day she went into the Home, I was away. It was Michele and Mark who took her there. To the place of old men and women, drooling wrecks, Alzheimer's cases. Jewish old people's homes had unusual problems. There was a Holocaust survivor there, severely damaged by dementia. When they took him to the shower he thought he was being led to the gas chamber.

I got back and the phone was ringing. 'They've made a new woman of me,' she said. 'I'm ready to go back to Bournemouth now.' They had, in a way. She was fed three times a day, properly medicated, no longer had to struggle to preserve herself intact for daily life.

'No, Mum, you can't go home.'

'Do you mean I've got to stay here for the rest of my life?'

I did not want to tell her, yes. There was silence at my end.

'You bitch,' she said.

1998
The Separated

Tim Lott

January

It is a short January day, unseasonably warm. The afternoon is getting dark and it isn't yet four o'clock. The house is a three-storey, a family house.

On the top floor: two bedrooms, slumber, awakenings from dreams, small excitements becoming sadnesses.

On the middle floor: a sitting room, with a third bedroom behind, this time strewn for play. There are children's paintings, colourful messes on the walls, toys. The children, sisters, one four and one two years old, are absent on a visit to their grandmother.

On the ground floor: the guts of the house. A whitewashed bathroom, evacuations, submersions, the faint scrape of razors across a leg or a face. Behind the bathroom, a small concrete yard where a cigarette is sometimes taken, out of sight of the children. You can sit on the blue plastic sandpit, moulded in the shape of a clam. Inside, the main room on this floor has a flat-pack kitchen, carelessly assembled, varnished gappy floorboards, a sofa made grubby with the food the children spill. There is a table in the style of a Fifties diner at the front, filling the curved space in the bay window. It is a basic metropolitan home, not luxurious, a little dirty.

The couple inside have just returned from a day at the winter sales. The man is on the short side, losing hair, his face wearing a bloom of frustration. The woman is dark-haired, Mediterranean, almost too slender. Pretty, appearing in any light far younger than she actually is. Her face is pale—always avoiding the sun—and her body is quite still.

There are seven or eight moths floating in the room. They made a nest here three months ago, and will not be discouraged by the remedial sprigs of lavender that are carefully placed on mantels, fireplaces and window frames. The moths move too slowly. You can easily catch one in your hand and destroy it with the tiniest movement. The man does this now, with an infant's sense of satisfied cruelty.

The couple are squared-up to each other, about five feet apart. The man is speaking loudly and purposefully. He knows exactly what he is saying and that perhaps he shouldn't be saying it, but he can't find the will or interest to prevent himself.

Words are now in the air, like the moths. Or not so much like moths, but small black birds.

'I fucking hate you. You fucking cunt.'

His unintended mission completed, the man walks out of the room. The words are still reverberating in his head. He leaves in order to calm himself. He knows he has gone much further than he has ever been in such a transaction between himself and his wife of six—is that right?—yes, six years. Six and a half, he thinks. He feels himself strangely excited by the freedom of the moment, while simultaneously shamed. The words have crossed several long-established borders that have previously contained their arguments. It is as far away as they have been from the starting line, or some imagined zone of healing and reconciliation. The man has never struck his wife, but imagines that this is how it must feel. He is shocked that it feels this pure, that it feels this real.

Five, maybe ten minutes have passed. He has been pacing the first-floor front room, tripping over, then cursing, stray dolls, cute dinosaurs, a battery-powered tyrannosaurus with soft teeth and a single eye. He gathers himself, and starts the journey down the stairs. This is difficult. He knows the space he has left will be transformed in some way he does not yet understand. He doesn't know what he is going to say.

His wife doesn't seem to have moved from where he left her. She is waiting for a resolution of some kind. Her mouth is set in an unmoving, crimson line. The man has to go and pick up the children in a few minutes. Things cannot be left as they are.

The man's voice is vibrating perceptibly when he speaks. He had only imagined that he had calmed down. The man says:

'I just want to say one thing.'

He looks at her face for the first time. It is blank.

'I'm calm now. And settled. And I just want to say. I want you to know that...'

He imagines that she is expecting him to apologize. He hopes so, so that she will be caught on the wrong foot.

'I want you to know that I meant every word that I just said. So wake up and smell the fucking coffee—before it's too late.'

And with this, he makes to leave with what he hopes to be a flourish. He likes the sound of his last sentence. It is an expression his younger brother uses, and he has borrowed it for this purpose. But his wife remains neutral, and rather than looking shocked or annoyed, looks perplexed. She says, in a voice he has heard so much, so often, it has become, for the most part, inaudible:

'What does that mean?'

The man is irritated that the flow of his exit has been interrupted.

'What does what mean?'

'*Wake up and smell the coffee*. What does that *mean*? I don't understand.'

It's a phrase she has never heard before, and in the heightened emotion of the moment she's unable to infer its meaning. So then the man has carefully to explain the phrase to her, so that the flourish with which he hoped to leave the house is deflated into lameness. He shakes his head in disgust and astonishment—not at his wife, now, but at invisible half-imagined gods. For even now, in the heat and heart of collapse, in the furnace of his temporary hate—strictly temporary, for he likes his wife often enough, well enough—they still can't understand each other. That his simple threat and insult, his searing warning, is met again with the endless tattoo that passes between them, publicly, privately, internally, verbally, symbolically, literally.

I don't, I don't, I don't *understand* you.

Exercises in Words

The man is a writer. This is a word he privately savours, always careful to distinguish it, sniffily, defensively, from the description 'journalist', the coin of whose trade, he believes, are mute facts skilfully assembled, opinions racked in a penny store, the minting of smart turns of phrase which are insufficiently true. *Writer*. To use that word accurately about himself he considers to be his greatest achievement, in a life full of garish stumbles, mistakes and small terrors.

He has a certain reputation for writing pieces of a confessional nature, exposing his tenderest parts, like a courting mandrill, for public inspection. Some find this tasteless. So occasionally, he writes about his life as if it were fiction. One or two commentators think that this is simply a stylistic conceit. But this is not, in fact, the case. It is the man's way of taking refuge, a protective coating over what is too raw. It is also a way, he hopes, of sparing himself embarrassment. The fear of embarrassment, he thinks, is one of the world's most underrated forces.

He often wishes that he could turn his life into fiction, or be given the option to claim it as fiction. It's what he does in his head all the time. Laid out like that, it acquires a grace and tidiness that real life lacks. The man's ugly abuse offset by considerations of style, structure and imagined elegance of grammar.

But what he writes is printed in his memory. It happened, though not exactly like that, not just-so, though this is exactly how he remembers it happening. His wife's memories, his children's, will be different.

The couple in his story, the story in his head, are himself and his partner. The 'third person', this godlike perspective, can only do so much to distance him from reality, to grant him absolution. He is Tee, and his wife is Ess. They have been married six years. Six and a half. It has all been coming a long time. Perhaps since that summer day, July 1, 1991, when he kissed her under the bridal veil, feeling, even then, a sense of theatre, of acting.

She was stiff with tension, frozen at the altar.

More Exercises: Again with Words

The man, Tee, considers it vital to the successful execution of his skill that he can see what lies underneath the skin of people. That, at the very least, he can make good guesses. He prides himself on his expertise at communication.

Communication. The man and the woman both know now that things are extreme, stretched dangerously. Tee thinks of a balloon expanding towards a pin. That frail tightness.

Family therapists—so the man and his wife are told—use a well-tested exercise which is designed to *facilitate communication*. These are the words that are used. The man finds it an ugly phrase, with a grain running through it implying homilies and mocked-up concern. Nevertheless, the balloon is about to burst. Unusual remedies, they accept, may be necessary. Both parties— for parties are already how he styles themselves in his mind, as if flexing for formal negotiation—recognize that they need help to find ways over the fences they have erected against understanding each other.

For the man, this fence is made of condescension, an adopted superiority. For the woman it is made of silence, or shouting. Both are expressions of a rearing, kicking anger at something, possibly something deep in the past, that manifests itself perpetually in the present. Or is history, the man wonders, just a way of getting them both off the hook? More and more nowadays, he thinks so.

The exercise, then. The exercise is simple, and, so they are assured, effective. One half of the couple begins a conversation. The other half, instead of answering verbally, writes their reply on a piece of paper, then immediately shows their written answer to the speaker. And thus the conversation progresses. One partner is therefore always silent, their voice converted into text. The couple rotate their roles as speaker and writer, on a daily basis.

The husband and wife gravely try the exercise. Half an hour, four times a week, after the children have gone to bed. A file begins to accumulate of all the arguments that have been eating up the marriage like famished tapeworms. The man stares at a ream of paper, some sides covered in his handwriting—big, intimidating—some sides decorated with hers, smaller, flowing.

He sees scraps of his own scrawled sentences. Only half the conversation, of course, his half. The half which is spoken by Ess is missing, unrecorded, and can only be inferred or remembered.

It's a very hard thing for me to express...somehow it bleeds you dry...your obsessive rituals...do something about what?...of course...but how can I when I don't know its source?...anything else would be asking the impossible...I have to find a way of averting my eyes...how have you done it all your life?...if you can tell me how you can do it, then maybe I'll know how I do it... Not true...! I thought I had accepted your limitations and that you had accepted mine...now it turns out that you don't. Result? War…I don't know.

It comes across as mostly nonsense. Yet reading the scraps is strangely satisfying, sometimes even, he thinks, they read like an oblique poem. In his mind, he calls it 'Sometimes'.

Yes.

Sometimes.

Yes.

Badly.

I don't know.

Why do you think?

The questions are all missing. In life, the other way round. He looks at the other pieces of paper, covered with his wife's handwriting. Now it is his voice that is absent. Perhaps there are some clues here.

Then why are you getting uptight?…you make me feel I should be so grateful…you make me feel guilty. I'm tired…I've always felt it was unfair…I did not say that…what would I be, a housewife, a 'mother'?—NOT ENOUGH. Was that a question, does it require an answer?…OK let's drop it. All I know is that you are different from other fathers…I hate your…stickler for the rules…I'm not a child I don't need boundaries. You can be so rigid sometimes.

He sees a pattern emerging, eventually. Each argument has had a life almost as long as the marriage, repeating, never even mutating much, just kicking along, separately alive, dedicated to its own survival in some obscure way. Seeing those screeds of part-arguments laid out now on paper is salutary. How inescapable those little whorls of ink and dots and lines seemed, how they stretched out and linked like tiny binding tethers.

They are both growing weary of this exercise, which seems less and less like a game, although it has worked in some way, by forcing them to confront the tight patterns that rule their lives. The patterns seem immutable.

A time comes when they have not performed the exercise for several days. Then, one night three days after the man's forty-second birthday, they resume.

A record remains of this night, the record, as it turns out, of the end of their marriage. Sometime later, the man picks up this

325

last scrap of paper and attempts to decode it, to remember the missing questions.

The first answer is:

Pretty bad.

It is written in the hand of Ess, so it is clear that Tee is doing the talking. The question, he remembers clearly, is, 'How are you feeling?'

The next answer is:

I wish I could answer that. We're on different planes—taking different journeys—not meeting anywhere.

The question there is, 'What's the matter?'

He goes on, filling in the gaps as best he can (his wife remembers some questions differently).

Him: *Are you as frightened of this conversation as I am?*

Her: *Yes. Is that why you didn't want to have it?*

Him: *I did want to have it.*

Her: *I hate these 'communications'. It's brought it to a head.*

Him: *I want to ask you one question. It's important that you answer honestly. Do you really really love me, or are you just keeping the marriage afloat because the alternative seems unbearable?*

The man remembers a tiny gap here before she starts writing. She shows him her words on the sheet of paper.

It's the second. But then I also believe(d) you don't love me.

He stares at the paper. Now he feels he knows what she wants. And whether she wants it or not, it's done now.

Well. There's nothing more to say then.

He acknowledges the courage the woman has shown in making her answer. He remembers that they sat there, perfectly still and silent, until the man began to sob, softly at first, then more loudly. The woman reached across to console him... They held each other like that for a short while. For a minute or so, perhaps.

The man had not cried such tears in the marriage—no tears at all, that he can remember—since one day, four or five years previously, when, standing in their kitchen alone, he suddenly stopped his trivial tasks, sat down and began to weep, inexplicably, for some twenty minutes, then resumed his tasks.

This time, though, was different. This time, the cause was all too clear.

The Separated

The man finds this separation an unpredictable experience. Yet it is not the first time it has happened—once before, almost exactly a year ago, they parted, for a matter of six weeks. But this occasion already feels different. No clenching of teeth, or utterances of determination. Just the sense of things now taking their proper course. It feels as if a great weight has been lifted, his interior cleansed by the first batch of deeply shed tears.

That night, the man struggles to unpack a sofa bed on the first floor. The man thinks that he will never share a bed with his wife again, and it does not seem so strange. Perhaps he has been more absent than he has been capable of admitting to himself.

It has been agreed that he will move out of the house in two weeks' time.

He pulls the mechanism of the bed to about a quarter of the way out. It often sticks like this. He wrestles and struggles with it, pulling wildly, nearly toppling the sofa over. It will not come loose. The man becomes enraged; the mechanism has momentarily become his marriage: stiff, stuck, cursed, immovable. Now he attacks it like a glowering enemy, but it remains immobile. The man lets loose a stream of curses, then packs the bed away, and falls on to a single line of sofa cushions, defeated.

He thinks of explosions underground. The system, he thinks, lying there in the darkness, has been building up pressure for so many years, then suddenly a hole appears, then another, then the whole thing blows, and you're soaked, soaked through, and it's dreadful, you might be swept away, but there's an ecstasy in it too.

It is a short-lived feeling. During that first night alone, he hears one of his children crying. He rushes upstairs to see if she wants milk, or if he can cover her with a blanket or bring her a toy. Then halfway up the stairs, he realizes it may not be either of his children, but his wife.

He keeps himself warm against the chill inside him by repeating over and over an incantation.

327

The present will sink into the past. Everything passes. Things will change. Death and birth and death and birth and death and birth.

He stands looking at his children breathing in their bunk beds. He imagines something here for them has been irretrievably shattered, but that that something may have been a bad thing. Something will be remade. It may be better. He hopes so, but cannot guarantee it.

He fears losing his children. He fears so many things. But at the same time, he feels brave, and far beyond any kind of backslide.

During the next day, the man finds himself beginning idly to calculate the odds—already!—of starting again with someone else, some day, far in the future. There is no one remotely on the horizon. Neither he nor his wife were unfaithful to each other during the marriage, despite occasional flirtations.

What are his chances? He is not young. He is ordinary looking, too stocky. Yet he feels confidence, some sense of power. It is, he realizes, the power of indifference. The strength of loving his children removes other needs. The power of moving himself forward through this situation to the other side makes him feel that choice is within him, no longer buried and latent, but exposed like a vein pulsing in his brow.

He does not do any more crying, except when he tells his younger brother. Then he falls once more into racking sobs. His brother puts his arm round him as if he were the elder, and holds him. When he lets go, Tee is calm.

He tries to convince himself: The children are all right, children are tough.

The last time they split up, the eldest daughter was assailed by asthma, began to suck her thumb, piss herself. On one occasion she smeared shit all over the wall. Her silent, furious protests at feared chaos.

Two nights on. The man hears a movement, in the darkness. He walks into his eldest daughter's room. She is sitting bolt upright, still asleep, but with her eyes open. She says just this:

'Daddy.'

Then lies down again and is silent.

The next day, the younger child, who has been told nothing yet—who cannot possibly understand anything yet—says:

'Where's Daddy's house?'

Then she says:

'Daddy's crying, Mummy's crying, Ruby's crying, Cissy's crying.'

No one has cried in front of her. She is two and a half years old.

The man is not superstitious, but he shares Shakespeare's belief that misfortunes come not as single spies. Everywhere he looks, connections are being unmade—friends parting, death intruding, couples disintegrating.

On one side of the house the neighbours are getting divorced, on the other side they have separated just this week. Another two friends have left or been left by their partners. The world seems to operate in these ebbs and surges.

On the fifth day, death begins to worry his elder daughter.

'You're not going to die, are you Daddy? I hope Mummy isn't going to die.'

She starts crying.

'What's it like to die, Daddy?'

'It's like going to sleep.'

This doesn't satisfy her.

'But...but then you don't wake up!'

And she cries bitterly once more. The man is lost for consolation, because what she says is so terrible and true.

Another time, she says:

'I want my real mummy.'

This daughter sometimes separates her parents into two. When her mother was angry with her, she would say: 'I want my good mummy,' thinking her bad mummy had appeared instead. Now she wants her real mummy, that is to say, the happy one.

Will I lose them? he wonders, for the hundredth time. Then he doesn't allow himself this thought any more. It scares him too much. He has never loved anything in his stupid life so much as his children. This, he supposes, is a banal, commonly repeated sentiment, but it is true, as true as anything can be.

The next night, the man thinks of other women he might

hold in bed. But the thought doesn't excite him or interest him. He has always found his wife attractive, and the sex has been more than good. But he is numbed anyway by the prospect of that much intimacy.

He is frightened, but not nearly as frightened as he had thought he might be.

On the seventh day he studies bank balances. There is two months' money left. But he refuses to let it worry him. He has come to believe in putting a certain amount of faith in the future. Not an intemperate amount. Just so much. It's going to be tough though. Money, atypically he understands, is one of the things he and his wife never quarrelled about. Their arguments were more about deafness, their inability to hear each other, and blindness, their inability to see each other.

The eighth day. Illusion is always pecking at the edges of their separation. More than once, the woman says to the man:

'Well, we can still go out together.'

And he thinks but does not at first say:

No, no we can't.

Things have changed, more than them simply occupying a different physical space. They are separate now. They are in this weird non-place, where they are not lovers, but more connected than friends, but at the same time not friends. They are suddenly The Separated, a class of relationship which is uneasy and vexed.

The same day, the man buys the woman flowers, worrying about what will seem respectful and concerned without being romantic, that will show a common cause. Roses, carnations, tulips, lilies are all wrong. He settles in the end for ginger-flowers which are red, spiky, outside the normal run of things.

At times, she quizzes him.

Who have you told? What did they say? What did they think? Who did you tell today? Who did you tell yesterday?

He grows irritated. He is tired.

When he does tell his friends, there is no great surprise or shock as there was last time they parted. They have been nudged off the front page to the bottom of page five. It's a filler, a par. They are not fresh news. Probably people buried them a year ago, when they were unable to bury themselves. Nobody even seems sad. Nobody says, as they did before:

'Are you sure?' Or:

'What about the children?'

People now shrug as if it's no big deal. His male friends do seem not much bothered. They don't come around, don't call much. Embarrassed, perhaps. Bored, more likely. He is writing a book about male friendships. He thinks the writer's thought, the consolation, that always comes with pain:

Well. It's good material.

New ways of censoring emotions come to him. If he feels cheerful, he is afraid to show it, in case it is an affront to the woman, in case she thinks he is not grieving sufficiently. But the grief comes in fits and starts, in moments and shadows. The rest of the time, things are normal. They both can still laugh.

More than a week has passed now. He will soon move out of the house. The children need to be told. Both the man and his wife are frightened of this prospect.

The eldest girl is getting upset. She doesn't want to be in her own bed but to sleep with one of them. Tee repeats to himself over and over again the most fundamental lesson he has learned in his life—that nothing is good or bad of itself. That even the worst things can have good consequences sooner or later, and vice versa. That one cannot guess the result of one's actions, or describe what might have happened if those actions had not been taken. All one can ever do is respond to the demands of the moment and take the consequences as and where they fall.

The elder daughter says:

'I don't want to be married when I grow up, and I don't want to have children.'

He says:

'You don't have to if you don't want to. You don't have to marry anyone and you don't have to stay married if you do.'

That night, he can hear the couple next door shouting, screaming, throwing things at each other, and he remembers himself saying:

'You fucking cunt.'

The great communicator. He thinks: Do any of us have any hope of communicating finally? How do you do it? And how do you love? And are they, finally, the same thing?

Sometimes a fear runs through him like a gale. When you have been mad, as once he was, this fear can never leave you.

The ninth night, the elder girl walks into the living room.

'Why are you sleeping down here?'

'Because Mummy snores.'

She laughs, and goes back to bed.

His health is suffering. He's shot his back. He spends every night sitting, bathetically, with a packet of frozen peas strapped to the skin behind him. He will scream in pain for no apparent reason, shocking passers-by. It is as if the emotional pain is being displaced to his middle to lower spine.

He has developed a cough. On one occasion he hawks up a gobbet of crimson blood, which he holds on his fingertip and examines, fascinated at the iridescent quality of its colour. He has a mysterious rash on his foot which will not clear.

He reads sad books. Holocaust literature, then Harold Brodkey's *This Wild Darkness*, the story of the writer's dying from Aids.

Another night. The woman is asleep. He has to avoid looking at her face. He glances at it, then glances away. She's wrapped in a tartan blanket like the one his parents used to wrap him in for car journeys. Perhaps it is even the same blanket—he cannot remember whether his mother gave it to him.

She hugs herself, dreaming. He looks away, for fear he will be overwhelmed by sadness. Her face is beautiful, he finds it beautiful, and sad. He wonders who she was. Now he supposes he shall never know, then thinks, too intellectually, defensively:

But what does the question mean?

He thinks: We blundered about together, trying to make some sense of things, to find an accord. Things were often a mess, but not always. There were fine times, clichés. Drunken Mediterranean summers. A day at the park with the kids. Just watching TV.

He thinks of John Updike's words—'growth *is* loss. There's no other way.'

His life has felt slightly unreal for a long while and he wishes it to take on the quality of reality. Already that is happening.

Things are thickening, clarifying. Something is dying in him, something is embryonic. Perhaps that is the nature of every moment.

The evening of the next night, two days before the man is finally leaving the family home, the man and the woman have to tell the children what is happening. They have to think of a plausible story, that is true enough, but not incomprehensibly true.

The children are watching a cartoon, a videotape of *The Simpsons*, when the man comes in from his office. The man and woman snap at each other two, three times in the first few minutes. Both are nervous. They want to get it over with.

They leave the children watching the cartoon, then go downstairs and try to agree a party line—how much truth to tell, how much to withhold, how kindly they can tell certain truths, how some unkind truths must be shown. They cannot agree anything consistent, and mither and squabble. It is because of their fear.

The two parents sit down and pause the video. The man sets about it immediately. He tries to explain that they will now have two places to live instead of one. He dresses this up as an addition rather than a subtraction. He explains that their father will no longer spend the nights there, but at the other place. This place, he will show them tomorrow.

He takes them upstairs. It is actually possible to see the flats into which he is moving from the top-floor rear window. He points the building out to them, and the church spire that sits behind it. He says that they will be able to wave to him.

The elder child seems puzzled, but more or less unconcerned. The younger doesn't understand a word of what is being said. The most uncomfortable moment is when the elder looks up at the man, brightly, and says:

'Will you ever come and sleep here again?'

And he takes a deep breath and says firmly:

'No. Never.'

Such a crushing, bitter word. The girl says:

'Ohhhhh.'

In a small, disappointed way, as if denied a sweet or a piggyback.

333

The awful finality of it. But the girl doesn't seem to mind. The man feels worried that he has failed. He tries to explain to the girls, drawing on reserves of popular wisdom, that they're not 'to blame'. He simultaneously worries that even mentioning the word 'blame' might sow an idea that otherwise would have been absent. Also it suggests that something bad has happened, and this is not how they are presenting these events.

Everything's so delicate, like the inside of a ticking, sprung watch. The man is desperate to avoid letting loose the wrong words, which will somehow permanently imprint themselves in the children's minds. Demons may be created, may be conjured here, at this moment, in this room. So care, care.

After a while there seems to be nothing to say. The two girls grow restless. They turn back to the cartoon. His wife says, kindly:

'You did very well.'

And he feels so grateful for her support, and proud that he has managed. At the same time he knows that it is an infinitesimal first step, knows there are aching dark fields in front of the children that they do not realize or sense.

He tells the elder girl three times before she goes to bed that he will take her tomorrow to see the flat. She is excited.

The next day, the last but one, he takes the children up to the new place. It is on the top floor of a stucco terrace, with big picture windows overlooking West London. The sky is huge through these windows, dwarfing all else. The children are happy and excited. It is a nice flat, small. He brings toys to establish one room as their territory, spreads them out on the floor as if laying garlands. He worries as they run around that they will collide with the landlady's furniture.

The next day is an ordinary Saturday. The man takes the children to an adventure playground in the morning. In the afternoon, the woman takes them to a park. It is the man and the woman's last night together.

After the children have gone to bed, they open a bottle of champagne. Ess makes dinner, the last supper. It is a good evening, peculiarly relaxed. They try to celebrate the time they have had together, even now that it is finished. But after a while, the talk simply begins to run out. Silences now are already more insupportable than they were before, contain more tension and ungrounded electricity. The man thinks: You run out of road so quickly when there are no quarrels to bind you.

The woman says:

'Why don't we go upstairs and have a game of cards?'

Reassured by the banality of the idea, they go upstairs, but they can't find the cards. Nine o'clock. The woman decides to go to bed. The man gets ready to unfold the sofa bed. The last night under this roof. There's a moment when they almost have sex, but each knows it would be merely nostalgia. Yet both weaken nonetheless, but at different times, so it doesn't happen.

On the sofa bed that night, the man is surprised to find that he cannot locate a sense of tragedy inside him. He expects it, but it does not come. There is a deeper sense of the rightness of the course of events. Their marriage wasn't even a particularly bad one, he supposes. Neither was unfaithful to the other, they never fought about money, they never came to blows, they were both concerned with each other's welfare.

But for him communication is an obsession, a neurosis almost; without it he feels himself panting for breath, dying. The woman is cautious of it, finds it painful to give up too much of what her secret self believes and intuits. She has been hurt as a child, awfully.

He thinks: We each had different solutions to the solitude of our lives, and they did not mix. I battered on her door, threatening, or so it seemed to her. So she put on another bolt, and another.

The next morning the man is packing, putting everything into bags. It takes no time at all. The couple have an argument in the morning, one of the endlessly recurring ones, as recorded on paper, one of the arguments that landlocked them in the marriage. And he thinks to himself: Soon, we won't have to do this any more.

And relief again spreads throughout his body, like a small narcotic rush.

The end of the day. The girls have been put to bed. Just as the man makes to leave, with his baggage, he hears the elder one calling him back. He had thought her to be asleep.

He goes to her bedroom, and the girl, who is sitting up on a wooden bunk bed, grabs his single hand tightly with both of hers. And she looks at him, and at that moment on her child's face there is a look that seems to him like that of a grave adult. Her tiny fists. She looks him right in the eyes, and says: 'I love you, Daddy.'

This is something, unlike her young sister, she almost never says. I love you. It feels to the man as if someone or something is talking through her. Trying to reassure him, after all the reassuring he has been trying to do.

The girl lets go of his hand, lies down and closes her eyes.

February

It is Sunday in the man's new flat, where he lives now alone, without the clamour of a family, the tussles and screams and regular morning-to-dusk love and fury.

He thinks: Why did we get married?

People, he knew, thought that he and Ess were unsuited. Perhaps the two of them sought out each other's damage. Perhaps it was all just a genuine misunderstanding, an accident. But the explanation he prefers is this: that they didn't make a mistake, that they set out on a course together that had the seeds of its unhappy conclusion in it, but that was not the same thing. A failed marriage was not necessarily a mistake.

They had many good times, happy times. Helped as well as harmed each other. They had...an experience. They lived life, their own, each other's. They attacked each other, defended themselves, sometimes defended each other and attacked themselves.

What others called failure he thought of as life's essential roughage.

It changed him, the man thinks. It changed her, he hopes. The change was painful sometimes, certainly. But can that be cause for regret?

They have two daughters. This love burns as bright as phosphorus inside them both. Their adults' love, they hope, is not so far regressed that they would let their differences damage the children. But then they imagine that all newly separated couples have this belief, and many are found wanting all the same.

What was left between them, other than this insoluble glue? Concern for each other still, flickering affection. Anger of course, rivers, straits and oceans of it, that ever-present binder and repellent, directed at his 'laziness', her 'martyrdom', his 'selfishness', her 'compulsions'. The deeper cause was what the deeper cause always is, the man guessed—the mutual unwillingness to let go of the patterns of thinking and behaving that they mistakenly thought protected them from what it was they feared, what everyone fears: that they were not good people, that their very selves were in jeopardy, that nothing was certain. That they were not in control.

1999
Hawk
Joy Williams

Glenn Gould bathed his hands in wax and then they felt new. He didn't like to eat in public. He was personally gracious. He was knowledgeable about drugs. He loved animals. In his will, he directed that half his money be given to the Toronto Humane Society. He hated daylight and bright colours. His piano chair was fourteen inches high. His music was used to score *Slaughterhouse-Five*, a book he did not like. After he suffered his fatal stroke, his father waited a day to turn off the respirator because he didn't want him to die on his stepmother's birthday. When Glenn Gould wrote cheques he signed them Glen Gould because he was afraid that by writing the second n he would make too many squiggles. He took prodigious amounts of valium and used make-up. He was once arrested in Sarasota, Florida, for sitting on a park bench in an overcoat, gloves and muffler. He was a prodigy, a genius. He had dirty hair. He had boring dreams. He probably believed in God.

My mind said *You read about Glenn Gould and listen to Glenn Gould constantly but you don't know anything about music. If he were alive you wouldn't have anything you could say to him...*

A composer acquaintance of mine dismissed Glenn as a *performer*.

Glenn Gould loved the idea of the Arctic but he had a great fear of the cold. He was a virtuoso. To be a virtuoso you must have an absolutely fearless attitude toward everything but Glenn was, in fact, worried, frightened and phobic. The dogs of his youth were named Nick and Banquo. As a baby, he never cried but hummed. He thought that the key of F minor expressed his personality.

You have no idea what that means my mind said. *You don't really know what it is he's doing. You don't know why he's brilliant.*

He could instantly play any piece of music from memory. On the whole he did not like works that progressed to a climax, and then to a reconciliation. The Goldberg Variations, which Glenn is most widely known for, were written by Bach for harpsichord. Bach was visiting one of his students, Johann Goldberg, who was employed by a Count von Keyserling, the

340

Russian ambassador to the court of Saxony. The Count had insomnia and wanted some music that would help him through the dark hours. The first notes of the Goldberg Variations are inscribed on Glenn's tombstone.

My dog rose from his bed and walked beneath the table, which he barely cleared. He put his chin on my knee. He stood there for a few moments, not moving. I could see nothing but his nose. I loved kissing his nose. It was my hobby. He was a big black German Shepherd with accents of silver and brown. He had a beautiful face. He looked soulful and dear and alert. He was born on October 17, 1988 and had been with us since Christmas Day of that year. He was now almost nine years old. He weighed one hundred pounds. His name was Hawk. He seemed to fear nothing. He was always looking at me, waiting for me. He just wanted to go where I was going. He could be amusing, he had a sense of humour, but mostly he seemed stoic and watchful and patient. If I was in a room, he was in that room, no other. Of course we took long walks together and many cross-country trips. He was adept at ferry crossings and checking into motels. When he could not accompany me, I would put him in a kennel, once for as long as two weeks. I felt that it was good for him to endure the kennel occasionally. Life was not all good, I told him. Though mostly life was good. He had had a series of collars over the years. His most recent one was lavender in colour. He had tags with his various addresses and phone numbers on them and a St Francis medal with the words PROTECT US. He had a collection of toys. A softball, and squeaky toys in the shapes of a burglar, a cat, a shark, a snowman, and a hedgehog that once made a snuffling noise like a hedgehog but not for long. They were collected in a picnic basket on the floor and when he was happy he would root through the basket and select one. He preferred the snowman. His least favourite was a large green and red toy—its shape was similar to a large bone but it was an abstraction, it lacked charm. Hawk was in a hundred photographs. He was my sweetie pie, my honey, my handsome boy, my love. On the following day he would attack me as though he wanted to kill me.

As regards to life it is much the best to think that the experiences we have are necessary for us. It is by means of experience that we develop and not through our imagination. Imagination is nothing. Explanation is nothing. One can only experience and somehow describe—with, in Camus's phrase, *lucid indifference*. At the same time, experience is fundamentally illusory. When one is experiencing emotional pain or grief, one feels that everything that happens in life is unreal. And this is a right understanding of life.

I loved Hawk and Hawk loved me. It was the usual arrangement. Just a few days before, I had said to him, This is the life, isn't it honey. We were picnicking on Nantucket. We were on the beach with a little fire. There was a beautiful sunset. Friends had given us their house on the island, an old farmhouse off the Polpis Road. Somehow, on the first night at the house, Hawk had been left outside. When he was on the wrong side of a door he would never whine or claw at it, he would stare at it fixedly. I had fallen into a heavy sleep.

I was exhausted. I was always exhausted but I didn't go to a doctor. I had no doctor, no insurance. If I was going to be very sick, I would just die, I thought. Hawk would mourn me. Dogs are the best mourners in the world, as everyone knows. In my sleep, in the strange bed in the old farmhouse, I saw a figure at the door. It was waiting there clothed in a black garbage bag and bandages. Without hesitation I got up and went to the door and opened it and Hawk came in. Oh I'm so sorry, I said to him. He settled down at the foot of the bed with a great comfortable sigh. His coat was cool from the night. I felt that he had tried to project himself through to me, that he had been separated from me through some error, some misunderstanding, and this, clearly, was something neither of us wanted. It had been a bad transmission, but it had done the job and done it without frightening me. What a resourceful boy! I said to him. Oh there are ghosts in that house, our friends said later. Someone else said, You know, ghosts frequently appear in bandages.

Before Hawk, I had had a number of dogs that died before their time, from grim accident or misfortune, taken from me unprepared in the twinkling of an eye. *Shadrach, Nichodemus,*

Angel... Nichodemus wasn't even old enough to have learned to lift his leg. They were all good dogs, faithful. They were innocents. Hawk was the only one I didn't name from the Bible. I named him from Nature, wild Nature. My parents always had dogs too, German shepherds, and my mother would always say, You have to talk to a dog, Joy, you've got to talk to them. It ended badly for my mother and father's dogs over the years and then for my mother and father. My father was a Congregational minister. I am a Christian. Kierkegaard said that for the Christian, the closer you keep to God and the more involved you get with him, the worse for you. It's as though God was saying...you might as well go to the fair and have a good time with the rest. Don't get involved with me—it will only bring you misery. After all, I abandoned my own child, I allowed him to be killed. Christianity, Kierkegaard said, is related only to the consciousness of sin.

We were in Nantucket during the *dies caniculares*, the dog days of summer, but it was a splendid time. Still, there was something wrong with me. My body had turned against me and was full of browsing, shifting pain. The pain went anywhere it wanted to. My head ached, my arms and legs and eyes, my ribs hurt when I took a deep breath. Still, I walked with Hawk, we kept to our habits. I didn't want to think about it but my mind said you have to, you have to do something, you can't just do nothing you know... Some days were worse than others. On those days, I felt crippled. I was so tired. I couldn't think, couldn't concentrate. Even so, I spent long hours reading and listening to music. Bach, Mahler, Strauss. Glenn thought that the 'Metamorphosen' of Strauss was the ultimate. I listened to Thomas de Hartmann play the music of Gurdjieff. I listened to Kathleen Ferrier sing Mahler and Bach and Handel and Gluck. She sang the famous aria from Gluck's opera, *Orfeo ed Euridice*—'What is Life'. We listened to the music over and over again.

Hawk had engaging habits. He had presence. He was devoted to me. To everyone, this was apparent. But I really knew nothing of his psychology. He was no Tulip or Keeper or Bashan who had been analysed by their writers. He knew sit, stay, down, go to your place. He was intelligent, he had a good memory. And surely, I believed, he had a soul.

The friends who had given us the house on Nantucket insisted that I see a doctor about my malady. They made an appointment for me with their doctor in New York. We would leave the Island, return to our own home for a few days, then put Hawk into the kennel and drive into the city, a little over two hours away.

I can't remember our last evening together.

On the morning my husband and I were to drive into the city, I got up early and took Hawk for a long walk along accustomed trails. I was wearing a white sleeveless linen blouse and poplin pants. My head pounded, I could barely put one foot ahead of the other. *How about Lupus?* my mind said. *How about Rheumatoid Arthritis? Well, we'll know more soon...* We drove then to the kennel. It was called Red Rock and Hawk had been there before, they liked him there, he'd always been a gentleman there. When we drove in, Hawk looked disconsolate yet resigned. I left him in the car while I went into the office. I was looking for Fred, big, loud, gruffly pleasant Fred, but he didn't appear. One of his assistants did, a girl named Lynn. Lynn knew Hawk. He's only going to be here for one night, right? Lynn said. I went out to get him. I put the leash on him, his blue, rather grimy leash, and he jumped out of the car and we walked into the office. Lynn had opened another door that led to a row of cement runs. We stood in that doorway, Hawk and I. All right then, I said. I was bent forward slightly. He turned and looked at me and rose and fell upon me, seizing my breast. Immediately, as they say, there was blood everywhere. He tore at my breast, snarling, I think, I can't remember if he was snarling. I turned, calling his name, and he turned with me, my breast still in his jaws. He then shifted and seized my left hand, and after an instant or two, my right, which he ground down upon, shifting, getting a better grip, always getting a better grip with his jaws. I was trying to twist his collar with my bleeding left hand but I was trying not to move either. Hawk! I kept calling my darling's name, Hawk! Then he stopped chewing on my hand

and he looked at me coldly. Fred had been summoned by then and had a pole and a noose, the rig that's used for dangerous dogs, and I heard him say, He's stopped now. I fled to the car. My blouse was soaked with blood, it was dripping blood. I drove home sobbing. I've lost my dog, I've lost my Hawk. My mind didn't say anything. It was all it could do to stay with me as I sobbed and drove, my hands bleeding on the wheel.

I thought he had bitten off my nipple. I thought that when I took off my blouse and bra, the nipple would fall out like a diseased hibiscus bud, like the eraser on a pencil. But he hadn't bitten it off. My breast was bruised black and there were two deep punctures in it and a long raking scratch across it and that was all. My left hand was bleeding hard from three wounds. My right hand was mauled.

At home I stood in the shower, howling, making deep ugly sounds. I had lost my dog. The Band-Aids we put over my cuts had cartoon characters all over them. We didn't take our medicine cabinet very seriously. For some reason I had papered it with newspaper pictures of Bob Dole's hand clutching its pen. I put clean clothes on but the blood seeped around the Band-Aids and stained them too. I put more Goofy and Minnie Band-Aids on and changed my clothes again. I wrapped my hand in a dish towel. Hawk's water dish was still in the kitchen, his toys were scattered around. I wanted to drive into the city and keep my appointment with the doctor, he could look at my hand. It seemed only logical. I just wanted to get in the car and drive away from home. I wouldn't let my husband drive. We talked about what happened as being *unbelievable*. We hadn't yet started talking about it as being a *tragedy*. I'll never see him again, I've lost my dog, I said. Let's not talk about that now, my husband said. As we approached the city I tried to compose myself for the doctor. Then I was standing on the street outside his office which was on East Eighty-fifth Street trying to compose myself. I looked dishevelled, my clothes were stained, I was wearing high-top sneakers. Some people turned as they were walking by and made a point of staring at me.

He was a cheerful doctor. He put my hand in a pan of inky red sterilizing solution. He wanted to talk about my malady, the symptoms of my malady, but he was in fact thinking about the hand. He went out of the office for a while and when he came back he said, I've made an appointment for you to see an orthopaedic surgeon. This doctor was on East Seventy-third Street. You really have to do something about this hand, the first doctor said.

The surgeon was of the type Thomas Mann was always writing about, a doctor out of *The Magic Mountain*, someone whom science had cooled and hardened. Still, he seemed to take a bit of pleasure in imagining the referring doctor's discomfort at my messy wounds. People are usually pretty well cleaned up by the time Gary sees them, he said. He took X-rays and looked at them and said, I will be back in a moment to talk with you about your hand. I sat on the examining table and swung my feet back and forth. One of my sneakers was blue and the other one green. It was a little carefree gesture I had adopted for myself some time ago. I felt foolish and dirty. I felt that I must not appear to be very bright. The doctor returned and asked when the dog had bitten me and frowned when I told him it had been six hours ago. He said, This is very serious, you must have surgery on this hand today. I can't do it here, it must be done under absolutely sterile conditions at the hospital. The bone could become infected and bone infections are very difficult to clear up. I've reserved a bed in the hospital for you and arranged for another surgeon to perform the operation. I said, Oh, but... He said, The surgery must be done today. He repeated this, with beats between the words. He was stern and forbidding and, I thought, pessimistic. Good luck, he said.

The surgeon at Lennox Hill Hospital was a young good-looking Chinese man. He spoke elegantly and had a wonderful smile. He said, The bone is fractured badly in several places and the tendon is torn. Because it was caused by a dog's bite, the situation is actually life-threatening. Oh, surely... I began. No, he said, it's very serious, indeed, life-threatening, I assure you. He smiled.

I lay in a bed in the hospital for a few hours and at one in the morning the hand was operated on and apparently it went well enough. Long pins held everything together. You will have some loss of function in your hand but it won't be too bad, the doctor said, presenting his wonderful smile. I used to kiss Hawk's nose and put my hands in his jaws in play. People in the hospital wanted to talk about my dog biting me. That's unusual, isn't it, they said, or, That's strange isn't it, or, I thought that breed was exceptionally loyal. One nurse asked me if I had been cruel to him.

My hand would not be the same. It would never be strong and it would never again stroke Hawk's black coat.

When I was home again, I washed Hawk's dishes and put them in the cupboard. I gathered up all his toys and put them away too. I busied myself thinking I would bury all his things. Meanwhile he waited at the kennel for me to come and get him, like I always had. I was taking Vicadon for the pain and an antibiotic. In a week I would begin taking another antibiotic and an anti-inflammatory drug for my malady. I lay about, feeling the pain saunter and ping through me. My arms felt like flimsy sacks holding loose sticks. If the sticks touched one another, there would be pain. I went back to listening to Glenn Gould and reading about Glenn Gould which is what I had been doing when Hawk and I were last together. I played Glenn Gould over and over. Glenn never wanted to think about what his hands and fingers were doing but as he grew older he became obsessed with analysing their movements. He felt that if he performed with a blank face, he would lose his control of the piano. Frowning and grimacing gave him better control of his hands. My mind said *You would not be able to defend or explain Glenn Gould to anyone who didn't care for him.*

Hawk had to remain in the kennel for fifteen days for observation, it was the law. It was the same number of days we had spent so happily on Nantucket. My husband spoke to Fred. You should talk to Fred, he said. When I called, I got Lynn. She spoke to me in a sort of light-hearted way.

She seemed grateful that I had held on to Hawk during the attack. I was too confused by this comment to reply to it. She said, After you left he attacked the noose but then he calmed down in the cage after we washed the blood off of him. He ate some food. Some dogs get a taste for biting, she said, after they start to bite. Everything she said was wrong.

Finally, she said, He seems to be in conflict. The word seemed to reassure her, it gave her confidence. I couldn't understand a thing she was saying. I wanted someone to tell me why my beloved dog had attacked me so savagely and how I could save both of us. He's just in a lot of conflict now, the girl said. Maybe he had some separation anxiety. He seemed all right for a while after we washed the blood off him, I don't know what to tell you.

Finally, Fred got on the line. He's just not the same dog, Fred said. I know that dog, this isn't him. When I had the noose on him he was attacking the pole and looking right at me. There was no fear in his eyes, there was nothing in his eyes. I'm no doctor, Fred said, but I think it's a brain tumour. I think something just kicked on or clicked off in him and you'll never know when it will happen again.

I said, He was a perfectly healthy, happy, loving dog.

This isn't your dog here now, Fred said.

I couldn't bear to call Fred every day. I called him every other day.

He has good days and bad days, Fred said. Sometimes you can walk right up to the cage and he just looks at you or he doesn't even bother to look at you. Other times he flings himself at the chain link, attacking it, trying to get at you. Some days he's a monster.

I thought of Hawk's patience, of his happiness, of his dear, grave face. Sometimes, when he slept, he would whimper and his legs would move as though he were walking quickly in a dream. What do you think he's dreaming about, I would ask my husband. Then I would call his name, Hawk, Hawk, it's all right, and he would open one startled eye and look at me and sigh, and then he would be calm again. I couldn't bear the thought of him waiting in the kennel for me to pick him up. I was not going to pick him up. I would have him put down, put to sleep, euthanized, destroyed. My love would be murdered. I would murder my love.

The days dragged on. Fred said, He's unreliable. I have no doubt that if you told him to do something he didn't want to do, he could attack you. Anything could set him off, he could turn on anybody. If you slipped and fell, if you were in a helpless position, he could kill you, I have no doubt of it. That's a tough dog. Fred fancied German shepherds and had several of his own whom he exhibited in shows. He's not the same dog any more, Fred said.

I did not really believe this, that he was not the same dog. I did not think that he had a brain tumour. I thought that something unspeakable and impossible and calamitous had happened to Hawk and me. My husband said, You have to remember him the way he was, if you just dwell on this, if this is all you remember from all the wonderful times you had with him, then shame on you. My husband said, I love him too, I miss him, but I'm not going to mention him every time I think of him. You can talk about him all you want and I'll talk with you, but I'm not going to bring him up again, it makes you too upset.

Upset? I said.

On the fifteenth day, Fred would put a soporific in Hawk's food and then the vet would arrive and give him a lethal injection. His brain would die and his heart would follow. It would take ten seconds. So often I had sat with Hawk while he ate. He would eat for a while and then pick up a toy and walk around the room with it and then eat some more. Oh, that's so good, I said to him while he ate. Isn't that good? Oh, it's delicious…

Fred said, I know this is difficult. If he had been run over by a truck, it would be a different matter, you would grieve for him. This is a harder grief.

If I talked about something else at home or if I ate something or if I had a Martini again, if I took the time to make a Martini rather than just slosh some gin in a glass, my husband said— You seem a little better.

I tried to imagine that Hawk was attempting to reach me teleneurally during these days. I went to all his places, for they were my places too, and tried to listen but nothing was coming through. I didn't expect his apologies of course. For my part I forgave him, but I was going to have him murdered too. We had loved one another and we would never meet again. He never came to me in dreams. I was granted nothing, not the smallest sign.

We had to go to the vet to sign the paper authorizing euthanization. The vet's name was Dr Turco. There had been Dr Franks and Dr Crane and Dr Yang and Dr Iorbar in my life in the last days and now there was Dr Turco. In the parking lot there was a young man with a white pit bull in the back of his pickup truck. He was fumbling with the dog's leash somewhat and it was taking me a while to get out of our car with my hand in the cast and my aching, crippling malady, my mysterious malady, whatever the hell it was. I passed the dog, sturdy and panting, cute in his ugliness, white and pink with dashes of black about him, a dog with his own charms. Hi there, I said to the dog. The young man seemed unfriendly, he did not seem as nice as his dog. They followed my husband and myself into the vet's waiting room, the dog sliding and scrambling across the waxed floor, his nails clicking.

My mind said *The vet may have an explanation for what happened, an answer. Perhaps some anecdotes at the very least will bring you peace.* Dr Turco said, Fred tells me that Hawk has become quite dangerous.

I said, It was an aberration, a moment's madness seized him. Could it be a brain tumour?

The vet paused. It's possible... he said, indicating that it wasn't very likely. He said, So sad. My sympathy and respect for your decision.

It's unusual, isn't it? I asked, for a dog to attack his owner?

It's quite unusual, the vet said. I've never known a dog to attack its owner. Excuse me for just one moment.

He left the room. My God, I said to my husband, did you hear that! He didn't say that, my husband said in anguish. He did! He just did! I said. I'll ask him when he comes back, my husband said.

I've never known personally of it happening, the vet said, in the course of my practice. I'm sure it's probably happened. I'm so sorry.

I signed the paper with my left hand. My signature looked

totally unfamiliar to me. Above it, printed by some other hand, was Hawk's name and breed and age and weight. As we returned to the parking lot the young man we had seen with the pit bull was coming back to his truck from the rear of the vet's office. He was cradling a black garbage bag in his arms, his lips pressed to it. He placed it in the back of the pickup, got into the cab and sat there for a moment. Then he rubbed his eyes and drove away.

On the sixteenth day, my husband went to the kennel to pay for Hawk's residency there and to pick up his leash. Then he went to the vet and paid for the euthanization, for the cremation that hadn't happened yet. He brought home Hawk's lavender collar from the vet with his tags on it and the St Francis PROTECT US medal. I said, That's not Hawk's leash. I wanted to bury Hawk's leash with his ashes and his toys but I wanted to keep his collar with all the photographs I had of him. That's his leash, my husband said. They bleached it to get the blood out.

Silver Trails is a pet motel but it also has a crematorium and a cemetery where the pictures of beloved pets, made weatherproof in a silvering process, are mounted on a curved tile wall. The wall was supposed to be capable of withstanding freezing temperatures but it has not and some of the tiles are cracked. All the dogs shown have been 'good' and 'faithful'. The wall is in a fragrant pine grove and on the pathway to it there is a plaque which the owners of Silver Trails are very pleased with. It says IF CHRIST HAD HAD A LITTLE DOG IT WOULD HAVE FOLLOWED HIM TO THE CROSS. There is no devotion, it is known, like a dog's devotion. Dogs excel in love.

Hawk had been taken from Red Rock to the vet's but it would be several more days before he was brought to Silver Trails. Actually, only living dogs come to the place so named. Dead dogs come to Trail's End.

I was waiting for someone to call me and say, Your animal will be ready after four, which, when the day arrived, is what they would say. Hawk still did not come to me in dreams. I dreamed instead about worrying that I had not told my mother. She would feel so badly about Hawk. Surely I must have told her, but I had forgotten if indeed I had. I wasn't sure. Awake, everywhere I looked, I thought Hawk should be there. He should be here with me. How strange it all is, how wrong, that he is not here. My mind said *He wants to come back, he wants to come back to his home and be with you but he can't because you killed him, you had him killed…* My body was my malady, my tedious non-life-threatening banal malady, but my mind was like Job's wife whose only advice to him was to curse God and die. I felt that I wanted to die.

I was utterly unhappy and when, according to Kierkegaard, one becomes utterly unhappy and realizes the absolute woefulness of life, when one can say and mean it, life for me has no value, that is when one can make a bid for Christianity, that is when one can begin. One must become crucified to a paradox. One must give up reason.

I listened to Kathleen Ferrier sing from *Orfeo ed Euridice* in her unearthly contralto.

What is life to me without thee?
What is left if thou art dead?
What is life, life without thee?
What is life without my Love?

In the myth of the great musician, Orpheus played music that was so exquisite that not only his fellow mortals but even the wild beasts were soothed and comforted by it. When his Eurydice died, he sang his grief for her to all who breathed the upper air but he was not able to call her back so he decided to seek her among the dead. It ended badly, of course, though not typically so.

The lovely Kathleen died when she was forty-one years old. Glenn died when he was fifty-one. My mind said *You haven't done much with your life, think of what those two could have done if they had lived on, you couldn't even keep your own pet from tearing you apart, or what do they call them now, pet, companion animal…*

There was no consolation. Hawk had been my consolation. When the phone rang, a woman's voice said, Your animal will be ready after four. I arrived at Silver Trails and I was directed to a building with a not unsubtle smokestack. I was told to speak with Michael. But Michael was not there. Michael? I called. I could hear a lawnmower in the distance and over the sounds of the lawnmower were the sounds of the live dogs barking.

I walked into the building which had two rooms, then a larger room, open like a garage. There was a stubby tunnel-like object there, the crematorium oven. There were twenty filled black garbage bags secured with twine on a table and a large sleek golden dog lying free. He was a big dog, lying with his face away from me. He looked fit and not old. One of his ears was folded back on itself in a soft, sad way. I walked outside and just stood there. I didn't know what to do with myself any more. Eventually the lawnmower grew closer with the boy named Michael on it. I've come for my dog's remains, I said. His name is Hawk. The boy led me into the building but he closed the door to the big room. He drew back a curtain that ran along a wall and there were dozens of small black shopping bags on the shelves, the size bag that might contain something lovely, special from a boutique. There was a label on each bag that said TRAIL'S END and it had the name of a dog and then the owner's name. Inside the bag was a blue-and-white tin with a vaguely Oriental motif of blue swallow-like birds flying. The boy and I searched the shelves for the proper bag. Here he is, I said. The boy pointed to another bag. There's another Hawk, he said. He had a strange, half-smiling grimace. There was grass in his hair and grass stuck to his T-shirt. This is my Hawk, I said, there's my name too. I gestured at the shelves. So many! I said. There's so many!

Oh sometimes all four shelves are full, the boy said.

At home, I sat on the porch and with great difficulty pried open the lid of the tin with its foolish scene. I used a knife around it. There was cotton on the top and beneath it was a clear bag of ground bones. Hawk's ashes weighed more than those of my mother or my father. We all end up alone, don't we, honey, I said.

And then, in time, my little dream.

Hawk and I are walking among a crowd in near darkness. I

am a little concerned for him because I want him to be good. He can hardly move among the people in the crowd but he pays them no attention. He is close to me, he is calm, utterly familiar, he is my handsome boy, my good boy, my love. Then, of course, I realize that these are the dead and we are both newly among them.

2000
Editing Vidia

Diana Athill

Good publishers are supposed to 'discover' writers, and perhaps they do. To me, however, they just happened to come. In 1956, four years after the launch of André Deutsch Limited, of which I was a director, Mordecai Richler (whose first novel we had just published) introduced me to Andrew Salkey. Andrew was a writer from Jamaica who was then keeping a roof over his head by working for the BBC's Caribbean Service and who was always generous towards other writers. When he heard that I was Mordecai's editor he immediately asked if he could send me a young friend of his who regularly freelanced for the same service and had just written something very good. A few days later V. S. Naipaul came to a coffee bar near our office and handed over *Miguel Street*.

He was in his very early twenties and looked even younger, but his manner was grave—even severe—and unsmiling. This I attributed to nervousness—but I felt that it was the nervousness of someone essentially serious and composed, and that it would be impertinent to think in terms of 'putting him at his ease'. It was a surprise to discover that *Miguel Street* was funny: delicately funny, with nothing overdone. It was a portrait of a street in Trinidad's Port of Spain, in the form of stories which each centred on a street character; its language that of the street, and its balance between amusement and sympathy perfectly judged. I was delighted by it, but worried: it was a publishing dogma to which André Deutsch strongly adhered that stories didn't sell unless they were by Names. So before talking to him about it I gave it to Francis Wyndham who was with us as part-time 'Literary Adviser', and Francis loved it at once and warmly. This probably tipped the balance with André, whose instinct was to distrust as 'do-gooding' my enthusiasm for a little book by a West Indian about a place which interested no one and where the people spoke an unfamiliar dialect. I think he welcomed its being stories because it gave him a reason for saying 'no': but Francis's opinion joined to mine made him bid me find out if the author had a novel on the stocks and tell him that if he had, then that should come first and the stories could follow all in good time. Luckily Vidia was in the process of writing *The Mystic Masseur*.

In fact we could well have launched him with *Miguel Street*, which has outlasted his first two novels in critical esteem, because in the Fifties it was easier to get reviews for a writer seen by the British as black than it was for a young English writer, and reviews influenced readers a good deal more then than they do now. Publishers and reviewers were aware that new voices were speaking up in the newly independent colonies, and partly out of genuine interest, partly out of an optimistic if ill-advised sense that a vast market for books lay out there, ripe for development, they felt it to be the thing to encourage those voices. This trend did not last long, but it served to establish a number of good writers.

Vidia did not yet have the confidence to walk away from our shilly-shallying, and fortunately it did him no real harm. Neither he nor we made any money to speak of from his first three books, *The Mystic Masseur, The Suffrage of Elvira* and *Miguel Street*, but there was never any doubt about the making of his name, which began at once with the reviews and was given substance by his own work as a reviewer, of which he got plenty as soon as he became known as a novelist. He was a very good reviewer, clearly as widely read as any literary critic of the day, and it was this rather than his first books which revealed that here was a writer who was going to reject the adjective 'regional', and with good reason.

We began to meet fairly often, and I enjoyed his company because he talked well about writing and people, and was often funny. At quite an early meeting he said gravely that when he was up at Oxford—which he had not liked—he once did a thing so terrible that he would never be able to tell anyone what it was. I said it was unforgivable to reveal that much without revealing more, especially to someone like me who didn't consider even murder literally unspeakable, but I couldn't shift him and never learned what the horror was—though someone told me later that when he was at Oxford Vidia did have some kind of nervous breakdown. It distressed me that he had been unhappy at a place which I loved. Having such a feeling for scholarship, high standards and tradition he ought to have liked it…but no, he would not budge. Never for a minute did it occur to me that he might have felt at a loss when he got to Oxford because of how different it was from his background, still less because of any form of racial insult: he appeared to me far too impressive a person to be subject to such discomforts.

The image Vidia was projecting at that time, in his need to protect his pride, was so convincing that even when I read *A House for Mr Biswas* four years later, and was struck by the authority of his account of Mr Biswas's nervous collapse, I failed to connect its painful vividness with his own reported 'nervous breakdown'. Between me and the truth of his Oxford experience stood the man he wanted people to see.

At that stage I did not know how or why he had rejected Trinidad, and if I had known it, still wouldn't have understood what it is like to be unable to accept the country in which you were born. Vidia's books (not least *A Way in the World*, not written until thirty-seven years later) were to do much to educate me; but then I had no conception of how someone who feels he doesn't belong to his 'home' and cannot belong anywhere else is forced to exist only in himself; nor of how exhausting and precarious such a condition (blithely seen by the young and ignorant as desirable) can be. Vidia's self—his very being—was his writing: a great gift, but all he had. He was to report that ten years later in his career, when he had earned what seemed to others an obvious security, he was still tormented by anxiety about finding the matter for his next book, and for the one after that...an anxiety not merely about earning his living, but about existing as the person he wanted to be. No wonder that while he was still finding his way into his writing he was in danger; and how extraordinary that he could nevertheless strike an outsider as a solidly impressive man. (Since writing this I have read the letters which Vidia and his father exchanged while Vidia was at Oxford. *Letters Between a Father and Son* fully reveals the son's loneliness and misery, and makes the self he was able to present to the world even more extraordinary.)

This does not mean that I failed to see the obvious delicacy of his nervous system. Because of it I was often worried by his lack of money, and was appalled on his behalf when I once saw him risk losing a commission by defying *The Times Literary Supplement*. They had offered their usual fee of twenty-five pounds (or was it guineas?) for a review, and he had replied haughtily that he wrote nothing for less than fifty. 'Oh silly Vidia,' I thought. 'Now they'll never offer him anything again.' But lo! they paid him his fifty and I was filled with admiration. Of course he was right: authors ought to know their own value and refuse the insult of derisory fees.

I was right to admire that self-respect, at that time, but it was going to develop into a quality difficult to like. In all moral qualities the line between the desirable and the deplorable is imprecise—between tolerance and lack of discrimination, prudence and cowardice, generosity and extravagance—so it is not easy to see where a man's proper sense of his own worth turns into a more or less pompous self-importance. In retrospect it seems to me that it took eight or nine years for this process to begin to show itself in Vidia, and I think it possible that his audience was at least partly to blame for it.

For example, after a year or so of meetings in the pubs or restaurants where I usually lunched, I began to notice that Vidia was sometimes miffed at being taken to a cheap restaurant or being offered a cheap bottle of wine—and the only consequence of my seeing this (apart from my secretly finding it funny) was that I became careful to let him choose both restaurant and wine. And this carefulness not to offend him, which was, I think, shared by all, or almost all, his English friends, came from an assumption that the reason why he was so anxious to command respect was fear that it was, or might be, denied him because of his race; which led to a squeamish dismay in oneself at the idea of being seen as racist. The shape of an attitude which someone detests in themselves, and has worked at extirpating, can often be discerned from its absence, and during the first years of Vidia's career in England he was often coddled for precisely the reason the coddler was determined to disregard.

Later, of course, the situation changed. His friends became too used to him to see him as anything but himself, and those who didn't know him saw him simply as a famous writer—on top of which he could frighten people. Then it was the weight and edge of his personality which made people defer to him, rather than consideration for his sensitivity, and it was easy to underestimate the pain and strain endured by that sensitivity when he had first pulled himself up out of the thin, sour soil in which he was reared and was striving to find a purchase in England where, however warmly he was welcomed, he could never feel that he wholly belonged.

During the Sixties I visited the newly independent islands of Trinidad and Tobago twice, with intense pleasure: the loveliness of tropical forests and seas, the jolt of excitement which comes from *difference*, the kindness of people, the amazing beauty of Carnival (unlike Vidia, I like steel bands; oh, the sound of them coming in from the fringes of Port of Spain through the four-in-the-morning darkness of the opening day!) On my last morning in Port of Spain I felt a sharp pang as I listened to the keskidee (a bird which really does say '*Qu'est ce qu'il dit?*') and knew how unlikely it was that I should ever hear it again. But at no time was it difficult to remember that mine was a visitor's Trinidad and Tobago; so three other memories, one from high on the country's social scale, the others from lower although by no means from the bottom, are just as clear as the ones I love.

One. Vidia's history of the country, *The Loss of El Dorado*, which is rarely mentioned nowadays but which I think is the best of his non-fiction books, had just come out. Everyone I had met, including the Prime Minister of Trinidad and Tobago, Eric Williams, and the poet Derek Walcott, had talked about it in a disparaging way and had betrayed as they did so that they had not read it. At last, at a party given by the leader of the opposition, I met someone who had: an elderly Englishman just retiring from running the coastguard. We were both delighted to be able to share our pleasure in Vidia's book and had a long talk about it. As we parted I asked him: 'Can you really be the only person in this country who has read it?' and he answered sadly: 'Oh, easily.'

Two. In Tobago I stayed in a delightful little hotel, where on most evenings the village elders dropped in for a drink. One such evening a younger man—a customs officer in his mid-thirties seconded to Tobago's chief town, Scarborough, from Port of

Spain—invited me to go out on the town with him. We were joined by another customs officer and a nurse from the hospital. First we went up to Scarborough's fort—its Historic Sight—to look at the view. Then, when conversation fizzled out, it was suggested that we should have a drink at the Arts Centre. It looked in the darkness little more than a shed, and it was shut, but a man was hunted up who produced the key, some Coca-Cola and half a bottle of rum...and there we stood, under a forty-watt lamp in a room of utter dinginess which contained nothing at all but a dusty ping-pong table with a very old copy of the *Reader's Digest* lying in the middle of it. We sipped our drinks in an atmosphere of embarrassment—almost shame—so heavy that it silenced us. After a few minutes we gave up and went to my host's barely furnished but tidy little flat—I remember it as cold, which it can't have been—where we listened to a record of 'Yellow Bird' and drank another rum. Then I was driven back to the hotel.

The evening's emptiness—the really frightening feeling of nothing to do, nothing to say—had made me feel quite ill. I knew too little about the people I had been with to guess what they were like when at ease: all I could discern was that my host was bored to distraction at having to work in the sticks; that he had been driven by his boredom to make his sociable gesture and had then become nervous to the extent of summoning friends to his aid; and that all three had quickly seen that the whole thing was a mistake and had been overtaken by embarrassed gloom. And no wonder. When I remember the Arts Centre I see why, when Vidia first revisited the West Indies, what he felt was fear.

Three. And it is not only people like Vidia, feverish with repressed talent, who yearn to escape. One day I was trying on a swimsuit in a store in Port of Spain when I overheard a conversation in the changing-cubicle next to mine. An American woman, accompanied by her husband, was also buying something, and they were obviously quite taken by the pretty young woman who was serving them. They were asking her questions about her family, and the heightened warmth of their manner made me suspect that they found it almost exciting to be kind to a black person. When the customer had made her choice and her husband was writing a cheque, the saleswoman's voice suddenly changed from chirpiness to breathlessness and she said, 'May I ask you something?' The wife said, 'Yes, of course,' and the poor young woman plunged into desperate pleading: please, please would they help her, would they give her a letter inviting her to their home which she could show to the people who issued visas, she wouldn't be any trouble, and if they would do this for her... On and on she went, the husband trying to interrupt her in an acutely embarrassed voice, still wanting to sound kind but only too obviously appalled at what his entirely superficial amiability had unleashed. Soon the girl was in tears and the couple were sounding frantic with remorse and anxiety to escape—and I was so horrified at being the invisible and unwilling witness of this desperate young woman's humiliation that I abandoned my swimsuit, scrambled into my dress and fled, so I do not know how it ended.

Vidia had felt fear and dislike of Trinidad ever since he could remember. As a schoolboy he had written a vow on an endpaper of his Latin primer to be gone within five years (it took him six). He remembered this in *The Middle Passage*, his first non-fiction book, published in 1962, in which he described his first revisiting of the West Indies and did something he had never done before: examined the reasons why he feared and hated the place where he was born.

It was a desperately negative view of the place, disregarding a good half of the picture; and it came out with the fluency and force of something long matured less in the mind than in the depths of the nervous system. Trinidad, he said, was and knew itself to be a mere dot on the map. It had no importance and no existence as a nation, being only somewhere out of which first Spain, then France, then Britain could make money: grossly easy money because of using slaves to do the work, and after slaves indentured labour which was almost as cheap. A slave-based society has no need to be efficient, so no tradition of efficiency exists. Slave-masters don't need to be intelligent, so 'in Trinidad education was not one of the things money could buy; it was something money freed you from. Education was strictly for the poor. The white boy left school "counting on his fingers" as the Trinidadian likes to say, but this was a measure of his privilege... The white community was never an upper class in the sense that it possessed superior speech or taste or attainments; it was envied only for its money and its access to pleasure.'

When this crude colonial society was opened up because the islands were no longer profitable and the British pulled out, what Vidia saw gushing in to fill the vacuum was the flashiest and most materialistic kind of American influence in the form of commercial radio (television had yet to come) and films—films at their most violent and unreal. ('British films,' he wrote, 'played to empty houses. It was my French master who urged me to go to see *Brief Encounter*; and there were two of us in the cinema, he in the balcony, I in the pit.') Trinidad and Tobago was united only in its hunger for 'American modernity', and under that sleazy veneer it was split.

It was split between the descendants of slaves, the African Trinidadians, and the descendants of indentured labourers, the Indians, both groups there by an accident of history, neither with any roots to speak of. In *The Middle Passage* Vidia called the Africans 'Negroes', which today sounds shocking. Reading the book one has to keep reminding oneself that the concept of Black Power had yet to be formulated. Black people had not yet rejected the word 'Negro': it was still being widely used and 'black' was considered insulting. And in this book his main criticism of Trinidadians of African descent is that they had been brainwashed by the experience of slavery into 'thinking white'— into being ashamed of their own colour and physical features. What he deplored—as many observers of West Indian societies had done—was precisely the attitudes which people of African descent were themselves beginning to deplore, and would soon be forcing themselves to overcome.

The Indians he saw as less unsure of themselves because of the pride they took in the idea of India; but he also saw that idea as being almost meaningless—they had no notion of what the subcontinent was really like. It was also dangerous in that it militated against attempts to bridge the rift. Theirs was 'a peasant-minded, money-minded community, spiritually static, its religion reduced to rites without philosophy, set in a materialist, colonialist society. The Trinidadian Indian was a 'complete colonial, even more philistine than the white'.

He sums up his account of racial friction thus: 'Like monkeys pleading for evolution, each claiming to be whiter than the other, Indians and Negroes appeal to the unacknowledged white audience to see how much they despise one another. They despise one another by reference to the whites; and the irony is that their antagonism should have reached its peak today, when white prejudices have ceased to matter.'

This was a fair assessment: everyone, apart from Tourist Board propagandists, to whom I talked about politics deplored this racial tension, and most of them either said outright, or implied, that blame lay with the group to which they did not belong. No one remarked on the common sense which enabled people to rub along in spite of it (as they still do), any more than Vidia did. The rift, which certainly was absurd and regrettable, became more dramatic if seen as dangerous, and therefore reflected a more lurid light on whoever was being presented as its instigator. People did make a bid for the outsider's respect—did 'appeal to the unacknowledged white audience'. But to what audience was Vidia himself appealing? It was *The Middle Passage* which first made black West Indians call him 'racist'.

The book was admired in England and disliked in Trinidad, but it was not addressed to the white audience in order to please it. Its whole point was to show that Caribbean societies are a mess because they were callously created by white men for the white men's own ends, only to be callously administered and finally callously abandoned. Vidia was trying to write from a point of view above that of white or brown or black; he was trying to look at the people now inhabiting the West Indies with a clear-sighted and impartial intelligence, and to describe what he saw honestly, even if honesty seemed brutal. This he felt, and said, had to be done because a damaged society shuffling along with the help of fantasies and excuses can only become more sick: what it has to do is learn to know itself, and only its writers can teach it that. Caribbean writers had so far, he claimed, failed to do more than plead their own causes. If he expected Trinidadians to welcome this high-minded message he was naive—but I don't suppose he did. He was pursuing his own understanding of the place, and offering it, because that is what a serious writer can't help doing. If anyone resented it, too bad.

Of course they did resent it—who doesn't resent hearing disagreeable truths told in a manner verging on the arrogant? But I think the label 'racist' which they stuck on him was, so to speak, only a local one. I saw him as a man raised in, and frightened by, a somewhat disorderly, inefficient and self-deceiving society, who therefore longed for order, clarity and competence. Having concluded that the lack of these qualities in the place where he was born came from the people's lack of roots, he overvalued a sense of history and respect for tradition, choosing to romanticize their results rather than to see the complex and far from admirable scenes with which they often coexist. (His first visit to India, described in *An Area of Darkness*, left him in a state of distress because it showed him that an ancient civilization in which he had dared to hope that he would find the belonging he hungered for, could be just as disorderly and inefficient as the place where he was born.) Although both England and the United States were each in its own way going to fall short of his ideal society, Europe as a whole came more close, more often, to offering a life in which he could feel comfortable. I remember driving, years ago, through a vine-growing region of France and coming on a delightful example of an ancient expertise taking pleasure in itself: a particularly well-cultivated vineyard which had a pillar rose—a deep pink pillar rose—planted as an exquisite punctuation at the end of every row. Instantly—although it was weeks since I had seen or thought of him—he popped into my head: 'How Vidia would like that!'

But although I cannot see Vidia as racist in the sense of wanting to be white or to propitiate whites, I do think it is impossible to spend the first eighteen years of your life in a given set of circumstances without being shaped by them: and Vidia spent the first eighteen years of his life as a Trinidadian Indian. Passionate though his determination to escape the limitations imposed by this fate was, and near though it came to achieving the impossible, it could not wholly free him from his conditioning.

In Chapter One of *The Middle Passage*, when he has only just boarded the boat train which will take him to Southampton, there begins the following description. Into the corridor, out of the compartment next to Vidia's, had stepped 'a very tall and ill-made Negro... He went to the window, opened the ventilation gap, pushed his face through, turned slightly to his left, and spat. His face was grotesque. It seemed to have been smashed in from one cheek. One eye had narrowed; the thick lips had bunched into a circular swollen protuberance; the enormous nose was twisted. When, slowly, he opened his mouth to spit, his face became even more distorted. He spat in slow, intermittent dribbles; and when he worked his face back in, his eyes caught mine.'

Vidia makes a slight attempt to give this man a role in the story of his journey by saying that he began to imagine that the poor creature was aware of him in a malign way, that after that one glance, in the buffet car there he was again...but in fact once he has been described the man has no part to play, he is done with; in spite of which Vidia could not resist placing him right at the start of the book and *describing him in greater physical detail than anyone else in all its 232 pages*. I am not saying that this man was invented or that he may have been less dreadfully unattractive than we are told he was; but by choosing to pick him out and to *fix* on him, Vidia has given an indelible impression less of the man than of his own reaction: the dismayed recoil of a fastidious Trinidad Indian from what he sees as an inferior kind of person. And I believe that if I were black I should from time to time, throughout his work, pick up other traces of this flinching presence hidden in the shadow behind one of the best English-language novelists we have. And even as part of the white audience I cannot help noticing the occasional touch of self-importance (increasing with the years) which I suspect to have its roots far back in the Trinidad Indian's nervous defiance of disrespect.

Vidia's mother, handsome and benignly matronly, welcomed his publishers very kindly when they visited Trinidad, and gave the impression of being the beloved linchpin of her family. When I first met them, long before they had been stricken by the close-together deaths of one of the daughters and of Shiva, Vidia's younger and only brother, they impressed me as a flourishing lot: good-looking, intelligent, charming, successful. A married daughter told me that Mrs Naipaul 'divides her time between the temple and the quarry'—the latter being a business belonging to her side of the family, in which she was a partner. That she was not simply a comfortable mother-figure became apparent when she told me that she had just got home from attending a seminar on welding and was very glad that she hadn't missed it because she had learned enough at it to be able to cut the number of welders they employed at the quarry by half. Soon afterwards she threw more light on her own character by making a little speech to me, after noticing my surprise when she had appeared to be indifferent to some news about Vidia. She had been, she said, a well-brought-up Hindu girl of her generation, so she had been given no education and was expected to obey her parents in everything, and that was what she did. Then she was married ('And there was no nonsense about falling in love in those days'), whereupon it was her husband she had to obey in everything, and that was what she did. Then she had her children, so of course it was her job to devote herself entirely to them and bring them up as well as possible, and that was what she did ('and I think I can say I made a good job of it'). 'But then I said to myself, when I am fifty—FINISH. I will begin to live for myself. And that is what I am doing now and they must get on with their own lives.'

It was an impressive little thumbnail autobiography, but it left questions in my mind. I had, after all, read *A House for Mr Biswas*, the novel Vidia had based on his father's life, and had gained a vivid picture of how humiliated Mr Biswas had been after his marriage into the much richer and more influential Tulsi family—although I don't think I knew at that stage that Seepersad Naipaul, Vidia's father, had once had a mental breakdown and had vanished from his home for months.

Clearly this attractive and—I was now beginning to think—slightly formidable woman was greatly oversimplifying her story, but I liked her; as I told Vidia when, soon after this, he asked me if I did. 'Yes, very much,' I said; to which he replied: 'Everyone seems to. I hate her.'

I wish I had asked him what he meant by that. It was not the first time that I heard him, in a fit of irritation, strike out at someone with a fierce word, so I didn't think it was necessarily true (and anyway, dislike of a mother usually indicates damaged love). But uncertain though I remained about his feelings towards his mother, I knew that he loved his father, who had died soon after Vidia left Trinidad to come to Oxford. He wrote a moving introduction to the little volume of his father's stories which he gave us to publish in 1976, and he spoke about the way his father had introduced him to books. Seepersad Naipaul had possessed a remarkably strong and true instinct for writing which had overcome his circumstances to the point of giving him a passion for such English classics as had come his way, and steering him into a writing job on the local newspaper. He had passed his passion on by reading aloud to Vidia and Kamla, the sister nearest to him, making the children stand up as he read to keep them from falling asleep—which seems to have impressed the importance of the ritual on them rather than to have put them off. Seepersad's own few stories were about Trinidadian village life, and the most important lesson he gave his son was 'Write about what you know', thus curing him of the young colonial's feeling that 'literature' had to be exotic—something belonging to the faraway world out of which came the books he found in the library. And I know of another piece of advice Seepersad gave his son which speaks for the truth of his instinct. Vidia had shown him a piece of would-be comic writing, and he told him not to strive for comedy but to let it arise naturally out of the story. It is sad to think of this man hobbled by the circumstances of his life (see *A House for Mr Biswas*) and dying before he could see his son break free. The mother was part of the 'circumstances' and the child sided with his father against her, of that I feel sure.

I cannot remember how long it was—certainly several months, perhaps even a year—before I learned that Vidia was married. 'I have found a new flat', he would say; 'I saw such-and-such a film last week'; 'My landlady says': not once had he used the words 'we' or 'our'. I had taken it for granted that he lived in industrious loneliness, which had seemed sad. So when at a party I glimpsed him at the far end of a room with a young woman—an inconspicuously, even mousily pretty young woman—and soon afterwards saw him leaving with her, I was pleased that he had found a girlfriend. The next time he came to the office I asked who she was—and was astounded when he answered, in a rather cross voice, 'My wife, of course.'

After that Pat was allowed to creep out of the shadows, but only a little: and one day she said something that shocked me so much that I know for certain that I am remembering it word for word. I must have remarked on our not meeting earlier, and she replied: 'Vidia doesn't like me to come to parties because I'm such a bore.'

From that moment on, whenever I needed to cheer myself up by counting my blessings, I used to tell myself: 'At least I'm not married to Vidia.'

It did not exactly turn me against him, I suppose because from the beginning I had thought of him as an interesting person to watch rather than as a friend. The flow of interest between us had always been one way—I can't remember ever telling him anything about my own affairs, or wanting to—so this odd business of his marriage was something extra to watch rather than something repellent. Had he ever loved her—or did he still love her in some twisted way? They had married while he was at Oxford: had he done it out of loneliness, to enlarge the minuscule territory he could call his own now that he was out in the world? Or was it because she could keep him? She was working as a teacher and continued to do so well into their marriage. Or was it to shelter him from other women? He had once asked a man of my acquaintance: 'Do you know any *fast* women?' which my friend found funny (particularly as he was gay) but which seemed touching to me. As did Vidia's only attempt to make a pass at me. Pat was away and I had asked him to supper. Without warning he got to his feet, came across the room and tried to kiss me as I was coming through the door carrying a tray loaded with glasses. It hardly seemed necessary to put into words the rebuff which most of him was clearly anxious for, but to be on the safe side I did. Our friendship, I said gently, was too valuable to complicate in any way—and his face brightened with relief. That someone so lacking in sexual experience and so puritanical should have to resort to prostitutes (as he told the *New Yorker* in 1994, and as a passage in *The Mimic Men* suggests) is natural; though I guess he did so infrequently, and with distaste.

The little I saw of Vidia and Pat together was depressing: there was no sign of their enjoying each other, and the one whole weekend I spent with them they bickered ceaselessly, Pat's tetchiness as sharp as his (developed as a defence, I thought). When he was abroad she was scrupulously careful of his interests; she did research for him; sometimes he referred to showing her work in progress: he trusted her completely, and with reason, because he was evidently her raison d'être. And she made it unthinkable to speak critically of him in her presence. But always her talk was full of how tiresome it was for him that she was sick in aeroplanes, or fainted in crowds, or couldn't eat curries…and when I tried to introduce a subject other than him that would interest us both, such as West Indian politics or her work as a teacher, she never failed to run us aground yet again on some reference to her own inadequacy. At first I took it for granted that he had shattered her self-confidence, and I am still sure he did it no good. But later I suspected that she had always been negative and depressing, someone who enjoyed being squashed.

In *A Way in the World*, writing (as usual) as though he were a single man, Vidia described himself as 'incomplete' in 'physical attractiveness, love, sexual fulfilment'. How terrible for a wife to be publicly wiped out in this way! Everyone who knew the Naipauls said how sorry they were for Pat, and I was sorry for her, too. But whatever Vidia's reason for marrying, he cannot have foreseen the nature of this sexless, loveless (on his part) union with such a discouraging little person. He, too, probably deserved commiseration.

When his Argentinian friend Margaret first came to London he brought her to lunch with me. She was a lively, elegant woman who, though English by descent, was 'feminine' in the Latin-American style, sexy and teasing, with the appearance of having got him just where she wanted him. And he glowed with pride and pleasure. Afterwards he said he was thinking of leaving Pat, and when I was dismayed (could she exist without him?), said that the thought of giving up 'carnal pleasure' just when he'd discovered it was too painful to bear. Why not stay married and have an affair, I asked; which he appeared to think an unseemly suggestion, although it was what he then did for many years. What happened later I don't know, but in the early years of their relationship there was no sign of his squashing Margaret. He did, however, make one disconcerting remark. Did I not find it interesting, he asked, that there was so much cruelty in sex.

What began to wear me down in my dealings with Vidia (it was a long time before I allowed myself to acknowledge it) was his depression.

With every one of his books—and we published eighteen of them—there was a three-part pattern. First came a long period of peace while he was writing, during which we saw little of him and I would often have liked to see more, because I would be full of curiosity about the new book. Then, when it was delivered, there would be a short burst of euphoria during which we would have enjoyable meetings and my role would be to appreciate the work, to write the blurb, to hit on a jacket that pleased both him and us, and to see that the script was free of typist's errors (he was such a perfectionist that no editing, properly speaking, was necessary). Then came part three: post-publication gloom, during which his voice on the telephone would make my heart sink—just a little during the first few years, deeper and deeper with the passing of time. His voice became charged with tragedy, his face became haggard, his theme became the atrocious exhaustion and damage (the word damage always occurred) this book had inflicted on him, and all to what end? Reviewers were ignorant monkeys, publishers (this would be implied in a sinister fashion rather than said) were lazy and useless: what was the point of it all? Why did he go on?

It is natural that a writer who knows himself to be good and who is regularly confirmed in that opinion by critical comment should expect to become a best-seller, but every publisher knows that you don't necessarily become a best-seller by writing well. Of course you don't necessarily have to write badly to do it: it is true that some best-selling books are written astonishingly badly, and equally true that some are written very well. The quality of the writing—even the quality of the thinking—is irrelevant. It is a matter of whether or not a nerve is hit in the wider reading public as opposed to the serious one which is composed of people who are interested in writing as an art. Vidia has sold well in the latter, and has pushed a good way beyond its fringes by becoming famous—at a certain point many people in the wider reading public start to feel that they *ought* to read a writer—but it was always obvious that he was not going to make *big* money. An old friend of mine who reads a great deal once said to me apologetically, 'I'm sure he's very good, but I don't feel he's for me'—and she spoke for a large number of reading people.

Partly this is because of his subject matter, which is broadly speaking the consequences of imperialism: people whose countries once ruled empires relish that subject only if it is flavoured, however subtly, with nostalgia. Partly it is because he is not interested in writing about women, and when he does so usually does it with dislike: more women than men read novels. And partly it is because of his temperament. Once, when he was particularly low, we talked about surviving the horribleness of life and I said that I did it by relying on simple pleasures such as the taste of fruit, the delicious sensations of a hot bath or clean sheets, the way flowers tremble very slightly with life, the lilt of a bird's flight: if I were stripped of those pleasures…better not to imagine it! He asked if I could really depend on them and I said yes. I have a clear memory of the sad, puzzled voice in which he replied: 'You're very lucky, I can't.' And his books, especially his novels (after the humour which filled the first three drained away) are coloured—or perhaps I should say 'discoloured'—by this lack of what used to be called animal spirits. They impress, but they do not charm.

He was, therefore, displeased with the results of publication, which filled him always with despair, sometimes with anger as well. Once he descended on me like a thunderbolt to announce that he had just been into Foyles' of Charing Cross Road and they didn't have a single copy of his latest book, published only two weeks earlier, in stock: not one! Reason told me this was impossible, but I have a lurking tendency to accept guilt if faced with accusation, and this tendency went into spasm: suppose the sales department really had made some unthinkable blunder? Well, if they had I was not going to face the ensuing mayhem single-handed, so I said: 'We must go and tell André at once.' Which we did; and André Deutsch said calmly: 'What nonsense, Vidia—come on, we'll go to Foyles' straight away and I'll show you.' So all three of us stumped down the street to Foyles', only two minutes away, Vidia still thunderous, I twittering with nerves, André serene. Once we were in the shop he cornered the manager and explained: 'Mr Naipaul couldn't find his book: will you please show him where it is displayed.'—'Certainly Mr Deutsch' and there it was, two piles of six copies each, on the table for 'Recent Publications'. André said afterwards that Vidia looked even more thunderous at being done out of his grievance, but if he did I was too dizzy with relief to notice.

Vidia's anxiety and despair were real: you need only compare a photograph of his face in his twenties with one taken in his forties to see how it has been shaped by pain. It was my job to listen to his unhappiness and do what I could to ease it—which would not have been too bad if there had been anything I *could* do. But there was not: and exposure to someone else's depression is draining, even if only for an hour or so at a time and not very often. I felt genuinely sorry for him, but the routine was repeated so often... The truth is that as the years went by, during these post-publication glooms I had increasingly to force myself into feeling genuinely sorry for him, in order to endure him.

Self-brainwashing sometimes has to be a part of an editor's job. You are no use to the writers on your list if you cannot bring imaginative sympathy to working with them, and if you cease to be of use to them you cease to be of use to your firm.

Imaginative sympathy cannot issue from a cold heart so you have to like your writers. Usually this is easy; but occasionally it happens that in spite of admiring someone's work you are—or gradually become—unable to like the person.

I thought so highly of Vidia's writing and felt his presence on our list to be so important that I simply could not allow myself not to like him. I was helped by a foundation of affection laid down during the early days of knowing him, and I was able to believe that his depressions hurt him far more than they hurt me—that he could not prevent them—that I ought to be better at bearing them than I was. And as I became more aware of other things that grated—his attitude to Pat and to his brother Shiva (whom he bullied like an enraged mother hen in charge of a particularly feckless chick)—I called upon a tactic often employed in families: Aunt Emily may have infuriating mannerisms or disconcerting habits, but they are forgiven, even enjoyed, because they are so *typically her*. The offending person is put into the position of a fictional, almost a cartoon, character, whose quirks can be laughed or marvelled at as though they existed only on a page. For quite a long time seeing him as a perpetrator of 'Vidia-isms' worked rather well.

In 1975 we received the thirteenth of his books—his eighth work of fiction—*Guerrillas*. For the first time I was slightly apprehensive because he had spoken to me about the experience of writing it in an unprecedented way: usually he kept the process private, but this time he said that it was extraordinary, something that had never happened before: it was as though the book had been given to him. Such a feeling about writing does not necessarily bode well. And as it turned out, I could not like the book.

It was about a Trinidad-like island sliding into a state of decadence, and there was a tinge of hysteria in the picture's dreadfulness, powerfully imagined though it was. A central part of the story came from something that had recently happened in Trinidad: the murder of an Englishwoman called Gail Benson who had changed her name to Halé Kimga, by a Trinidadian who called himself Michael X and who had set up a so-called 'commune'. Gail had been brought to Trinidad by her lover, a black American known as Hakim Jamal (she had changed her name at his bidding). Both of the men hovered between being mad and being con men, and their linking-up had been Gail's undoing. I knew all three, Gail and Hakim well, Michael very slightly: indeed, I had written a book about them (which I had put away—it would be published sixteen years later) called *Make Believe*. This disturbed my focus on large parts of *Guerrillas*. The people in the book were not meant to be portraits of those I had known (Vidia had met none of them). They were characters created by Vidia to express his view of post-colonial history in places like Trinidad. But the situation in the novel was so close to the situation in life that I often found it hard to repress the reaction: 'But that's not true!' This did not apply to the novel's Michael X character who was called Jimmy Ahmed: Jimmy, and the half-squalid half-pathetic ruins of his 'commune', is a brilliant and wholly convincing creation. Nor did it apply to Roche, Vidia's substitute for Hakim Jamal. Roche is a liberal white South African refugee working for a big commercial firm, whose job has involved giving cynical support to Jimmy. Roche was so evidently not Hakim that the question did not arise. But it certainly did apply to Jane, who stood in for Gail in being the murdered woman.

The novel's Jane, who comes to the island as Roche's mistress, is supposed to be an idle, arid creature who tries to find the vitality she lacks by having affairs with men. Obtuse in her innate sense of her superiority as a white woman, she drifts into such an attempt with Jimmy: an irresponsible fool playing a dangerous game for kicks with a ruined black man. Earlier, Vidia had written an account for a newspaper of Gail's murder which made it clear that he saw Gail as that kind of woman.

She was not. She was idle and empty, but she had no sense of her own superiority as a white woman or as anything else. Far from playing dangerous games for kicks, she was clinging on to illusions for dear life. The people she had most in common with were not the kind of secure Englishwomen who had it off with black men to demonstrate their own liberal attitudes, but those poor wretches who followed the American 'guru' Jones to

Guyana in 1977, and ended by committing mass suicide at his bidding. She was so lacking in a sense of her own worth that it bordered on insanity.

It was therefore about Jane that I kept saying to myself, 'But that's not true!' Then I pulled myself together and saw that there was no reason why Jane should be like Gail: an Englishwoman going into such an affair for kicks was far from impossible and would be a perfectly fair example of fraudulence of motive in white liberals, which was what Vidia was bent on showing.

So I read the book again—and this time Jane simply fell to pieces. Roche came out of it badly, too: a dim character, hard to envisage, in spite of revealing wide-apart molars with black roots whenever he smiled (a touch of 'clever characterization' which should have been beneath Vidia). But although he doesn't quite convince, he almost does; you keep expecting him to emerge from the mist, while Jane becomes more and more like a series of bits and pieces that don't add up, so that finally her murder is without significance. I came to the conclusion that the trouble must lie with Vidia's having cut his cloth to fit a pattern he had laid down in advance: these characters existed in order to exemplify his argument, he had not been *discovering* them. So they did not live; and the woman lived less than the man because that is true of all Vidia's women.

From the professional point of view there was no question as to what I ought to do: this was one of our most valuable authors; even if his book had been really bad rather than just flawed we would certainly have published it in the expectation that he would soon be back on form; so what I must say was 'wonderful' and damn well sound as though I meant it.

Instead I sat there muttering 'Oh my god, what am I going to say to him?' I had never lied to him—I kept reminding myself of that, disregarding the fact that I had never before needed to lie. 'If I lie now, how will he be able to trust me in the future when I praise something?' The obvious answer to that was that if I lied convincingly he would never know that I had done it, but this did not occur to me. After what seemed to me like hours of sincere angst I ended by persuading myself that I 'owed it to our friendship' to tell him what I truly thought.

Nothing practical would be gained. A beginner writer sometimes makes mistakes which he can remedy if they are pointed out, but a novelist of Vidia's quality and experience who produces an unconvincing character has suffered a lapse of imagination about which nothing can be done. It happened to Dickens whenever he attempted a good woman; it happened to George Eliot with Daniel Deronda. And as for my own attitude—I had often seen through other people who insisted on telling the truth about a friend's shortcomings: I knew that *their* motives were usually suspect. But my own were as invisible to me as a cuttlefish becomes when it saturates the surrounding water with ink.

So I told him. I began by saying how much I admired the many things in the book which I did admire, and then I said that I had to tell him (*had* to tell him!) that two of his three central characters had failed to convince me. It was like saying to Conrad, '*Lord Jim* is a very fine novel except that Jim doesn't quite come off.'

Vidia looked disconcerted, then stood up and said quietly that he was sorry they didn't work for me, because he had done the best he could with them, there was nothing more he could do, so there was no point in discussing it. As he left the room I think I muttered something about its being a splendid book all the same, after which I felt a mixture of relief at his appearing to be sorry rather than angry, and a slight (only slight!) sense of let-down and silliness. And I supposed that was that.

The next day Vidia's agent called André to say that he had been instructed to retrieve *Guerrillas* because we had lost confidence in Vidia's writing and therefore he was leaving us.

André must have fought back because there was nothing he hated more than losing an author, but the battle didn't last long. Although I believe I was named, André was kind enough not to blame me. Nor did I blame myself. I went into a rage. I fulminated to myself, my colleagues, my friends: 'All those years of friendship, and a mere dozen words of criticism—*a mere dozen words!*—send him flouncing out in a tantrum like some hysterical prima donna!' I had long and scathing conversations with him in my head; but more satisfying was a daydream of being at a huge and important party, seeing him enter the room, turning on my heel and walking out.

For at least two weeks I seethed...and then, in the third week, it suddenly occurred to me that never again would I have to listen to Vidia telling me how damaged he was, and it was as though the sun came out. *I didn't have to like Vidia any more!* I could still like his work, I could still be sorry for his pain; but I no longer faced the task of fashioning affection out of these elements in order to deal as a good editor should with the exhausting, and finally tedious, task of listening to his woe. 'Do you know what,' I said to André, 'I've begun to see that it's a release.' (Rather to my surprise, he laughed.) I still, however, failed to see that my editorial 'mistake' had been an act of aggression. In fact I went on failing to see that for years.

Guerrillas was sold to Secker and Warburg the day after it left us.

A month or so after this I went into André's office to discuss something and his phone rang before I had opened my mouth. This always happened. Usually I threw myself back in my chair with a groan, then reached for something to read, but this time I jumped up and grabbed the extension. 'Why—Vidia!' he had said. 'What can I do for you?'

Vidia was speaking from Trinidad, his voice tense: André must call his agent *at once* and tell him to recover the manuscript of *Guerrillas* from Secker and Warburg and deliver it to us.

André, who was uncommonly good at rising to unexpected occasions, became instantly fatherly. Naturally, he said, he would be delighted to get the book back, but Vidia must not act too impetuously: whatever had gone wrong might well turn out to be less serious than he now felt. This was Thursday. What Vidia must do was think it over very carefully without taking action until Monday. Then, if he still wanted to come back to us, he must call his agent, not André, listen to his advice, and if that failed to change his mind, instruct him to act. André would be waiting for the agent's call on Monday afternoon or

Tuesday morning, hoping—of course—that it would be good news for us.

Which—of course—it was. My private sun did go back behind a film of cloud, but in spite of that there was satisfaction in knowing that he thought himself better off with us than with them, and I had no doubt of the value of whatever books were still to come.

Vidia never said why he bolted from Seckers, but his agent told André that it was because when they announced *Guerrillas* in their catalogue they described him as 'the West Indian novelist'.

The books still to come were, indeed, worth having (though the last of them was his least important): *India: a Wounded Civilization, The Return of Eva Perón, Among the Believers, A Bend in the River* and *Finding the Centre*. I had decided that the only thing to do was to behave exactly as I had always done in our pre-*Guerrillas* working relationship, while quietly cutting down our extra-curricular friendship, and he apparently felt the same. The result was a smooth passage, less involving but less testing than it used to be. Nobody else knew—and I myself was unaware of it until I came to look back—that having resolved never again to utter a word of criticism to Vidia, I was guilty of an absurd pettiness. In *Among the Believers*, a book which I admired very much, there were two minor points to which in the past I would have drawn his attention, and I refrained from doing so: thus betraying, though luckily only to my retrospecting self, that I was still hanging on to my self-righteous interpretation of the *Guerrillas* incident. Vidia would certainly not have 'flounced out like some hysterical prima donna' over matters so trivial. One was a place where he seemed to draw too sweeping a conclusion from too slight an event and could probably have avoided giving that impression by some quite small adjustment; and the other was that when an Iranian speaking English said 'Sheep' Vidia, misled by his accent, thought he said 'ship', which made some dialogue as he reported it sound puzzling. To keep mum about that! There is nothing like self-deception for making one ridiculous.

When Vidia really did leave us in 1984 I could see why—
and even why he did so in a way which seemed unkind,
without a word of warning or explanation. He had come to the
conclusion that André Deutsch Limited was going downhill. It
was true. The recession, combined with a gradual but relentless
shrinkage in the readership of books such as those we published,
was well on the way to making firms of our size and kind
unviable; and André had lost his vigour and flair. His decision
to sell the firm, which more or less coincided with Vidia's
departure, was made (so he felt and told me) because publishing
was 'no fun any more', but it was equally a matter of his own
slowly failing health. The firm continued for ten years or so
under Tom Rosenthal, chuntering not-so-slowly downwards all
the time (Tom had been running Seckers when they called Vidia
a West Indian, so his appearance on the scene did nothing to
change Vidia's mind).

A writer of reputation can always win an even bigger
advance than he is worth by allowing himself to be tempted
away from publisher A by publisher B, and publisher B will then
have to try extra hard on his behalf to justify the advance: it
makes sense to move on if you time it right. And if you perceive
that there is something going seriously wrong with publisher A
you would be foolish not to do so. And having decided to go,
how could you look in the eye someone you have known for
over twenty years, of whom you have been really quite fond,
and tell him, 'I'm leaving because you are getting past it'? Of
course you could not. Vidia's agent managed to conceal from
André what Vidia felt, but André suspected something: he told
me that he thought it was something to do with himself and that
he couldn't get it out of the agent, but perhaps I might have
better luck. I called the agent and asked him if there was any
point in my getting in touch with Vidia, and he—in considerable
embarrassment—told me the truth; whereupon I could only
silently agree with Vidia's silence, and tell poor André that I'd
been so convincingly assured of the uselessness of any further
attempt to change Vidia's mind, that we had better give up.

So this leaving did not make me angry, or surprised, or even
sad, except for André's sake. Vidia was doing what he had to

do, and it seemed reasonable to suppose that we had enjoyed the best of him, anyway. Many years later Mordecai Richler, in at the story's end, oddly enough, as well as its beginning, told me that he had recently seen Vidia with his new and much younger wife, Nadira (they met in Pakistan in 1995 and married the next year, soon after Pat's death). He was, said Mordecai, 'amazingly jolly'; and I was pleased to find that this news made me very glad indeed.

About the Writers

Diana Athill was one of the most respected editors in British publishing during her fifty-year career at André Deutsch in London. 'Editing Vidia' is taken from her memoir *Stet*, which is published by Granta Books.

Jurek Becker (1937–1997) was born in Lodz in Poland. His novels include *Jakob the Liar* and *Sleepless Days*.

Isaiah Berlin (1909–1997) was the first President of Wolfson College, Oxford. His works include *Karl Marx: His Life and Environment*; *The Hedgehog and the Fox*; *Four Essays on Liberty* and *Russian Thinkers*.

Abraham Brumberg writes on Russian, East European and Jewish affairs. His books include *Poland: Genesis of a Revolution*.

Bill Buford was the editor of *Granta* from 1979 to 1995. He is now the Fiction Editor of the *New Yorker*.

Raymond Carver's (1938–1988) story collections include *Cathedral*; *Will You Please Be Quiet, Please*; *What We Talk about When We Talk about Love* and a collection of his fiction and prose *Call If You Need Me*.

Seamus Deane's novel *Reading in the Dark* was shortlisted for the Booker Prize in 1996. He is the editor of the *Field Day Anthology of Irish Writing*.

Mircea Dinescu was under house arrest in Romania in 1989 for criticizing the Ceaucescu regime. He is a poet.

Hans Magnus Enzensberger's collections of essays include *Civil Wars: from LA to Bosnia* and *Zig Zag*. He lives in Munich.

James Fenton is a poet and critic and, formerly, a foreign correspondent. He writes regularly for the *New York Review of Books*. His most recent book is *The Strength of Poetry*.

Richard Ford's novels include *The Sportswriter* and *Independence Day*, which won the Pulitzer in 1995. His new collection of stories, *A Multitude of Sins*, will be published in 2001.

Martha Gellhorn (1908–1998) was born in St Louis, Missouri. Her books include a collection of her war reporting, *The Face of War*, and *A View from the Ground*, both published by Granta Books.

Amitav Ghosh was born in Calcutta in 1956. His books include *The Circle of Reason*, *The Glass Palace* and *In An Antique Land*.

Nadine Gordimer won the Nobel Prize for Literature in 1991. Her novels include *July's People* and *The Conservationist*. Her collected non-fiction is titled *Living in Hope and History: Notes from Our Century*.

Linda Grant's novel, *When I Lived in Modern Times* (Granta Books) won the Orange Prize for Fiction in 2000. 'Are We Related?' became part of her memoir *Remind Me Who I Am Again*, also published by Granta Books.

Werner Krätschell was a Dean in the German Protestant Church in 1989 and a leading critic of the Communist regime.

Günter Kunert was expelled from the East German Social Democratic Party in 1976 for protesting against the expulsion of Wolf Biermann.

Hanif Kureishi's novels include *Intimacy* and *The Buddha of Suburbia*. His screenplays include the Oscar-nominated *My Beautiful Laundrette*, and *Sammy and Rosie Get Laid*.

Primo Levi (1919–1987) was born in Turin and trained as a chemist. He was deported to Auschwitz in 1944. His books include *The Periodic Table*; *If Not Now, When?* and *The Drowned and the Saved*.

Norman Lewis was born in 1908. He is the author of thirteen novels and fourteen books of travel and memoir. His fifteenth, *A Voyage by Dhow*, will be published in 2001. He lives in Essex.

Tim Lott's memoir *The Scent of Dried Roses* won the PEN/J. R. Ackerley Award for Autobiography. His first novel is *White City Blue*.

Adam Mars-Jones was one of *Granta*'s Best of Young British Novelists in 1993. His books include *Lantern Lecture*, which won the Somerset Maugham Award, *Monopolies of Loss* and *The Waters of Thirst*.

Leonard Michaels's novel *The Men's Club* was published in 1981.

Jonathan Miller is a writer and director who has directed operas and plays throughout the world. He lives in London.

Lorrie Moore's novels include *Who Will Run the Frog Hospital?* and *Anagrams*. 'Agnes of Iowa' is also published in her third short-story collection, *Birds of America*.

Harold Pinter is the author of twenty-nine plays including *The Caretaker*, *Betrayal* and *No Man's Land* and twenty-one screenplays.

Salman Rushdie's novels include *Midnight's Children*, which won the Booker Prize in 1981, *The Satanic Verses*, *The Moor's Last Sigh* and most recently *The Ground Beneath Her Feet*.

Josef Škvorecký was born in 1924. He left Czechoslovakia after the Russian invasion of Prague in 1968 and emigrated to Canada.

Stephen Spender (1909–1995) the poet coedited both *Encounter* and *Horizon* magazines.

George Steiner's collected fiction is published as *The Deeps of the Sea and Other Fiction*. His books include *The Death of Tragedy*, *After Babel* and most recently *Grammars of Creation*.

Joy Williams has published three novels and two volumes of short stories. Her fourth novel, *The Quick and the Dead* is published in 2001.